MW01644512

USA TODAY BESTSELLING AUTHOR

LAYLA FROST

From The Pervy Heart of The Author

To **Layla Frost's Cupcakes**, thank you for your patience. Your encouragement. Your, uh, gentle insinuation that you wanted Lars' story. Maybe. A little...Okay, thank you for demanding I write this story. I hope you love Joss and Lars as much as I do. And I hope you love the trip back to Sweets You Rock bakery and the Hyde Garage. Everyone is there and as gossipy as ever.

Thank you to **Layla's Naughty Review Team** for going with the flow and being flexible with me.

Thank you to **Brynne Asher** and **Sarah Curtis** for being my ride or dies. I am lucky to have you.

As always, thank you to **M** for all you do. You keep the house running smoothly. You know what to say and do before I even know I needed it. You keep me hydrated and fed with delicious burrata because you know cheese is the way to my heart.

But the good dickin' down doesn't hurt, either...

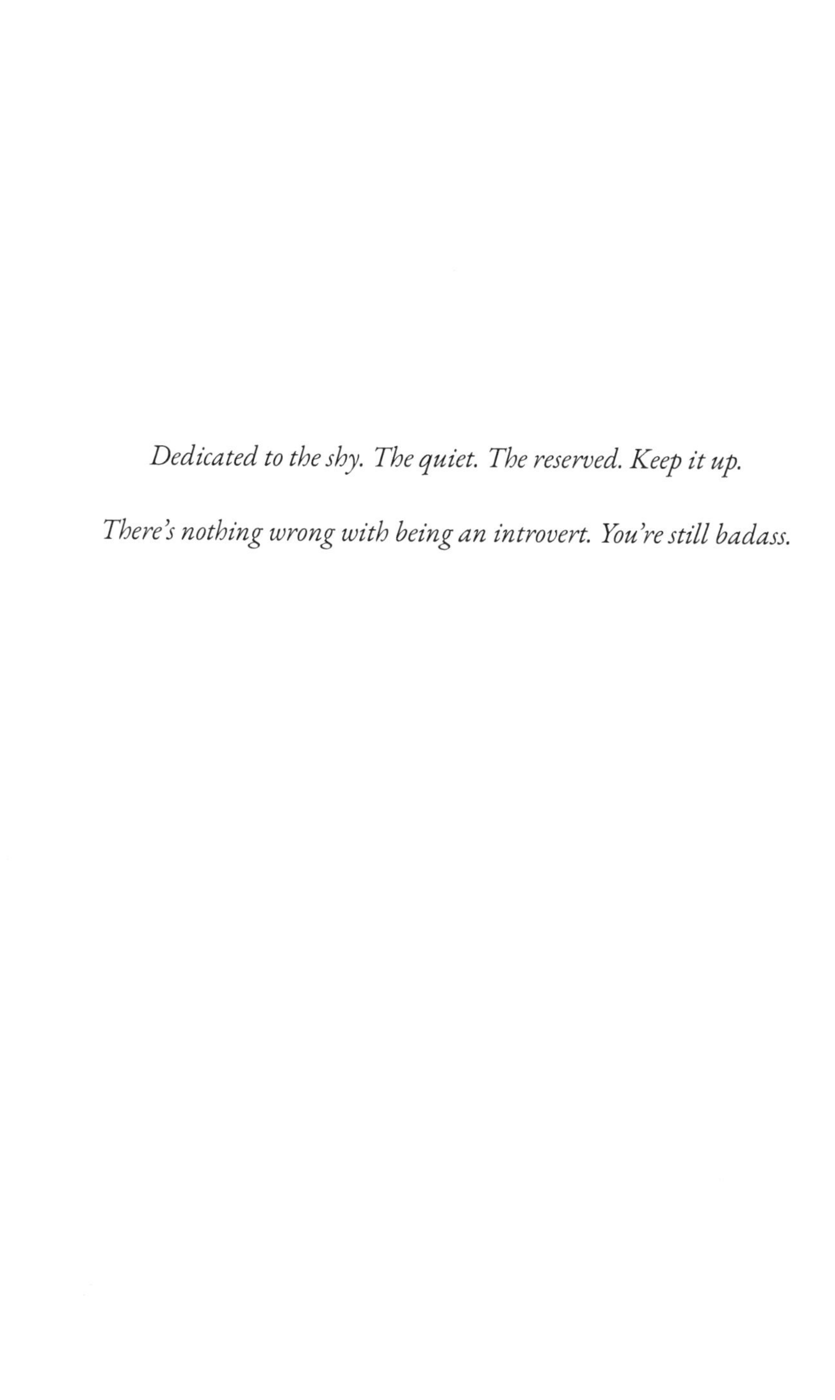

Dedicated to the shy. The quiet. The reserved. Keep it up.

There's nothing wrong with being an introvert. You're still badass.

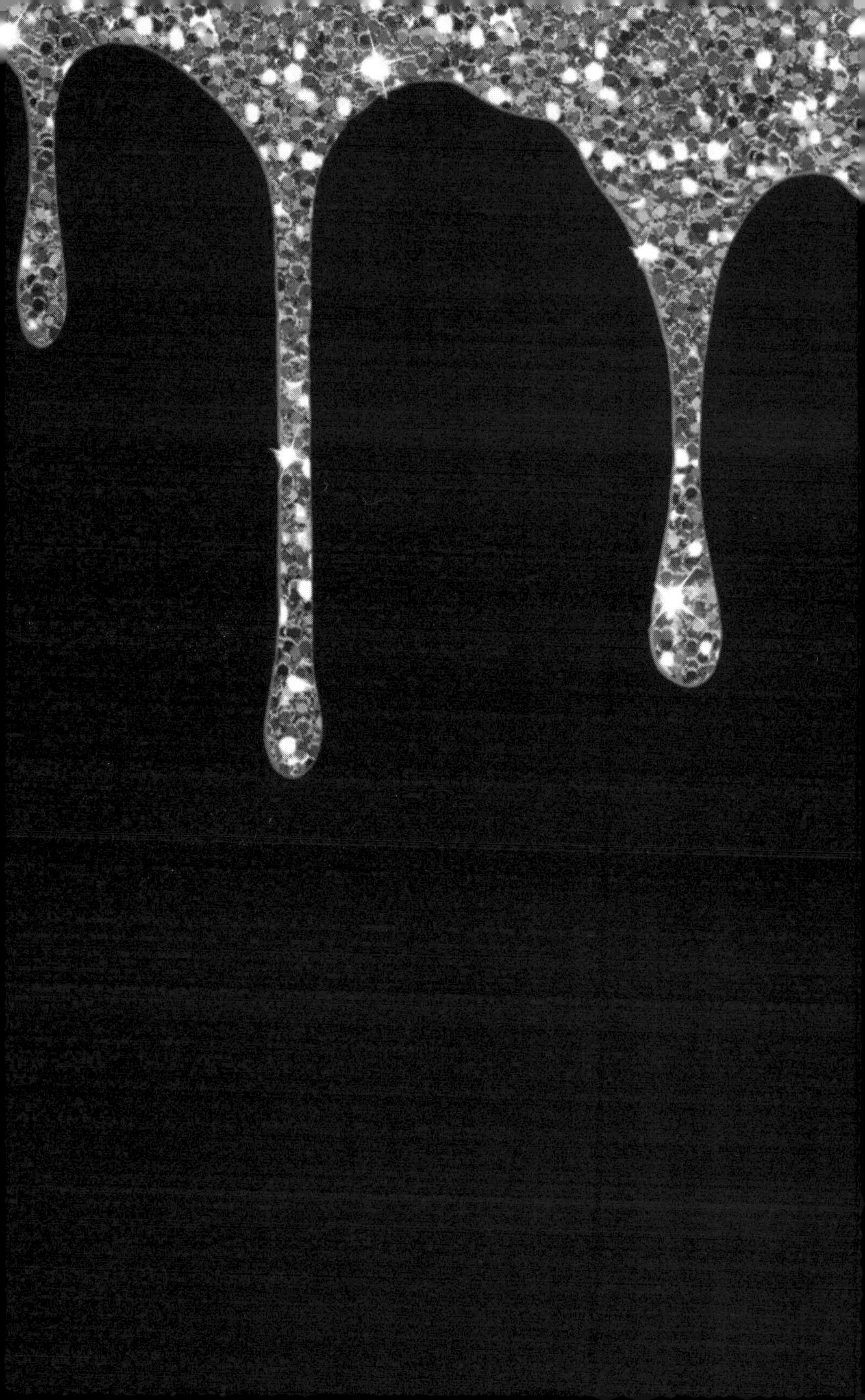

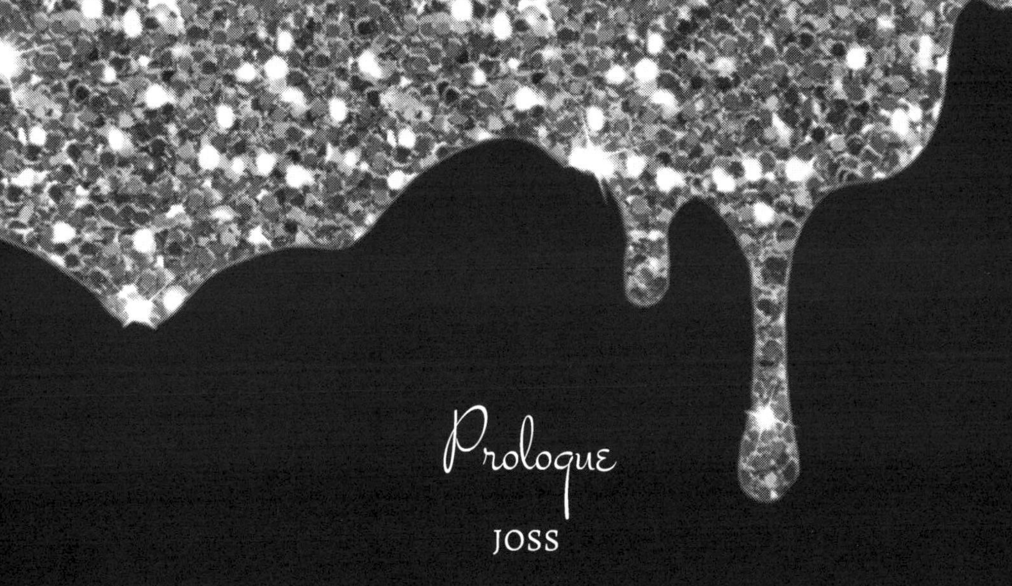

Prologue

JOSS

ONE YEAR AGO

PLEASE, DON'T BE BAD.

Please.

Like, the most please with a brick finish, repurposed wood detailing, and a cherry on top.

But when the mortgage broker handed me a paper with the estimated closing cost breakdown and monthly payments, I saw the cost of my dream home wasn't simply bad.

It was worse.

So much worse.

Disappointment filled me as I blinked at the number, silently pleading for some of the pesky digits at the end to drop away. When it remained the same, the layer of resentment that hovered around me grew thicker, pressing in.

I'd told Peter I didn't want to see the house.

I'd told him it was out of my budget.

I'd told him I didn't want to fall in love with something I couldn't have.

But I might as well have been talking to the beautifully rustic brick finish.

Because Peter was... well, *Peter* about it. He'd made the showing appointment without telling me. Then he'd claimed to be taking me to lunch but instead we went to said showing. Because, according to him, I was being irrational for not going to see it.

He didn't get it. If I never saw it in person, I could pretend there was some massive flaw. Maybe the paint was faded. Maybe the listing photos were taken at deceiving angles to make it look bigger. Maybe there was water damage, a permanent smoke stench, and rats.

But thanks to his heavy-handedness, I had seen it. And it'd been as spacious and gorgeous as the undeceiving pictures had shown—more so, maybe. No damage. No flaws. No rats.

Not one measly cobweb.

Nothing but perfection.

Just as I'd feared, I'd fallen in love. The house was everything I'd ever wanted and then some.

Or should I say, and then *sum*.

As in a huge sum of cash.

Like he sensed my crushing disappointment and internal freak out, my fiancé leaned closer to whisper, "We can afford this."

I so couldn't. Even using my inheritance from my grandparents to cover closing costs and a sizeable down payment, the numbers staring at me were daunting.

"This is almost my entire monthly salary," I pointed out.

"*We* can do it."

"Take some time to think it over," the broker said, his tone and expression doing little to hide his boredom. He likely saw similar scenarios all day long. "But you should know, it's a seller's market right now. Good houses are going fast. If you want it, let Martina know soon."

I wanted it.

I wanted it *so* bad.

The gorgeous house was outside the city but still had all the traditional charm Boston was known for. It was big enough for us to grow into, with a yard and so much space.

It was a stark contrast to our shoebox of an apartment with barely enough room to move around without feeling on top of each other—and not in a good way. The tiny patches of weeds that grew between the cracks in the sidewalk were as close to a lawn as we had.

Standing, I shook the broker's hand before gathering the papers, my coffee, and bag. The entire time, my thoughts raced.

On one hand, I knew I couldn't afford the place. I *knew* it.

On the other, I wanted it.

Desperately.

So badly, my brain refused to accept the truth. Illogical regret squeezed my stomach as I thought about every impulse purchase I'd ever made, no matter how small. Because, sure, not splurging on that one dinner three years ago would totally have made a difference.

My head was a mess of numbers and budgets and ideas to scrimp and save, but it was pointless. It wasn't as if I had a couple hundred grand stuffed between my couch cushions like lost loose change.

Once we were in Peter's car, he turned to me and smiled. "Call Martina." When I didn't move, he pushed, "What're you waiting for?"

A miracle windfall.

He glanced in the rearview mirror and fixed his already perfectly groomed blond hair. "Hun, we can do this. It's perfect timing. We can move, decorate, even remodel the bathroom and kitchen before the wedding."

That wasn't saying much. We could do pretty much anything before the wedding since we were contenders for the *Longest Engagement Ever* record.

Six years and running.

"I don't want to rush into anything. There will be other houses," I pointed out, even as my heart broke a little.

"But not this house." His gaze shot to me and narrowed, hurt clouding his handsome face. "Is this because of the mortgage?"

Yes.

Definitely.

As soon as the thought ricocheted through my head, guilt followed like the damage from an emotional bullet.

In his early days at the PR firm, Peter had been anxious to prove he was just as good as the other hotshots. Wining, dining, golf lunches—the best of the best everything. He'd overextended himself, sinking his credit score in the process. I hadn't known how bad it'd gotten until the collection letters had rolled in. One after another after another million—or so it'd seemed.

It'd been *bad*.

Like always, his parents swooped in to rescue him from the consequences of his own actions, but by that time, the damage had been done. His credit was such garbage, there'd been no way to get preapproved with both our names on the loan.

He would be able to help with payments, but it was up to me and my stellar credit to burden the risk.

Not that I'd phrase it like that to him, of course. He was already defensive about it, and even hinting at my feelings would cause a battle that wasn't worth fighting.

His lips curled in a slight frown as he looked at my eyes.

Not into them.

At them.

It didn't matter that I'd been wearing my new volumizing mascara for over a week, he'd clearly just noticed. I could almost hear his thoughts.

She's wearing too much makeup.

Her lashes look like spider legs.

Blah, blah, pffffft.

Peter didn't like too much makeup. He also didn't like unnatural hair colors, fussy clothes, or anything wild. In his mind, natural was best.

The girl-next-door to complement his All-American handsomeness.

There were times I wondered if he'd find me more attractive if I wore an Amish dress and bonnet.

It was on the tip of my tongue to tell him if he didn't like my makeup, he didn't have to wear it. But *I* was going to do what I wanted.

It's not worth the fight.

His frown smoothed out. "We'll set the date for next year. That will give us enough time to get everything done. When we get back from our honeymoon, we'll already be settled into our life together."

That bullet of guilt hit my belly when I realized his mind wasn't on critiquing my makeup, it was on our future.

Our future *together.*

God, I'm such a bitch.

Panic prickled the back of my neck, but I pushed it down. "Okay, I'll call Martina."

Cupping my cheek gently, Peter gave me a quick, chaste kiss before repeating, "What're you waiting for?"

I pulled out my cell and dialed our realtor.

"Good afternoon, this is Martina."

"Hi, this is Joss Lennon."

"Joss, what can I do for you?"

Inhaling deeply, I forced the words out. "We'd like to put in an offer."

SIX MONTHS LATER

PARKING MY CAR in front of a seemingly empty warehouse, I grabbed my cell and checked the screen.

According to the health app that was synced with our smart watches, Peter was in the middle of yet another intense workout that had his heart rate elevated.

Only he wasn't at the gym. Nor was he in a stressful meeting—though his last text had claimed he'd be in one all afternoon. Nope, *Find My Phone* said he was parked on the other side of the warehouse.

Maybe he's just jacking off.

Taking the one-hand-band on the road.

With an increasing frequency, Peter would lock himself in his home office at night, claiming he had to work. My phone would alert me he was *exercising*, and his step count and heart rate would skyrocket.

Either he was the new Usain Bolt or only his dominant hand was getting a workout.

It'd taken me a few times to realize what he'd been up to, but I'd never called him on it. Peter would've gotten defensive, flipping it on me. Making it my fault he was forced to literally take matters into his own hands, until I was left feeling like I had to apologize for not meeting his needs or whatever.

It wasn't worth the fight because I hadn't really cared. We'd never been especially physical, so my vibrator got plenty of use. Maybe not daily—and never when he was home—but I had my own solo time, so who was I to judge?

When his heart rate had spiked during a workday, I'd wondered if he was having a little afternoon delight with himself in his office. But then I'd noticed his steps hadn't changed, just his heart rate. I'd dismissed it as stress or a tech glitch.

But three weeks in a row at the *exact* same time?

Yeah, there were coincidences and then there was willful ignorance.

Forcing myself out of the car, I aimed for stealth, but with my clumsy steps and pounding heart, I was certain anyone in a mile radius was aware of me.

I was wrong.

Because as I rounded the building and saw Peter in his parked car, it was obvious he wasn't aware of anything around him.

Well, anything other than the gorgeous woman who was riding him.

I stopped in my tracks as I stared into the driver's side window, watching it all unfold like a voyeur. A sense of surrealness coated me, like I was dreaming. Or having a nightmare. My brain went blank except for one bizarre thought.

That bastard is letting her be on top.

Peter *never* let me be on top. He was a missionary kinda guy. Which, like the lack of frequency, I'd convinced myself was fine. Normal. Expected even.

Things cooled.

They faded.

They grew comfortable.

Except he didn't look cool right then, with his head tipped back. Nothing about the technicolor woman and their steamy bliss seemed faded. And fucking in the front seat of the car wasn't exactly comfortable, either.

They weren't in the midst of pleasant, efficient sex—only ever on a bed and only ever in one position. They were *fucking.* And they were doing it in a way that would send someone's heart rate through the roof.

In the million scenarios my brain had imagined, I'd pictured him with a faceless *girl-next-door*. No matter what other details my brain filled in, that part had remained the same. I'd thought if he were cheating, it had to be with his dream girl. That she'd be so perfect for him, he hadn't been able to resist.

But there was nothing about the woman that matched his preferences.

Not her hair color.

Not her makeup.

Definitely not her tattoos.

And that pissed me off more than what they were doing. Especially those gorgeous tattoos, dammit.

Every time I'd mentioned wanting a tattoo, even a tiny one, he'd make some shitty passive-aggressive comment. Like most things with him, it'd been easier to just let it go. It wasn't worth the fight.

I should've fought since he clearly wasn't as against them as he'd claimed.

I should've fought because I wanted one.

I just should've fought.

With trembling hands, I pulled my phone out and recorded a short video for proof in case he was feeling extra gaslighty and wanted to fight me for the house or my car or anything else. I wouldn't put it past him to try to use everything I loved as leverage. The footage was shaky, as though it were from a bad horror flick, but that didn't matter. It was clear who they were and what they were doing.

Tucking it away, I didn't bother being stealthy as I approached the car.

They were too occupied to notice.

Not until I knocked on the window. Their eyes darted to me as they frantically tried to cover up. When Peter saw it was me, he launched the woman off his lap, her hip hitting the horn and making them both jump. He hadn't thought the maneuver through, though, because it wasn't like I hadn't seen her on him. And without her body blocking the way, he'd exposed his softening dick.

At least he wore a condom.

Bile rose in my throat, the terrifying images and warnings from high school Health class filling my head. Condoms weren't one hundred percent effective—and who knew if he wore them every time. Plus, this could be one girl in a long line of many.

He could *have* something.

Which meant I could, too.

I need to be tested. Like, immediately.

Fighting to keep from getting sick, I waited for him to roll down the window.

"Joss, it's not—"

"We set a date," I seethed, my voice low, even, yet still filled with fury. "We sent invites. We had our wedding shower. People have made travel arrangements. All our deposits are..."

And that's when it hit me.

I wasn't upset about him cheating. Hurt, yes. A blow to the ego? Oh, hell yeah. Bitter and resentful that he was sleeping with a tattooed goddess with wild hair who skyrocketed his heart rate?

Fuck. Yes.

But more than any of that, I was inconvenienced.

Embarrassed.

And, if I were being honest, relieved.

God, how did it get so bad?

How had I allowed myself to settle so much?

"Joss, hun, I can explain. It's... I just... You..."

"*Me* what?"

His face grew redder and more panicked. "We've been together since high school. You're the only person I've been with and—"

"Only person you *had* been with." I pointedly glanced toward the redressing woman and then back to him. "Past tense."

"This is... It's stupid." He tucked himself away and zipped his slacks. I was hoping he'd catch skin and pull the beans above the frank, but no such luck. "A mistake. Let me explain."

I was insulted he thought I was stupid enough to even listen to his justifications.

Based on the woman's blatant indignation, she was equally insulted he'd referred to her as a mistake.

He didn't deserve our forgiveness, and I hoped like hell she was strong enough to fight his charm.

"How long?" I asked.

"It doesn't—" he started, but I wasn't talking to him.

Realizing my eyes and question were aimed at her, the woman answered, "Since his friend's bachelor party."

His wince—the one that could be seen from Pluto—showed he knew he was screwed in a variety of different ways. Because none of his friends were engaged. None. And the only bachelor party he'd been to?

His own.

Oblivious to the bus she'd just thrown him under, she continued. "I was one of the dancers."

Dancer*s*.

Plural.

Plural dancers he'd sworn he hadn't had.

I hadn't asked. I wouldn't have cared if he and his douchey bros had party bussed to every strip club in the Boston area—that was what bachelor parties did. But he'd said strippers were cliché. He'd claimed he wasn't into that. He'd told me all about how they'd spent the night at the casino, losing money at poker and drinking expensive scotch. *He'd* been the one to volunteer the information. The *lie*.

One of many he'd been repeating for an entire month.

She studied me for two-point-five seconds before surmising the truth. "It was his party."

"Yup."

I didn't blame her for falling for his BS. Peter was persuasive. He was charming. His boyish good looks made him appear wholesome and trustworthy.

He would've made a hell of a politician.

She turned a vicious glare his way. "They said it was some other guy."

God.

God.

They.

His friends knew me. We'd attended functions together. Had dinner or drinks together. They'd been to my house often. Sitting on my couch. Eating my snacks. Drinking my booze. Talking my ear off about their work crap that I didn't care about until I'd wanted to punch their arrogant faces.

And they'd done that knowing that Peter had cheated on me. Knowing they'd *helped* him do it.

It was infuriating and mortifying.

At the thought of my house, I hissed, "Where?" I needed to know that he hadn't brought her there. Into my gorgeous home I loved so much.

"Hun, it's..." Peter's excuses fell on deaf ears as he tried to talk over the woman.

"My apartment or here when he didn't have time to make the drive."

Thank God. I don't have to move.

Just him.

He can move all the way to hell for all I care.

"How often?" I asked.

Again, he tried to speak over her when she said, "A handful of times. But we texted and he bought private cam shows. A lot."

Bought.

While I'd been fighting off financial panic attacks every time I paid a bill, he'd been paying for cam shows.

I thought about how frequently he'd escaped into his home office. His one-handed exercises. "Around seven at night?"

He paled at the realization I knew what he'd been *up* to. Surprise widened his eyes until they looked like they'd pop out.

The nightly jack-off sessions hadn't been sponsored by KY Jelly and Pornhub.

They'd been because of another woman. A flesh and blood woman who he'd also had sex with.

I had my confirmation.

No doubts.

No wondering.

No lingering what-ifs.

I was done.

Removing my engagement ring, I clutched it in my fist until the gold band dug in. At the feel of it—and my suddenly empty ring finger—long overdue tears burned my eyes.

During high school, Peter had worked with me at my dad's hardware stores, saving all through junior and senior year to surprise me with the ring right after our graduation ceremony. The diamond was tiny and the band was thin. But I'd loved it so much. After he'd started making good money, he'd offered a million times to upgrade it, but I'd always turned him down. I wanted the one he'd saved so long to give me.

When his tall, lanky teenage boy body had shakingly lowered to one knee.

When his handsome face had nervously smiled up at me, his eyes shining with love and hope.

When he'd first asked me to be his wife.

When we'd had dreams, a plan, and our entire lives ahead of us.

Before he'd thrown it all away.

It wasn't just the cheating. That may have been the last straw, but it was just one in a bale of many. In his quest to be a power player, he'd changed. He had to have a certain look. A certain personality. A certain vibe.

A certain *life*.

He'd become image obsessed, deceitful, and selfish.

And I was done making excuses for it. For him.

I wanted to jam the ring down his throat, but I settled for tossing it through the open window.

"Jossy Bean," he said, the seldom used nickname cutting me like a million daggers. "I'm sorry. *Please*. I love you."

He didn't. Not in the way he should've. And as I stared at a man I barely recognized, I realized I didn't love him in that way, either.

But I did love myself.

Which was why I turned and walked back to my car with my chin held high.

Numb and overwhelmed, I drove around the corner and parked. Once my hands stopped shaking so badly, I texted my sister.

Me: Have Benny change my locks.

Ruth: Shit. I'm so sorry. I didn't think he was actually doing anything. I honestly can't believe this.

When I'd told Ruth my suspicions, she'd had a never-ending rolodex of excuses and alternatives. She'd thought I was crazy, reading too much into a coincidence. Even still, her and her husband had agreed to wait at my house for me with new locks and a big bottle of rum.

Ruth: Come home, we'll get drunk.

Me: Nothing has ever sounded better.

Putting the car into drive, I headed to the house I now lived in alone.

And rum.

A lot of rum.

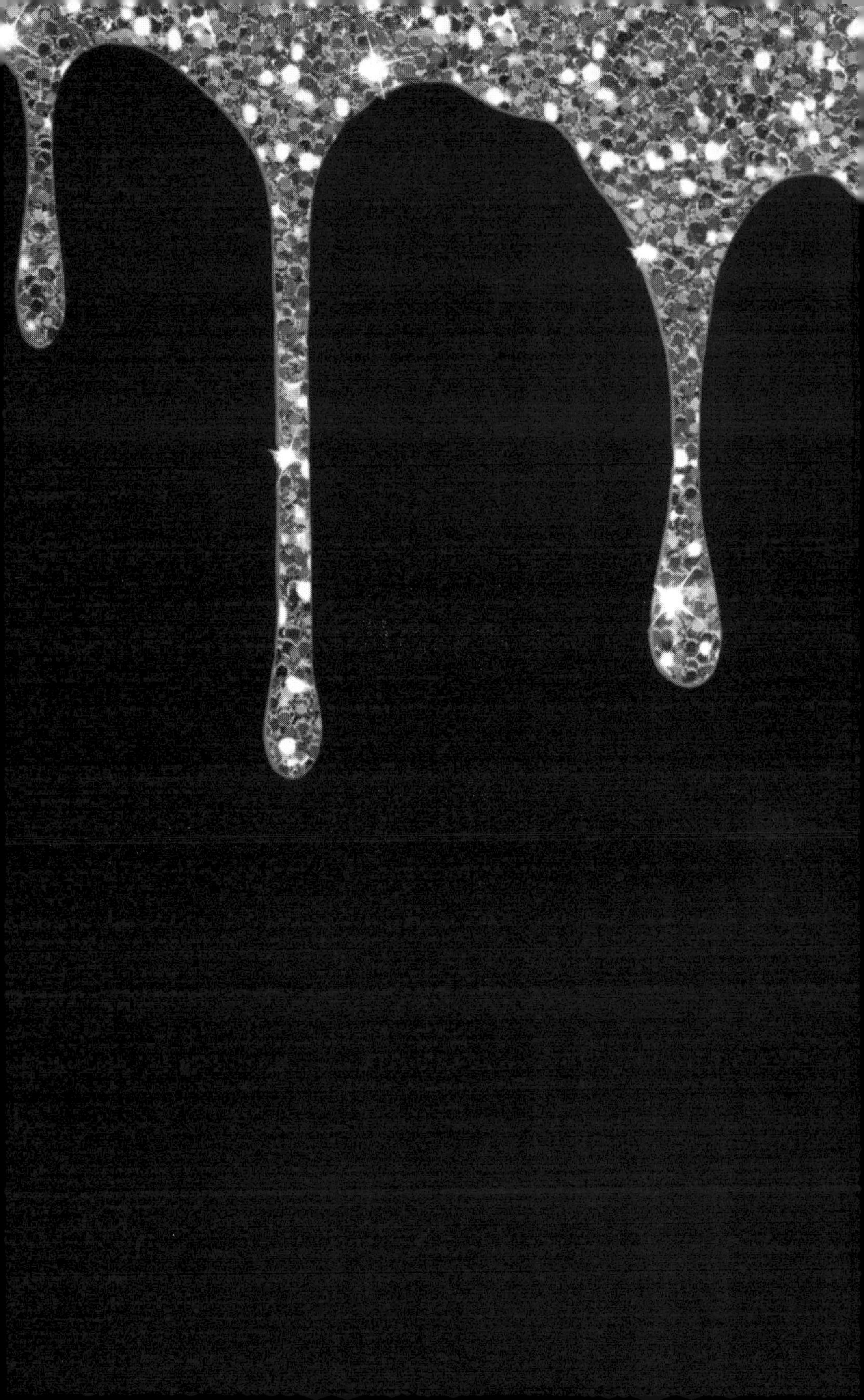

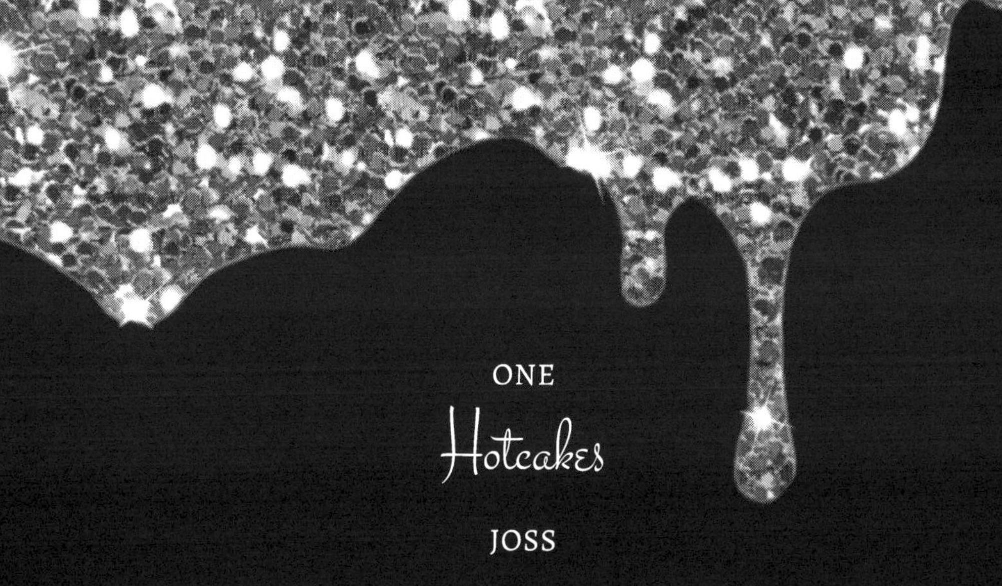

ONE
Hotcakes
JOSS

"EARTH TO JOSS. Come in, Joss."

At my boss' teasing voice close to my ear, I jolted and spun, nearly knocking the tray of chocolate chip cookies out of her hands.

"Shit." I reached out to steady it.

"You good?" Piper's concern was aimed at me and not the near tragic demise of her delicious cookies.

"Yeah, sorry, spaced out."

After a long moment, a smile tipped her lips. "Then can you open the display case and scooch?"

I belatedly realized I was still just standing there, helping her hold the tray she didn't need help holding. "Right."

Once I opened the door, she slid the fresh goods into place before turning to me, her smile growing and turning wry. "So... whatcha thinkin' about?"

The same thing I thought about every Saturday—and most other days, too.

Lars.

Ultra hottie with a razor-sharp edge.

In the few weeks I'd worked at Piper's bakery, Sweets You Rock, he had come in every Saturday like clockwork. Well, technically, he'd gone to Hyde—the connected custom garage that was owned by Piper's husband, Jake. Before he left, though, he always popped in for a cookie.

And I always looked forward to the brief interaction even though we barely spoke. He scared me.

But in a *really* good way.

A way that sent a thrill down my spine and got my blood pumping.

I didn't tell Piper any of that, of course. If she knew, she'd try to work her matchmaking magic. Or she'd tell Jake. Since gossip flew through that garage faster than the stereotypical high school girl's locker room, everyone would know about my crush within the hour.

Yeah, big ol' no thanks to *that*.

"I'm thinking I need more caffeine," I said instead, which wasn't a lie.

I'd had yet another nearly sleepless night. It was becoming increasingly common. Even when I crashed by nine, I could only sleep for a few hours before my mind woke me. I would toss and turn, overthinking and stressing until sleep was a distant dream.

Going to Piper's state of the art coffee maker, I poured a fresh cup, avoiding her studious gaze.

Even though I was three years older than her—twenty-four to her twenty-one—I often felt like I was the younger one. It wasn't just because she was a business owner. Or my boss. Or because she was married to a badass who was wildly in love with her. Or because she was a badass in her own right, with a plethora of gorgeous tattoos and a killer rockabilly-esque style.

It was her whole vibe. She had an old soul. Responsible and mature and too damn sharp. I knew if she kept looking at me, she'd be able to read the truth all over my face.

To distract her, I asked, "Any new recipe ideas I should be aware of?"

That was enough to get her off the trail and on to something that lit her pretty eyes with passion. "It's in the very beginning phases, but I'm toying around with adding marshmallow treats to the menu. They're low cost but could be sold for a decent price, so it's a good cost margin. And they're easy."

"Easy is always a plus in my book."

Weekday morning, I was in before five to get things started before going to my main job as a kindergarten teacher. It made for a long day, but I loved both jobs, so it was worth it.

As were the two paychecks.

On Saturday, I was still there before five but worked until we closed at three—or earlier if we inevitably ran out of everything.

My skills were limited to customer service, working the cash register, and baking—so long as the recipes were clear. The projects that involved piping frosting, molding fondant, or designing were beyond my capabilities.

Marshmallow treats were definitely in my wheelhouse.

"What do you think of starting with two flavors?" Piper asked. "Maybe a traditional and a fruity one with sprinkles. If they do well, we can add more. Or do a rotation like the cupcakes."

That was another thing I adored about Piper. She was my boss. It was *her* bakery. Yet she always asked my opinion. She took my suggestions. She said 'we' and 'us' instead of just barking orders for me to follow.

"I love that idea, but I think we could go bigger," I told her honestly. "The original and fruity, but also a chocolate and something wonky that rotates."

She grinned wide, and I could practically see the possible combinations rolling through her head. "That'll be perfect. If they don't sell, we pawn them off on the boys and move on."

The boys were far from boys. They were *men*. Mega hotties who worked at the garage and frequently snuck in to swipe snacks. Piper's desserts made the bakery popular, but the frequent hottie sightings didn't exactly hurt business.

My eyes went to the door that connected Sweets You Rock's waiting room to Hyde's. "I don't think there'd be much pawning or manipulation needed. Those guys are bottomless pits."

"True. I often wonder what it would be like to have leftovers so I could run a day-old special."

"You'll never find out." I took a long drink of my coffee and mulled everything over, my own excitement growing to match Piper's. "I really think this idea will work. Once you have a recipe nailed down, I can make the batches in the morning."

"You don't have to do that. You already do so much."

"It's kinda my job," I pointed out. "Plus, this really is an easy addition. I can whip up batches while I'm waiting for cookies to bake. It's perfect."

Although she'd tried to decline the help, relief flowed across Piper's expression. "Have I mentioned how freakin' lucky I am that Harlow sent you to me?"

"Technically, it was Kase."

The world really was small, and, for once, I was grateful for it. I'd gone to high school with Harlow—Piper's best friend. We'd reconnected when I'd taught her little sister. When Harlow and her man—who was Jake's best friend and right-hand—had seen me scouring the help wanted ads, Kase had shared about Piper's desperate need for a reliable employee.

It'd been kismet because I'd been in desperate need of a reliable employer.

"Well, he steals a ton of cookies, so we're even. Speaking of..." Piper glanced at the time. "I better open up before the boys get in. Otherwise the paying customers won't have a chance to get anything."

Going around the counter, she unlocked the door and flipped the sign to open. Within minutes, a customer came in.

Then another.

And another.

And a whole hell of a lot more.

For a few hours, a steady line of customers stretched out the door, everyone after their morning muffin, weekend treat, or a view of the Hyde men.

Once it finally died down enough to breathe, Piper turned to me. "You got this for a minute? I want to bring Jake a coffee."

"I'm good," I said, knowing full well it'd be much longer than a minute. By the time she did get back, his coffee would be cold and her lips would be swollen from fooling around.

"Thanks, I'll be right back," she lied. Maybe not intentionally, but it was a lie all the same. She headed into the kitchen, where there was a door that connected her space to his office.

I bet their heart rates skyrocket just from being around each other.

Pushing down the toxic thought, I took advantage of the lull by restocking the case and tidying up after the tornado of chaos. I was in the middle of resetting the small, brightly colored tables when I heard it.

Lars' motorcycle.

The immediate recognition was a sad indication of how obsessed I'd become. A plethora of motorcycles and cars came to Hyde every day, but I was still able to tell when it was his. His bike had a distinct sound. Like its owner's voice, the low rumbling sank into my bones, traveling through me.

I was officially crazy.

I was also officially so nervous, my heartbeat seemed to echo in the small storefront.

Because that Saturday was different.

I was going to actually *talk* to him.

Nothing major. I wasn't going to spill my guts and admit how hot I thought he was. I wasn't going to tell him his dark blue eyes sucked me in and made me feel like there was no one else around. Or that when he ran his hand across his dark, buzzed hair, my mind went stupid.

I was going to say hi and ask about the parts he'd been picking up from Hyde. I'd heard enough of the constant stream of shop talk to know it was a good opening. Even Key—the quietest of all the Hyde men—got chatty when talking about cars.

It would be easy. I could handle simple small talk.

Probably.

Or maybe I'd just hide in the kitchen for the rest of the day.

That was an option, too.

I thought I had time to decide since Lars usually visited Hyde first. But as I was bent over the table to grab the shredded cupcake wrappers someone had so kindly left behind, the bells chimed behind me. I glanced over my shoulder to see his large frame filling the doorway and his eyes aimed my way.

Specifically, at me with my ass in the air.

Standing fast, my thighs bumped the side of the table, and I nearly toppled it. By the time I steadied it and turned, he'd already moved close.

Way close.

"Eep," I squeaked, startled at his sudden nearness.

Not the smooth opening I'd planned on.

He didn't seem fazed by my squeak or his closeness.

I, however, was fazed enough for both of us.

Craning my neck to look up at him, his blue eyes were even more mesmerizing than they were from across the counter. Shadowed and dark and edgy—just like the man himself.

Remembering my master plan, it seemed like as good a time as any to execute it. "Hi."

So captivating.

How will he resist such wit?

Such charm?

Such flawless conversational skills?

Rather than return my greeting, he just stared down at me for a long, intense moment. When he finally broke the charged silence, it was to glance to the side and ask, "Legs here?"

Legs was his nickname for Harlow, dating back to her brief stint as a dancer in his strip club.

Before I could answer, the door chimed behind him and a customer came in. I used the momentary distraction to put some space between us before I did something stupid—like spew my attraction.

Or just kiss him.

Because, *God*, with him standing so close, smelling like leather, man, and a hint of smoke, I really freakin' wanted to kiss him.

I walked behind the display, speaking as I moved. "No, Kase took the day off, so they're doing… whatever."

Knowing them, it was a safe bet they were still in bed—and not necessarily to sleep.

When I looked back at him, a frown twisted his mouth and there was a flash of something on his face.

Disappointment.

Is he upset that Harlow isn't here?

Wait… does he like *her?*

It wasn't out of the realm of possibilities. For one thing, Harlow was smart, funny, a smidge nerdy, and absolutely gorgeous. For another, they did have a history, albeit minor.

One night, over copious amounts of drinks, Harlow had regaled Piper and me with the tale of her first—and only—kiss with Lars. It'd been before Kase, and they'd quickly realized there was no spark there.

Finding someone attractive wasn't the same as being attracted to them.

But I only knew her side of the story. Maybe while she'd moved on to her soul mate, Lars had been left wanting her. Pining for her. Waiting for his chance.

Mind reeling, I went through the motions as the customer cleared out the rest of our cinnamon rolls.

Once it was just Lars and me again, I tested the waters. "Did you need something?"

The tiniest hint of a smirk pulled at his lips. "I need… a lot."

Oh goodness.

For such an innocuous response, his words packed a punch.

A punch that left me fighting to stay on topic while my brain and body very much wanted to imagine all the things a man like him needed.

Reminding myself he might be wanting those desires met by a very taken woman, I fished a little more. "I meant from Harlow."

"No."

I was unsurprised by his clipped answer. It wasn't like he would want me to pass her a note asking if she liked him, check yes or no.

He didn't say anything more, so I opened the display door and pulled out the small paper bag I'd stashed to the side.

His eyes dropped to my outstretched hand and then back to me, though he made no move to take it.

"Chocolate chip was selling like crazy today. I saved one for you before we sold out."

When he still didn't take it, I wondered if my assumption he'd stick with chocolate chip was wrong.

"You can have something else," I offered, "but we're picked over. I'm pretty much down to just my hot cakes." Inwardly cringing, I amended, "All I have left are hot cakes in the back."

That doesn't sound much better…

That time, his mouth didn't curl into a hint of a smirk. No, it curved into a full, wolfish grin. "Chocolate chip is good, hotcakes."

My brain fritzed out at the unexpected playfulness of the nickname.

Taking the cookie, he turned and went through the door to Hyde's waiting room without another word and just a cool flick of the wrist wave.

I watched him go, my thoughts racing. *If* he had feelings for Harlow and everyone found out, the implosion that would occur in the tight friend group would be catastrophic. Or maybe apocalyptic if he was stupid enough to act on his feelings.

Well, I finally talked to him.

Only now I kinda wish I hadn't.

Lars

What the hell am I doing?

I had a shit-ton of work to do. Or a shit-ton of sleep I could've been getting.

Instead of doing something productive with my limited time, I'd gone to the bakery just so I could get a glimpse of the sweetness behind the counter—and I wasn't talking about the desserts.

Joss.

Shy.

Gorgeous.

Too fuckin' good for me.

That didn't stop me from wanting her.

That didn't stop me from becoming damn near obsessed with her.

It sure as hell didn't stop me from *needing* to kiss her—especially when I'd walked in to see her gloriously rounded ass in the air as she'd bent over the table. And, after confirming we were alone, kissing her was exactly what I'd been about to do.

Un-fuckin'-fortunately, the old lady hoarding cinnamon rolls had interrupted before I could. Maybe it was for the best because, based on the way Joss had hurried her fine ass around the counter to put distance between us, it was safe to say she didn't feel the same need for me.

Not yet, at least.

I took the cookie out of the bag as I walked into the Hyde waiting room to find Eli working at the computer.

"Hey, what's..." he started before his eyes narrowed. "Is that chocolate chip?"

"Yup."

"Joss said they were out."

I liked that Joss had thought to set aside the cookie for me. I liked it a hell of a lot more that she hadn't given it up when the greedy Hyde bastards came sniffing around.

It made me wonder what else she'd give to me and only me.

I took a big bite and bragged, "She was saving it for me."

"That goes against bakery rules," he grumbled like a petulant child.

"Sucks to be you."

"Maybe if I turn on the charm..."

My hand curled into a fist, crumpling the paper bag.

He shook his head. "Never mind. She's hot, but not my type. I'm not about to be a cookie gigolo."

Good. Fuckin' keep it that way.

Not looking too closely at the anger and jealousy that hit my gut like a right hook, I asked, "Where's Jake?"

Eli lifted a brow, his tone heavy with implication. "Office."

Right.

Owning a strip club meant I saw a lot of poor bastards who hated their wives. Hated their lives. Hated themselves. I'd already been jaded on relationships and seeing that shit every day hadn't helped. But after being around Jake and Piper—then Kase and Harlow—I'd realized not everyone was destined to be miserable, lying sacks of shit.

I was turning into a true fuckin' romantic.

"What do you need?" Eli asked. "Other than to rub it in that you got the last cookie."

"Jake ordered me a set of dual head pipes."

He clicked a few buttons on the computer. "Chrome?"

"Matte black."

"That'll look sick. Lemme grab them."

It might look sick, but there was nothing wrong with my current head pipes. I didn't need new ones.

What I needed was a better excuse to come in to see Joss. Better yet, to find my damn balls and ask her out.

Otherwise, I'd be stuck with my own right hand and enough parts to open my own warehouse.

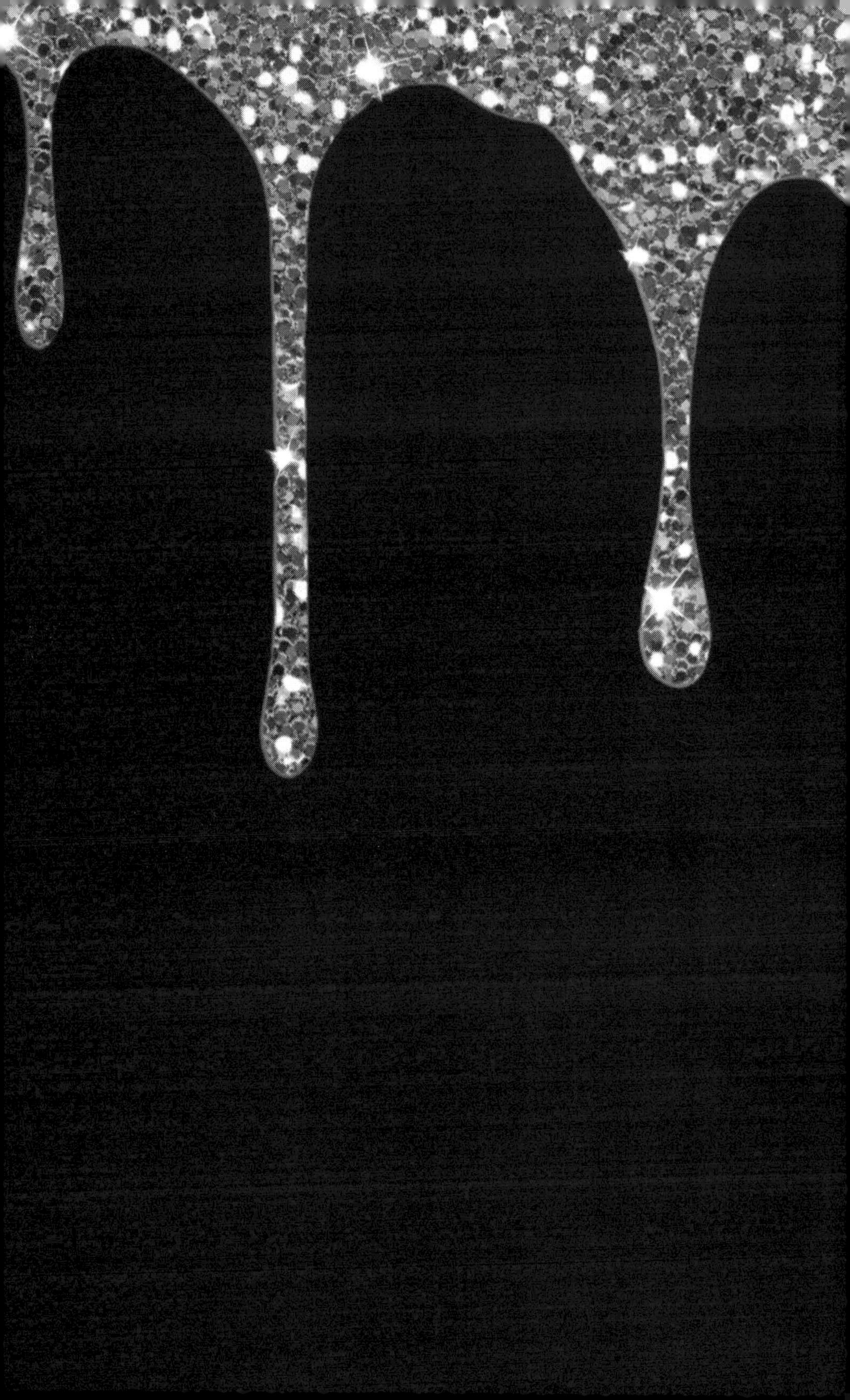

TWO
A Black Sheep with a High Horse

JOSS

WHY DO I HAVE TO LIVE CLOSE TO MY FAMILY?

Why couldn't I have been one of those kids who moved across the country for college and then stayed there? Or maybe traveled the world with just a backpack and no ties.

I would love to be on the other side of the world right now.

"Josie, did you hear me?" my mom asked.

"No," I lied, not making eye contact as I focused way harder than necessary on peeling a carrot.

My mom had always been able to tell when me or my sisters were lying. As a kid, I'd been absolutely certain she had lie detection software installed in her eyes.

As an adult, I was still, like, eighty percent sure she did.

With a motherly—meaning exasperated—sigh, she repeated her stupid question. "I asked if you've talked to Peter."

Only in my nightmares.

"No, Mom. And I won't, so I'd appreciate it if you stopped asking."

For the love of pot roast, mashed potatoes, and the holy Pyrex, please stop.

Peter was a topic I wanted to avoid like the plague.

Actually, more than the plague.

The plague was better than thinking about Peter-Peter-Stripper-Eater.

"It's been a few months," she pointed out, not dropping it. "I'm sure he's had enough time to regret his... indiscretion."

Funny, because I'm *sure he's had enough time to bury his mediocre dick in every stripper in the metro Boston area.*

Maybe farther.

"Mom," Ruth warned, shooting her a look.

"She just doesn't want Joss to be alone," our other sister, Nora, said, unsurprisingly having Mom's back while she talked about me like I wasn't there.

"She's only twenty-four. I think she's got a good couple of years before she has to stock up on cats," Ruth shot back, unsurprisingly having my back.

Not that she always sided with me, per se. True to middle child form, she was the peacekeeper and went with whoever needed backup in order to ensure harmony. But since Nora and Mom usually ganged up on me, that left her on my side by default.

As annoying as they were—and, trust me, they were annoying—they just wanted me to be happy. In their minds, that meant living a similar life to them.

And I was *way* behind their schedule.

After my parents got married at nineteen, Mom had dedicated her entire adult life to raising us girls and being a homemaker extraordinaire. Even right then, in her apron and perfectly coiffed Mom-bouffant, Mary Lennon looked as though she'd stepped out of a sitcom from the fifties—right down to the roast in the oven.

Nora was thirty-five, married with three kids, and living her best president-of-the-PTA life.

Ruth was thirty-one, married with two kids, and living her best stay-at-home-mommy life.

Then there was me.

The black sheep of the family.

The spinster-in-training with no kids and not a strapping husband in sight.

Which meant they pestered me. A lot. First, for Peter and me to set a date. Then, they wanted to know why the date was so far in the future. Finally, what I was doing with my post-Peter life.

Even with their frequent nagging and not-so-silent judging, it was easy to see my happiness mattered. That they wanted what they—very mistakenly—thought was best for me.

Since Peter hadn't made me happy, and he sure as hell wasn't the best for me, her suddenly pushing him on me made no sense.

Eyes narrowed, I studied her, hoping her lie detecting ability was hereditary. "Why're you asking about Peter?"

A small, wistful smile curved her lips. "You guys were just so good together."

Right up until he started shoving his little Peter into another woman.

"I'm not saying you have to marry him tomorrow," Mom continued, "but I'm sure he's tried to contact you."

He had. Frequently. I'd blocked him online, only for him to create new profiles to message me. I hadn't replied to a single one and had simply deleted and blocked. He'd get the hint eventually.

"It's not gonna happen," I muttered, chopping a carrot with a little more force than necessary. The fact it was phallic shaped was probably a coincidence.

She made a noncommittal noise, but thankfully let the subject drop as she dumped the cucumber slices into the large salad bowl before pulling the roast from the oven. Like their food senses were tingling, the backdoor flew open and five ravenous children ran or toddled in.

"Wash hands and set the table," Nora shouted over the roar of voices, swatting away little fingers that reached for veggie scraps and warm rolls.

Just as quickly, the chaos rolled out, the loud slamming traveling through the house on the way to the bathrooms.

Oh.

Right.

This is why I live close by.

The adults in my family drove me nuts, but my five nephews—Parker, Jasper, Paxton, Owen, and Logan—owned my heart. I was crazy about them. Sometimes literally. I was the overly enthusiastic aunt at every sporting event, school concert, science fair, and birthday. Sunday dinners with them were more than worth the headache.

Usually.

Unless my mother kept bringing up Peter, in which case, I'd be forced to host sleepovers at my place in order to get my nephew fix. Sure, last time that'd resulted in a stained carpet, a hole in my couch, *two* broken doors, and a weeklong headache. But if I wrapped everything in bubble wrap—including them—it'd probably work.

Maybe.

Even if it didn't, it'd still be worth it.

Carrying the salad to the huge table, I set it down before returning to the kitchen to get more food.

Mary Lennon did not mess around when it came to Sunday family dinner.

Once the table was covered in more comfort food than an army could consume and everyone was sitting, the full chaos began. Dishes were passed around in a whirlwind of delicious smells. Clusters of conversation took off as if it'd been years since we'd been together rather than a week. I ignored the adults and tuned into the boys, who loudly made fart jokes and threatened to throw their veggies at each other.

It was perfect.

That was, until my dad cleared his throat.

Thanks to an abundance of experience with that particular noise, trepidation filled me. I hesitantly glanced in his direction to see where his focus was aimed.

Oh. Joy.

Me.

He skewered me with a look. "Josie, your mother tells me you've got a new job."

All eyes darted to me.

Mine, however, shot to Ruth and narrowed in a glare that promised retribution. She was the only one who knew about my job at Sweets You Rock, which meant she'd blabbed.

She gave me a small, apologetic shrug that I did *not* accept.

"Are you going to tell us about it?" my dad prodded. It may have *sounded* like a question, but I wasn't fooled.

Noah Lennon was a force to be reckoned with. He owned a chain of four hardware stores that were right out of Small-town Americana. It didn't matter how out of place they were in the flashy city or how many big-box retailers tried to squeeze him out, his stores remained the preferred choice of many. According to signage Dad proudly displayed, people liked the care, knowledge, and quality they got from Lennon Family Hardware.

Like his stores, Dad was old fashioned. When he asked a question —no matter how loaded—he expected an answer.

"It's a new bakery. They have the best chocolate chip cookies. I'll bring some next week."

My futile attempt to bribe and distract predictably didn't work, and Dad asked, "How long have you been working there?"

"A month."

My mom froze with a forkful of salad halfway to her mouth. "A *month*?"

"Just part-time. Usually only Saturdays," I lied, hoping she was too upset to detect it.

She made a murmur of disapproval.

Dad didn't murmur his disapproval. It rang loud and clear. "*Why* are you working there?"

If my parents got even a teensy whiff of my financial trouble, they'd flip their lids worse than the time Ruth got caught making out in a car with the neighbor boy.

It hadn't mattered that she and Benny were in their twenties *and* engaged.

From the beginning, my parents had been adamantly and vehemently against me buying my home. I'd heard their never-ending arguments. Their concerns. Their pragmatic and logistical evisceration of my financial standing.

But at the time, I'd thought it was okay. I'd thought I had Peter's income as a safety net. I'd bought into his bullshit about how we were a team and doing it together, so my solo finances hadn't mattered.

If it weren't for the fact I didn't want anything to do with him, I'd have made him fork over some cash to cover his part of the bills. But I knew if I cracked open that window of communication, he'd try to bust down the wall like the Kool-Aid Man.

It'd be very *oh no* and not at all *oh yeahhhh*.

I'd rather pawn my every worldly possession than talk to him.

And I'd do the same ten times over before I admitted to my parents they'd been right. They wouldn't just gloat. They'd become overbearing to the point of smothering. My mom would insist on seeing every aspect of my finances so she could come up with one of her signature budgets that would exclude anything slightly fun or convenient. My dad would bring over every realtor and try to strongarm me into selling.

Or, worse, he'd demand I come work for him—which would be one step above hell. A *very* small step. I loved my dad, but he wasn't the easiest person to get along with. Especially when it came to work. I'd spent my teen years busting my butt at his stores, and that wasn't an experience I was racing to repeat. Dad didn't do nepotism or favoritism. He'd made his girls work the bad shifts, do the worst jobs, and held them to a higher standard than the other employees.

According to him, it built character.

According to me, it also built resentment and an unhealthy mental space.

Plus, I already had a second job I loved. The bakery was on the opposite side of the spectrum. It was chaotically fun and filled with delicious eye candy. It left me happy even in my exhaustion. Not to mention, Piper paid me far above minimum wage, was flexible with my schedule, and wasn't an overbearing boss.

And she needed me just as much as I needed her.

Which was the part I shared. "It's my friend's shop. She's had trouble finding reliable employees. You know how that is."

Mom may have had lie detection eyes, but Dad had *resting-disappointment-face* that worked like a truth serum. He gave me a skeptical look as he stared me down, waiting for me to break.

I stayed strong, and instead shoved a forkful of roasted veggies into my dry mouth. They tasted like sawdust, but I forced myself to casually chew.

With a gruff harrumph, he let it go and turned his attention to Nora and Dan's home improvements. He grilled them on seemingly every screw size they were using before moving on to Ruth's potential car upgrade. Since Benny agreed with Dad that she needed a practical minivan and not the cool SUV she wanted, I didn't envy the overbearing double-teaming she had to deal with.

No, I basked in her discomfort. It wasn't the retribution for her big mouth that I'd be delivering when she least expected it, but it did soothe my anger. A bit.

But I should've remembered that karma was a mega-bitch. Enjoying her pain welcomed it to return to me.

"Joss…" my mom started, studying me with an intensity that made me brace and preemptively get annoyed. "Since you won't talk to Peter, does that mean you're seeing someone new?"

Everyone quieted, waiting expectantly for my answer. Even the kids seemed to instinctively know something big was happening.

"No. It means I'm not subjecting myself to his pointless excuses," I gritted out.

I waited for her argument, but it was my nine-year-old nephew, Parker, who spoke. "Mom said Auntie Josie is gonna end up alone 'cause she's too sensitive and independent."

"Parker," Nora yelped at her son, bolting out of her seat and spilling her wine in the process.

"What? That's what you said. You told Dad that it doesn't make sense that she's so d-word proud and always on her horse because her life is a *mess*." He put so much nine-year-old attitude into that one word, it made me wonder how emphatically my sister had said it.

By the time Nora made it to him, he'd already finished his sentence, but she covered his mouth anyway.

He wiggled away, his words coming out muffled. "Can I see your horse, Auntie Josie?"

My stunned gaze went to Nora, taking in the guilt coating her tight expression.

It hurt to see.

Scanning the rest of the adults at the table, I didn't see surprise. No outrage on my behalf. No indignation. None of them leaping from their chairs, frantic to come to my defense.

Each of their faces was coated in matching guilt that made it painfully obvious they shared Nora's opinion of me. Knowing the way they were, it was also likely they'd all shared said opinion amongst themselves.

And that didn't hurt.

It fucking *killed*.

"Joss, I—" Nora started, but I didn't want to hear it.

I hauled ass to the door, my thoughts a mess of storm clouds that grew so dark, they began leaking from my eyes. If I had any kind of luck, my exit would be like the dramatic ones in movies. The ones where whoever called after the escapee but for some reason never actually followed to stop them.

I should've known better. The previous year of my life had made it clear that if it weren't for shit luck, I'd have no luck at all.

Sure enough, just as I stepped onto the porch, Nora's hand wrapped around my arm. "Joss, stop."

Whipping around, I hissed, "Sorry, I can't hear you up here on my high horse."

Ruth came behind her, and I had no doubt the rest would be there soon. They'd gang up, throwing barbed wire apologies that would slice and sting—the kind that offered example after example of why they were right.

Tearing my arm out of Nora's grasp, I took a step away and opened my mouth before closing it again. It wasn't worth it.

Because I knew—in my battered and wounded heart—she wasn't completely off base in her assessment.

I was everything she'd said. And since my second job was more necessary than even Ruth knew, I was more of a hot mess than they already believed.

Unable to face that *or* them, I turned, jogged down the steps to my car, and ignored the voices behind me as Ruth worked to keep everyone off my back.

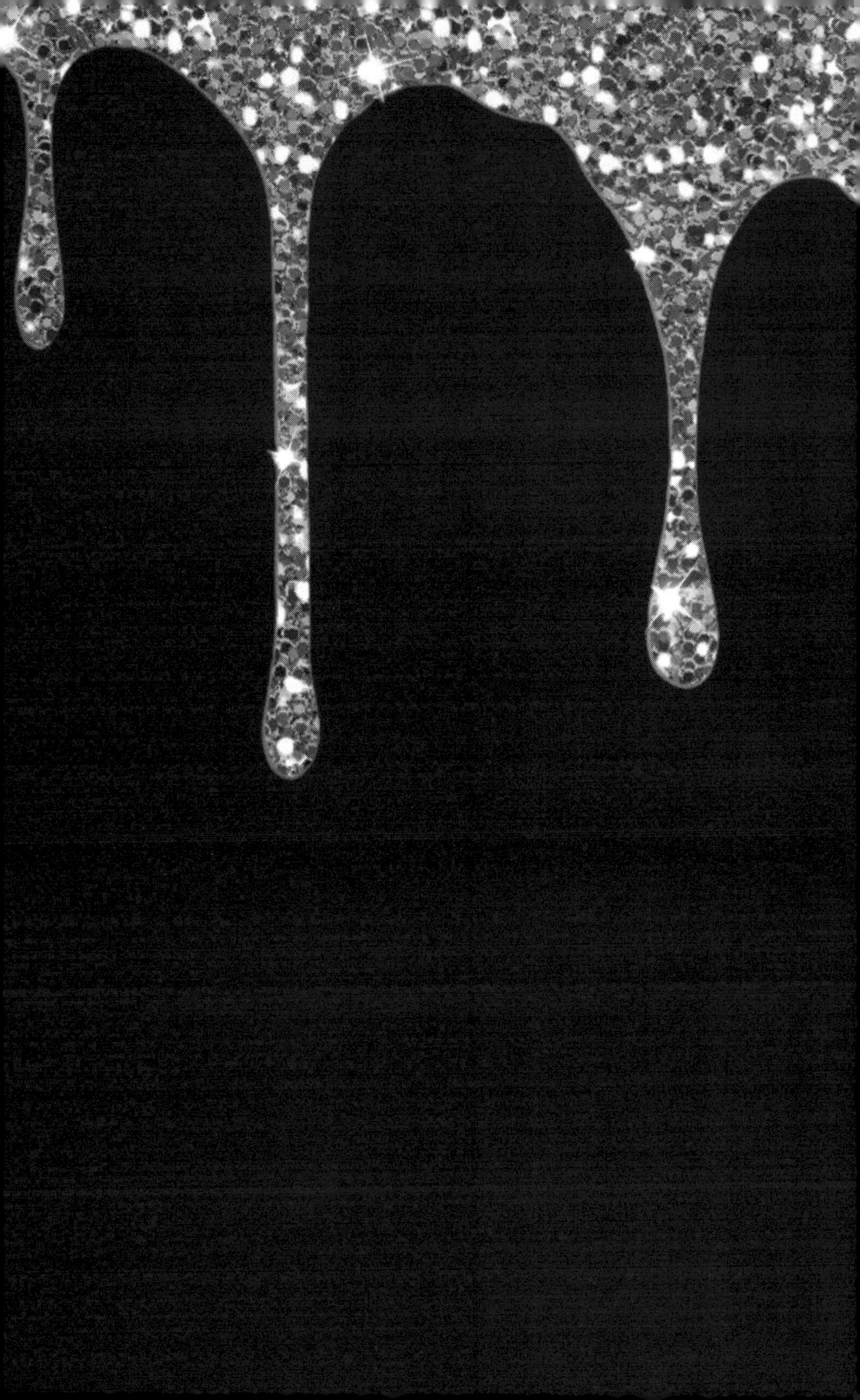

THREE

Wacky Lars Day

JOSS

RUTH: YOU HAVE to answer us eventually.

Joke's on them. I really don't.

Discreetly checking my phone during Fantastic Friday Free Fun—otherwise known as *It's the end of the week and the kids need some extra play time*—I swiped away the text from Ruth.

Since the epic disaster that was Sunday dinner, I'd yet to talk to my family. I didn't answer their numerous texts, Facebook messages, or calls. I knew I was feeding into Nora's claim I was too sensitive, but I didn't care. There was nothing wrong with being sensitive.

Just like there was nothing wrong with needing time and taking it.

"Miss Lemon!" a shrill shout came from across the room.

Hurriedly tucking my phone away, I rushed over to the play kitchen center where a ruckus was brewing. Other nosy kiddos circled as two of my kindergartner friends were engaged in a fierce stare-off. Hannah was rocking an epic stink eye as she glared at where Samuel stood near the toy oven.

"What's happening?" I asked.

Hannah grew flustered as she tried to put all her five-year-old emotions into words. "Uh... soooo... I was... And then he... And I... Miss Lemon."

"Le*nn*on," I corrected. And would keep correcting even though I'd inevitably be *Miss Lemon* all year. "Take a deep breath and start at the beginning."

"Miss Le*nn*on," she corrected with the same emphasis, "Samuel isn't playing right."

"It's free time, Hannah. There is no right or wrong way to do it."

"But he's cooking our baby!"

Okay, I stand corrected. Cooking a baby definitely leans toward the wrong way to play.

My eyes dropped to the baby doll in the oven. We'd only been in school for a couple weeks, but I had a good grasp on the kids' big personalities. And though I'd *never* have favorites because teachers didn't do such a thing… Samuel was totally my favorite. I couldn't help it. He was the sweetest little boy. He was funny and had a dry wit beyond a typical five-year-old. I was pretty certain that roasting a doll wasn't a warning sign of a budding serial killer, but that kind of play was unusual for him.

Crouching in front of him, I kept my tone light. "Whatcha cooking, buddy?"

Tears filled his big brown eyes, though the stubborn set of his thinned lips and lifted chin showed how hard he was working to hold them in.

"Feel your emotions, Samuel. But don't worry, you're not in trouble," I reassured him. "I just want to know what you're cooking."

His eyes darted to Hannah and then back to me. "Baby's backs. My dada cooks on the grill. They're messy."

"Baby back ribs?" I asked. "The meat with all the BBQ sauce and bones?"

He nodded frantically. "We love them, I wanted to make them for Hannah 'cause she said I was playing the dada. And dadas gots to keep their women fed and happy."

Attaboy, Dad.

I reeeeally *can't wait to meet Samuel's parents at open house.*

"Ribs are delicious, but they're *not* made with babies." I reached into the basket of play food and pulled out a plastic burger. "How about you cook burgers instead?"

"I like burgers."

"Who doesn't?"

He grabbed the burger and a frying pan, setting them on the stove before pulling the baby out of the oven. Although he'd been attempting to cook her, his new handling of the doll was sweet and gentle. He propped it on his hip while he moved around, pretending to add every fake sauce and condiment the kitchen contained.

I kept an eye on them for a minute, making sure Hannah was settled, too. She sat at the table, exaggeratedly sipping at the plastic milk while watching Samuel cook.

Living the dream.

Seeing as the freak-out was finished, I relaxed.

It lasted all of two minutes before another high-pitched, hysterical cry filled the room.

Thank God it's Friday.

CAN I GO back to Friday?

Staring down at my shoes, I stupidly blinked as if one would magically change.

Spoiler alert—it didn't.

I'd heard of people accidentally wearing a brown shoe with a black one. Rounded toe with pointed. Heck, even different brands but in the same color.

But that would've been too boring for me.

Noooo, I had to go all out in my faux pas by putting on a hot pink Chuck and a black Vans. They were nowhere near the same color. They weren't the same style. And they certainly weren't subtle enough to go unnoticed.

I knew that for a fact because Piper had complimented my bold wardrobe choice within seconds of entering the kitchen.

It would've been one thing had I been at my teaching job. I could've switched some stuff around, read *Wacky Wednesday*, made it a whole impromptu theme of the day. I, however, had to go and pull the fashion blunder on the worst day.

Saturday.

Bakery day.

Lars day.

Why aren't the pants that completely cover shoes back in style yet? High-waisted skinny jeans had their turn. It's JNCO's time to shine again.

"I… can't believe I left the house like this," I muttered, cursing my four AM wakeup. No one's brain operated at full capacity under those circumstances.

Piper checked the time. "I don't mind what's on your feet. Actually, I think you look cool. Very punk rock. But I don't want you feeling uncomfortable all day. I can take over the rest of your prep and get one of the boys to help so you can run home and change."

"You won't have anything left to sell if you do that," I pointed out.

"Meh, it's fine. They can't eat the entire inventory." She glanced around the counter loaded with trays of unbaked cookies I'd been prepping—Frosted Flakes with white chocolate chips. "Only, like, half."

I was tempted. But driving home, switching shoes, and driving all the way back would take time. That was time someone else would have to help, and, no offense to the guys, they weren't very good at it. Between what they dropped, ate, and forgot to charge for, Piper really would be out half her sales for the day.

Not to mention, my lost wages.

"It's fine. I'm back here or behind the counter all day. No one will see."

I'll just hide if Lars comes.

The timer went off, and I moved to take the last few batches of sugar cookies out before popping in some trays of the Frosted Flakes ones. "We'll be too busy for me to even think about it."

"If you're sure…"

"I'm sure."

I was also right.

From the time Piper unlocked the door and flipped the sign to open, it was a seemingly never-ending stream of customers with little to no break in between. Even in the craziness, the mood was good. Fun, even. Most people were happy to wait because they knew it'd be worth it. Of course, there were the few inescapable complainers who felt they should get a discount or freebie for their time, as if they were being forced to wait there.

A couple likely would've turned into threats of bad online reviews and annoying I-want-to-speak-to-the-manager hassles had Harlow not shown up with Kase and immediately jumped behind the counter. She didn't work for Piper in any official capacity, but she was a good friend who helped on Saturday mornings in exchange for an unlimited supply of Piper's coffee.

Even with the extra set of hands, though, it was a madhouse.

"I need to hire another employee," Piper said while boxing up a custom cake order. She scanned the full room. "Maybe two or three."

She had a counter gal—Becca—who worked weekdays, but I'd only met her in passing since she only worked when her kids were in school. Which, of course, was when I didn't work because *I* was in school.

"Oh!" The older woman I was cashing out grinned. Only instead of looking like a wholesome grandma, there was a wicked glint in her eyes. I knew what was coming before she hitched a thumb over her shoulder. "How about some of those men from next door? I bet they'd be able to help with any heavy lifting you have."

Piper smiled as she shook her head. "My muffins and cupcakes may be fully-loaded, but I don't think they require that kind of muscle."

"It was worth a shot."

"No way," the younger woman with her added. "If those men were around all day, the lines would be even longer."

She fanned herself, paying zero mind to what anyone might think of her being a dirty bird. I aspired to be like her. "But what nice scenery to enjoy while we wait."

I finished cashing her out before letting Harlow take over so I could go into the back to pop more cookies in. Coming out with a loaded tray, I said, "Last batch of chocolate chip for the day. I'm going to set one aside for..."

My words trailed off as I froze. Like he'd materialized from my thoughts, Lars stood in the pretty storefront. He should've looked ridiculous. This tall, insanely built man in faded jeans, a white tee, a worn leather jacket, and biker boots amongst bright tables and glitter cupcake décor.

But he didn't look ridiculous. He looked like he belonged. He was at ease. In charge. Like he controlled any room he was in, his dangerous vibe filling it as thoroughly as smoke from a fire.

Smoke that filled my lungs, swirling around my heart and parts farther south until I couldn't catch my breath.

Stroking his hand across his buzzed head, he brought it down to rub his neck as his gaze slid down my body. His ever-present cocky smirk grew to a grin. "Dig the look, hotcakes."

So distracted by all that was Lars, my mismatched shoes had somehow managed to slip my mind. Embarrassment burned my cheeks, but that didn't stop the return of my nickname from making my stomach feel as warm and melty as one of the chocolate chip cookies I carried.

It was a recipe for drama to pine for a man who was pining for another man's woman. Hell, it was convoluted just saying it. But, oh man, lucky me.

I was clearly *great* at following all recipes, not just ones for baked goods.

"Hotcakes?" Harlow stage whispered to Piper, who just shrugged.

I was saved from having to explain the shoe situation to him because Lars moved his attention to Harlow. "Hey, Legs. Sasha's been up my ass to ask you a question."

Zoning in like it was the most complicated task in the world, I hurried to bag up a cookie and put it on the display case before sliding the tray in.

And then I might as well have sprouted feathers with how fast I fled to the kitchen like the big chicken I was.

It wasn't like I was totally abandoning my work. Like most Saturdays, the kitchen looked as if a baking bomb had detonated. I took a few minutes to straighten up before risking a glance out the door to see that Lars was gone.

I should've gone home and changed my damn shoes. Preferably right as he'd pulled in.

Grabbing the last of the muffins, I returned to the storefront, praying to the gossip gods no one questioned me about Lars or my hasty getaway.

I should've known better.

Because the second she saw me, Piper's painted red lips tipped into a sly smile. "So... Hotcakes, huh?"

If she was aiming for nonchalant, she'd missed by a long, vanilla-scented mile.

"I misspoke when he was in last week," I explained, getting it over with. "Apparently, the nickname is going to stick."

And me and my stupidly swooning stomach don't mind.

"Yup, you're never getting rid of it," Harlow confirmed. "I'm pretty sure I'll forever be Legs. Although, that may be mostly because he knows it bugs Kase."

I held back a frown of concern for my friend's relationship. Yup. Just concern. And not at all the pang of jealousy as I wondered whether Lars was purposefully trying to sabotage Harlow and Kase's relationship.

Okay, fine, a little of that. But mostly the concern thing.

Which was why I asked, "Have you ever asked Lars to stop?"

"Why would I? It's entertaining. Plus, Kase gets all growly and possessive and..." Her words trailed as her smile shrank from amusement to wistfully secretive.

The pang in my chest grew to a sharp stab. I envied Harlow as much as I envied Piper. I'd never had anything like what they had with their men. If Peter had been pissed about something like that, he wouldn't have been sweet and possessive in his jealousy. He'd have taken it out on me with the silent treatment interspersed with passive aggressive comments.

"Do you want Lars to stop calling you hotcakes?" Piper asked.

I shifted to look at her, only to see alarm tightening her features. It made me wonder how long she'd been watching me.

And how badly I'd done hiding my toxic emotions.

Before I could answer, she tilted her head toward the garage. "I can have Jake casually bring it up in a subtle, non-threatening kinda way." She shrugged. "Or in a totally threatening way, if you'd prefer. Either works."

"No, it doesn't bother me."

"Let me know if you change your mind. I wouldn't be a very good boss if I let you be uncomfortable. You'd have to report me to HR and

I don't even have an HR. I'd have to hire an outside company just for you—"

"It's honestly fine," I said through my laughter. "I lucked out. It could've been something way worse, like dump cakes."

"Or Fire Crotch," Harlow muttered, referring to the *suuuper* flattering and professional nickname gifted to her by one of the anchors at the news station she worked at.

"Yup, hotcakes is sounding better and better by the minute."

Especially when Lars says it in his low, gravelly voice.

The door behind us swung open, and I glanced back to see which man it was so I knew what they were after. If it was Jake, he was after Piper. If it was Kase, he was after Harlow. And if it was anyone else, they were after whatever baked goods we had left after the morning crush.

In basically a blur of pretty blue eyes, pulled back dreads, tattooed skin, and paint splattered clothing, Kase made a beeline for Harlow. As soon as he was within reach, he snagged her shoulders and pulled her to him, as if he couldn't wait those extra two steps. He cupped her cheeks and kissed her in an inappropriate way that was still so beautiful, it made my chest ache. He tore himself away just enough for them to have a whispered conversation that I bet involved a lot of innuendo and dirty talk.

Their heart rates are probably through the roof just from talking.

Scowling at myself, I started scrubbing the counter with more force than necessary, as though it'd personally insulted me and owed me money. But my sour mood wasn't the poor counter's fault. I was mad at the bitterness that filled my clenched stomach and brain with its poison.

I'd just gotten my emotions tamped down when the door swung open again, and Jake stalked in.

I picked the wrong place to work. I don't need True Love Bakery. I need Jilted Lovers Rum Bar.

"Hey, baby," Piper greeted, smiling at him as though they'd been separated for years and years. "What'd Lars need?"

His brows lowered. "Dunno, didn't see him. I've had my hands shoved in a Vette's engine all morning."

"Kinky."

"I'll show you kinky..." With that, Piper was up and over his shoulder before he carried her into the kitchen. They'd likely end up in his office where he'd inevitably end up in... well, in someplace I didn't want to think about.

Soft applause came from a table where a man and two women were squeezed in on one side of the table so they could watch everything play out at the counter.

"You should start selling admission and popcorn." The man lifted his coffee. "This place is better than TV."

Rated MA-TV, but yeah.

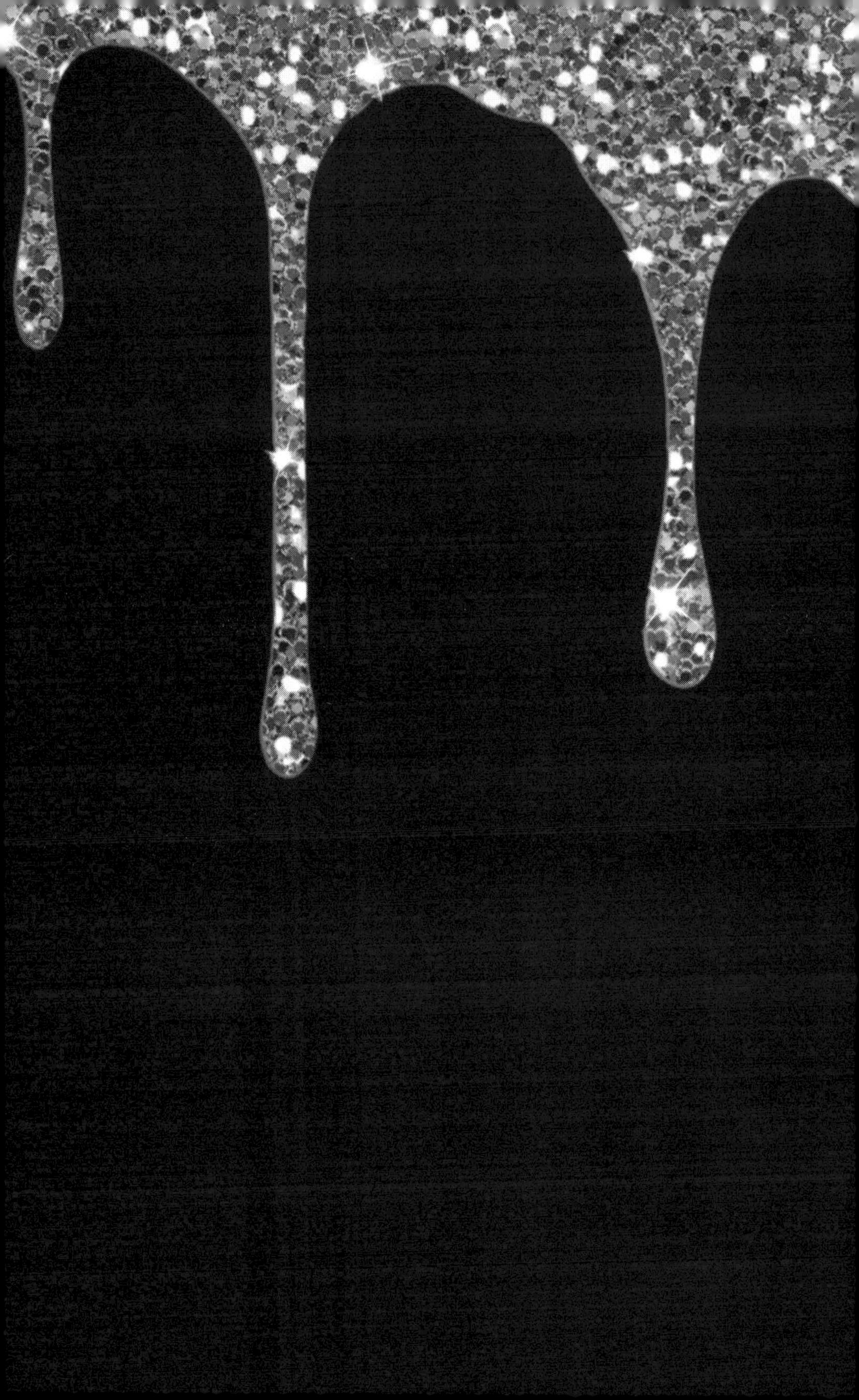

FOUR

You Can't Sugarcoat a Stolen Cookie

JOSS

IT'S AMAZING HOW THIS SCHOOL WEEK MANAGED TO *break the laws of time and physics to last for five years rather than five days.*

Trudging up my porch steps on Friday afternoon, I was beyond exhausted. My mind was so focused on the well-earned rum and Diet Coke waiting for me inside, I almost missed it.

A pile of vegetables and a loaf of homemade bread sitting on my little outdoor table.

If that didn't scream *Mom*, nothing did.

I gathered the goodies and headed inside. Killing the security alarm, I set the veggies on the coffee table, plopped onto the couch, and immediately busted into the bread.

If this is banana bread, I'll peel down the foil and eat the whole thing like it's an actual banana.

Unfortunately, my hopes and mood both crashed when I saw it was lemon poppyseed. Still good, but not my favorite.

It was, however, Peter's favorite.

I wasn't sure if it was a coincidence or Mom's attempt at bread related matchmaking. My money was on the latter. It was just like her to think I'd see his favorite bread and magically forget I also saw him kneading another woman's ass like sourdough.

My family and I had been locked in a tense standoff since the Great Sunday Dinner Debacle. I'd texted Ruth a few times because if I'd remained totally radio silent, Mom and Dad would've sent out the National Guard, Army, Navy, and some other secret government agencies I wasn't privy to.

But the veggies and bread may as well have been a wartime mediator. Mom was done letting me stew. And, honestly, I was surprised she'd stayed away as long as she had before making a peace offering, Lennon-style. It meant if I didn't meet her halfway, I was no longer the wounded party.

I was the bad guy.

Since there was no way in hell I was letting that happen, I called her as I popped a bite of bread into my mouth.

"Hello?"

"Hey, Mom. How're you?"

"Better now that I'm finally hearing from my youngest daughter. A daughter I carried and birthed and nursed and—"

"I know, I know. I've been busy."

Also, your eldest is a crap-talking beyotch and none of you defended me.

"You sound exhausted," she said. "Are you sleeping enough?"

"Just a long week. The kids are still getting into the swing of being back at school."

Mom launched into... well, full-on *Mom Mode*. "Be sure you're getting enough sleep. And drink more OJ and take your vitamins. You know how germy little kids can be. And wear a heavy coat, not just your hoodies."

If she starts telling me to eat more kale, I'll hang up.

Super food, my ass. Super-nasty food is more like it.

Even as I rolled my eyes, I did it smiling. She may be a pain in my ass, but my mom meant well. She loved me, and that feeling was mutual.

"I will." Changing the subject, I asked, "How's the fall garden coming in?"

Mom filled me in on her garden and book club, and neither of us touched on the Sunday dinner drama. That was the Lennon way. We moved on and glossed over it—there was never any growth or change.

After a short while, she sighed. "Well, I better run. Your father and I are going to dinner, and I need to fix my hair."

No need to rub it in, we all have crazy social lives, Mother.

I myself have wild Friday night plans to drink alone while I binge Netflix.

"That sounds like fun," I said instead.

"With the Michelsons," she added.

The Michelsons were my parents' neighbors. Mr. Michelson was fine enough, in a boring-as-hell way. Mrs. Michelson was rude, gossipy, and walked around like she was queen of the cul-de-sac. In stereotypical bored suburban housewife fashion, she spent her days policing her neighbors to ensure her property value didn't drop a single nickel. It wasn't as if they were living in a mega mansion, so I wasn't sure where her sense of entitlement and superiority had come from.

But I sure knew where I wanted to tell her to stick it.

"That sounds like fun," I repeated, that time with sarcasm dripping like thick molasses.

"Joss Lennon, be nice," my mom said, her tone filled with warning before it lightened. "But I *am* hoping it'll be an early night. That woman is exhausting."

I laughed. "Okay, I'll let you get ready. Thank you for the bread."

Even though I wish it was banana.

My food disappointment was replaced by food longing when she said, "I'm making your favorite Caprese chicken for dinner on Sunday, so make sure you come hungry."

Her not-so-subtle message was received—I was expected at Sunday dinner.

Not giving me the chance to get out of it—not that I was going to, I really did love that chicken—she rushed out, "Okay, love you, Josie. I'll give Dad your love, too. Bye."

And then she hung up on me.

To go get ready for her night out.

Leaving me to my own crazy night of Netflix.

Sighing, I tossed my phone down and thought about maybe, possibly, potentially, contemplating getting dressed to go to Rye instead.

Rye was a cool, grunge—but not grungy—bar owned by the Hyde gang's friend, Rhys. And Rhys was a hot guy with dimples deep enough to dive into. Harlow bartended there occasionally, mostly on the busy weekends. I was pretty sure she was working that night. And if she was there, Kase would be parked on a stool to keep an eye on her—both because he was mildly obsessed with staring at his fiancée, and because he was protective as hell.

Maybe a night at a bar is just what I need.

Maybe I should text Piper and see if she's going so we can make it a mini girls' night.

Maybe others in the group will be there.

Others like, oh, I dunno... Lars.

Scowling, I dropped my head back and closed my eyes.

I needed to get over my stupid crush. Not only was it not reciprocated, it really seemed as if he had feelings for someone else. A *taken* someone else. That was a load of drama I didn't need.

Being smart for once, I wasn't going to go out in the hopes of seeing him.

I was going because I wanted to. Because I deserved it after such a long week. Because I wasn't living to my full potential as the black sheep of my family if my parents partied harder than I did.

This is it.

Tonight is the turning point. No more bitterness over Peter. No more wasting my youth on Netflix and early bedtimes.

And no more crushes on unavailable men who are surrounded by hot strippers and hung up on another woman.

I'm moving on and getting wild.

I stood and glanced down at my sensible sneakers, jeans, and loose top.

Okay, I'm getting changed and then I'm moving on and getting wild.

WHOSE IDEA WAS it to make Friday nights come before Saturday morning?

And whose brilliant idea was it for me to go out on a Friday when I work early Saturday?

Oh.

Right.

It was mine.

Well, the choosing-to-go-out part. I don't control the days of the week.

Yet...

Fighting a yawn, I rushed around Sweets You Rock. My brain was dead with a rum hangover and sleep deprivation, but my body was the MVP, literally carrying me through the motions. I hadn't even realized how much of the day had gotten away from me until I moved on autopilot to serve the next customer only to find there was none.

"Holy crap, it's almost two already," I noted.

"No," Harlow drawled, stretching. Thankfully, she'd decided to tag along with Kase that morning. Otherwise, it would've been *rough*.

Or *rougher*.

"No wonder my caffeine tank is on E. I'll be back. Maybe," she added as she went into the back.

Piper opened the display case to condense the few items that were left. She looked exhausted. More so than usual. "That was brutal. I have five interviews set up this week. Unless they're serial killers, I'm hiring them." She scanned the case before amending, "Actually, even if they're serial killers, I'll probably still hire them. They say Bundy was charming, I bet he could sell the hell out of some cinnamon rolls."

"Seeing as we ran out of cinnamon rolls before ten, I don't think you need help with that."

"True. Any chance you love me enough to stay late today?"

Assuming it was to help tame the chaos that was left behind after the insane day, I nodded.

"I'm gonna pop what we have left into the oven and then bring Jake a coffee... so long as Harlow left any. You good?"

I gestured to the mostly empty storefront where only a couple tables of people chatted and picked at their food. "Yeah, I think I can handle this rowdy crowd."

Piper followed Harlow into the kitchen, and I leaned against the counter to catch my breath. And then I lost it again when rumbles filled my ears and vibration rippled through my bones.

After a lot of thought—and even more rum—the night before, I'd reached an important decision.

I was over Lars.

I just needed my common sense to communicate that newly developed info to my body.

Because I wasn't a complete unfeeling monster, I'd still saved a chocolate chip cookie for him. I grabbed the bag from the case, set it on the counter, and turned around, pretending to be engrossed in the complicated task of folding boxes. I ignored the—albeit smaller than previously—cluster of butterflies that fluttered in my belly. I ignored the tiny hint of anticipation that skittered down the back of my neck. And when I heard the heavy fall of his shitkicker boots, I ignored that, too.

But he didn't ignore me. "Hey, hotcakes."

Barely glancing over my shoulder, I said, "Hi. Your cookie is right there."

"Right where?"

"The bag on the counter."

"If there's a bag on the counter, hotcakes, it's invisible."

I spun around to see he was correct. In the tiny window of time I'd turned my back, someone had helped themselves to a free cookie. "People really suck."

"Yeah," he agreed, not trying to sugarcoat it—because he had no sugary treat to coat it with.

"Sorry, that was the last one, too. You want something else?"

A smirk curved his lips as he ran his hand across his short hair and down his neck. Had I not been mostly over my crush, I'd have noticed how sinisterly hot it made him look. "Yeah, but that's okay. You'll owe me."

With that, he turned and walked into the garage.

I'm over my crush.

I'm over my crush.

I'm over my crush?

Lars

FUCKIN' HELL, I was pathetic.

I was a grown ass man and Joss was just a little thing, but I was running outta the bakery like a coward. If I didn't get away, I'd have admitted what I wanted more than any damn cookie.

A kiss.

Just one taste of her lips that I knew for a fact were sweeter than any baked good.

I also knew one kiss would never be enough for me. But, based on the fact she barely glanced my way, one kiss would likely be too much for her. I might want her so badly it fuckin' hurt, but I wasn't gonna sexually harass her at work. I'd be no better than the pricks at Wicked who took shit too far.

Cookie-less, kiss-less, and ball-less, I walked into Hyde just as Jake came from the back. It was obvious what he'd been up to—and not just because his overgrown blond hair was in disarray.

"What's up?" he greeted.

"I always took you for a coral or maybe a light pink," I said. At his brow raise, I gestured to my mouth. "You got a little something."

Grabbing a chrome part from the stack on the counter, he held it up and used it as a mirror. "Shit." He scrubbed at the red lipstick with the back of his hand, which only worked to smear it across his cheek and into his stubble. "Gimme a minute, yeah?"

When he returned with a clean face, I said, "Take it since she has time to share her lipstick with you, that means shit is good."

After the bakery and garage opened, both places had been slammed. And had stayed slammed. Jake had mentioned she had help on the weekdays, but the weekends were an issue.

"Finally," he said. "Loaning my guys to her every Saturday may have caused an uptick in female patrons, but it'd also caused a serious hit to her inventory. Thank Christ for Joss. I'd say I'm grateful for all the shit that went down with her house and fiancé, but that'd make me a prick."

In our brief weekly interactions, I'd picked up a lot about Joss. She was twenty-four—a whole damn decade younger than me. She was also a teacher, hot as fuck, sweeter than any damn baked good, and quiet in a way that made me wanna see how wild she got when she let loose. But there was a lot about her I didn't know.

For instance, that she'd been engaged.

Or maybe she still was since he hadn't said *ex*.

I worked to keep my voice neutral. "Didn't realize she was engaged."

"Don't know the details, just that some shit went down a few months ago, and she's been bustin' her ass to fix it."

Damn.

Even if she wasn't still engaged, she was clearly hung up on the dickhead. Why else would she want to fix things between them?

Maybe that's why she was always so desperate to get away from me. Or that was my pride talking, and she just wasn't into me.

Either way, I was fucked.

Or *not* fucked, in my case.

Xavier came from the back. "You here for your panel?"

I lifted my chin.

"You keep this up, there's not going to be a factory part left on your Harley."

He wasn't kidding. But while my other recent purchases had little to do with upgrades and more to do with seeing the brunette next door, the new instrument panel was actually necessary.

Mine had cracked last time I'd had to lay my bike down. As far as I was concerned, it wasn't needed. The road and instincts told me how fast I should be going.

The state of Massachusetts disagreed. If I wanted my Harley to be road legal, I needed to swap out the broken panel.

I lifted my shoulder in a half-assed shrug. "What else am I gonna do with all my minutes of free time?"

"You could try getting yourself a woman," Jake said, cashing me out with a hefty friend discount.

"Don't have your luck."

"No one has my luck 'cause no one has a woman like mine."

I ran my palm across my buzzed hair. "I'm telling you, man, I just need to grow out my hair. You and Kase have good hair and good women. Can't be a coincidence."

"Yeah, your lack of hair is the problem. Nothin' to do with you being too busy to date."

"Who said anything about dating?"

But it was bullshit. I wanted to date.

I was just the dumb bastard who wanted to date a woman who was hung up on a different dumb bastard.

Jake let it drop and said, "Based on your minutes of free time, I take it Wicked is still packed."

"You'd be correct. Tried to get Sasha to take over papers, but she made a bigger mess of shit than I did. Now I'm sorting through her clusterfuck and my own, all while making sure shit doesn't implode around me."

"You should hire Joss."

The image of Joss up on my stage, shaking that rounded ass and smiling at someone—*anyone*—else made me fuckin' livid.

Hard as steel but fuckin' livid.

"Don't quite think the schoolteacher is a Wicked girl," I said through gritted teeth.

"Not as a dancer. Hire her to do your paperwork. She got all Piper's books organized and color-coded. If she can tame that growing shitstorm, she'll be able to handle your stuff, yeah?"

It was a bad idea.

A really fucking bad idea.

I'd have to be a moron to invite that kinda torture into my space.

That didn't stop me from lifting my chin. "I'll ask."

Because it was an opening. May have been a round opening and a square peg, but I would make it work 'cause I wanted time with her.

Time I'd use to find out about that bastard fiancé and how I could get rid of him.

When did I get so damn pathetic?

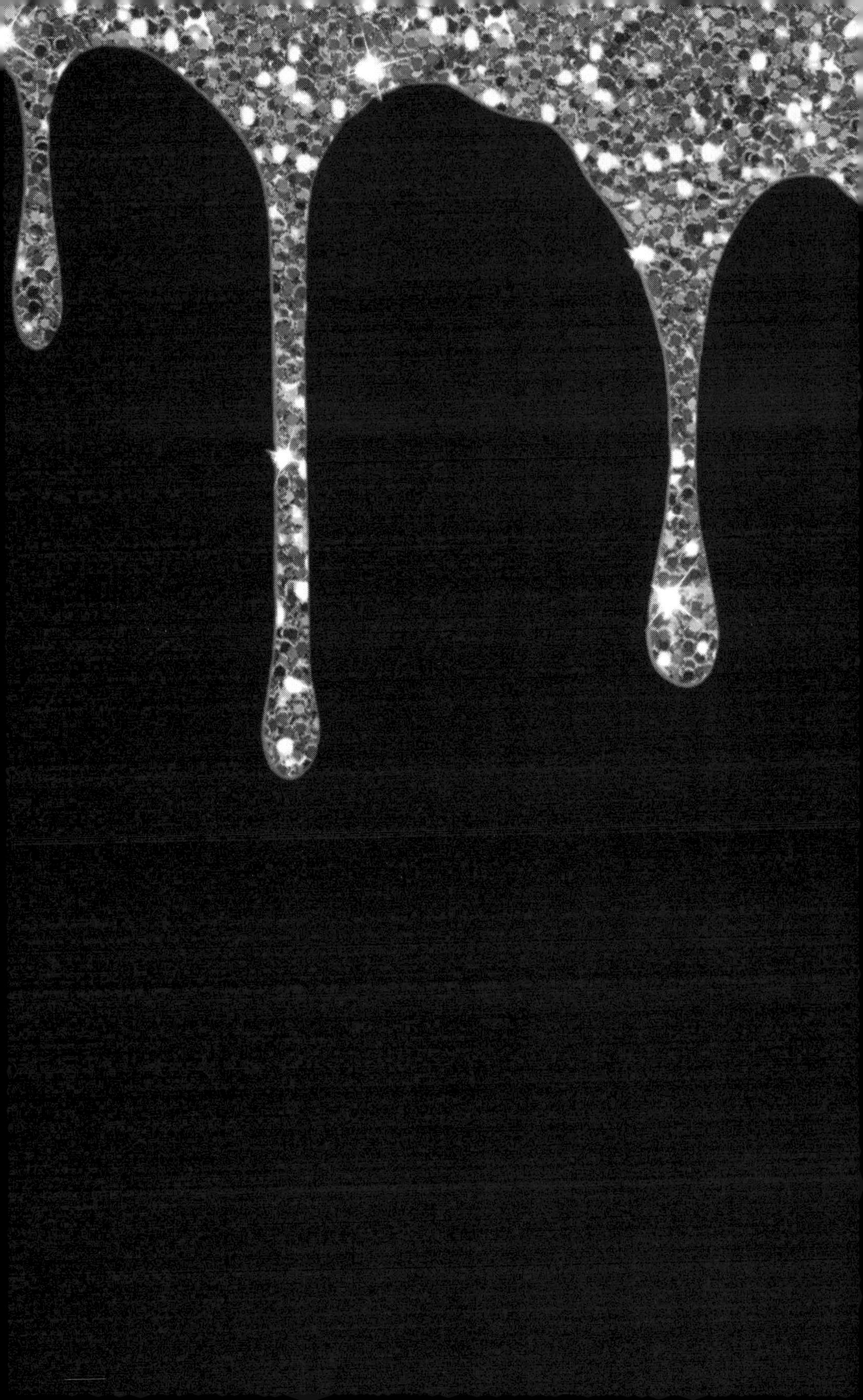

FIVE
Don't Forget Your Strip Club Permission Slip

JOSS

"HOW DO YOU FEEL ABOUT STRIP CLUBS, HOTCAKES?"

I almost dropped the cupcake tray I was holding.

When I'd heard the door behind me, I'd assumed it was a customer, not Lars returning after going to Hyde.

I sure as hell hadn't expected him to ask my thoughts on adult entertainment venues.

Turning around to face him, I shrugged. "I wouldn't know, I've never been. Not exactly a good spot for a kindergarten field trip. Too many slippery poles and glitter shrapnel. No permission slip in the world would cover that kind of risk."

His midnight blue eyes widened slightly, and he gave a low chuckle.

I liked that I'd been the one to elicit it almost as much as I liked the way it sounded.

"Full of surprises," he murmured. "Shame you're..."

My defensive hackles rose. "Shame I'm *what*?"

"Nothing. Like it better this way," he bizarrely answered—or non-answered—before giving me conversation whiplash. "Jake said you worked some magic on the bakery's bookkeeping."

I didn't bother to be modest. Although Piper had a good setup in place for a smaller operation, her business had grown too much for the basic system. She had a CPA and multiple computer programs but getting her side of things streamlined had still taken some work. I had a lot of experience thanks to all the long hours at Lennon Family Hardware with my stubborn dad's old-school systems. And I had a whole lot of chill and patience thanks to school. Which is why I said, "I keep fifteen five-year-olds organized and on task. A little paperwork was basically a vacation."

"What a coincidence." His mouth curved into a smirk. "My back office looks like it's run by fifteen five-year-olds."

"So it's all hand turkeys and crayon scribbles?"

That didn't make him smirk. He outright grinned, and God, it was sinister and beautiful. I wasn't sure how someone could look so dangerous while smiling. He was like the very best kind of villain in a movie. Viewers were supposed to fear him. Instead, they wanted to fix him. Claim him.

But never soften him.

An inkling of disappointment crept up my spine. Lars was off-limits for a variety of sensible reasons, but that didn't change the fact I wished I was the kind of woman who could get a guy like him. Not as anything serious. I doubted I'd be rushing into a new relationship—if ever.

But something casual. A weekend. Hell, even one night.

Rather than adding another side hustle, I should've been setting aside my free time to go out. I clearly needed a social life, a reality check, and an orgasm... or ten.

And not necessarily in that order.

All I want is a night of no settling, no regrets, no rules, and no expectations. Just fun and wild and countless orgasms.

"Do you have time?" Lars asked.

It took me a moment to realize his question had nothing to do with my thoughts of countless orgasms.

"It depends on what your expectations are. If you need it done this week, I won't be able to help."

"Lived with it this long, hotcakes." Blue eyes searing into me, his voice dropped. Just a little. Just enough to be rougher. Intimate. "I'll greedily take as much as you wanna give me."

I knew what he meant, but because I was a living and breathing woman, my mind teamed up with my hormones to process his fully-loaded words in a different way. The visual filled my head, overheating my body and tingling through my veins.

I had to remind myself—repeatedly—he wanted to hire me to do a job.

And not the hand or blow variety.

My loss of words was thanks to his unintentional and easy to twist declaration, but he must've taken it as indecision because he sweetened the pot. "I'll pay you a shit-ton to make it worth your while."

I bristled at that. Nora had been right about me being too damn proud. At least, I hoped that was the word Parker wouldn't say, and not douchey, dick-headed, or some other more offensive D-word.

Whatever it was, it probably still applied. I *was* proud.

"I'll work for a fair price," I said. "Doing your books isn't worth a *crap-ton*."

Amusement glittered in his dangerous eyes and made his lips tip. "Didn't say crap-ton. Said shit-ton."

"It isn't worth that, either."

"You haven't seen how bad it is yet."

"I have open house on Monday, but I can start Tuesday afternoon."

"Tuesday works. Gimme your phone."

I pulled my cell from my back pocket, unlocked it, and handed it over.

"We'll go over everything when you get there." He handed me my phone. "Park in the back lot and call me, I'll come let you in."

"Got it," I said.

"Looking forward to it, hotcakes."

Anticipation buzzed through me as I watched him go, leaving me feeling as though I'd chugged an espresso while overdosing on cupcakes for a massive sugar and caffeine rush. I told myself it was because I was happy to pad my bank account.

I was a bad liar.

With a sigh, I went into the kitchen just as Harlow and Piper came crashing through the door that led to Jake's office. From the matching flushed excitement on their faces, I thought for sure the men would follow, chasing their women. Instead, they stopped short when they saw me.

"So..." Harlow drawled, looking around. "What'd Lars want?"

If Harlow had no chill, Piper had negative chill. She wasn't even trying for casual. Ever the romantic, her face lit, and I could practically see the cartoon hearts floating from her eyes. "Did he *finally* ask you out?"

Ha. Yeah right.

"No, it's nothing like that. He wants to hire me."

Both women froze and looked at me with matching shock, their eyebrows nearly at their hairlines.

Realizing their assumption, I clarified, "He asked me to help with Wicked's bookkeeping like I did here."

Not that they'd judge if I were stripping. To ease her financial anxiety thanks to the sudden death of her father followed by her mother's illness, Harlow had walked that road in stilettos and pasties. It wasn't the most logical or even necessary step, but anxiety wasn't about logic or necessity. It was about needing some semblance of control when everything felt uncontrollable.

Something I understood.

And Piper never judged anyone.

Harlow's expression fell faster than the cake I'd forgotten to put baking soda in. She quickly rallied herself, but she and her face were bad liars. "That's cool."

"What is it?" I asked.

"Nothing."

On the off chance it was hereditary, I summoned some of my dad's *resting-disappointment-face* and waited for her to break.

Surprisingly, it worked and she admitted, "I thought there was a vibe between you two, but he never mixes his personal life with business."

Piper opened her mouth and closed it before opening it again to gently remind Harlow, "You worked with him when there was that thing..."

Harlow waved away the comment. "It wasn't a full thing, more like a *thi*. It doesn't count."

Maybe not to you...

"There's no vibe. No *thing*. Not even a *thi*." I slammed a dirty pan into the sink. "I'm not looking to date anyway. I'm fine."

Totally fine.

Totally fine and fucking dandy as shit.

"Who said anything about dating?" Piper waggled her brows as she helped me tidy up, although she was much quieter about it. Until she wasn't. "Okay, Lars is out. Whatever. There are a plethora of hot alphas."

Harlow cut in. "Oh! You know Nox? Big guy, big beard, big dick energy? His business partner-slash-friend is planning on coming into town. All the fun, none of the commitment since he lives in Ireland. I'm betting he could whisper all sorts of things in that accent of his that'd make your underwear fling itself across the room."

I'd only met Killian Nox and his new woman, Augusta—or Gus, as she went by—a couple times in passing. But the man was a badass with a capital *Beast*. If I hadn't seen how tender and sweet he was with Gus, he'd almost be more intimidating than Lars.

Almost.

I was assuming anyone Nox worked with was equally intense and scary—the opposite of what I needed in my life.

"I'll pass," I said.

Piper tapped her chin. "There's Nox's employee or bodyguard or whoever he is. Uhhh, Beck?"

Harlow made wide eyes. "Kase wouldn't go into details, but he said that dude has some interesting... er... preferences."

"Okay, crossing him off?" Her statement came out like a question as she glanced at me for confirmation.

If unkinky was known as vanilla, I was less than that. I was ice-flavored ice cream. If I was a spice, I'd be flour. About as exciting and freaky as untoasted low-carb, white bread.

"Off the list," I agreed.

"Jake's had this biker club as new customers lately. The president is hot. And if he's not your type, he has a broody brother."

Broody men, just what I need in my life.

"I'm good. Honestly."

"Fiiiine," Piper drawled, knowing when to drop it. Unfortunately for Harlow, Piper turned her attention that way. "Soooooo... how're wedding plans?"

"My mother will be the death of me. She's spent more money at craft stores this month than seems humanly possible. Her house looks like the messy Bizarro World version of Pinterest. She's got all these half-finished samples for homemade centerpieces and décor. I don't have a crafty bone in my body!"

Remembering how mangled her little sister's art projects always came out, I could only imagine. "It runs in the family."

"See? It's going to be awful. People will assume a rabid polar bear broke in and trashed the wedding hall."

"Have you talked to her?"

Harlow had a lot of soft spots—for Kase, her little sister, and her friends. But other than her one for Kase, none of them came close to the one she had for her mom. Because of her mom's Multiple Sclerosis, Harlow had taken over the protective role, hovering and worrying over each flare up and possible regression. She claimed she'd eased up as of late, but that only made me wonder how bad she'd been before.

Bad in a good way, of course.

Just as expected, Harlow smiled and shook her head. "No, she's having fun, so it's fine. She'll come around when she sees how disastrous it looks. She'll just rack up a lot of frequent shopper points until then."

"Maybe I can send over some of those awful life-hack videos I've seen to keep it interesting," Piper put in.

Harlow grabbed a rag and threw it at her friend. "Don't you dare."

Piper dodged it and grinned. "I could introduce her to Etsy."

"You're no longer invited to my wedding."

With the heat off me, I enjoyed the easy friendship and chaos around me. By the time Harlow left, flipping the sign to *Closed* on her way out, the place was a disaster. Well, just the front. The back wasn't a disaster.

It was worse.

The entire kitchen looked like a sugar bomb went off. Piper was established enough to clean as she cooked. At the most, we were left with tidy piles of messes. But not that day. There'd been no time for organized destruction.

It was just a mess.

I welcomed the distraction, getting lost in dishes, scrubbing, and organizing. Cleaning was a way more productive option than second guessing my decision to take a side hustle at Wicked.

Okay, fine, I did both.

After a bit, Piper stuck her head in. "There you are. Can you come out here when you get the chance?"

I finished stacking the Swiss roll pans and wiped my hands before going into the storefront to see Piper sitting at one of the tables with a woman I didn't know. Or maybe I did. She looked vaguely familiar. Around my age, her light brown hair was pulled back in a low ponytail, and she was dressed in a blouse and slacks. Since no one at the garage or bakery ever dressed professionally, she stood out.

Piper pulled out the chair next to her and gestured for me to sit. "Meet Sophie."

Nope, doesn't ring any bells.

"Hi," I said to the woman.

We chatted for a few minutes—longer than I cared to admit—before it hit me.

It was a job interview.

Sophie was one of the five interviewees Piper had mentioned.

To be fair, my interview had consisted of telling Piper I could follow a recipe and then her plying me with cupcakes as a bribe to take the job—her words, not mine.

Seeing her perform an actual interview, albeit still a casual one, wasn't something I was familiar with. And by the time I'd realized what was happening, it was done.

"I'll be in touch," Piper told Sophie at the end of it.

She gave us both a small smile. "Thanks for your time."

Once she was gone, Piper turned to me. "So, what do you think?"

"About?"

"Hiring her."

I blinked at my boss. I should've been used to the way she asked my opinion and listened to my input, but I wasn't. I doubted I ever would be. My dad ruled his hardware stores as a dictator, with his word being law. And schools were run by administrators and lawmakers who hadn't stepped foot in a classroom in decades—or *ever*.

So Piper including me in something as massive as a new hire was, well, *massive*.

"It's *your* bakery," I said.

She rolled her eyes. "Yeah, but her availability is before her day job, so you'd be the one working early morning prep with her. If you don't think you'll vibe, I'll keep looking."

"No, she seems great."

"I agree. Her portfolio was good, she seems sweet, and she swears she always follows recipes *exactly*."

That was a big one for Piper, and part of the reason I worked out so well. A lot of bakers liked to experiment like mad scientists. All well and good, but not if they were changing the recipes customers waited in long lines to get their hands on.

"Plus," Piper continued, tapping her pen on her coffee cup, "she barely even looked when Xavier and Key swung by to scavenge for scraps, so it doesn't seem like we're gonna have another Nicole..."

Nicole was an employee before me who'd only lasted a week—*barely*. Piper was a laidback and fun boss, but even she had her limits. Flat-out ignoring customers every time one of the Hyde men came around was well past those limits.

Employees needed to multitask and ogle the men *while* serving customers. Like a professional.

We talked for a few more minutes, my chest warm and content the whole time. If I didn't love teaching so much—plus that whole pesky mortgage thing—it would be tempting to quit so I could work full-time at the bakery.

Piper really was the absolute best boss.

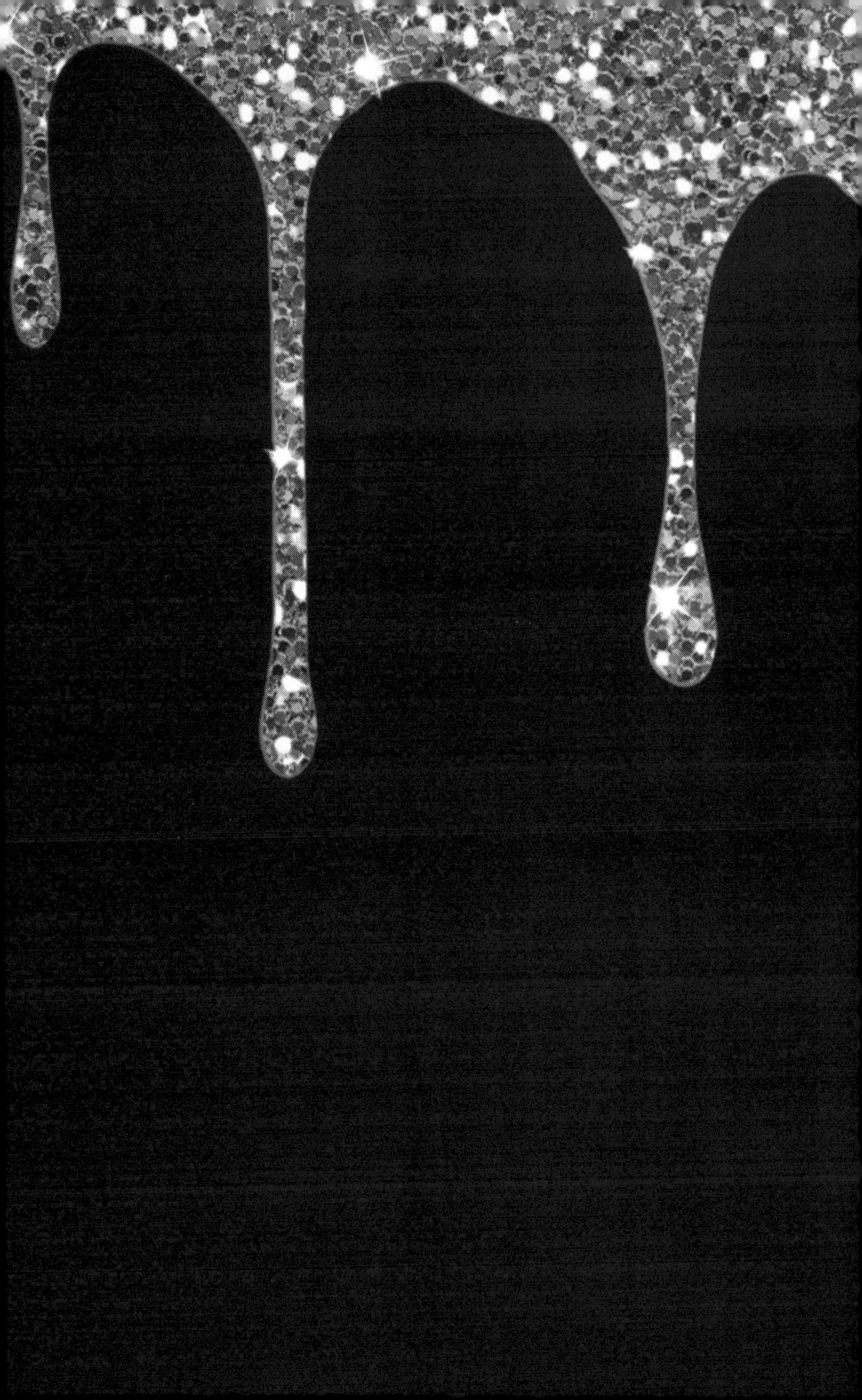

SIX
Ain't No Math for the Wicked
JOSS

I LEFT AN ELEMENTARY SCHOOL AND DROVE TO A STRIP club.

I wasn't sure if that was the worst setup to a joke or what, but it was a drastic transition. Although, according to Lars, I would be stepping into similar chaos, though that remained to be seen.

Honestly, after the insanely long week—and, yes, it was only Tuesday—I was looking forward to the break. I'd spent Monday night listening to fourteen sets of parents tell me how perfect their little angel was. The exception had been Samuel's parents, who'd openly admitted he could be a butthole, but at least he was entertaining about it.

It sealed the fact Samuel *and* his parents were my favorites.

Compared to that headache, tackling office work was exactly the mind-numbing dullness I needed.

The only hint of trepidation came from being around Lars. Seeing him at the bakery made me nervous enough. Entering his world wasn't just a big leap out of the bakery. It was a massive step into the wild side.

And wild was not a word I'd ever use to describe myself.

Pulling into the front of Wicked, I slowed down as I scanned the building. I wasn't sure what I'd expected, but it was nice.

Better than nice, actually.

The expansive parking lot was clean and lined with well-maintained shrubs. There were no letters hanging crookedly from the unlit sign or faded and torn posters advertising nude women and discount buffets, and no neon sign blinking with *Girls! Girls! Girls!*

Kinda underwhelming for my first foray into adult entertainment, but whatever.

Continuing around the gray brick building, I pulled into a spot and grabbed my phone. I was about to connect the call when I glanced toward the building and saw the recipient already standing outside.

Leaning against the wall, Lars had a cigarette hanging from his lips. Even though it was still sunny out, he was shrouded in a shadow with smoke billowing around him.

Dark.

Mysterious.

Seductive.

He looked as though he'd stepped out of a gritty Noir film. Like he should've been wearing a trench coat while he called me *dame.*

My eyes moved up to find his were already aimed my way. A smile curved his lips, and I sent a silent prayer into the universe that it wasn't because he'd caught me checking him out.

Hurrying before I made an awkward situation worse, I grabbed my bag and got out, approaching the monster in the shadows.

"You showed," he said, flicking the half-smoked cigarette to the side in a cool way.

"Those are bad for you," I blurted before immediately wishing I could rewind time to suck the words back in. Or maybe have the universe strike me down and be done with it already.

Anything was better than being Goody Two-shoes Joss who lectured her new boss about his habits.

Thankfully, rather than telling me to ride off on my high horse, Lars' lips tipped in a smirk. His voice was low and gruff when he said, "But it's the bad shit that's the most fun."

The weighty, intimate way he spoke sent a tremor down my spine and a surge of envy through me.

I wanted to do something bad rather than always walking the straight and narrow on the boring side of life.

"Lemme show you the office." Lars opened the door behind him, kicking a wedge of wood out of the way. Letting me enter first, the heavy door slammed behind us.

Ominous.

The long hall was lined with signed photos of celebrities that'd partied at Wicked. I don't know why that surprised me. I knew of a flashier club across the city that got a ton of publicity—some paid for, some courtesy of the crime blotter. Opposite Wicked, that place looked every bit the stereotypical, skeezy strip club. I'd have figured that'd be the hot spot for celebrity debauchery.

But what did I know?

My gaze landed on the swinging door at the end of the hall. Based on the music thumping on the other side, I guessed it led out to the main room.

Curiosity poked at my brain, becoming more insistent until it was a stabbing I couldn't ignore. It settled in my stomach, mixing with anticipation. Without thought, I took a single step. A tiny one. I just wanted a peek. A glimpse into the other side of life.

"They were in last month," Lars said, making me jolt as guilt flooded me, though I'd done nothing wrong.

Well, unless I was counting the seven deadly sins, because lust and envy had totally joined forces with my usual pride.

He must've thought I was distracted by the picture—as opposed to having a mini-existential crisis right there in the hallway—because he pointed to a couple other frames housing photos of the same angsty rock band.

"That's so cool," I said, though I had no clue who the band was. I was up to date on the latest kid's movie soundtrack and annoying gimmick songs my students wanted to hear on repeat, but I was woefully out of touch with mainstream music. After a long day, I usually drove home in welcome silence.

The music in the other room changed, growing louder to drown out the sudden burst of applause. I stared at the door, as if it would turn transparent and give me the view I was, for whatever reason, desperate to see.

"Ready, hotcakes?"

When I looked back at Lars, he was holding open a different door.

No wickedness for Joss Lennon.

Nope.

The exciting world of paperwork and math awaits me.

Exhaling, I followed him into the room before my steps came to an abrupt halt.

Okay, I was wrong. It's not going to be as boring as I thought.

Lars had warned me it was a disaster. What he hadn't said was that it was a disaster's disaster. The desk alone was piled with a mess of papers, books, and other unknown terrors. That didn't even include what horrors the filing cabinets may or may not include. Some were wedged shut with folders begging to be neatly filed peeking out.

"Told you," Lars said.

"What do you want me to do?" I scanned the chaos again as ideas began to form.

His voice was low, the edge rough like gravel. "Everything."

It was a good sign I'd finally gotten my crush under control, because his innocuous word didn't run amok with my libido. My excitement wasn't of the erotic variety and my focus wasn't on the man standing next to me.

All I wanted to do was get my hands on the chaos—not the chaos maker.

"Can I change your system?"

He gestured to the mess. "Not much of a system to change."

"So, I can implement one?"

"As long as it's simple and quick to use, have at it."

"Do you use a computer program?"

"Already loaded up."

I dragged my focus away from the mess to see Lars was still glaring at it. I knew he'd said he hated it, but the amount of pure loathing that coated his expression was enough to make my breath catch.

Had he been anyone else, I'd have taken at least a few steps away or maybe just sprinted out the door. That's how freakin' scary he looked. But since it was Lars, and I knew down to my bones he wouldn't turn that dangerous vibe my way, I stayed in place.

Barely a moment later, his face smoothed out and it was as if that rage had never been there. "You get paid every Thursday. I can do it all legal, with new hire papers and direct deposit, but I'd rather keep it cash."

Since cash meant less to claim on my taxes, I was all for that. "Cash works."

He lifted his chin. "Work after school Monday through Thursday, as much or little as you want. No Fridays or Saturdays 'cause it's a fucking madhouse here. Only come in through the back door and never the front. There's always a bouncer outside the changing room down the hall. You need me, send him."

I hadn't planned to actually go to the front, despite my curiosity. Call it cowardice or self-preservation or whatever. I knew if I went out there, I'd feel lacking. And I had no interest in hurting my own feelings.

But his rules to ensure I stayed hidden hurt. Like he knew as well as I did that I didn't belong in that world.

His world.

Think of the money.

Cold, hard cash.

"Got it." I rounded the desk to get to work before he could suggest I wear a cloak and half mask like I was the Phantom of the Opera.

There was a knock, and I glanced up before doing a double take.

A gorgeous woman in the tiniest skirt, a strip of fabric for a top, and a leather biker vest stood in the doorway. Her curious gaze took me in before she focused on Lars. Tossing her sexy black and blue hair over her shoulder, she snapped, "Crystal is late. Again."

"I'll handle it," Lars said.

"We've got stage duty together throughout the night and a party at ten."

He thought for a moment, his hand rubbing the top of his head. "Take the stage on your own. Have Sia work the party with you."

"Got it. Thanks, boss." She strutted away with enough sway and attitude in her walk, it was hypnotic.

But when I looked at Lars, his eyes weren't on the work of art that was her dance-toned ass.

They were on me.

He was probably waiting to see if the goody two-shoes bolted at the first sign of a bare midriff covered in body glitter.

I grabbed a stack of papers and met his gaze without flinching. I hoped the nonverbal action was enough to make it clear I was sticking around. "Anything else I need to know?"

"Yeah." He smiled. "Glad you're here, hotcakes." With that, he turned and strode from the room.

Also with that, I knew I could do the job without turning into an idiot. My crush was officially dead. Squashed. RIP, six-feet-under, DOA, *dead*. Because the sincerity in his voice and the easily manipulated words could've made the butterflies riot, but I'd officially beaten them to death.

About time.

PAPERWORK MIGHT NOT BE AS crazy as the fun that was happening in the main room, but it was consuming. I wouldn't have noticed it was dinner had Lars not shown up with tacos—something I'd told him wasn't necessary. I'd planned to just finish one last thing, but time must've gotten away from me. I hadn't even noticed he'd returned until he cleared his throat.

He opened his mouth to speak, but before he could, something started beeping. It was a shrill sound I'd never heard. It took me a moment to realize it was coming from my purse.

More specifically, my phone.

What the hell?

I grabbed it out just in time for the noise to cut off and ringing to begin. A pit formed in my stomach as I read the caller ID.

"Hello?" I answered, my gaze going to Lars. He'd been leaning against the door jamb, relaxed like he'd been there a while. At the anxiety he likely read on my expression, there was nothing casual about his tense body or the alert that lit his sharp gaze.

"Miss Lennon, this is Mass Home Security. We just received an alert that your alarm has been triggered. Are you at home?"

I shook my head before remembering I was a moron and he couldn't exactly see me. "No, I'm not."

"Okay, we'll dispatch the police to your address."

We stayed on the phone a minute longer while he verified my info. As he spoke, I grabbed my purse and stood, approaching the door. Rather than stepping aside so I could pass, Lars put his hand on my lower back, guided me out into the hallway, and out to my car. I unlocked the door and hung up with the security company before looking at Lars. Since he was standing way close, I had to crane my neck.

I was about to apologize for leaving the office a mess, but he jerked his chin toward my car interior, nonverbally telling me to get in. Once I did, he said, "I'll follow you there."

My brows raised. "You don't have—"

"I'll follow you there," he repeated in a voice that brooked no argument. Also brooking no argument? The fact he'd closed the door and walked away before I even had the chance to speak.

A moment later, a car that was too dark to see flashed its lights. I inhaled deep and tried to calm the adrenaline coursing through my body as awful scenarios raced through my head.

My concern wasn't about material goods. I wasn't exactly housing The Hope Diamond and a priceless collection of van Goghs. It was the idea of someone breaking into my space. My home.

The thought was so... violating.

Trying—and failing—not to panic, my already battered heart clenched when I neared my house and saw the flashing lights. I parked on the street, vaguely aware of Lars pulling up behind me. My focus was on my home.

It's still standing, and no one is cuffed in the back of the cop car. Both are good signs.

Maybe.

I climbed out and Lars was there, his hand on my lower back again as we approached the waiting officer.

"You the homeowners?" the older man asked, giving us a cursory glance.

"Yes," Lars said at the same time I said, "No. Well, yes. Me. But not..." I trailed off and just muttered, "Yes."

It was easier than delving into who we were to each other—something that, depending how in depth I went, may have required one of those whiteboard, string charts they used at the police station on TV.

The cop didn't pay attention, uninterested in my rambling as he gestured to his approaching younger partner. "This is Officer Daniels. Give him your key, and he and the other officers will do a walkthrough." Once I handed off my key—and said a silent prayer I hadn't left anything intimate sitting out—the older man crossed his arms. "There's no sign of a break-in, or even an attempt. Doors are still locked. Security company said the alarm came from one of the first-floor window sensors. Our guess is all this wind rattled it too hard." He skewered me with a look, and it was as if he was channeling my dad. "Those windows are older than you, young lady. You need to get them replaced."

Yeah, I'll jump on that with all the extra money I have.

I didn't have to force any sort of half-assed promise to get on it because Officer Daniels was back. "All clear."

After getting more information for the paperwork they were clearly thrilled to fill out, they told me to call if I noticed anything amiss before leaving.

My shoulders slumped with relief as tremors started through my body.

I'd almost forgotten Lars was there as silent support until he wrapped an arm around me. "Adrenaline is wearing off."

That explained why I felt like I'd run a marathon on an empty stomach.

Helping me up the steps, he stopped us on the porch. "Wait out here, I want to do a sweep."

"The cop—"

"That twelve-year-old boy scout barely spent two minutes in there."

"No!" I squeaked in a panic. Lars stopped and turned a raised brow my way as I inhaled deeply. "It's fine. I'm fine. Everything is fine. Honestly. I appreciate you coming, but you heard the cops. It was the wind."

He must've seen there was no way I was letting him into my house. I'd have literally thrown myself in the doorway to stop him. I mean, it wouldn't have actually stopped him, but it would've slowed him down for a second or two. Mildly inconvenienced him.

Because some random baby-faced cops seeing my dirty laundry or vibrator wasn't a big deal. But Lars? I didn't want him seeing any of that.

And I also didn't want to examine those feelings.

Lifting his chin, he backed away, reiterating the cops' instructions but adding I should call him, too.

Then he was jogging down my porch steps to his car.

So much for a boring night of paperwork...

Lars

SHE DIDN'T WANT me inside.

No. It was more than that. She'd looked ready to tackle me down to keep me from going inside her house. Was all for her jumping me, but not like that. The panic in her eyes?

Fuck.

Maybe her place was a pigsty. Maybe she had panties and bras and shit all over the place.

Or maybe it had something to do with the fiancé.

I watched as she went inside before pulling away from the curb. Making a few turns, I parked.

A few car lengths from the spot I'd just left.

Killing the engine, I sat back and settled in.

Isn't stalking if I'm making sure she's safe.

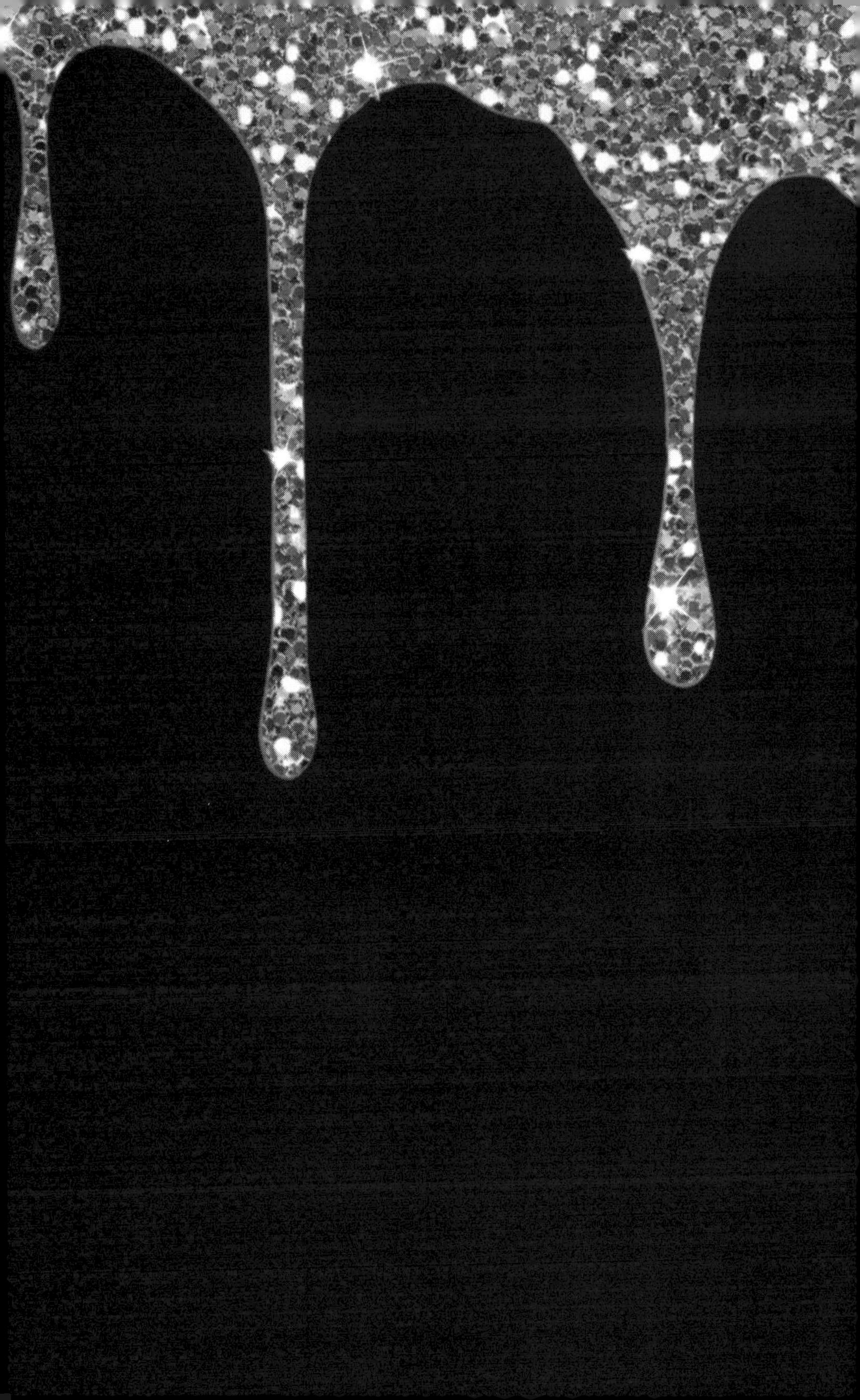

SEVEN

It's Important to Have Goals

JOSS

I YELPED.

Loudly.

Embarrassingly.

Startled, I looked up from a stack of papers to meet Lars' gaze. His *amused* gaze, letting me know my yelp had likely been louder than I'd realized

Two days.

I'd been working for him for two days—and not even full days.

That was long enough to have me questioning if my crush was really extinct.

I'd thought I was smarter than foolish feelings that would lead to very real pain. But my common sense and self-preservation were no match for a man like Lars. Him having my back with the alarm fiasco hadn't been a fluke. He was that protective. Thoughtful. Funny. *Intense.* Not to mention, hotter than any one man had the right to be.

When I'd taken the job, I had assumed I would barely see him since he had a business to run and sexy, nearly nude women to supervise. I'd been wrong. He'd popped in and out of the office often, sometimes staying for chunks of time to utilize said office. And being around all that badass heat wore away at me. It made me forget I was a smart woman who knew better. It made me forget all the multitude of reasons why liking him was a disaster in the making.

But it did make me finally see how and why a woman could go stupid for a man.

His tattooed hand was still gripping my ponytail that he'd gently tugged to get my attention.

And, oh hell, did he have it.

The tiny pull zipped from my scalp down to tighten my nipples and make me squeeze my thighs together. I'd never experienced such an intense and immediate surge of electricity shooting through my body, but I'd also never had my hair pulled—by a growly man or otherwise.

Hoping like hell he didn't have any kind of arousal detection skills, I removed an earbud. "What's up?"

"Food."

"No, it's..." My words trailed off when I glanced at the time on the computer and saw it was a couple hours past my usual dinner time.

Time flies when you're up to your neck in invoices.

I was about to reach for my purse—and the protein bar I kept in there—when the smell of something savory and delicious and *curry* penetrated my overwhelmed brain.

Summoning up every bit of somberness I could despite the drool filling my mouth, I glared up at Lars. "Did you not hear what I said yesterday?"

That being when he'd delivered me tacos for dinner, and I'd told him it was unnecessary.

"I heard," he confirmed.

"Then why—"

"Heard, just didn't listen." Showing not one iota of guilt or remorse at that fact, he put a bag of takeout on the papers I'd been working on and then set a glass emblazoned with the Wicked logo next to it. I already knew it'd be Diet Coke because I'd mentioned it was my favorite the night before, and Lars was nothing if not observant.

Case in point, the Indian food I couldn't stop myself from unbagging despite my glaring and protests. "I brought something for dinner. You don't have to feed me. I'm just like any other employee—"

"Independent contractor," he interrupted.

Again.

Seems the Hyde habit extends to other alphas in their group. Annoying.

Not that I was actually annoyed, per se. More confused.

"What?" I asked.

"I'm not your boss. You're not an employee. You're an independent contractor."

"Isn't that basically the same?"

"No."

"Okay," I drawled. "Then I'm like any other independent contractor. You don't have to get me dinner."

"Don't have to," he said before smirking, "but I'm gonna do it anyway."

Before I could argue—mostly because I was staring at that damn mouth of his—he turned around to leave.

"Wait," I called.

Opening the door, he paused and looked over his shoulder.

"Are you not eating with me?" Realizing how that could be taken, I gestured to the containers. "There's enough to feed an army."

"Wish I could, hotcakes, but I gotta get back behind the bar."

I ignored the pang of disappointment that hit my chest. "I can't eat all this."

My stomach decided to protest that statement with an embarrassingly audible groan.

I could tell from the twitch of his lips that Lars had heard, but he didn't give me grief about it or my heated red cheeks. "Eat what you can then put the rest in the walk-in fridge to take home later. Or give it to Frankie. He's probably standing around just to smell it."

"Am not," Frankie—one of the bouncers—said from the hall, proving he was indeed close.

Lars left me to my feast, closing the door behind him.

That he'd known Indian food was my favorite was impressive. That he'd known my favorite order—paneer makhani, garlic naan, and kheer for dessert—was downright magical.

Almost as magical as the feeling of him pulling my hair.

Had my mouth not been stuffed full of bread and curry, I'd have called myself an idiot—and I wouldn't have even cared if Frankie heard me. I really was one for thinking I could do the job unaffected.

Leave it to Lars to put the *romance* in necromancy. Because in just a couple days working in his space, I was beginning to fear my crush was back from the dead.

LARS

WHAT WAS I thinking offering her this job?

When Jake had suggested the idea, I'd known it was a mistake. That it'd be fuckin' torture. But I hadn't given a damn. For one, I got more time with Joss—pitiful as shit for me to want that so bad, but it was what it was.

For another, I needed the help.

When I'd gotten the idea to open Wicked, my cousin had helped me secure the funding. 'Cause un-fucking-surprisingly, all the suited bankers who lined the stage night after night weren't exactly creaming themselves to invest in the strip clubs they loved to visit. They were even less enthusiastic when the loan holder was an ex-con fresh out of prison on an assault charge.

In exchange for him signing his name on a bunch of papers, Eddie had gotten a hefty cut every week. When he'd asked for more responsibility, I'd started teaching him how to run shit. The plan—before it *and* Eddie both went to shit—had been for him to eventually run his own location. When I'd handed over the reins on some of the back of the house duties, I'd put my trust in him.

Trust I never gave easily.

I'd relearned that lesson fast.

'Cause it turned out, his idea of being hands-on in the business had only involved the dancers and not the actual business. He hadn't managed his shit as well as he'd let on while he was alive, and he sure as shit hadn't left it organized after he'd died.

If his strung-out, triple-crossing body wasn't already buried in an unmarked grave, I'd have put a bullet in him myself for the shitshow he'd left.

Every time I thought I had it under control, I found a new bundle of discarded but important papers. A new bill he'd hidden. A new money trail that led to his bookie, dealer, or some other piece of garbage.

To be real fuckin' blunt, I was one frustration away from taking a torch to the club and walking away without a backward glance.

Which was why I'd thought Joss helping at Wicked outweighed the torture of having her close.

I'd been dead wrong.

It'd only been a few days, but I was coming out of my skin wanting to touch *her* skin. Having her in my space when I couldn't do that was a fresh new hell. But I was dealing with it.

And I was doing that by jerking off thinking about her more than before—which had already been a pathetic amount—and by becoming more obsessed.

Still counted as dealing with it.

I'd underestimated how hard it would be to go about my night when I knew she was in my office. I was supposed to be taking liquor inventory, but my mind was on her ass in the next room.

Literally.

I stood there, staring at the gin bottles, but I wasn't counting. Instead, I was racking my damn brain trying to come up with a reason for her to bend over the desk. Because the image of her rounded ass bent over the table at Sweets You Rock had set itself as my brain's background, home screen, and screensaver. If I could see her like that on *my* desk, I'd have jack-off fuel for years to come.

Deciding I'd figure out an excuse when I got in there, I tossed my clipboard down and headed for my office. Just as I was approaching, the door swung open, and Joss let out a startled yelp.

I had a habit of making her do that, and it wasn't one I intended on breaking. I liked the cute-as-fuck noise and the way she looked up at me with those big, brown eyes.

"My bad," I said, though I didn't mean it.

Even with her alarm going off, Joss had stayed past dinner on Tuesday. Wednesday was even later. Assuming it'd be a regular thing, I'd planned to order again, making sure no one bothered me so I could eat with her.

Since it wasn't even six and she was already in her hoodie and gripping her purse, my threats about being interrupted had been for nothing.

"Giving up already?" I asked.

I wouldn't blame her—it really was a fuckin' disaster in there. I would just come up with a new way to get close to her. And a new excuse to get her bent over my desk—which was apparently my life's sole mission.

She smiled and it hit me in the gut like it always did. She was so damn... pretty. "Just for the day. I have some last-minute things to do for tomorrow. It's Friendship Friday, so I made small cardboard cutouts of best friend book characters and..." She paused for a second before finishing, "And I'll be back on Monday."

"What were you gonna say?"

Waving a hand, she grimaced. "Nothing important, I—"

"Everything you say is important."

"It's really—"

Putting my hands to the door frame, I leaned closer and repeated, "What were you gonna say?"

Her eyes narrowed, but she didn't back away. "You interrupt a lot."

I smirked down at her. "Wanna give me detention?"

She fought a smile. "Bad manners usually means no recess."

"Can't have that, play time is my favorite." Her lips parted, and I took a second to memorize her expression before ordering, "Tell me what you were gonna say."

"I was just saying I have to put the finishing touches on the character cutouts. We're going to read their stories and talk about how friends help each other. The kids like visuals."

I like visuals, too.

Especially of you, bent over my desk, taking me and begging for more.

Fighting a hard-on from that thought, I said, "Bet if there were more teachers like you, kids would actually enjoy school."

I hadn't realized it was that big of a compliment, but at my words, Joss grinned up at me, excitement shining in her sweet brown eyes. "That's what I want. To make learning fun. I hated school, and I don't want my students to go through that daily dread."

That surprised me. Joss seemed like she would have had straight-As, been class president, in all the extracurriculars, easily gliding through school as the good girl everyone liked.

"Did you like school?" she asked.

"Loved learning, hated the rules," I shared.

Her lips tipped, her voice laced with sarcasm. "I'm shocked."

There was a lot I was learning about Joss.

She was motivated, bordering on stubborn as shit while she worked through piles of papers.

She was also not used to people doing nice things for her—and, again, she was stubborn as shit about it. When I'd dropped off dinner or a refilled drink, she'd fought me or insisted the cost come out of what I was paying her, which was not happening.

And even though Wicked was as far from a kindergarten class and PTA meetings as she could get, Joss didn't treat anyone with superiority. She didn't blink at fighting dancers or topless chicks running around with more drama than a daytime soap. She didn't cower from the bouncers, even though they were big, scary motherfuckers. All smiles and sweetness, she was nice to everyone she encountered.

Most of all, though, I'd learned that behind her shy, quietness was a shit-ton of snark and wit.

I liked it.

I liked it even more since it seemed like I got to see it more than anyone else.

Christ, I wanted to kiss her. Always, but especially right then with that damn smile pulling at her full lips and her playful voice in my head.

But I didn't do it.

Not yet, at least.

"Lemme grab your money," I said.

Her lips turned down, and there was a flash of something. If I didn't know better, I'd say it was disappointment. But if I let myself believe that—believe she wanted me to kiss her even half as bad as I wanted to—my carefully constructed plan would fly right out the window.

Whatever the expression, it was gone just as fast as she stepped out of the way.

A sick anticipation flowed through me as I walked to the desk and grabbed her envelope. Un-fuckin'-fortunately, I didn't get another glimpse of her snarky fire because she tucked it into her bag without opening it.

Gesturing to the desk, she said, "I tried to get my stacks out of the way until Monday, but I'm pretty sure it's messier now than when I started."

That was the damn truth. My office had already been a disaster zone. After her working, it looked like a fuckin' bomb went off.

I didn't say shit. She could dump the papers into a trash can and take a lighter to it for all I cared. I'd even give her the lighter.

"Text if you can't find something," she continued. "I know it doesn't look like it, but I'm making progress."

"It looks good," I lied.

"Thank you for lying to make me feel better," she shot back, calling me out.

"Okay, it looks like hell, but I get it. We did updates out front a couple months ago, and the place was so trashed, I didn't think it'd ever be done." My lips curved up and I put heat into the words when I finished, "But it was worth the wait when it finally came together."

A tinge of pink hit her cheeks, and her lips parted in an invitation I wasn't sure she knew she was making. One I wasn't sure I was strong enough to decline. Before I could push, the swinging door slammed open.

"Boss," Tank—one of the bouncers—called. "Need you out here."

In the brief moment my head had been turned, Joss had snuck by and snagged Frankie to walk her out. With a view of her profile, I watched as she smiled up at him. Jealousy burned in my gut, but I let them go because the growing shouts from the main room said I had other shit to deal with right then. Plus, all the other shit I had to do before I made my move.

First, I had to find out what the deal with the fiancé was. Since no man had been there when her alarm had gone off—or the rest of the night while I'd been parked out front—and she never mentioned anyone, it was a safe bet they'd split. But Jake had said she was working to fix shit. I needed to know why she was hung up on an asshole who was stupid enough to let her get away.

Next, I had to figure out how to *unhang* her from that bastard.

Last—and hardest—I had to con her into thinking it was a good idea to take a walk on the wrong side of the tracks with a bastard like me.

Until then, I'd take it slow, and get her sweet smiles and humor while I did.

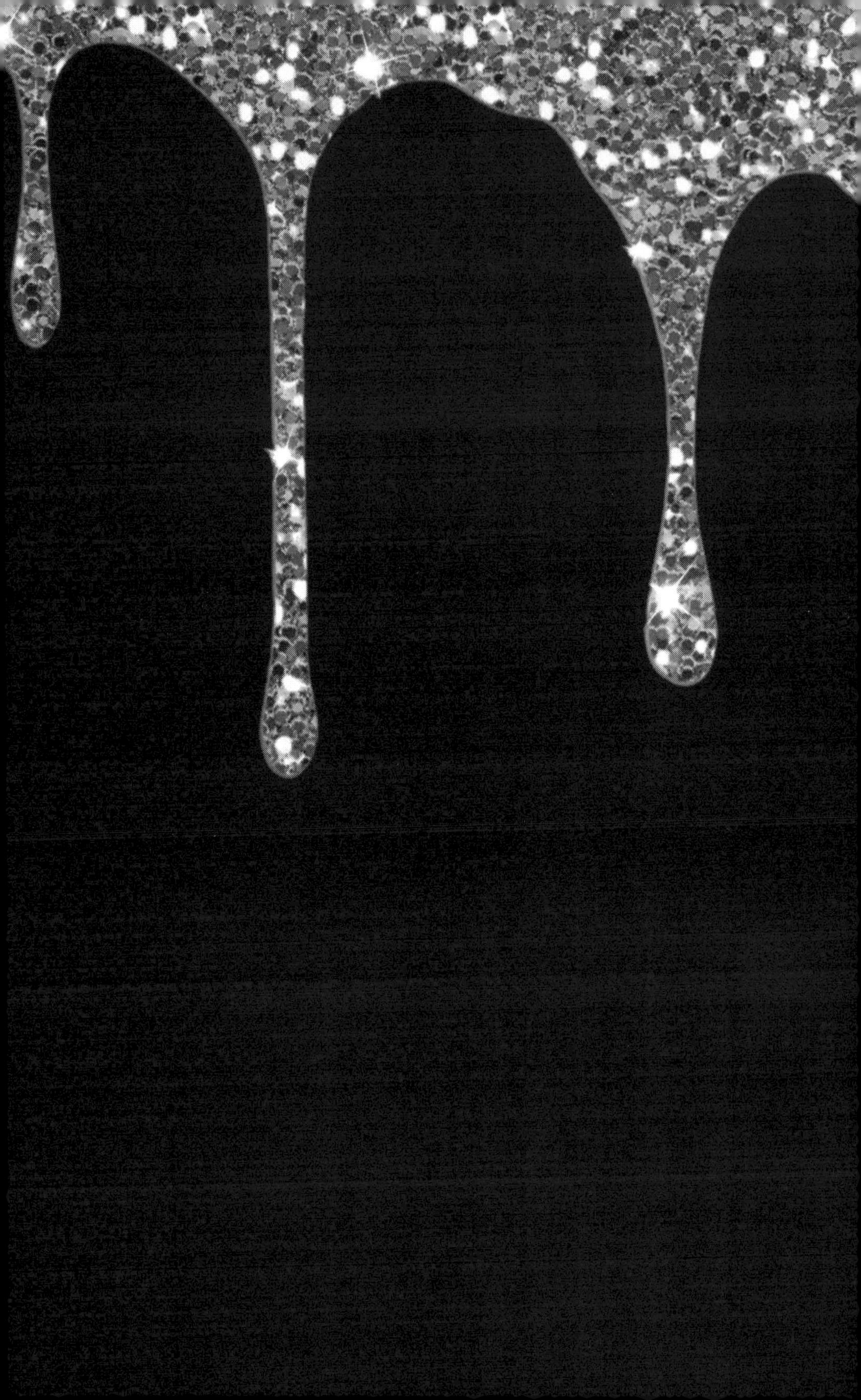

EIGHT
You Can Ride a Horse to a Dating Pool
JOSS

I WAITED.

And waited.

And freakin' waited.

As I stood behind the counter of Sweets You Rock, my attention was partially on the customers ordering their usual plethora of goodies, partially on Piper filling me and the newly-hired Sophie in on a plethora of gossip, but mostly it was aimed outside as I listened to the plethora of vehicles.

Listened for a very specific motorcycle.

Only instead of the pleasant rush as I waited for my glimpse of a badass hottie, my anticipation was fueled by anger and indignation.

And it was putting me in a nasty mood.

I was beginning to worry he wasn't going to show, and my bad mood would fester until it had an outlet. On the plus side, maybe my vibe would keep my family off my back for Sunday dinner.

Who was I kidding? If anything, they'd pick up on it and bug me until I snapped. Then it'd turn into a drama I'd have to apologize for.

I'd just about given up hope when I heard the telltale rumble. I finished packing some of our new—and very popular—marshmallow treats into a box and practically threw it at the customer. Grabbing the small bag I'd tucked to the side, I looked at Piper. "Can I take a quick break?"

Rather than the expected mischievous smile and curiosity, concern—with a fair amount of curiosity—filled her expression. She nodded as she grabbed her cell. "Sophie is crumb coating a cake in the kitchen, so I'll have one of the guys come over."

By the time Lars' large frame filled the doorway, I was nearly to him.

His stupid-handsome face was already filled with stupid amusement—like he'd been anticipating the showdown just as much as I had. "Hey, hotcakes, what's—"

I put my hand to his hard chest. "Outside. Now."

"Whatever you say." He walked backward a few steps before turning. Without thinking, I snagged his wrist and pulled him, as though he'd try to escape.

As if I could stop him if he tried.

Because I'm so menacing and all.

Once we were around the corner, I released his hand and pulled the envelope from my back pocket, shoving it at him.

His unsurprised gaze dropped to where I pressed the envelope against his abs then rose to meet mine.

"Take this back," I ordered.

He didn't ask what it was. That and the smile he was failing to hide confirmed he'd expected the altercation. "Pretty sure it's against the law to take back paychecks."

"Then it's a good thing we're doing this all under the table. And it's only half."

Caught up in finishing Friendship Friday crafts, I hadn't looked at the contents of the envelope until I was at the bank after school. My shaking hands had almost spilled the cash. I'd been so thrown, I was probably on some money laundering or drug ring watchlist somewhere thanks to my bizarre behavior.

I'd counted out half the money to deposit into my account while stashing the other far-too-generous half to return. And if I were being honest, the portion I'd kept was still too much.

Steeling my spine and drawing from my stubborn pride, my voice was firm—even as the fictional bank account in my head silently wept. "I took the job to help and earn a little extra cash. I'm not a charity case."

"No one said you were."

"This is almost as much as I make at my day job."

"Always heard teachers were underpaid."

He wasn't wrong.

"Maybe," I admitted, "but it's not up to you to bridge that pay gap. I—"

"Have been doing a shit-ton of work and there's still a shit-ton left. You've already caught two suppliers I'm paying too much to every damn month, and that's been going on for a year. You've earned every damn dollar I paid you."

"It's too much."

"Not in my book. And since it's my business, I get final say."

My eyes narrowed. "Then I quit."

At that, my bank account didn't weep. It cursed me to hell and back.

Lars didn't look pissed, concerned, or defensive. His lips curled up into a cocky smirk that screamed *checkmate* in a game of chess I hadn't known we were playing. "No, you don't."

I was wrong. It wasn't chess, it was poker because he'd easily called my bluff.

Too much pride and not enough sense, I dug my heels in to die on a mountain I had no interest in climbing. "Yes, I do."

"No." He took a step forward, and even though it took every last ounce of willpower I had, I held my ground. His smile grew. "Wanna know how I know you're not quitting?"

"No," I lied. "But I'm sure you'll tell me."

Reaching up, he grabbed a lock of hair from my ponytail. As though he were feeling the most extraordinary silk, he gently twisted it around his fingers, his eyes following the movement.

The look on his face.

His casual, yet intimate touch.

And the fear he was about to call out my crush, yanking it into the stark light of day so he could use it against me...

All of it worked together to freeze my lungs until my head swam.

Finally meeting my gaze again, he gave my hair a brief but oh-so-pleasurable tug before releasing it. "Because that clusterfuck is a challenge. And you don't back down from those."

Relief loosened in my chest, and my lungs emptied with a soft *whoosh*. "You don't know that."

"Tell me I'm wrong."

I could, but I'd be lying.

"You're underestimating how proud and stubborn I am," I said instead, my words something between an admission and a gloat.

"Only a dumbass would underestimate you." His voice lowered, far too gravelly for my sanity. "And that same stubborn pride is exactly why you won't walk away."

If I were smart, I would do just that. I'd walk away from it all. The job at Wicked. My money-sucking dream house.

From him.

But no matter how many times I told myself I should, I didn't.

Couldn't.

I was clearly the dumbass.

Clueless to how layered his declaration was, he continued. "I paid you what's fair. You're helping me out more than you know. I can't tame that shit, and every time I try, I make it worse."

"So hire an office manager."

"I did hire one—*you*. That's why I'm paying what the job deserves and not taking advantage."

Huh. I didn't think about it as something official like that.

Then he brought out the big guns. "And I don't trust anyone else with that shit. I trust you."

From the bit I'd gathered, his cousin had been the one to screw up and screw him over so disastrously. It made sense he'd be hesitant to put his business in a complete stranger's hands.

"Fine." Like I had any sort of leverage, I added a stipulation. "But no more buying me dinner."

"We'll see."

"No, we won't. I'll bring something from home on the nights I'll be there late."

"Whatever you say," he muttered, not bothering to hide how full of it he was.

Frustrated—but also grateful and content about how it'd worked out—I pocketed the envelope before handing him the bag I'd nearly forgotten about. "I have to get back in there."

"I'll see you Monday." There was no question in his tone, the words coming out firmer than I was capable of.

That didn't stop me from trying. "With no dinner."

I knew it wasn't effective when he muttered, "We'll see."

He'll be the death of me.

At least I'll have some cash for a cushy casket.

I was almost to the door when Lars called, "Hotcakes."

Biting back a smile, I schooled my features and spun around. "Yeah?"

He held up the marshmallow treat. "Where's my chocolate chip?"

"Chocolate chip cookies are for people who don't irritate me."

He stared at me for a few stretching seconds before taking a big bite. "Good thing I like these, too, 'cause I'm bettin' I'll piss you off a lot."

"Good to know. I'll switch to raisin cookies."

The smile dropped off his face. "That's cold, hotcakes."

Rather than speaking, I turned and gave him a flick of the wrist wave over my head. I doubted I looked anywhere near as cool as he had when he'd done it, but it seemed like the cool way to end the convo.

Like, a figurative mic drop or when badasses don't look back at an explosion.

Going into the bakery, I saw the line had died down enough that I didn't feel guilty for abandoning my post. It also meant Piper would have time to grill me, but I had a shiny distraction up my sleeve.

Her pretty eyes scanned me, first and foremost the concerned friend. "Everything okay?"

I gave her a reassuring smile that wasn't even the slightest bit forced. It was, however, a little giddy thanks to the money in my pocket and the butterflies in my stomach.

Oh God, I need an internal bug zapper to get rid of these suckers.

"All good. Just had some office manager questions for him."

Office manager. Yup, definitely like the sound of that.

"How's that working out?" she asked. "Must be a lot more interesting than here. My benefit package doesn't include nipple pasties."

Key, one of Jake's employees, looked over from where he was manning my spot at the register. "Neither does Hyde's. I need to contact my union rep and right that wrong."

Since he was even quieter than I was, any time I heard Key's dry wit, I was surprised.

Laughing, I suggested, "Hold out for the glitter, too."

"Good call." He shot me a wink before returning to what he was doing.

Like the other Hyde men, Key was hot, though not my type. That said, his wit mixed with that wink elevated him to extra hot.

Answering Piper's question, I said, "I only work in the back office, so it's not that exciting. Plus, I'll take free pastries over pasties any day."

"Hard to argue with that," Piper agreed.

"But I'm enjoying the new challenge. I got things running too well here. It's boring."

That part was a lie, of course. We were too busy to be bored.

With the reassurance that all was well in Booby-ville, her expression morphed to conniving—of the matchmaking variety. "So... how is Lars?"

"Barely see him," I lied. Not wanting to talk about the nothing-burger that was my relationship with Lars, I busted out the distracting shiny. "Do you know anyone you can set me up with?"

Holding a cinnamon roll in one hand and a bag in the other, Piper froze. "Seriously?"

"Yeah."

A smile split her face. "I have *so* many questions. I don't even know your type. Or what kind of thing you're looking for."

"Something *casual*," I emphasized before she could start planning a wedding. "I want to inch my way into the dating kiddie pool, not dive in to drown in the deep end."

Again.

"Got it, got it. Hmmm."

"There's no rush—"

"I know someone," Key said.

Well, that was fast.

Which is good.
Super good.
Time to get back on the...
Horse.
Yup. The horse.

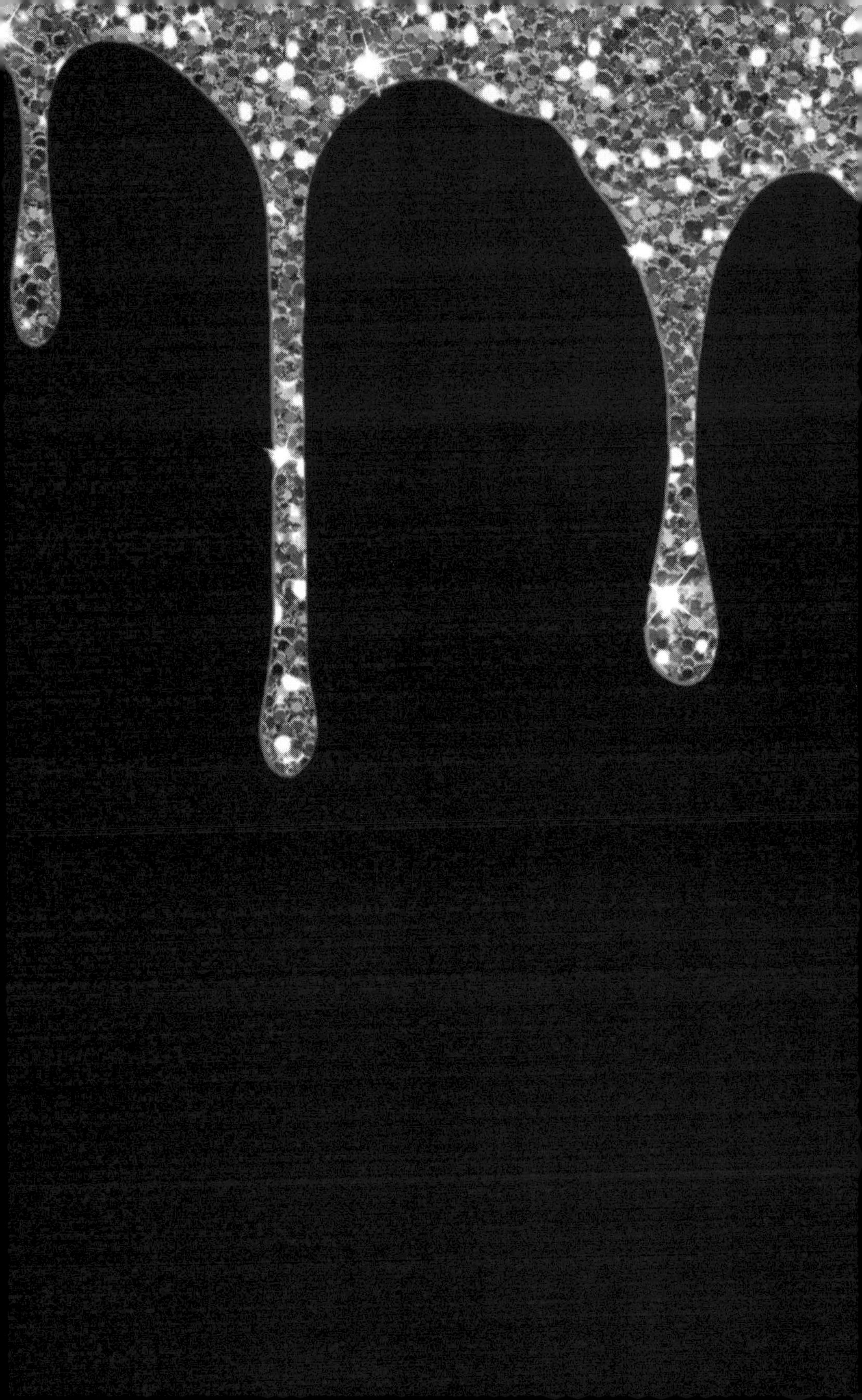

NINE
Mystery Date
JOSS

WHEN I'D ASKED TO GET SET UP ON A DATE, I HADN'T fully considered the ramifications.

Those being that I'd actually have to *attend* said date.

Standing outside a restaurant that was hipper than I'd expected, I contemplated sneaking back home to my poly relationship with Ben and Jerry. The pint of delicious ice cream sounded way better than small talk with a mystery date. Key had been the one to make the arrangements—I had no clue who I was even meeting—so I could just claim I thought I'd been stood up.

Or that I'd gotten stuck in traffic.

Or come down with the plague.

Anything but the truth, which was that I was a giant coward.

In my defense, I hadn't been on a first date since high school. That had led to my one and only serious relationship.

To say I was rusty was an understatement—a drastic one.

I'd forgotten how choosing an outfit and getting ready became a stressful exercise in self-doubt. I'd have thought it'd be easier as an adult with more wardrobe choices, but nope. Totally the opposite. And all that pre-date drama wasn't even taking into consideration what would happen once I walked inside.

I had no clue how to act on a first date as an adult. I couldn't rely on the same stimulating topics—such as Ms. Ellar's sucky math class or which cheerleader was dating which football player. I'd have to find something else to talk about.

And, unfortunately, my life heavily revolved around which kindergartners were on the outs, which dancers were on the outs, and what the top selling pastry was.

None of it made for the most interesting conversation.

Well, maybe the dancers and the pastries, but only if I was supplying samples of both.

Which I wasn't, though bringing some of Piper's desserts would've been smart. It was hard to make a bad impression when I started with *literal* brownie points. Since all I brought was myself, I gathered my nerve and walked inside to get it over with.

Rather than taking up a table while I waited for a man who might never show, I'd already decided to sit at the bar. I didn't have to bother with that, because as I approached the hostess, someone called, "Joss."

I turned toward the deep, masculine voice.

Wait.

Whaaaaaat?

Lars

Fuckin' Fridays.

Making my way through the crush of people at Rye, I spotted Kase, Jake, Piper, Xavier, and Eli at a couple tables pushed together. Harlow, Rhys, and some other chick were working behind the bar. I scanned the table and crowd, searching for pretty brown eyes and a sweet, shy smile, but came up empty.

She's not here.

Maybe I can back away before anyone sees I'm here.

No such fuckin' luck, though. Kase chose that moment to tear his attention away from staring at his fiancée to look my way, lifting his chin.

One drink, then I'll fake a work emergency.

I regretted the thought as soon as I had it. Not because I was being a dickhead, though I sure as fuck was. But thinking shit like that issued a dare to the asshole world, and it was probably only a matter of time before Sasha called with actual bullshit I'd have to deal with.

It wasn't that I didn't like the group. I actually really fuckin' liked them. Kase and I went back to our days on the inside with Nox. Once we'd gotten out, Kase had gone his way to find his family at Hyde and then with Harlow. I'd been happy for him and hadn't blamed him for distancing himself.

He'd deserved that good after spending time in hell for a sin that wasn't his.

After some shit had gone down with Harlow, her piece of shit stepfather, my piece of shit cousin, and a somehow even shittier piece of shit drug runner, I was no longer on the outside. I'd been pulled into their circle.

Since I liked them—and because the circle included Joss—I couldn't say I minded.

But if I wanted to deal with crowds of drunk douchebags, I could've stayed at Wicked. Instead, I'd put Sasha in charge so I could spend my Friday dealing with the same bullshit in a new location.

For what?

The chance to see Joss.

Christ, I wasn't just a dickhead, I was a pathetic one.

My ass had barely touched the stool when a bourbon was set in front of me.

"Wow, you left Wicked on a Friday. Think the place will survive?" Harlow asked.

Kase shifted to the side so she could settle between his spread thighs. "Better question, can *you* survive a night away from it?"

"I'm sure we'll both make it through this difficult separation," I deadpanned before saying hey to the rest of the table.

And belatedly noticing two empty stools on the opposite end.

Maybe Joss is coming.

"You know," Piper started, pulling away from the hold Jake had on her to sit up straighter, "if you're worried about the club, we could always take this party there."

"No," Jake, Kase, and I bit out at the same time.

Deflated, she sunk back into her husband's touch. "It would be fun."

Jake looked one step away from murder at the idea. "No, it'd be a fuckin' fight waitin' to happen."

"We to the fighting part of the night already?" Nox asked, settling his woman into one of the empty stools before taking the other one. "Lemme get a couple scotches in me first, aye?"

Damn. Empty seat wasn't for Joss.

Picking up my bourbon, I downed half in one go, planning my exit as everyone congratulated the newly engaged couple.

Once it settled, Gus, Nox's new fiancée, asked, "Why're we fighting?"

Piper gave a dramatic sigh. "They won't let us go to the strip club."

Gus spun to face Nox as his expression turned just as pissed as Jake's. Before she could speak, he shook his head. "Nah, mo chuisle, don't get any fookin' ideas."

"But it'd be fun."

"That's what I said," Piper agreed.

Harlow tried to move away, but with the grip Kase had on her ass, she didn't make it far. "I've gotta grab drinks," she said through a laugh, though she wasn't exactly fighting his hold.

"And I've gotta grab..." The rest of his words were muttered quietly, which was likely a good thing based on the way her skin flamed nearly as red as her hair.

She half-assedly slapped his chest and even more half-assedly tried again to shift away.

I averted my gaze, only to land on Jake in a similar clinch with his wife and Nox in one with his soon-to-be wife.

Yeah, a night out with one married couple and two engaged couples was a genius fuckin' way to get my mind off my shitty love life.

I moved my focus to Xavier and Eli, the only other single people at the damn love fest. Eli was talking about some destination wedding he had to travel to as they eyed the women who were trying to grab their attention.

If I was smart, I'd have been doing the same so I could try to clear the futile fantasies of pretty brown eyes from my head.

But when it came to Joss, I was far from smart. I didn't *want* to clear them.

I wanted to make them a reality.

Kase finally let Harlow go, though his gaze stayed locked on her until she was through the crowd and behind the bar. "We're gonna have to find a new joint if she's gonna keep jumping back there to help every time we come in."

Piper sighed. "I already suggested we go—"

"Sweets," Jake growled, pulling her off her stool and onto his lap.

"You can't blame me for messing with you when you make it so fun."

"Shit still bad with staffing here?" I asked.

Kase lifted his chin. "Swear he hires five new bartenders just for ten to quit."

"I get it," I said, my shoulders bunching just thinking about Wicked. I rotated through dancers faster than they rotated thongs. High turnover wasn't uncommon, but shit was getting ridiculous.

Harlow returned a few minutes later with a loaded tray of drinks, including a new bourbon for me even though mine was only half gone.

It only took a few minutes after that for the conversation to split like it usually did. The guys talked shop and the women...

The women were fuckin' funny as shit.

It was no wonder Joss got along with them, though I didn't think she shared her humor as openly. No, I seemed to be the only one who got to hear her snark—something I liked a whole fuckuva lot.

I stayed in the middle, chiming in about my Harley upgrades while keeping an ear on the women to hear their jokes. Jokes that were so dirty, they'd make grown men blush.

When Xavier brought up a car he and Key were restoring in their free time, I scanned the area. "Where *is* Key?"

The women's conversation stopped abruptly, and I glanced over in time to see Piper and Harlow share a look.

"He's... on a date," Piper said slowly—an answer that didn't explain why they'd gone tensely silent.

Or why they were studying me like I was a wild animal about to attack.

I wasn't the only one not in the know because Jake asked, "With who?"

"Joss."

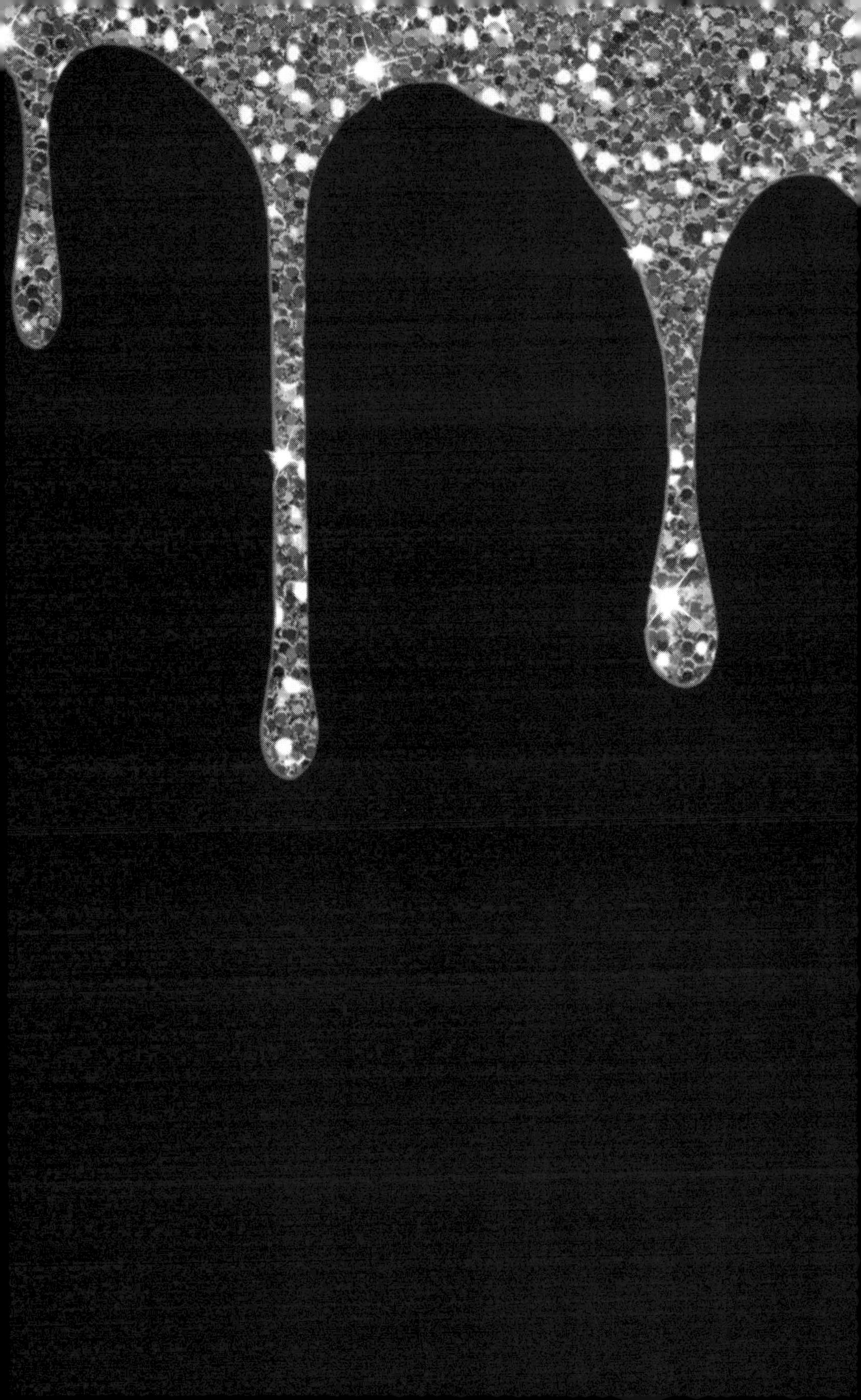

TEN

Door Number Two

JOSS

MY MYSTERY DATE IS *KEY?*

The quietest of all the Hyde men approached, looking handsome and cool in dark jeans and a black shirt. He gave me a half-hug. "Hey. You look beautiful."

I didn't have time to respond—not that I was sure I even could—before he lifted his chin at the hostess.

Stunned and silently freaking out, my feet moved on autopilot as I followed her with Key at my back. Amazing smells hit me as she led us through the maze of tables to what had to be the best one in the gorgeous restaurant. Tucked away in an intimate nook, it was positioned next to an enclosed fireplace filled with blue glass pieces, the reflection of the flames hitting each in a mesmerizing way. Like water and fire coexisting. On the other side was an expansive window with a view of the nightlife lights bouncing off the inky bay water.

It was almost mythical and ethereal and all the other *-al* words that still didn't come close to portraying just how beautiful it was.

Key pulled out my chair, and I sat automatically, my thoughts whirling as I took in the view and fire and *Key*.

Freakin' Key.

The hostess walked away, leaving me alone with Key.

Freakin' Key!

It wasn't that there was anything wrong with him. Far from it. He had that whole broodingly-intense-and-sensitive thing going. That just wasn't my thing. Not to mention, there'd be no balance between us. We weren't opposites or even opposite sides of the same coin. We were just the same.

Shy.

Quiet.

It'd be all silence, all the time.

And, for another not to mention that I was very much mentioning, I didn't think I was *his* thing. I'd seen him out with women and guys, so I knew his attraction came from who the person was and not what body parts were beneath their clothes. But he'd never given any indication there was even a spark of interest.

Needing a second to gather my thoughts, I focused on the menu, but my stomach was clenched so tight, nothing sounded even slightly appetizing. In my wildest daydreams—and there'd been a lot of them—I'd never imagined Key would set me up with himself.

The potential for an awkward and dramatic disaster was astronomical.

Aw, hell.

Lars

No.

No fuckin' way did I hear that right.

"What'd you say?" I gritted out.

"He and Joss are on a date," Piper said.

"Where?"

She shrugged like it wasn't the fuckin' craziest shit in the whole damn world. "I don't know. Somewhere nice because he had to pull strings to get the reservation. He..."

The rest of her words were lost in the blood pulsing through my ears and the jealousy tearing at my gut—as if I'd eaten a bowl of tiny circular saws like they were fuckin' Wheaties.

Yanking my phone from my pocket, I brought up his number in my texts.

Me: Where are you?

Nothing.

I wasn't surprised—if I had Joss sitting across from me, I wouldn't look at anything else, either.

"Her ex," I said suddenly, cutting off whoever had been talking.

"What about him?" Harlow asked.

"She's fixing shit with him."

Harlow and Piper shared another look before cracking up.

"No, no, *no*." Harlow turned to me, emphatically shaking her head. "Not unless she told you something *way* different than what she's told us."

"That's what Jake said."

Everyone's eyes went to him, and he held his hands up in the surrender position. "Never said that. Just said she was bustin' her ass to fix shit."

Harlow's expression tightened on her friend's behalf. Knowing the way she dealt with anger, it was a safe bet she was imagining kicking the fiancé in the nuts. "The only thing she wants to fix is the mess of a mortgage he dumped on her. If she was pining for that asshole, Piper and I would take turns smacking some sense into her."

"I'd pay to see that." Eli glanced around. "Lemme just find some mud or Jell-O first."

"Dude," Kase and Jake snapped in unison.

Lifting his beer, Eli told Piper, "You're right, messing with them *is* fun."

Usually, the whole scene would've made me sit back and enjoy watching Kase and Jake get riled, but I wasn't in the mood. "You don't know where Key took her?"

"No, but I can text her." A knowing smile spread across Harlow's face before she fucked with me. "Or I can just wait and get the details tomorrow at the bakery. Or Monday—"

"Do it." I knocked back my drink before adding, "You know, please."

No one asked about my sudden interest in Joss. They sure as shit didn't look surprised by it.

I'd thought I'd done a good job hiding the fact I was into her.

I'd clearly thought wrong.

Just like I'd been dead fuckin' wrong to let the fact she was far outta my league stop me from making her mine.

I sent three more texts to Key before calling.

Nothing.

Since I couldn't hunt them down or force him to return a damn message, I did the only thing I could do.

I got shitfaced.

And I planned.

Joss

"Relax." Key grabbed my attention and clued me in that I wasn't hiding my panic well—or at all. Usually being told to relax would make me want to throw him through the expansive window, but right then, it was a valid suggestion. "This isn't a date."

Since I specifically remembered asking to be set up on a date, that surprised me.

My eyes shifted to the side. "Is someone else coming?"

Or did someone back out and you're filling in so I wasn't left to gorge myself on free bread while I pathetically watched the door?

"No, but it's still not a date. It's..." A smile tipped his lips. "A push." At my slow, lost slow blink, he continued. "You haven't been on a date since your engagement ended, right?"

I was surprised he knew about my failed engagement, much less any other details of my personal life. It made me wonder how much he noticed when he was quietly blending in.

"This crosses off that awkward first one," he explained.

All week, the impending date had lurked in the back of my mind, leaving my nerves raw. More than once, I'd given myself a major tension headache from clenching my jaw.

But thanks to Key, my first foray back into the dating pool wasn't a high-pressure Olympic swim. It was just a float in the shallow end, complete with snacks and yummy drinks. It was enough to make all that anxiety flow from me.

In its place was warmth and gratitude. Key had been thoughtful enough to do that for me.

Before I could say anything more, the server came to take our orders. Key, like the other Hyde men, seemed to have a bottomless pit of a stomach. I wasn't sure how he'd eat all the food he ordered. I wasn't even sure it would fit on our table. I bit back a laugh at the image my brain formed.

When the server walked away with pages upon pages of items—only a slight exaggeration—Key took in my smile. "Something funny?"

"Just picturing the folding card table they're gonna have to drag out to hold your dinner."

"This place is too swanky for that. I think it'll be a conveyor belt like those sushi places in Japan."

I lost the battle with my laughter as I pictured our food looping around the fireplace while we frantically grabbed pieces—like the chocolate factory Lucy episode I used to watch with my Gram.

His phone chimed, but he didn't take it out of his pocket as he focused on me. "Tell me about your classroom."

It was more a command than a request—not that I was surprised. You could take the alpha out of the garage...

I shrugged. "It's not as interesting as working on expensive hotrods all day."

"All those tiny humans with no filters? They've gotta be like little drunks. That's more exciting than gear shafts, exhausts, and transmissions."

He had a point.

I started to tell him about some of the class antics—including Samuel's baby back rib confusion—when his phone rang. It stopped only to start again.

"You can answer that," I insisted.

Pulling his cell out, he glanced at it and his mouth pulled into a small smile—the Key version of a grin. But all he did was silence the phone before pocketing it again. "So has he tried to cook any more babies?"

"No, but he's started calling his pretend wives *babe* and some of the girls are less than thrilled. They think he's saying that they're babies."

"Between his pet-name game and his budding cooking skills, he'll be set when he gets older."

"According to what Samuel's dad taught him, men have to keep their women fed and happy. So, yeah, he's definitely got a better grasp on things than some adult men I know."

It wasn't long before the server returned with food that smelled heavenly. Happily digging in, Key asked more about school, my life, and everything else under the sun.

It was the best not-a-real-date a girl could ask for.

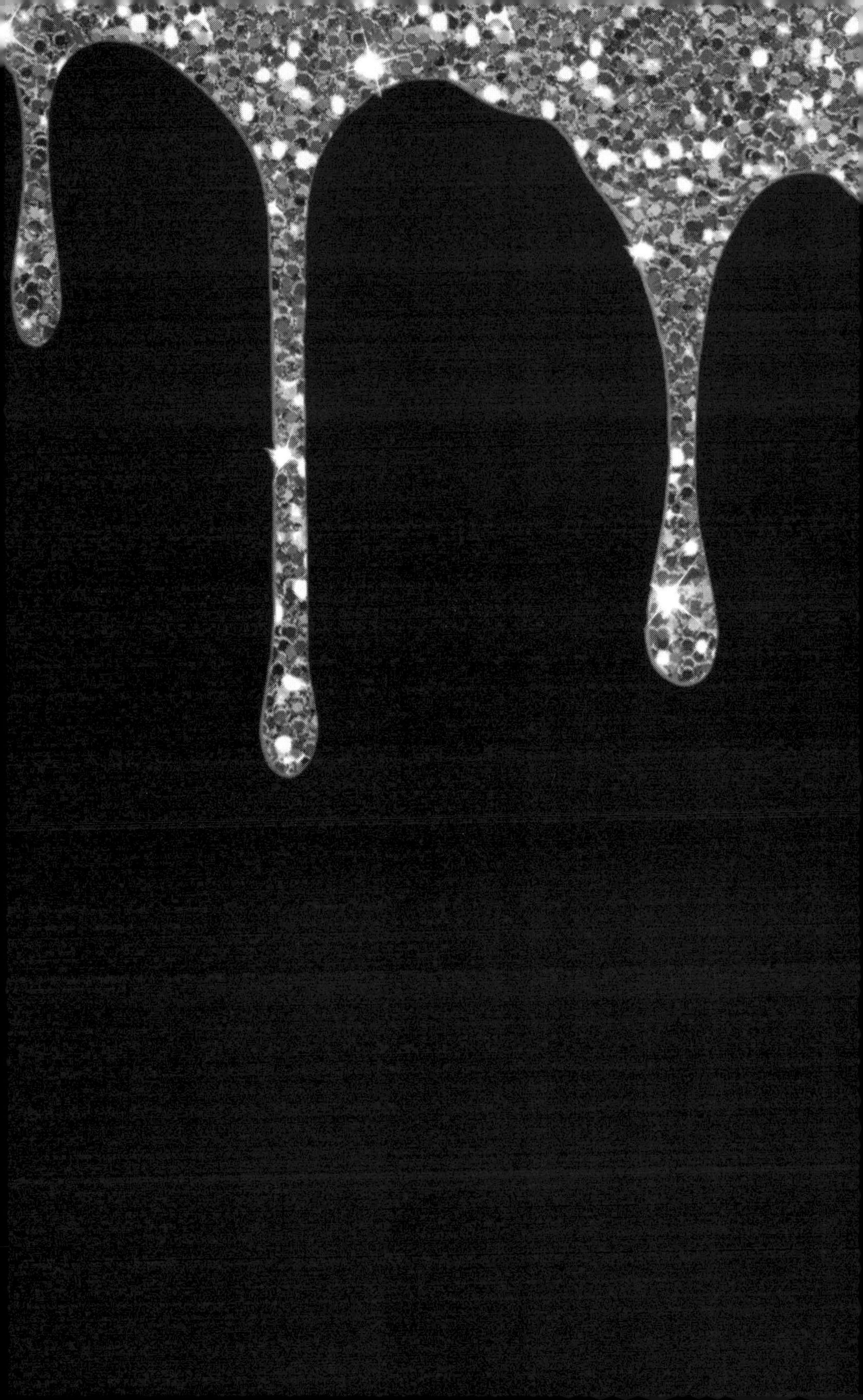

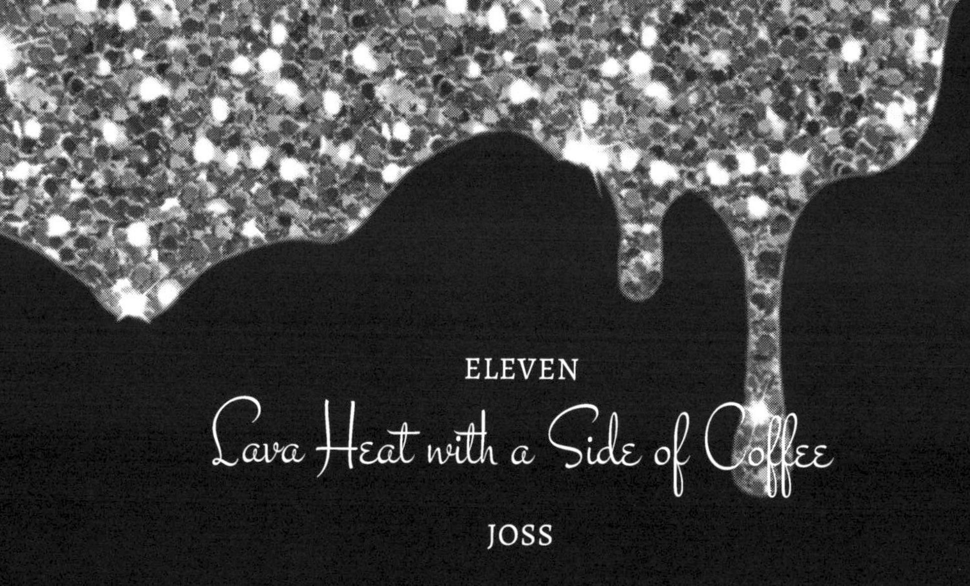

ELEVEN

Lava Heat with a Side of Coffee

JOSS

I NEED COFFEE.

I need my coffee to have coffee.

I need a coffee to get up the energy to go grab another coffee.

Based on the way I was dragging, my brain and body were in agreement that I was not made for wild Friday nights. Key and I hadn't even stayed out late, but since I was usually asleep on the couch by nine on the weekend, it felt like I'd been out until three rather than eleven.

It'd been fun and well worth the rough morning.

Kinda.

Okay, it would be worth it once I got more caffeine into my system.

Unfortunately, we were smack dab in the middle of our peak busy time. I had no chance to step away to refill my cup.

I barely had time to yawn—not that I was letting that stop me.

I really was freakin' tired.

On the plus side, being slammed meant Harlow and Piper hadn't had any time to grill me on my not-a-date with Key. In fact, they'd been surprisingly tightlipped all morning.

"We're almost out of marshmallow treats," I noted, surprised at how quick they'd sold that morning. The adjusted, extra marshmallow recipe was even more popular than the original test run, but it was still some kind of record. "I'll whip up more."

And grab the most giant cup of coffee while I do it.

In fact, I might stick a straw in the coffee pot and call it a day.

"Sophie will get it," Piper rushed out fervently.

Even though Sophie hadn't made them before, she shrugged and started for the kitchen. It wasn't like they were complicated.

"I've got to grab a coffee first," I said. "Otherwise, I'm afraid I'll fall asleep against the display case and drool everywhere."

"Bring me one, too," Harlow said, earning a glare from Piper.

What the hell is going on between them?

Even Soph glanced between the two, her brows lowered. With the tension and dirty looks, it almost seemed like they were fighting, but Harlow wouldn't be there if they were.

Hauling ass to the back, I was almost done fixing the mugs when I heard it.

The rumbles.

The rumbles that, despite how dead I'd sworn my emotions were, traveled through my body, making anticipation and excitement flare to life.

Two weeks working in Lars' space. Hearing his loaded words. Staring into his midnight-blue eyes that were too sharp. Too intense. Too distracting. Getting his attention, his thoughtfulness, and his smiles.

Two weeks of him praising each millimeter of progress I made.

Of him gently tugging my ponytail—a ponytail I specifically wore so he would pull it.

It was no wonder I was going soft. Who could resist all that?

I was surprised to hear Lars so early—he didn't usually come in until the afternoon.

Carrying the coffee, I was careful as I pushed through the doorway so as not to spill even a single drop of the caffeinated lifeblood. When I raised my gaze from the cups, it landed on Lars as he stormed into the building. He was one man, yet he'd managed to fill the entire storefront and steal all the oxygen.

Or at least the oxygen from my lungs.

Frozen to the spot, my eyes widened as he stalked toward me, not stopping on the other side of the counter. He came right back, still not stopping until his massive body was nearly touching mine and he was cupping my cheeks.

His gaze roamed my face. It was intense bordering on a bit feral.

Holy caffeine and chocolate chip cookies.

"What're you—" I started when I couldn't take it any longer, but my question was cut off.

Because he lowered his head and pressed his lips against mine.

Kissing me.

Lars was kissing me.

I wanted to memorize each little detail.

Every scent and sound and nuance that I'd want embedded into my brain for the rest of my life.

But I couldn't.

His deep kiss consumed me, wiping out all thoughts of anything other than how amazing his mouth felt on mine. And how mind-blowing it was to *finally* feel it. Not a fantasy. Not a daydream. Not an idle wonder that floated through my head when I studied his mouth as he spoke to me.

Lars Luthor was actually—*finally*—kissing me.

I was vaguely aware of someone taking the coffee cups out of my hands. Perfectly timed, too, because I'd been about to drop the hot nectar, thereby ruining the kiss with shards of ceramic and second-degree burns.

With my hands free, I was able to do something else I'd been dying to.

I touched him.

Well, I gripped the sides of his tee to hold myself up while I took everything he had to give, but still. Contact was made.

Contact he apparently enjoyed as much as me, because he groaned and shifted closer, pressing tight until I felt his hard muscles and his harder... *everything*.

As if my veins were filled with live electricity, a shock jolted through me. It was quickly followed by a surge of lust, the lava heat of it mixing with the electricity until I was coming out of my skin.

In the absolute best way.

Too soon—or maybe not soon enough since I'd completely forgotten we were in public—Lars tore his mouth away. He took a step back but kept hold of my face. That and my death grip on his shirt were the only things keeping my wobbling legs from giving out. His dark blue eyes dropped to my lips, his jaw clenching and his fingertips digging in as he silently stared for a moment. "Picking you up at six."

His mouth took mine in another hard but way too fast kiss before he released his hold and turned to stalk out. Just like that.

No question.

No confirmation.

He told me we were going on a date.

And I couldn't freakin' wait.

After a long, hazy moment of staring unseeing in front of me, I turned to find eyes on me.

A lot of eyes.

The storefront was also eerily quiet, making me realize the kiss hadn't drowned out the noise—there hadn't been any in the first place.

After a long moment, one of our regulars broke the silence. "Well, it's about time! I've been waiting every single Saturday for him to do that."

You and me both, ma'am.

You and me both.

Piper, Harlow, and Sophie looked as if they'd perish on the spot if they didn't ask me a million and ten questions. They'd just have to deal with the torturous wait, because without the distraction of hot and heavy kissing, the long line of customers demanded our attention.

Jumping back to it, I rushed around like a chicken with my head cut off to get caught up.

But I did it replaying the kiss and anticipating my impending date.

And I did it no longer needing the energy boost from my coffee.

I still drank it, of course.

I wasn't a monster.

"THAT WAS SO FLIPPIN' hot," Harlow said with no segue the moment Sophie flipped the closed sign.

She wasn't wrong.

I knew Harlow was practically bursting with questions and thoughts and excitement. But I had something else on my mind first.

Once the high of the kiss faded and my mind started working again, I grew suspicious. Piper had been acting pretty damn shifty about keeping me in the storefront. Almost like she'd known something was going to happen.

Turning to face her, I narrowed my eyes. "Did you know Lars was coming in?"

Her own gaze darted away as she badly tried to hide a smile. "I may have suspected."

"How?"

"He came to Rye last night." She tapped away at the register to close out the sales as she talked, telling me about his reaction to my date with Key.

All those calls and texts Key was getting.

They were from Lars.

"He even asked me to text to find out where you were," Harlow said with a grin.

My lips tipped down. "I didn't get a text."

"I didn't actually send one." She shrugged. "He's been dragging his feet, he deserved to suffer a little longer."

"You're terrible," Piper said. That didn't stop them both from laughing.

When I didn't join in, mostly because my mind was still reeling at the dramatic one-eighty he'd seemed to make, Harlow skewered me with a sharp gaze. "You *are* into Lars, right?"

There were a million reasons why I shouldn't be. Including, but not limited to...

I was busy with work, work, and more work.

We were *so* different. Opposites may attract, but what about beyond that?

And was there even an attraction? For all I knew, he only wanted me after finding out about my non-date with Key. Was I a toy he had no interest in until someone else wanted to play with me?

It didn't help that my relationship history was limited to one large dumpster fire.

On that same note, Lars owned a strip club and my ex had cheated on me with a stripper. Not that Lars was anything like Peter, but maybe my pride or jealousy or logical part of my brain hadn't gotten that message. I'd just be suspicious and miserable.

I'd be the toxic one.

Last, and definitely most important, I wasn't sure I wanted to get involved with anyone. Physically or emotionally, period. I'd be inviting drama into the tight-knit group for a date? A booty call? A friend with benefits?

Despite all the reasons why it was a terrible idea, I met Harlow's inquisitive gaze and didn't hesitate before nodding.

I couldn't deny it. I was into Lars.

Both women grinned at me, their excitement clear. Even Soph looked ecstatic, and she didn't really know Lars or me. I expected more questions, but they didn't come. They had the reassurance that I was happy with the surprising turn of events and that was all they needed.

For then, at least.

I was sure that post-date would be a different story.

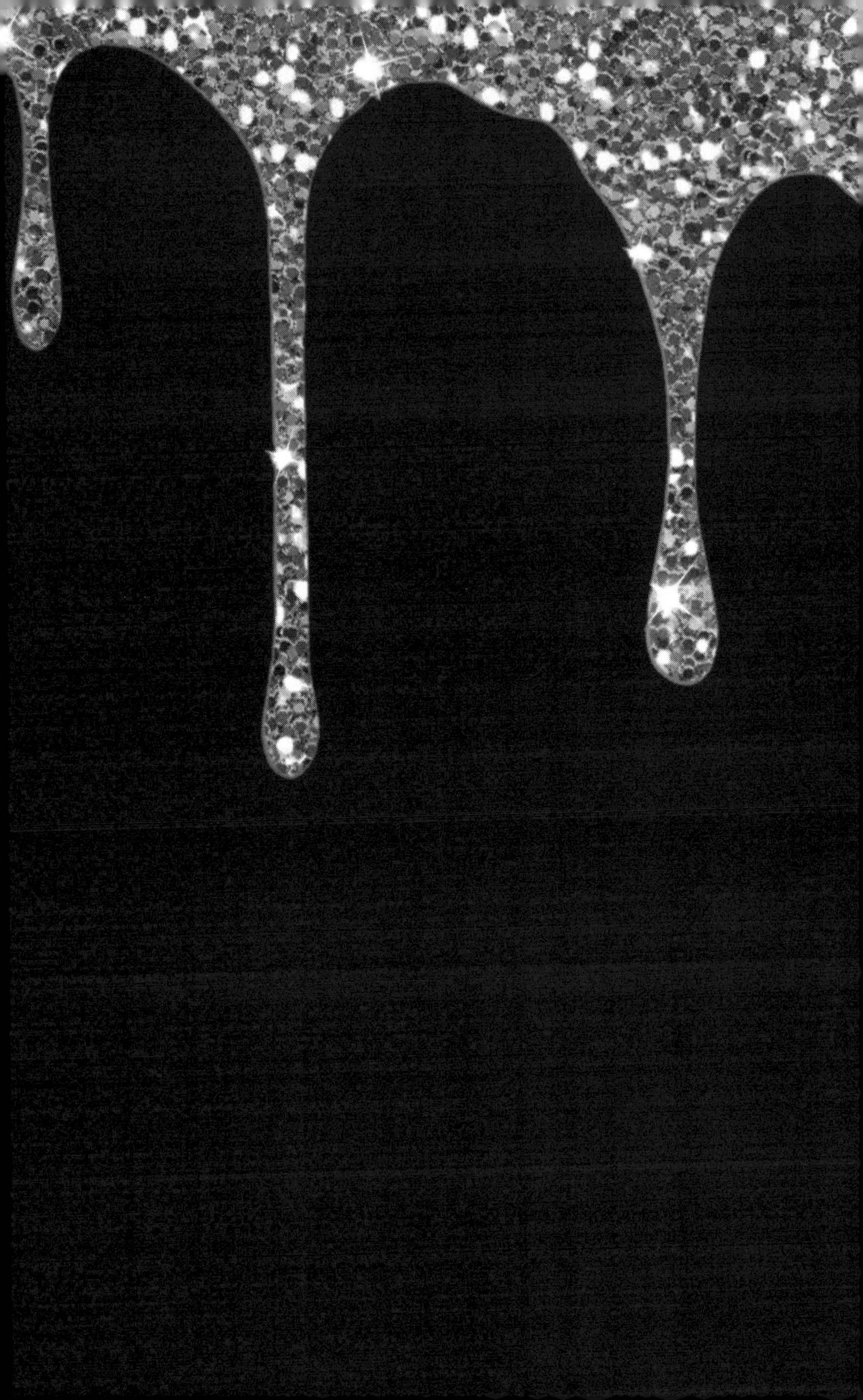

TWELVE
Hellhounds Love Pizza

JOSS

MAYBE IT WAS BECAUSE KEY'S NOT-A-DATE FIRST-DATE idea had really worked.

Or maybe it was that Lars had texted to say we were going somewhere casual, taking the guesswork out of date night preparations.

Or maybe it was just that it was with Lars.

Whatever the reason, I wasn't in a total panic as I waited for him. I was nervous, yes, but I was mostly excited. I'd had to force myself to sit so he didn't show up to find my nose pressed against the window like a hyper puppy.

That would've been too awkward to come back from.

Instead, I'd settled for straining to hear the telltale rumble. In my quiet neighborhood, I would be able to hear him coming a few streets away, giving me a minute or so to get my shit under control.

But there were no motorcycle sounds. Just a sudden knock on the door, making me jolt.

Please don't be Ruth.

Or Mom.

Or, even worse, Nora.

Oh God. Or worst of the worst…

Dad.

My family was known to drop by unannounced—likely to make

sure I hadn't withered away all alone, a husk of a spinster. I was already whipping up four different excuses to clear away whoever was out there. They would receive a personalized lie because I put care and effort into being the black sheep.

It was those little touches that made all the difference.

When I checked the peephole, my breath whooshed out to see Lars' handsome face staring back at me.

Not wanting to appear overzealous and desperate—though my heart rate would confirm I was both—I contemplated waiting a few beats.

I didn't have the chance.

"Open the door, hotcakes," Lars said.

I swung it open. "How'd you know I was there?"

He pointed toward the peephole. "Went dark."

Great, I'm not aloof or stealthy.

Oh well.

Turning, I grabbed my purse and keys. "Just making sure it was you."

His heat hit my back like a physical caress. I locked my knees to fight the urge to lean into him.

Something told me that if I did, we wouldn't go anywhere.

Though right then, with him so close, his hands on the doorjamb and his outstretched arms caging me in, I was having trouble figuring out why that would be a bad thing.

His minty breath skimmed my ear and made a chill run down my spine. "You expecting someone else?"

"Just the usual parade of men," I deadpanned. "I triple booked my schedule."

"Funny," he muttered, though his gruff tone said otherwise.

Turning, I rolled my eyes. "I just didn't hear your bike."

"Drove my car."

Bummer.

I'd been looking forward to the bike. Seeing Lars straddle the chrome and matte black beast, controlling it how he wanted...

His voice was low and as gravelly as an unpaved road when he asked, "You ever ride before?"

It took me a moment to realize he was referring to a motorcycle and not a muscular, powerful body.

Either way, the answer was the same.

"No."

"This drive is gonna be stop and go," he explained. "Not a good ride, and sure as hell not a good one for your first time. That should be special. Unrushed. I'll take you out when we can hit open road and just cruise. It'll be worth the wait. Promise."

My heart squeezed with excitement at the idea of spending hours on the back of his motorcycle. And my thighs clenched with a very different kind of excitement as I imagined doing what else his words conjured. Doing it for *hours*. Special. Unrushed. Worth the wait.

Does he do that on purpose, or are the dirty thoughts all my own fault?

We walked down the path to a cool as hell muscle car. It reminded me of Harlow's bluish-green car Kase had painted for her, though Lars' was matte black like his motorcycle. I wished I knew a single thing about cars, but my knowledge was limited to color, generic vehicle type, and whether their rear lights made them look like a face—a favorite game I played with my nephews.

I was really good at that game.

It may not have been the transportation I'd been hoping for, but it wasn't exactly lacking.

Lars opened my door before going around to the driver's side. Once he was in, I asked, "Where are we going?"

"You'll see."

"Ominous," I muttered.

"Exciting," he corrected. "Gotta keep you interested somehow."

Yeah, 'cause the insanely good looks, dangerous vibe, and cool personality aren't enough.

As he drove, Lars peppered me with questions about school and the bakery. I tried to ask him about Wicked, but he said, and I quote, "It's a fuckin' shitshow I don't wanna think about while I'm with you."

That may not have been the most flowery compliment, but it was an effective one, nonetheless.

After a short drive that turned into a longer one thanks to all that stop and go he'd predicted, we pulled up to our destination.

Bury the Hatchet.

Since it was highly unlikely he was taking me to a peace mediator—not unless he was holding a grudge about my raisin cookie threat—I turned a questioning look toward Lars.

"We're throwing axes," he explained, killing the engine and getting out.

"That's a thing?" I muttered to myself as I followed.

When we reached the brick building, Lars opened the door and stepped aside for me to enter first and see it was, in fact, a *thing*.

An intimidating, and possibly incredibly dangerous, thing.

Oh no. This could be baaaad.

"Have you done this before?" I asked, hoping like hell he wasn't an expert while I wasn't sure I could even throw an ax a couple feet in front of me.

Lars shook his head. "This is my buddy Demetrius' place. He's been on me to come, but I haven't had time."

Like he'd been standing around the corner, waiting for his cue, an extremely good-looking and *extremely* muscular Black man entered the crowded lobby. "Luthor!"

Keeping his hand on my back, Lars propelled me forward. He still didn't remove it as he shook the man's hand and made introductions.

No, he used that hold to curl me into him. My front plastered to his side, my hand automatically landing on his abs.

His impossibly hard abs that tensed at the contact.

Since I was so close, I could hear *and* feel his sharp inhale.

Brows raised and jaw literally dropped, Demetrius didn't miss the smooth maneuver.

Neither did my body.

At each point of contact, my skin became hypersensitive. I'd never been so acutely aware of my proximity to someone else. There was this crazy current traveling between us, but rather than electrical power, it fueled an insane amount of lust that stole my breath.

I moved my hand from his stomach to take Demetrius' outstretched one. When I dropped it awkwardly to my side, Lars didn't hesitate to grab it and press it back against him.

Demetrius again watched the action, though this time he did it with an outright grin. "I'd say it's about damn time you came to check out the business that *you* co-own, but from the looks of things, you've had better stuff to focus on."

Lars didn't bother to correct him that it was our first date. He just squeezed me tighter and said, "Told you I'd be a hands-off silent partner."

"Didn't realize hands-off meant never showing your ugly mug here, period."

Scanning the packed building that included a full lobby of groups waiting for their turn to hurl murder weapons, I smiled at Demetrius. "It doesn't look like you need his help anyway. Did you recently open?"

"Coming up on two years." He aimed another pointed look at Lars.

I shot him my own surprised one.

Lars lifted a shoulder. "Like I said, haven't had time."

A thought hit me, and I opened my mouth to blurt out the question suddenly burning on the tip of my tongue. It took all my self-control to hold it in, which meant I had very little rein on my fanciful imagination.

"I got your spot all set." Demetrius tilted his head for us to follow.

I watched people as we walked, hoping to pick up any and all helpful techniques in the short distance. The general method seemed to be drink beer, throw ax, hope for the best.

I could handle that.

Maybe.

Demetrius pushed through a heavy wooden swinging door that led to a private room clearly meant for parties.

Only instead of banners, streamers, or other party decorations, twinkle lights hung from the protective fencing, sexy music played low from hidden speakers, and bottles of beer were positioned just so in one of those ice buckets usually used for champagne. There were even a multitude of flowers spread throughout the room.

I mean, sure, they'd clearly been pilfered from the planters that lined the streets, and they were being held in pint glasses and a couple kitchen canisters. But that didn't lessen the pretty impact.

Lars scanned the room, taking in all the touches before muttering, "Subtle."

Demetrius gave an unapologetic grin. "After we talked, how could I not?"

I'd give up coffee and Piper's cupcakes to have been a fly on the wall during that discussion.

Not forever, of course.

But for a week or so.

That was still a great sacrifice.

Taking us to one of the alleys, Demetrius ran through a quick explanation and demo of how to throw, score, and not accidentally cut a head off. Once he was done—and I was less worried about accidental murder—he looked at me. "Any dietary or allergy restrictions?" At my headshake, he continued. "Got a taste for anything specific?"

Another headshake from me.

"I'll send out our best stuff."

"Aren't you gonna ask me?" Lars asked.

"No. Suck it up."

"Fuckin' rude."

I turned my patient-teacher-smile his way. "You get what you get, and you don't throw a fit."

Demetrius laughed as he headed for the door, but Lars didn't crack a smile.

Instead, his dark blue eyes were heated as he closed the distance between us. "When it comes to you, hotcakes, I'll take any-fucking-thing I can get, and I damn sure won't throw a fit."

With his tall, powerfully built body so close to mine, I had to crane my neck to meet the inferno in his gaze.

And in that moment.

That one single dot in the timeline of my life.

In that tiny span, I felt more intensity than I'd ever felt. More desire. More giddiness. More wanting. More excitement. More wild.

Just so much *more*.

I thought he was going to kiss me.

I wanted him to kiss me.

No.

I *needed* it.

My lips still warmed and tingled at the memory of his kiss that morning, and I was desperate to experience it again.

But before either of us could move, the door swung open and a server backed in, carrying a tray. When he spun around to face us, his steps faltered, and he nearly dropped the load. "Uhh, food. From the kitchen. From Demetrius... in the kitchen."

His stammered words and the bright red of his face showed that, despite the fact Lars and I weren't kissing, he knew he'd interrupted an intimate moment, nonetheless. His gaze darted from Lars to me before doing a double take and swallowing hard enough to be visible.

I tilted my head back to see Lars glaring daggers at the guy. Elbowing him in the ribs, I offered the server a reassuring smile. "Thanks. It smells amazing."

"Thanks, you too," he shot back instantly before visibly cringing, setting the tray down, and then practically running from the room.

"You scared the poor guy half to death." I shook my head as I stepped back and crossed my arms. "Are you proud of yourself?"

"A little, yeah."

I rolled my eyes and turned away.

Lars hooked a finger in my belt loop, using the hold to spin me back. "Didn't mean to terrify the kid, I was just pissed he interrupted before I could do this."

His head lowered, his mouth pressing to mine in a hard, searing kiss. I couldn't hold back my soft moan, but I thought the noise around us would drown it out.

I thought wrong.

At that little sound, Lars gave his own low, rumbling groan before deepening the kiss. His tongue pressed into my mouth to twirl with mine, and his hand slid from my belt loop to cup my ass. Too soon—and like it physically pained him—he tore himself away and stepped back.

I saw why when I glanced over at the swinging door and our audience.

"Hey, asshole," Demetrius said, "don't terrorize my employees with your scary-as-shit looks. They're hard to find as it is, and I'm pretty sure he's in the back trying not to shit a brick."

Lars' lips tipped as he raised his chin before Demetrius stormed away, loudly muttering curses aimed toward Lars.

I grabbed a beer from the ice—partially to hide my smile at his expense and partially because I needed to cool off. I didn't do a good job at either, because Lars came up behind me, reaching around to pluck the beer from my hand as he whispered, "Think that's funny?"

"Yup. They were inventive insults." When he backed away, I spun and watched him tip the long-necked bottle to his mouth, his muscular throat doing oddly attractive things in the process.

I'd never in my life thought of a neck as sexy. Just like I'd never in my life been jealous of a bottle.

Yet there we were.

With a sinfully sexy smirk, he lowered the bottle enough to run his thumb across his bottom lip as he stared down at me.

I'd spent a lot of time secretly watching Lars. Or thinking about him. Or thinking about watching him. Too much, in fact.

But never, in all the times I'd stared as I'd barely held in my drool, had he looked better than he did right then.

On my deathbed, I'd remember three things.

The cringy time I'd hugged my crush in ninth grade because I'd thought he was going in for one—he'd actually been reaching behind me to throw out a paper.

The more recent yet no less cringey time I'd worn two different shoes to Sweets You Rock.

And the way Lars was looking at me right then, his tattooed thumb dragging across his full lip. It was branded and imprinted in my memory for life.

"Christ, you're pretty," he rumbled, low and intimate.

Pretty.

Not hot.

Not sexy.

Not technicolor or heart rate raising.

Pretty.

I was growing to hate that word.

I forced a smile, and his gaze immediately dropped to my mouth, his brows lowering. Before he could speak, I spun and grabbed a new beer. "What're we playing for?"

"Fun?"

"Boring. There's gotta be a wager."

"Never struck me as competitive, hotcakes."

"I have two older sisters. Trust me, *everything* is a competition."

He looked thoughtful as he took a pull of his beer. "Top score after every throw gets to ask a question."

I was relieved he hadn't gone a different route, like strip ax throwing. If the poor server had been embarrassed interrupting an intimate hold, he'd have passed out seeing various states of undress. Especially since I was fairly certain I'd be the one stripping.

Plus, nudity and sharp projectiles were never a good combination.

I popped a spicy bite of cheesy tot heaven in my mouth before giving a firm nod. "Deal."

Lars gestured to the alley. "Ladies first."

Setting my stance, Demetrius' instructions looped through my head as I threw.

And hit the target.

Not just hit it. The ax landed close to the bullseye *and* stuck in the wood.

I spun around and grinned at Lars, a *squee* of proud excitement escaping me.

"Why do I feel like I'm being hustled, hotcakes?" There was no anger or misplaced toxic masculinity in his question. If anything, he seemed amused, proud, and— surprisingly—turned on. There was a fire in his gaze that had me fighting the urge to throw something again.

Maybe another ax to show off.

Or maybe just myself at him.

I switched places with him, taking a presumptuous victory drink as I watched him set himself. Then I nearly choked on my beer and my tongue as I watched his impressive muscles bunch and flex as he let the ax sail through the air.

When it hit the wood, it was close to the bullseye. Just not as close as mine.

He spun around and dipped his head. "Ask away."

I sorted through the lengthy list of questions I'd been mentally forming before picking one. I carefully kept any trace of ire, judgment, jealousy, and anything other than genuine curiosity from my tone. "What made you open Wicked?"

He paused for a second, studying me so intently, I was worried he could somehow see all *my* secrets. And since most of those secrets involved my borderline obsessive crush on him, I'd rather he not.

That kind of crazy should be let out slowly and methodically. Ease him into it.

When he finally spoke, it was to cautiously rumble, "You know I did time?"

I nodded. I didn't know the specifics, but I was aware Kase, Lars, and Nox had met in prison.

"I started working as a bouncer at a shitty club during high school." At my surprised brow hike, he shrugged. "I've always liked to fight, so I figured I'd make my hobby a career and get paid for it. A few years in, club traded hands and I found out the new owner was forcing the girls to do fucked up shit in exchange for the good shifts." Thankfully, he didn't elaborate on what that entailed, and I didn't ask. I just watched as his lips curled in a vicious smile. "A couple years locked up was a small price to pay for making sure he could never do it again."

That's scary.

And hot.

Scary hot.

"After I got out, there weren't a lot of job options. People aren't exactly lining up to hire ex-cons, and the ones who do treat 'em like shit 'cause they know they got leverage. So I opened Wicked. Girls got a place to dance where they were taken care of instead of taken advantage of, and I didn't have to work for anyone else." Another sinister smile shifted him from hot to dangerously hot. "And I still get to fight when the occasion arises."

Like the most primally erotic flip book, my mind raced with images of Lars using his powerful body like a weapon. All the flexing. Tensing. Slick muscles and raw aggression.

It should've been frightening. As in, the reddest of all red flags. But I was apparently colorblind. Or maybe red flag was just my new favorite color.

Realizing he was staring at me expectantly, waiting for my reaction, I found my voice in my desert dry mouth. "If you like to fight, why didn't you go into UFC or boxing?"

"Uh-uh. You already asked your question." He tipped his head toward the target, and I quickly reset and threw, landing in the second circle.

Shit, he's got this one.

He almost did, too, except his ax hit too hard and bounced back.

"Well?" I prompted.

"She's a shark. Definitely bein' hustled," he muttered before answering my question. "I don't have the mentality to fight for sport. Don't like rules and can't just go knuckles against some bastard for the hell of it."

"So you need a reason for violence."

"Pretty much."

We took our turns again, my mind already picking my next question. It was for nothing, though, because he beat me by a wide margin.

Sticking his ax in the stump holder, he grabbed his beer before facing me. "Why do you work at Sweets?"

There was a heaviness in his tone. An emphasis that said he wasn't asking why I'd chosen the bakery. He wanted to know why I needed a second job at all.

I could've gone the evasive route by claiming I liked working with Piper—which was technically true—and he probably would've let me get away with it. But he'd laid his cards on the table with his answer before opening the door to allow me to do the same.

So I did.

"I bought a house with my ex-fiancé. After things went south with him, I happily dropped the fiancé but kept the house. I came out ahead."

At my admission, there was no flash of surprise on his handsome face. Given how impossible it was to keep a secret in the Hyde group, I also didn't have a flash of surprise that he'd known about my failed engagement.

Dark-blue eyes scanned my face, searching for… something. Seemingly finding it—or maybe at the lack thereof—he gave a barely perceptible nod before grinning down at me. There was enough heat in his gaze to boil the queso on the bar behind me.

Needing to break the intensity of the moment before I flung myself at him, I flung myself at said queso instead. I dipped a chip, popping the whole thing into my mouth despite the fact my stomach was a whirlpool of emotions, and I had zero appetite. Though, once the salty, spicy, creamy flavor hit my tastebuds, that changed.

I wonder if it would be in bad taste to drink the whole bowl. Possibly with some sort of beer funnel system for quick consumption.

My lids closed on their own accord, and I barely bit back a moan. "Oh my God, this is amazing."

"It's the birria," someone said, making me jump. Opening my eyes, I saw Demetrius give Lars the finger before focusing on me. "We slow cook it daily, adding it and the consumé to our scratch-made queso."

I had zero clue what birria or consumé were, but I knew I'd like to marry them.

"Just making sure you're good," Demetrius said.

"Be a lot better if people stopped interrupting," Lars shot back, his voice practically at my ear rather than a few feet away. I glanced over my shoulder to see he'd closed the distance, stopping behind me with his body nearly touching mine.

"Then don't look like you're about to violate state laws and health codes."

"Perks of being co-owner." Lars said it as if he was joking, but when he winked down at me, there was little amusement and a whole lot of lust.

What is it about a wink that is so damn sexy?

Demetrius started out the door, calling over his shoulder, "I really am missing the *silent* part right about now..."

"How do you two know each other?" I asked when it was just Lars and me again.

"He used to be a bouncer at Wicked."

"Do you co-own other businesses?"

Lars lifted his chin. "When I got out of prison, my cousin helped me get the financing to start Wicked."

"The one whose mess I'm cleaning up?" I teased.

"The very fuckin' same." A sharp edge threaded his voice. Inhaling, he softened his tone and expression. "Before he died, he jacked my shit up more than you know. More than I know."

I gasped. "I didn't know he was dead. I'm sorry."

It was no secret Lars harbored a lot of anger toward his cousin—

anger that would likely remain unresolved thanks to no closure. But that didn't mean he wished death on his cousin.

Or so I thought.

"Don't be. That prick had it coming. Actually, he had worse coming." At my open-mouthed gape, Lars put a finger under my chin and pushed my jaw closed. "Eddie let power, money, and smack rot our relationship until there was nothing left."

"Then I'm still sorry, but in a different way."

He skimmed the knuckle of his bent finger along my jaw, feather-light but undeniably intimate. "Thanks, baby."

Awkward origin aside, I loved when he called me *hotcakes*.

But I could really freakin' lose my mind at his rough voice rumbling *baby*.

"Before shit went bad with him, Eddie had been the only person willing to give me a fresh start. I pay it forward by giving other ex-cons jobs or investing in them—without the bullshit strings attached."

He's a cinnamon roll.

A grumpy, dangerous, badass one, but still. A secret cinnamon roll.

Sensing he wouldn't appreciate—or even understand—the sentiment, I kept it to myself. "What other kind of businesses do you co-own?"

"Nice try." He stepped back and pulled an ax from the stump, handing it to me. "You've already asked more questions than you've earned."

I took my shot, my mind on his revelations, his voice calling me baby, and, in all honesty, the incredible queso. It must've been the lucky trifecta because the blade hit the center ring and stayed. My arms shot up as I jumped and spun to face Lars. "Woohoo!"

It was unfair to compare Lars and Peter, even in my own head, but I couldn't help it. Lars didn't get his boxers in a twist that I was kicking his ass. He didn't slam his bottle, make excuses, or lash out with passive-aggressive insults. And it'd be downright cruel to Peter. Because he'd never, *ever* match up to the kind of man Lars was.

That knowledge was confirmed when Lars' grin matched mine. No, actually, it was even bigger. "Good job, baby."

His words skittered down my spine, pooling with heat and wetness between my thighs.

Crazy enough, at the way his eyes widened before going hooded, it was almost as if Lars knew how he affected me.

Facing me, he wrapped one arm around my torso while the other threw the ax. His landed close, but it was no match for my bullseye. "Ask your question."

I'd planned to ask about his other businesses. Or his hobbies. Favorite... whatever. I wanted to know anything and everything there was to know about him.

But when I opened my mouth, I blurted, "Do you have feelings for Harlow?"

There was zero hesitation. "No."

The past was the past was the past. I didn't need to hear about his, and I was fairly certain he had no interest in hearing about mine. His answer was enough for me, but apparently he had follow-ups.

Lars' head tilted to the side as he studied me with his seemingly all-knowing gaze. "What makes you think *that*?"

"When you came into Sweets a few weeks ago, you asked if she was there and—"

"Yeah, she gave me a drink recipe. Sasha had been on my ass to get it, and I kept forgetting."

I shook my head. "A different time. I told you she wasn't there and then you looked... bummed."

His brows lowered, and a pang of worry swirled with jealousy in my chest. I much preferred the certainty I'd felt only moments before. Lars had been so firm in his assertion he wasn't into her but being cheated on had a way of shredding even the strongest self-esteem. Obliterating it.

Every time I thought my wounds had healed, a new doubt crept in to tear them open and freshen the pain.

After a long moment, Lars must've recalled what Saturday I was talking about because the side of his mouth lifted. "Wasn't disappointed about Harlow. Was fuckin' crushed that old lady came in before I could kiss you."

"You wanted to kiss me?"

"Technically, I wanted to see you bent over that table again. It's my new life mission. But since you hightailed that fine ass away from me like hellhounds were biting your ankles, took that to mean you weren't interested in me, my kiss, or bending over for me."

He said it jokingly, but there were layers in his tone. The obvious humor, the expected heat, and something more.

Something that was almost... vulnerable.

I didn't understand how Lars would think any woman in the world wouldn't be interested in him, his kiss, and bending over forward, backward, and every other direction to give him whatever he wanted. But that a man like him thought, even for the briefest moment, that I was out of his league or whatever? It may have made me a bitch, but it also made me feel good. Like, maybe we were on more even standing than my damaged ego had led me to believe.

"Gotta stop calling her Legs," Lars said, more to himself than me.

"What? Why?"

"Don't ever want you thinking there's anything more to the name."

I couldn't help it. I laughed. In his face. It was rude, but the mix of amusement and, honestly, flattery bubbled inside me until it had nowhere else to go but out.

"I'm not bothered by the name," I told him honestly and then divulged some insider information. "More importantly, Harlow likes how it riles up Kase, so you can't stop."

Oh no. The penchant for gossiping must have rubbed off on me.

He grinned at that before his expression turned solemn. "Thought for a second there was something there with her, but there wasn't. Never was, even without Kase. Harlow's cute, but you?" He speared his fingers into my hair, fisting the strands and forcing my head back. There was no gentle pull like when he tugged my ponytail. It was a sharp burn across my scalp, making goose bumps spread across my skin as I bit my lip to keep in a moan. Blue eyes, so dark, they were nearly black, studied me as if he were trying to commit every feature to memory. Sear me into his brain. Into his soul. "You're so fuckin' pretty."

When he'd called me pretty earlier, my heart had sunk with disappointment at the lackluster description. But I'd been wrong. There was *nothing* lackluster about the way he was looking at me.

I hoped my voice didn't come out as pathetically needy as I felt when I asked, "And that's good?"

"In my world, baby," he whispered roughly, "it's the fuckin' best there is."

No longer sinking, my heart soared in my chest, powered by the butterflies that were rioting inside me. I'd never felt such a rush of giddiness, arousal, and pure happiness.

The question that'd danced on the tip of my tongue in the lobby popped into my head. "Did you go to Rye last night to see me?"

It didn't matter that it wasn't my turn to ask questions, his answer was instantaneous. "Yes."

"And you took tonight off to take me here?"

"Yes," he repeated.

Lars was a workaholic. He was whatever was more than a workaholic. Him taking his two busiest nights off for me wasn't a big thing.

It was a *huge* one.

Clutching his shirt at his chest, I lifted onto my toes and pulled him down so I could press my lips to his. He didn't take over or deepen the kiss. He let me lead, and his bruising grip on my hips betrayed his restraint. I went slow, savoring the taste of him. The feel of him. I took my time, finally having a modicum of brain capability to commit the moment to memory. All those sensory bits I'd wanted to remember during our first kiss.

I'd have thought the bakery would've offered the best sensory experience, with the scent of vanilla and chocolate and butter and all the mouthwatering baked goods. But nope. Standing there, surrounded by freshly cut—and freshly stolen—flowers and all the reclaimed wood, there was no better olfactory representation of Lars and me.

Masculine and feminine.

Hard and soft.

Outright strong and deceptively resilient.

Lars' hands slid down to my ass, palming each cheek in a firm grip. His fingertips dug in, a burst of pleasure-pain brought me to my tiptoes as I molded myself to his body, searching for more.

Desperate to get closer.

At my whimper, the rein he had on his control snapped. His tongue thrust into my mouth to dance with mine. Dominating it and me. Inching me backward until my thighs hit something, he used his hold on my ass to lift me. My legs automatically wrapped around his muscular torso before he could settle me on a stool. When I tried to loosen them, his hands circled my thighs and pressed them back in place, holding them tightly. Like he craved the same closeness I did.

Like he was just as desperate for the reassurance that the powerful desire was reciprocated.

When he adjusted his positioning so his hips were pressed between my thighs, I got all the reassurance I needed. Hard, thick, *massive* reassurance that curved across his pelvis in a way that couldn't be comfortable. But it was sure as hell intimidating.

And enthralling.

Palms sliding up my ass, he continued until his hands pushed under my shirt. His calloused skin trailed along my sensitive sides. Goosebumps. Heat.

No.

Fire.

Lava in my veins and an inferno in his touch.

His hands stopped under my breasts, his thumbs resting just beneath their swells.

My breath caught, anticipation—or maybe lack of oxygen—made my head swim. I was worried I'd pass out before he moved again to touch me.

I *needed* him to touch me.

I was two seconds away from grabbing his hands and using them to cup my breasts myself when he finally stretched his thumbs up to brush across my hardened nipples. He swallowed my gasp as his own groan rumbled through me. I arched, pressing myself toward him. But rather than the increased contact I was silently pleading for, I lost it all.

His thumbs.

His hands.

His hard... body.

Lars' expression was tight, pained, as he took a few steps away. Space or not, the charged air between us left my body tingling. The way he was staring at me while his thumb rubbed his bottom lip wasn't helping matters.

Or maybe it was.

I wasn't sure what I wanted at that moment.

Reminding myself we were in public, I glanced over my shoulder, expecting to find the server or Demetrius there. But there was nothing.

Why the hell did he stop kissing me?

As if he could read my thoughts—or maybe my expression was as disgruntled as I felt—Lars said, "I keep kissing you, I'm not gonna be able to stop. And there's no way in fuckin' hell I'd risk anyone walking in to see what's *mine*."

Mine.

That one word.

That one *declaration*.

If his kiss and hard-on and branding touch hadn't shown he was into me, the resoluteness in that single syllable did it. It echoed through my head in a way I knew I'd always remember.

Especially when I was alone in my bed at night.

Though with the way arousal was pooled between my thighs, leaving me squirming and flushed, I hoped like hell I wouldn't be alone —first date or not.

Lars grabbed his beer and drank half in one go. Still holding the long neck of the bottle, he swept his thumb across his bottom lip, and my core clenched.

That image and his growly mine *will fuel my fantasies for years.*

"Don't look at me like that, baby, or I may go back on what I just said."

I blinked and rotated on the stool, grabbing my own beer. It didn't do much good, I was still so *thirsty*.

"Take your turn, hotcakes," Lars said, turning away.

But not before I caught a glimpse of him using the heel of his palm to adjust his hard-on.

Yup.

Still thirsty.

Managing to keep some semblance of public decency, I set my drink down and grabbed an ax. My throw went way wide. I blamed my tingling body and distracted brain and the fact that not even the delicious food on the table interested me anymore. I just wanted more of Lars' kisses.

"Good one." Lars grinned, lifting his beer to me. I thought he was being sarcastic until he pointed out, "You hit the kill shot. Automatic win."

I glanced back at the board and saw I'd landed solidly in the small circle in one of the upper corners. I vaguely remembered Demetrius saying something about it, but I hadn't paid much attention since I'd been more worried I wouldn't even be able to reach the board, much less a small circle.

"Ask away," he said.

There were a million and ten questions rotating through my head. Heavy questions. Invasive ones. Nosy-as-hell ones.

But we'd had enough seriousness for the night. We'd covered the important bases. Except one incredibly important one.

"What's your favorite color?"

Lars grinned at the softball question. "Black."

"I'm shocked. Shocked, I say."

That earned a chuckle. "Take your next turn, smartass."

Meeting his grin with my own, I went and grabbed my ax from the wood before burying it in a stump so I could finish my beer. "Victory drink."

Lars opened another bottle and handed it to me. "Well earned."

Again, it was unfair. It really was. Lars didn't deserve my mental comparison to Peter. Yet I couldn't help but notice the stark difference in... everything. In that specific case, though, in the way Lars was handling the defeat. It wasn't an act. There was no tightness in his jaw or by his eyes. His smile wasn't forced. No silence, no cutting comments, and no slamming tantrums.

Just fun.

So much fun.

And not even a tiny hint of settling.

Lars

Parking outside of Joss' house, I got out and rounded the car to help her out. Not 'cause she was drunk—though she was definitely riding the line—but because Demetrius had sent her home with so many to-go boxes, she wouldn't have to shop for a week.

"Thanks," she said through a yawn. And not her first, second, or even tenth one.

It was easy to see the shy teacher didn't spend her nights moonlighting as a party girl.

As we walked up the porch, I looked around again. She needed better lighting, along with the new windows that the cop had mentioned when her alarm had gone off. Her railing needed to be tightened. Plastic chairs and a table looked like they'd seen better days. There was a porch swing pushed to the side, but it sat in the box rather than hanging. And the faded box looked like it'd seen better days, too.

That said, given the decent size and the neighborhood, the place must've still cost a shit-ton. It was no wonder she'd been busting her ass to fix shit with that kinda mortgage.

Her ex is a dumbass to let her go and a prick to leave her to deal with all this.

She unlocked the door before turning to me. "Want to come in? I don't have beer, but I can fix a mean rum and Diet Coke."

I fought a grimace. Diet soda didn't belong anywhere near booze. Ever. But I knew that wasn't what she was offering. Or, at least, that wasn't the taste I'd have on my tongue if I walked inside her house. I reached out and dragged my knuckle along her jaw before tipping her chin up. "Not tonight, baby."

Thanks to her exhaustion—or maybe the alcohol in her system—the walls Joss kept high and reinforced with steel were lowered. Not completely, just enough to give me a quick glimpse of the small wince and the hurt that filled her big brown eyes before she looked to the side. Taking my denial as rejection, I could see *and* feel her pull away even though she didn't move an inch.

I'd be damned if I let that shit happen.

Fisting her hair, I gently tugged it back to force her to meet my eyes again. "Want to. Fuck, I've wanted to since the first time I saw you. Think about it—*fantasize* about it—more than I wanna admit. But you're wiped. And when I fuckin' finally get my shot with you, I want you awake and sober 'cause I'm gonna need time."

"Time?" she whispered, surprise and more than a hint of anticipation in the one word.

Christ, her ex really was a punkass bitch.

I lifted my chin. "A lot of it. Waited this long for you, I'm not about to rush it now."

She gave me a slow nod before blurting, "You fantasize about me?" As soon as the words were out, she pressed her lips together and her cheeks heated. "Never mi—"

I pushed in close so she could feel how hard my dick was. What effect she had on me. I knew it would make me sound pathetic as fuck, but when it came to Joss, I was, so I told her the truth. "Every morning in the shower. Every night in bed, exhausted but too hard to sleep until I wrap my fist around my dick, thinking of you. Every damn time I close my fuckin' eyes, you're there."

Leaning into me, her lashes fluttered as her hair pulled taut. I was surprised as hell by her reaction to the pulling, but I sure as fuck planned to do every damn chance I got. My dick jerked, ready to burst through my jeans. If it were capable, the thing would be cursing me for the case of blue balls I was willingly inflicting on myself.

My control is strong but I'm not superhuman. Time to go.

Like she read my thoughts, Joss asked, "Are you sure you don't want to come in?"

I released my hold on her and stepped back before the thin thread holding my control snapped. "Want that more than I want my next breath, baby, so do me a favor. Stop torturing me."

At her wide—and slightly evil—grin, I knew two things in my gut.

One, I'd do anything to keep her smiling like that—torture or not.

And two, she was out to kill me.

But I'd happily follow her fine ass to hell and back. 'Cause it'd be worth it.

She was worth it.

"Say goodnight, hotcakes," I ordered.

"Goodnight, hotcakes," she mimicked in a deep voice. But then she put her hands on my chest as she pushed up onto her toes. Pressing her lips to mine, she pulled back just far enough to say, "Thanks for the best date I've ever had."

She didn't give me the chance to respond before she slipped inside, her security alarm beeping.

I waited until I heard the system was rearmed and the lock clicked into place before jogging back down to my car.

Unlike Joss, I was used to late nights, so I headed for Wicked to help Sasha with the end of the night bullshit. Rather than thinking about whatever clusterfuck surely awaited, my mind was on the sweet schoolteacher.

And her piece of shit ex.

I wasn't sure if I wanted to break his fingers for touching what was mine or thank him for being such a douche that her expectations were set so low. 'Cause if throwing axes was the best date she'd ever had, he sure as shit hadn't treated her right.

But I would.

Or I'd kill myself trying.

It'd be worth it for that smile.

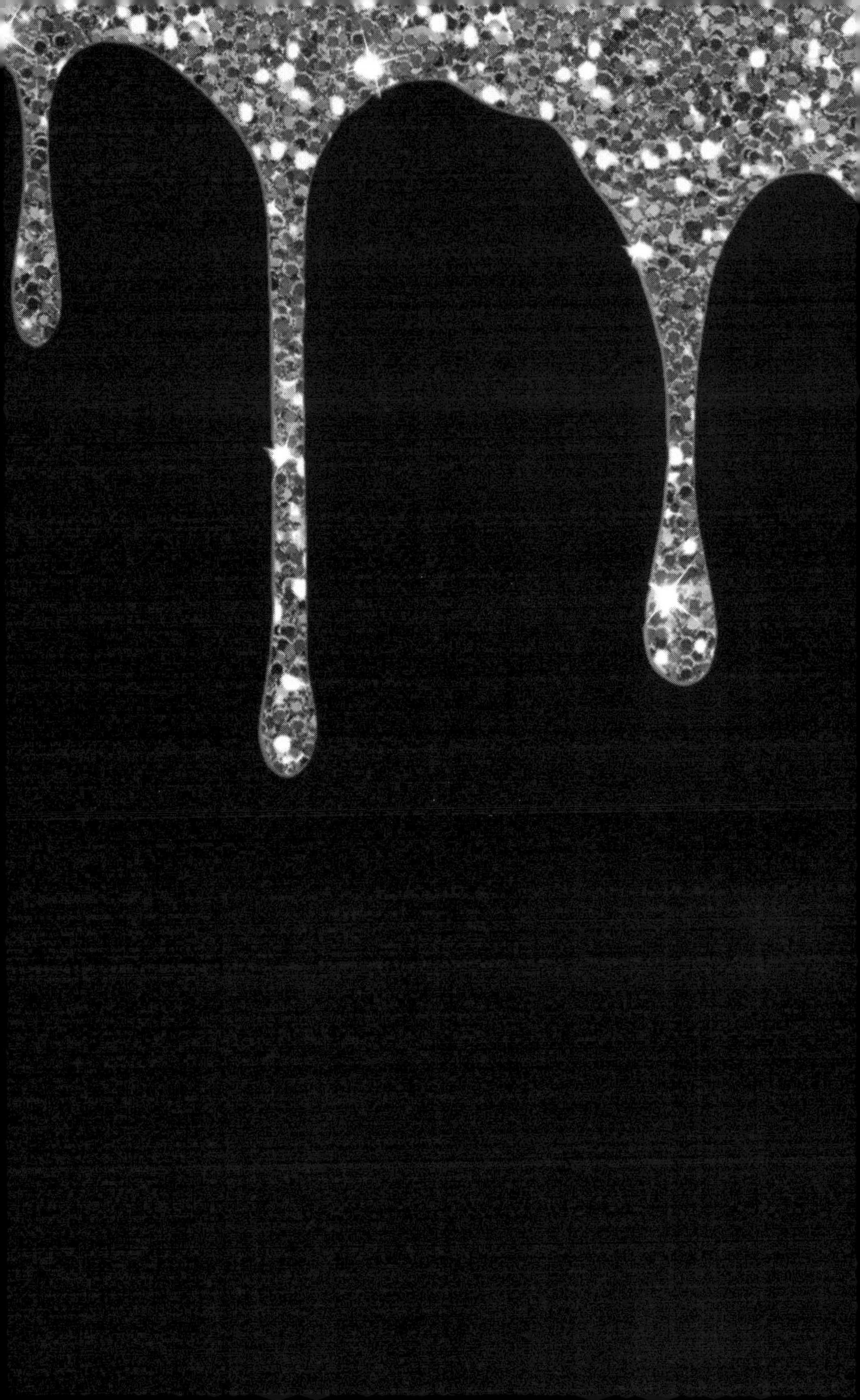

THIRTEEN

Dirty Deeds Done Near Sheep

JOSS

CRAP, I'M LATE.

I blamed Lars. First, he'd kept me out way late the night before, plying me with beer.

Okay, fine, I'd insisted on staying for one extra game that I'd managed to turn into more and more. And I'd been the one enjoying the beers while Lars had nursed one before switching to water.

God, he was such a gentleman. A gentleman with a wild side, filthy mouth, and kisses that made me wetter than I'd ever been.

While me staying out late had been my fault, I was still blaming Lars for me running late. More specifically, I blamed his text messages. No games, no waiting, no bullshit. I'd woken up to a sweet one telling me he couldn't stop thinking about me.

I wasn't sure if he'd meant that in a naughty way, but that was the way my hormones and I interpreted it. And if I was wrong, I didn't want to know. The visual had helped make my shower... interesting.

He'd continued texting me all day, sometimes in rapid succession and sometimes with time in between while he took care of Wicked shit. That meant I'd spent the day glued to my phone with a constant smile so big, my cheeks hurt.

Literally *hurt*.

All good things came to an end, and as I carefully backed out of my driveway, I was trying to figure out how to make a thirty-minute drive in ten.

In such a rush, I almost missed it.

The rumbles.

My breath caught, and I paused in the middle of the road to check my rearview mirror. Sure enough, a muscular beast riding a metal beast roared up, stopping next to my window.

Lars slid his aviators down to look at my back seat before meeting my eyes. "Big plans, hotcakes?"

"What're you doing here?"

"Was in the neighborhood, thought I'd swing by and see if you wanted to take that ride. See it's a bad time."

God, I wanted to. So bad. So, so bad. If it were any other Sunday, I'd ditch dinner without a second thought. But it wasn't any other Sunday.

I hoped my intense disappointment was obvious. "I've got to get to family dinner, and I'm already *way* late."

Before he could respond, my phone started ringing through my car's speakers. I glanced at the screen to see Nora's name before silently cursing.

Ruth, I'd answer.

Nora? No way in hell.

"I'll text you later," I said, wishing I had time to get out and kiss him. Like her mother-senses were tingling to tell her I was tempted to be even later, Nora's call ended just for my mom's to start. "Shit, I really gotta go."

I settled for blowing him a quick kiss before hightailing it out in my boring, practical car.

Stupid Sundays with my stupid family who I love... stupidly.

I made the drive in twenty-five minutes, which I still counted as a win. I was apparently the only one who held that opinion because as soon as I pulled into the driveway, my mom and Nora stepped onto the porch.

Matching looks of disappointment and all.

"About time," Nora huffed when I stepped out of the car.

"We were worried about you," Mom said, softening the situation as only a mother could do. Maybe she sensed that I was one minor inconvenience away from fleeing. Especially if that meant being on the back of Lars' bike.

I could really go for riding off into the sunset right now.

Opening my back door, I carefully grabbed the precious cargo Nora was actually concerned about. And then I nearly dropped it when a shrill, "Auntie Jossiiiieeeee!" cut through the air.

Nora caught Paxton just as he was about to launch himself off the porch. His excited little feet kept moving as if he were walking on air. "It's my birthday!"

"Is it? I don't think so. I feel like someone would've mentioned something."

Paxton made a sound that was somewhere between an outraged scoff and a *duh.*

Terrible-twos have nothing on the attitudey-fives.

He gestured to the Pinterest board that'd thrown up tasteful and stylish decorations all over Mom and Dad's yard. "Why else would it be decorated?"

"I thought those were for me!" I exclaimed with faux shock. "I just thought you were excited to see me."

"I ammmm," he drawled before grinning. "You've got my cake."

I freakin' loved my nephews, even when they were smartasses. Maybe more so when they were smartasses. It was like seeing a little glimpse of my black sheep self.

Hoisting the big box higher, I shook my head. "No, this one is mine. Yours is still in my car."

There was no way his mom was keeping hold of him. Paxton went flying down the stairs. I wasn't even sure his feet ever touched wood. He reached my car and squealed his delight.

Since I knew what he'd find, I'd braced. Nora and my mom, however, hadn't.

"Paxton, too loud."

"But there are so many!" He wiggled up onto the seat before sliding back down with enough balloons to lift an animated house. I honestly wasn't sure if the newly five-year-old weighed enough to keep from floating away.

"Really?" Nora sighed from the porch.

Unlike her artfully crafted décor, there was nothing tasteful about the balloons. They were bright and covered in cartoon characters and totally obnoxious.

In other words, they were perfect.

Paxton was so distracted by them, he hadn't even noticed the abundance of presents.

Nora just shook her head before opening the door. "Parker, come help your aunt. She's clearly lost her mind."

Exasperated or not, there was still a smile on her face as I carried the cake onto the porch.

"What?" I feigned innocence. "I stopped to grab candles and the balloons were there."

"And they just happened to get tied together on weights and shoved into your car?"

I gave a solemn nod. "I see this has happened to you before."

She took the black matte cake box from me before faltering. "Holy crap, this is heavy."

"Just wait until you see it."

I hadn't baked or decorated the cake. That'd been all Piper. But pride still bubbled in my chest as if I'd been the one to toil away at the stunning design.

I went back to the car to retrieve the cookies and presents while Parker helped carry the other party favors I'd grabbed. They were cheap and would likely break within the hour, but that was part of the fun.

As soon as Paxton saw the brightly wrapped presents, he tossed the balloon bundle to the side. "I love my biiiiirthday! Can I open them?"

"Not yet," my mom said before I could answer. Which was good because I'd have said yes. She took some of my load before kissing me on my cheek. "You look good."

"Thanks, Mom, you, too." I bit back a smile. "Must be all those wild nights out with the Michelsons."

She rolled her eyes. "If I have new wrinkles, we'll know who to blame. She already came over to... *comment* on the decorations."

The fact that Mrs. Michelson could find fault with the boring and minimal decorations said everything that needed to be said about her.

"So she's definitely not going to like the confetti cannons I bought for the boys?"

"Don't you dare give those to them. She would complain for

months." For once, Mom wasn't an older Nora. She was all *me* as an evil smile twisted her expression. "Actually, you know what? Let 'em loose by the road."

Laughing, I bobbled the boxes in my hold to give her a half hug before heading inside.

"Josie," my dad boomed from the living room.

I made my way in there, adding my presents to the stack on the folding table. Then I grabbed the smallest box and handed it to my dad.

"This what I think it is?" He didn't wait for an answer before opening that bad boy right up and grabbing a cookie.

Not just any cookie.

No, it was lemon with candied lemon zest and a light dusting of powdered sugar.

It'd initially been a diversion, but I'd kept my promise to bring cookies over. Dad had been ambivalent about the chocolate chip ones —a phenomenon I hadn't thought possible—but the lemon ones were a different story.

I was pretty sure he'd sell off one of his store locations for a lifetime supply.

"You going to help out at this bakery much longer?" Rather than the interrogatory tone and narrowed eyes I'd expected, his question was conversational.

And, dare I say, hopeful.

Piper really does work magic.

"Probably," I answered truthfully. I didn't mind the early mornings. I loved what I did *and* who I worked with. Plus, it'd suck to miss out on all the excitement, gossip, and hoopla of the Sweets and Hyde building. "Piper needs a reliable employee, and you know I learned from the best."

My smooth talk seemed to work, and Dad harrumphed—but with pride, not disapproval. "Make sure she's paying you fair. And on the record. You don't want to deal with the IRS if things go south. You know how they like to stick it to the little guy."

"I've got paystubs and everything."

It's my Wicked job that's under the table.

But not in the way I want it to be...

Not wanting to think about *that* while I was surrounded by family, I left my dad to his stash of cookies and went to find Nora before I missed her reaction to the cake.

"Joey, where'd you get that candy?" Ruth was calling out the backdoor.

I cleared my throat, not even pretending to be innocent.

"Another thing that just jumped into your car?" Nora asked dryly.

"How'd you guess?"

Ruth shot me a glare. "Joey doesn't react well to artificial dyes and too much sugar."

"Then he's really not going to enjoy this cake. I'll eat his piece."

Nora shook her head. "Stealing cake from a baby..."

"Stealing cake from a *kid*," I corrected. "He's four. At the worst, it's stealing cake from a toddler. And don't judge until you've had the cake. You'll want to hoard it, too."

Carefully, Nora opened the box and gasped. "It's gorgeous. This can't be real. Is this real?" She carefully undid the cardboard until it folded flat. "I can't believe someone made this."

The sheet cake was meticulously designed like a city building, including color variation for shadows and streetlights. Perfectly sculpted superheroes looked as if they'd sprang into action and had been frozen mid-fight.

"It looks fake," Ruth agreed, no longer shooting me daggers. "I mean that in a good way. I'm jealous. Bringing this means you've basically cemented yourself as the favorite aunt."

Piper's magic strikes again.

That pride swelled in my chest again. "Wait until you taste it."

But Nora didn't wait. Going for a hidden spot in the back, she swiped a little frosting before popping her finger into her mouth. "Oh. *Wow.*"

When Ruth tried to do the same, Nora slapped her hand. "Joss was right, I've decided to hoard it."

Ruth rolled her eyes and tried again, that time succeeding. "You weren't kidding." She turned her attention to me. "First the cookies and now this. How do you work around it all the time and not eat until you throw up?"

"It doesn't last long enough for me to. We sell out daily."

Or the men next door lend their assistance to prevent waste.

I wasn't about to tell them that, though. If they knew I was in close proximity to such attractive men on a near daily basis, they'd see marriage bells and baby booties on my horizon. Well, Ruth would. Nora could be a little more... judgmental. She'd likely try to warn caution around such tattooed, and therefore nefarious, characters.

They'd both shit bricks if they knew I was seeing a tall, sexy, tattooed, strip club owner.

Usually, I'd dread the drama. A lifetime of being keenly aware of their strong opinions had made me toe the line carefully. I'd gone with the flow because it was easier. It kept the peace. I hadn't wanted to *fight*. But when it came to Lars, I didn't care. I didn't care what my family thought. If they approved or not. I was an adult. I could do what I want.

Or who I wanted.

Before anyone else decided to sample the cake, I snapped some pictures for the bakery's socials. Then I went to hunt down the sticky, candy-coated birthday boy. "Paxton, come here."

He hauled ass toward me, sliding on the hardwood floor. His birthday hat was askew, the pointed tip bent. "Is it time for presents?"

"Not yet." I crouched. "Take a picture with your favorite aunt."

He didn't hesitate before coming to stand next to me.

"Wow, couldn't even pretend to mull it over," Ruth sighed.

"You gotta give 'em the good stuff," I gloated.

Paxton and I took a few pictures—one serious, one with me giving him cootie kisses on his cheek, and one with silly faces. That was as much as I got before he was on the move again.

Glancing over my shoulder for nosy family, I saw the coast was clear and brought up my messages with Lars. I sent all three pictures.

Lars: Christ, you're pretty. Dig the hat. You partying hard?

Me: Extra wild. Candy and cake and everything. May even have some organic, low-sugar lemonade.

Lars: Whoa now, badass. Don't get too crazy.

But I wanted to get crazy. Or at least crazy-ish. Crazy adjacent. Which was why I had a question to ask.

Me: Stop and go motorcycle rides suck, but what about nighttime ones?

Lars: My favorite. Why you asking, hotcakes?

I inhaled deeply, nerves and giddiness mixing within me until I felt as if I'd explode like a school project volcano. It wasn't that I thought he'd reject me or tell me I was being clingy. He'd been the one to come over, obviously not believing the BS three-day rule for contact after a date. It was just that being vulnerable was hard for me. Those still healing wounds and all.

Me: Because I want to see you and a ride sounds like a good excuse.

Me: Unless you have work tonight. We can totally do it a different time.

Luckily, it wasn't one of those stretches with a gap between responses. His text was immediate.

Lars: Been thinking about you every damn second since I woke up and seeing you for a minute didn't help matters. I'll get coverage. Text me when you're on your way home.

I'm totally ducking out early.
Maybe now.
Is now too early?

Me: Sounds good.

Lars: Can't wait, baby. Be ready to hold on tight.

The image of my front pressed to his back and my thighs bracketing his popped into my mind.

Definitely leaving A-S-A-freaking-P.

Tucking my phone away, I went to join in all the fun. Since I was an adult and it was a kid's birthday, that meant loads of prep, keeping my nephews away from the cake, keeping them away from the presents, and tidying up the chaos they left in their wake.

It was perfect.

At least until Mom tore her attention away from the elaborate veggie tray she was assembling in the shape of a cake.

It may have been a party for a five-year-old but that didn't mean Mary Lennon was phoning it in.

"You're in a good mood," she noted, her tone partially suspicious and partially happy. "I don't think I've seen you smile so much since Peter."

I couldn't help it. A noise somewhere between a scoff and a snort escaped. Peter had never made me smile like Lars. Maybe in the beginning, when we were young and stupid, but things had long cooled. Even the mention of him was enough to dull the effervescent excitement that bubbled in my chest.

For, like, two-point-five seconds. But then it was back—such was the power of Lars.

My mom aimed a disapproving glare my way at my very unladylike noise. Before she could chide me, though, my sister jumped in.

Not Ruth.

Nora.

"We're out of serving bowls," she said. "I'm just going to mix the olives and pickles."

"No," Mom gasped, jostling Nora out of the way. Nora shot a wink at me as Mom was distracted by explaining why mixing brines was akin to a crime against humanity.

Giving her a mental get-out-of-jail card for the next time she inevitably irked me, I made a speedy exit while I had the chance. I didn't get far before my dad and Benny intercepted.

Dad's stoic glare was full of accusation, like I'd committed some atrocity. "Your porch railing is still loose?"

Well, the two seconds of peace were nice while they lasted.

I had no clue how my dad knew about my wonky railing. My guess was Ruth had told Ben who'd in turn told Dad. I'd managed to temporarily brace it myself before his last visit, otherwise he'd have grabbed his tools from his truck and done it himself. Since his repairs tended to expand into bigger projects, I'd have ended up with a new porch. And I didn't want a new porch. I liked my old porch, loose railing and all. It had character.

I need to offer to babysit more if their peak excitement is discussing my home repairs.

"Ben and I will swing by one night this week," Dad continued. "You home by four?"

I would be if I went straight home from school. But I didn't. Not that I'd tell him that. If he'd been peeved to learn about my job at Sweets You Rock, he'd lose his absolute shit about Wicked—back office or not.

"I'm taking care of it," I told him with a smile that I hoped was more reassuring and less manic.

"No reason to pay some jackass for parts and labor. Ben and I can knock it out in a couple hours, and I'll give you the supplies at cost."

Typical Dad. No freebies for the Lennon girls. Freebies didn't build strength.

"I, uhh, want to do it myself," I claimed.

I didn't.

I'd happily pay some jackass for parts and labor if they did it quickly, efficiently, without it growing into a bigger project, and without them digging into my life.

But I knew my dad.

His bushy brow raised in a skeptical arch. "You do?"

No.

God no.

Nodding, I hoped like hell he believed my bullshit. I may have been willing to fight for my happiness a little more, but I wasn't actively courting drama. "I'm a homeowner now. I have to learn these things."

Dad beamed with pride. "Good for you, Josie. That's the way to do it. You need to borrow any tools?"

"Nope, I'm set."

Which wasn't a lie. Dad's gift of choice since I was ten was some set or equipment. I could likely rotate my tires, change my oil, fix a leaky faucet, and install a lovely shiplap accent wall with little prep.

I didn't necessarily *want* to do any of that, but that was beside the point.

With a nod of approval, Dad turned all his *Dad-ness* on someone else.

I made another hasty escape. Well, I tried to.

Because the serving bowl diversion had only worked for a few minutes, and then Mom cornered me again. "I baked some bread for you."

That was good news.

Usually.

But I didn't like the look in her eyes when she said it.

"Another loaf of banana chocolate chip."

Again, good news.

Or it should be. But something was rubbing me wrong, so I asked, "Another?"

"Yes, another. But I also—"

"You haven't made me banana bread in forever."

Or a few months, but in banana bread world, that is forever.

"Yes, I did," she said in that exasperated mother tone. "You even called me to thank me."

"That was lemon poppyseed."

"No, I made—" Her words cut off abruptly and her eyes widened. With a brittle smile, she forced a laugh. "Oh, that's right. I, uh, didn't have ripe bananas."

Mom may have had internal lie detection skills, but she didn't have any lie telling ones.

"Mom, what is..."

The supposed banana bread.

The actual lemon poppyseed.

Peter's favorite.

"Did you see Peter?" I hissed, my voice loaded with accusation.

My own mother. A Judas. A snake.

A Regina George.

"We had coffee," Mom admitted. There was a flash of guilt before she drew on that Lennon stubbornness and raised her chin. "He's been in our lives since he was a child. I'm friends with his parents. Just because you refuse to see him doesn't mean everyone has to."

"I won't see him because he *cheated* on me."

"It was a mistake," my mother snapped right back. "Pre-wedding jitters. He feels awful. Every time I see him, you're all he talks about. He worries about you. That you're working yourself sick at school and that bakery—"

"You told him where I work?"

Piper didn't mind entertaining scenes of gossip, playful drama, and PDA. But if Peter showed up, it would be none of those. Not unless choking a man with a muffin counted as affection.

"No, he told me." She said it like it was no biggie he knew that kind of information. Her expression was actually filled with soft tenderness when she added, "He's concerned."

Rage simmered through me so strong, I was practically vibrating. I'd never understood why people said they saw red until that moment. I could barely force the words through the thick anger that filled my chest.

"I never told him about the bakery. We were over and I'd already blocked him on all social media by the time I started working there."

Mom's brows raised, and the first hint of doubt flashed across her face before she smothered it and waved away the creepiness of that. "One of your mutual friends must've told him."

That was also impossible since I'd also cut off all our so-called *mutual friends*. They'd been the very same people who'd helped him cheat on me.

So either Ruth was also a Benedict Arnold who'd sold me out to my ex, or I had a social media leak who'd put two and two together when I'd shared some of the bakery's posts.

I needed to be more cautious.

And purge my friends list.

And grill Ruth.

Possibly throttle her.

"If you want to have coffee with Peter, I can't stop you." I choked down the pain from being stabbed in the back. It hurt so much worse because, for the briefest moment earlier, I'd seen some of me in Mom. I hadn't felt like the black sheep. "But don't tell him about me. Don't tell him about my life. We're never getting back together, Mom. *Ever.*"

"Can we save the rest of this conversation for a different time?"

Nora said, handing me a cup of clear liquid. I'd hoped it was vodka, but it was cucumber water. Gross. "Like *after* my son's birthday party?"

I wanted to say no. I deserved to be upset. Informing my ex about me was a big deal. I couldn't remember ever being so furious at my mom.

But Paxton's party was not the time or the place. And since I'd recently stormed out of a Sunday dinner, I couldn't do that, either. That was a once-a-year thing, or it would lose the dramatic effect.

With a tight nod, I mentally redeemed Nora's get-out-of-jail free card back and made yet another escape.

That time, I went somewhere safe.

To hang out with my nephews.

And their confetti cannons.

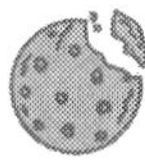

I COULD GET USED to this.

As soon as the insane thought popped into my brain, I scowled and literally shook my head, as if that would dislodge it. Or maybe completely erase it like an Etch-A-Sketch.

I wasn't getting used to anything. I was enjoying what we had for as long as we had it. Living in the moment.

Being wild and carefree.

So, while the sight of Lars waiting for me in my driveway was one of my new favorite things, I wasn't getting ahead of myself. Except, of course, allowing it to become my new favorite thing. But whatever.

I killed the engine and got out. I'd intended on closing the distance between Lars and me, but he obviously had the same idea. He swung his leg over to climb off and met me halfway. Like he couldn't wait the extra three seconds. He didn't speak and neither did I. Instead, our lips crashed in a kiss that screamed an eternity apart.

Pulling away, Lars dropped his forehead to mine. "Been thinking about doing that all fuckin' day."

"Me, too," I admitted. With Mom's betrayal, the knowledge I'd be riding with Lars had gotten me through the day. Well, that and my nephews trashing my mom's garden with the confetti cannon I'd provided.

Petty payback at its finest.

Standing fully but not backing away, he asked, "How was the party? Knock back those lemonades?"

"No, I stuck with water so I was clear-headed for our ride."

I'd meant it as a joke, but the air around us changed, becoming tense. Charged. As if both our minds shot to other things I'd need to be clear-headed for.

Because Lars wanted to take his *time.*

I was torn. I wanted to drag him inside. I was tempted to. If a ride with Lars would clear my head and shake off the bad day, a different kind of ride *on* Lars would likely shake off the bad year.

But I really was looking forward to my first time on a motorcycle.

Plus, it was a school night. If he backed up his claims of taking his time—and I knew he would—I'd be up way too late.

Napping under my desk while the kids caused chaos and destruction was frowned upon.

Responsible decision made, I tilted my head toward the shiny beast. "Ready?"

"Let's get you geared up, hotcakes." Lars grabbed a helmet from the satchel thingy attached to his motorcycle. When he stepped closer, I saw the gorgeous purple shimmer in the setting sun.

Since he didn't strike me as a shimmery kinda guy, a rush of jealousy shot through me. It knotted my stomach, and all the cake I'd eaten turned to concrete.

I'd thought my mom's ability to read my lies was impressive, but she had nothing on Lars' ability to read all of me, period.

He shifted the helmet that was way more expensive than I'd have guessed.

And I was able to gain that knowledge because the tag was still attached.

"Picked it up this morning just for you," he said. "It's why I was in the neighborhood."

I went for nonchalant even as the tension loosened from my muscles. "Cool."

"Christ, you're cute." He set the helmet on my head, tipping my chin up as he adjusted the straps. I didn't ask for more, but he gave it anyway. "Never had a woman on the back of my Harley. Even if I had, I sure as shit wouldn't give you a communal helmet."

No games.

No bullshit.

Just refreshing openness and honesty.

It was what my wounds and I needed.

"That's a relief. I thought I'd have to sign it out like a library book, and I don't have a pen for the checkout card."

"Smartass," he grumbled, but the smile on his face contradicted his tone. With my helmet on and properly tightened, he stepped back and shook his leather jacket off. It wasn't freezing, but it was definitely too cold for him to ride with just the thin hoodie he wore underneath.

"I can run inside and grab my coat."

He shook his head. "Coulda bought you your own when I got your helmet. Gonna have to pick one up. But for your first ride, wanted you in mine."

That he wanted me in his coat was possessive and hot and so sweet.

That he spoke of needing one for the future.

The way his tone had changed, growing rough and weighty, letting me know I wasn't reading too much into his insinuation.

All of it. Everything about his words burrowed inside me. Swirling around and warming me like no coat ever would.

I gave him my back as he helped me into the jacket. It smelled like worn leather, Lars' cologne, and a faint hint of tobacco. The mix made my head swim as arousal settled between my thighs.

With the way Lars so easily read me, I was glad he'd turned away to put his own helmet on. He situated himself before reaching out to help me climb on behind him. There was a small lip I perched my ass on, but I'd barely settled before Lars reached back and grabbed my hands. I let out a yelp as he tugged me forward until my front was plastered to his back. He pressed my hands to his abs.

Low on his abs.

So temptingly low on his abs.

I could feel his belt buckle, which meant if I dropped my hold an inch or so, I'd feel something a whole lot more interesting.

How the hell am I supposed to think about anything else?

"Ready?" Lars asked.

For a split second, I wasn't.

I'd never been on a motorcycle. I wasn't sure if passenger skills were a thing. I didn't want to be responsible for him crashing or damaging his bike in some way.

I also didn't want either of us to get injured. That would kinda suck.

Apprehension filled me. I wondered if riding a motorcycle was one of those things that was fun to imagine but not actually do.

Ugh, I'm being Goody Two-shoes Joss. Playing it safe.

Playing it boring.

How do I expect to have wild in my life when I'm too chicken to go get it?

"Ready." My voice was adamant. But all my confidence disintegrated when I jumped like a scaredy cat as it roared to life under us. But whatever.

Baby steps to badass.

I tightened my hold as we took off, deep breathing without it being obvious. Since my chest was pressed to his back, it was a tricky task to accomplish—and I doubted I was. After a minute that hadn't resulted in our fiery death, I pried my eyes open. A few minutes after that, my lungs began functioning normally. I kept my death grip on him—I wasn't stupid—but I relaxed. I lifted my head. I watched as the sights zipped by.

I wasn't even sure how long we rode. The suburbs faded away, replaced by the expressway. My physical grip and the metaphorical panicked one both tightened each time we buzzed by a tractor trailer, but it was only a short distance until we exited to peacefully cruise along the water.

There was something about the wind, the steady drone of the engine, and the open road that was therapeutic.

Freeing.

My mind cleared. My worries and festering anger were left in our dust.

It was just Lars and me.

Unintentionally—or maybe subconsciously—my hands lowered as I shifted. I froze at his hardness under my palm. I should've moved, if for no other reason than groping him at sixty miles per hour was dangerous as hell.

But I couldn't make myself pull away.

No, I pushed my palm down.

My stomach dropped to my toes when Lars slowed suddenly. My gaze shot over his shoulder to see what was wrong. I expected to find construction cones or an animal darting across our path.

But there was nothing.

It was just us, the open road in front of us, and the trees to the side.

Slowing to a crawl, Lars turned us toward the tree line. My hold tightened instinctively as the terrain became rougher. I was likely multiple feet below the stretching branches, but that didn't stop me from ducking like I was about to hit my head.

I could feel Lars' chuckle rumbling up his chest. I'd have smacked him for laughing at me, but I was too busy making sure I didn't eat dirt.

Stretching up slowly, I looked over his shoulder and nearly went back on that plan. Eating dirt was surely preferable to driving off the cliff we were heading toward.

Before I was forced to tuck and roll like I was in *Mission Impossible*, he slowed further until we came to a gentle stop. When I calmed my panic enough to look at the treacherous drop-off, I saw it wasn't a bottomless abyss I'd imagined. It was a gradual decline. We probably could have continued with little issue.

Okay, I may have been overreacting.

When Lars cut the engine, I expected to hear him laughing at me some more. Instead, he leaned to the side and gripped my thigh and arm. In a move that could only be described as magically acrobatic, he spun me around his body so my front was pressed to his and I was straddling him.

There wasn't a hint of humor in his expression as he tugged off his helmet before doing the same with mine. Reaching around me, he hung them from the handlebars before taking my cheeks in his freezing palms. I didn't even care that they were like icicles on my skin.

"Why'd we stop?" Not that I minded. The ride was fun, but the view from his lap was better.

"Because if I don't touch you in the next ten seconds, I'm gonna lose my motherfuckin' mind."

Holy.

Shit.

The need in his gruff voice sent a tremor down my spine, leaving goosebumps in its wake.

Cupping the back of my head, he leaned down, stopping with his lips a breath from mine. "Say no, and I'll start the engine right now. We'll get back on the road, and drive by the baby sheep a mile away."

"And if I say yes?"

"Then we're not going anywhere till I make you come."

My one word came out airy and soft, but it wasn't because of nerves. Or apprehension. Or doubt. It was the intense lust and anticipation that was stealing my breath.

"Yes."

In another impressively fluid movement, Lars dismounted, taking me with him. He lowered me to stand, his hands going to the button of my jeans before pausing. When I didn't stop him—no freakin' way in hell was I stopping him—he undid them before pushing the fabric to bunch around my ankles. Gripping my hips, he lifted me to sit sideways on the seat.

I thought he was going to touch me. I wanted him to touch me.

And he did, just not in the way I needed.

Just as he'd promised, he took his *time* as he kissed me. Like he was savoring every moment. Every touch. Every taste of my mouth and twirl of my tongue. Keeping hold of my head in one hand, he used the other to trail up my side, moving under my shirt. Up to my bra, back down to the band of my—thankfully cute—panties.

It was a maddening pattern. Never quite touching me where I was desperate for it as his lips, teeth, and tongue worked together to stoke my need higher than Everest.

If he doesn't touch me soon, I'll be the one to lose my mind. And maybe shove him down the hill.

His mouth skimmed down my chin, nipping at my jaw before continuing to my neck. He teased the sensitive skin there, but finally—freakin' *finally*—skimmed a hand up my thigh until his thumb was pressed to my slit. Moving over the cotton, he ran it up and down.

I was soaked. I had been since seeing him in my driveway and it'd only grown. There was no way he couldn't feel it.

"Fuck," he groaned against my neck like it was him being tortured. And that's what it was.

Unadulterated torture.

I was on the verge of tearing the interfering fabric apart with my bare hands by the time he tugged them down my legs. It didn't matter that it was cold out. His touch was hot enough to make me sweat. I'd happily strip down to nothing to get more of it.

He slid a finger through my wetness before pressing it inside me. "Fuckin' Christ."

"Oh," I whispered, nearly going cross-eyed at the way his palm rubbed my clit as his finger hit a magical place.

It was one noise that could barely qualify as a word, but it was enough. He didn't slow down, speed up, or move. He read my body, knew he'd hit his target, and he kept going until my legs shook and my ass came off the seat.

I was close.

So close.

It was embarrassingly fast, but I didn't care. I didn't care about anything other than coming. My thoughts went hazy, and I was at that edge...

Lars pulled away.

My disgruntled protest was cut off when he dropped to his knees and hauled me to the edge of the seat. The positioning was awkward with my pants around my ankles, but I didn't care. I'd have done a handstand on an actual steep cliff with one arm tied behind my back if it meant Lars' mouth was on me.

Holding my thighs wide, he used his thumbs to spread me. Slowly, he ran his tongue up my slit. His low moan vibrated against my clit, and my ass shot off the seat. I was worried I'd tip the bike, but not worried enough to have any semblance of control of my undulating hips.

Thankfully, the machine was sturdy. Or maybe it was just Lars' tight hold on me.

He took my nonverbal cues, spearing his tongue and working me hard. He shifted to suck and flick my clit as he slid a finger in. And then two. It wasn't long before I was riding that edge again. And just like earlier, the blessedly smart man knew to keep the steady pace that was doing delicious things.

Getting involved with Lars was like riding a motorcycle. It was new. Unknown. Kinda dangerous. I could end up eating dirt—physically or emotionally.

Or I could end up with something beautiful. For a day. A week. A month. Whatever.

As I came apart thanks to his skilled mouth and hands, I knew it was the latter. The peace I found on the back of the bike and the pleasure I found perched on it proved as much.

That some risks were *so* worth taking.

Lars slowed and softened his touch, leaving me floating on the clouds above us. Out of my body yet somehow aware of every last nerve ending and molecule. There, but not.

When it passed, leaving me a pile of sated goo, Lars stood and moved in tight. Rough denim scraped across my overstimulated core as he kissed me. I tasted him, myself, and sunlight on his skin. God, it was more intoxicating than all the rum and Diet Cokes in the world.

Pulling back, he helped me to my feet before kneeling to tug my panties and jeans into place. He kissed my stomach above my waistband and stood to tower over me again. I wasn't sure how much he could see in the dim light from his headlights, but I got the feeling it was still too much. He confirmed my suspicion when he rumbled, "You liked the ride."

It wasn't a question, but I still nodded.

"No." Fisting my hair—something I was glad was becoming a habit—he tipped my head up. "You *liked* the ride."

He was wrong. And, after a moment's hesitation, I told him as much.

"No. I *liked* being pressed tight to you."

It was the right thing to say. Holy shit, it was the right thing.

His lips curved into a hint of a smile as his eyes went deliciously hooded. I only got the incredible view for a moment before he kissed me again. It may have been a quick one, but it still left me ready for another orgasm.

More than ready.

I was desperate for it.

"Any chance tomorrow is one of those made-up school holidays?"

"Made-up?" I asked. "Like Teacher Enrichment?"

"Was thinking *Pretty Kindergarten Teachers Stay in Bed with Their Man Day*, but close enough."

Their man.

Their.

Man.

Just a phrasing.

Don't read into it.

It's a saying.

Or a joke.

Lars' gaze narrowed. "Don't know what just went through your head, hotcakes, but if you think I waited this long to *finally* fuckin' have you just to keep shit casual, you're outta your mind."

I bristled. "I'm not. But—"

"Say you don't want this." There was a challenge in his tone and a stubborn set to his sharp jaw. "'Cause I'm telling you, baby, there was nothing *casual* about my feelings for you before this pit stop. And now that I've got your taste on my tongue, I'm even more obsessed."

Usually I appreciated Lars' no-nonsense openness, but when he said stuff like *that*—stuff that made me breathless in the best possible way—it was overwhelming.

Taking my loss of words to mean I needed more convincing, he continued. "Not saying we're gettin' hitched tomorrow, but I'm also not fuckin' around. Too old for that shit. More importantly, I'm smart enough to recognize when I've already got *exactly* what I want. I don't play games. And sure as shit don't share. So when I finally get inside you, I'll do it knowing that pussy is mine and mine alone. And you'll take me knowing I've been yours since that first smile. Get me?"

What wasn't to get? After all, it wasn't as if he'd been vague or coy. In usual Lars-style, he'd bluntly laid it out. He preemptively mollified any anxiety that could form thanks to my wounds.

And the literal son of a bitch who'd given them to me.

Because I knew, down to my soul, I could trust Lars.

That didn't stop my curiosity from getting the better of me. "And if I don't?"

"Then I'll bust my ass to make sure you never want some other bastard in my spot. Lucky as hell to be here." He leaned down to nip my jaw. "I'm not letting go without a fight. And, baby?" With a twist of his fist, the burning tingle spread across my scalp before traveling down to tighten my nipples and leave an empty ache between my thighs. "I fight dirty."

I'd been vehemently determined to keep things light and breezy with Lars, but he wasn't making it easy. He was knocking down my walls like they were made of blocks. And not even Lego ones. More like the hollow cardboard blocks from my classroom.

A few words.

An intimate touch.

Hell, just one of his wolfish smirks was enough to make them fall.

So with the intense way he'd just verbally staked his claim, the bricks didn't teeter. They didn't knock down, little by little.

They were destroyed.

Decimated.

"I'll ask again..." He loosened his hold on my hair but kept me tight to him. "Get me?"

"I get you," I said softly.

"Good, baby."

I was fairly certain he was saying that it was good, but my brain—or maybe my libido—twisted it to him calling *me* good. If I'd been on the edge of combustion before, I was ready to tackle him to the ground—to the dirt and leaves and brush.

Before I could, he released me and stepped away. "Since it's not a day off tomorrow, let's get you home."

"What about..." I started, my words trailing off. I didn't play games, but I also wasn't as blunt as Lars.

Even in the minimal lighting, I could see the smile Lars was failing to hide. He wasn't going to let me off the hook that easily. "What about *what*, hotcakes?"

Infuriating man.

"What about *you*?"

"Christ, you're fuckin' killing me and my control. Not taking you for the first time with a quickie in the mud."

Does that mean it's an option down the line?

I've never had outdoor sex.

Palming my ass in one hand, his gaze locked on my mouth. "But you can bet your fine ass I'm gonna take you up on that offer your parted lips are making. And soon."

"When you have *time*?" I asked, partially teasing but also...

Not.

Because, unlike some men who liked to brag that they could go for hours—so long as it was measured in dog years where hours actually meant milliseconds—nothing about Lars said he was exaggerating. He and his big dick energy spoke for themselves.

Not to mention his actual big dick that was hard and stretched down his *thigh*.

When he said he needed time, I believed him. I was also beginning to believe I'd need to stretch first. Stock up on Gatorade. Maybe take a few days off.

"Exactly," he rumbled.

"I, uh, do have a question, though."

If he hadn't been standing so close, I may have missed the way he braced. "Yeah?"

I paused for a moment, just to mess with him. Sue me. Before I spoke, I inhaled deeply. Audibly. Then on a slow exhale, I asked my not at all dramatic question. "Can we still go see the baby sheep on the way home?"

Throwing his head back with a husky laugh, Lars used his grip on my ass to haul me to him so my forehead was pressed to his chest. It meant I got to hear and feel the laughter. "It's like that, is it? Don't forget payback's a bitch, hotcakes. And I already warned you... I fight dirty."

I'm in so much trouble.

But at least there will be orgasms followed by baby sheep.

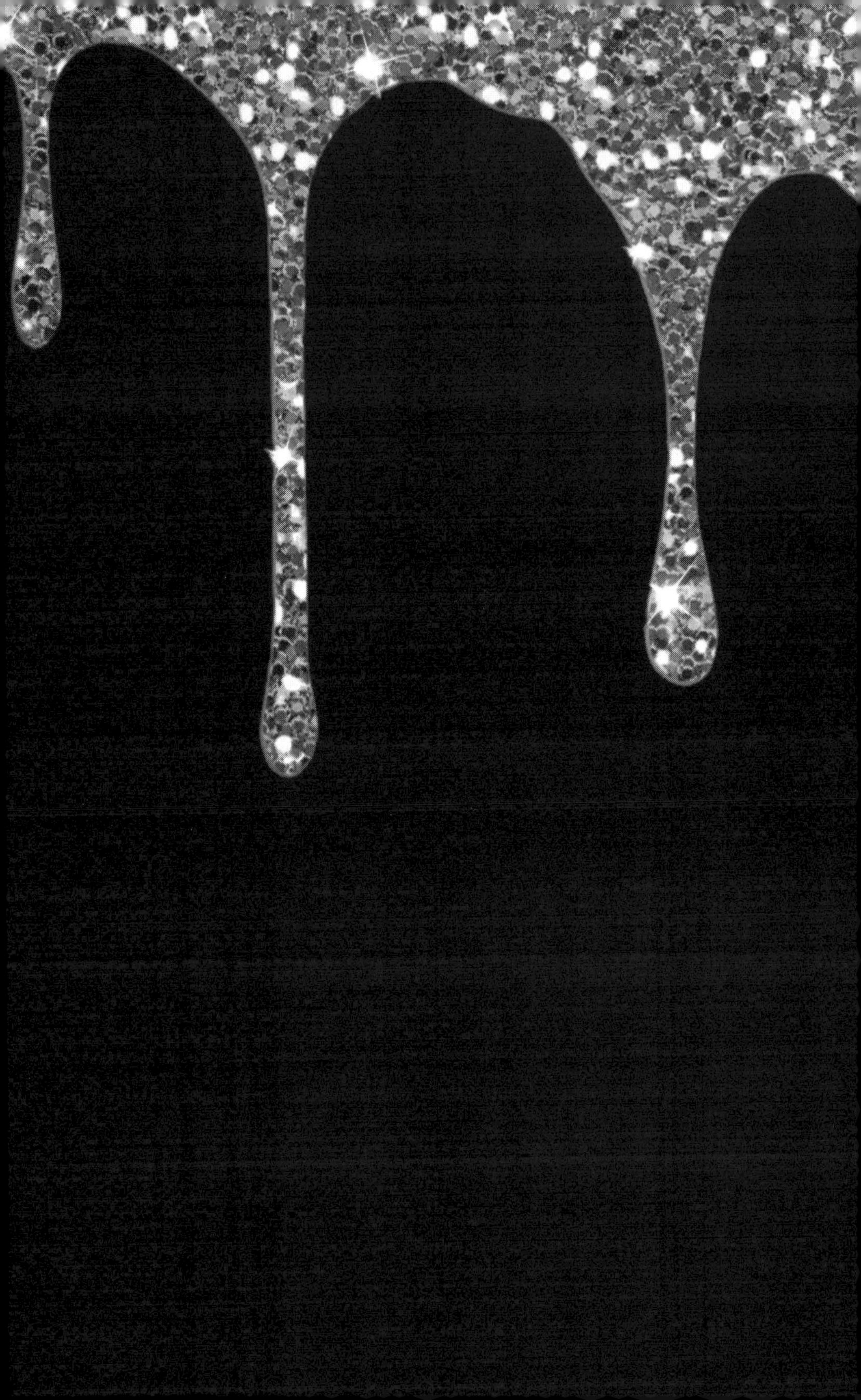

FOURTEEN

Coffee, the Anxiety Extender

JOSS

THERE WAS NOTHING.

Not a single thing.

Not one single, solitary thing in the entire universe that set anxiety off like a text from a boss asking to meet later.

Why later? Why not right then? Why not just make the meeting an email?

Surprisingly, the text that was short on letters but high on angst hadn't come from my principal or superintendent. It'd come from Piper.

And then she'd promptly ignored my responding messages. Girl hadn't even left my messages on read. She hadn't even looked at them.

I had no clue what it was about. I knew it wasn't just her wanting the details on my date with Lars. She'd just happened to come in way earlier than usual that morning. Strictly a coincidence, she'd claimed. Apparently, it'd been vital for her to drag her butt out of bed early, sit on the counter, and drink coffee while she peppered me with questions.

So, rather than heading straight from school to Wicked on Monday afternoon, I made a detour to Sweets You Rock. The storefront was already closed by that time, but the Hyde Garage was still slammed. I hoped that meant Jake was too busy to keep Piper... occupied in his office. My anxiety was already through the roof. I'd lose my mind waiting around to find out why I'd been summoned.

"You're too late," Piper greeted from behind the counter. It would've been ominous if she hadn't said it with a big smile. And an even bigger mug of coffee she held out to me.

"For?" I was still lost but no longer panicking. If Piper was firing me, at least she'd done it with coffee. There were worse severance packages.

"Another interview."

Of the five she'd had previously, only two had even shown up. And only one had been hired—Sophie.

"Am I that late?" I asked.

"No, it was that bad."

Yikes.

"What happened?"

"Jake happened."

That could mean anything. Maybe he scared the interviewee with his intimidating glower. Maybe he made her uncomfortable with the way he unabashedly groped Piper every chance he got. Or maybe...

"I'm surprised the building didn't flood while she was staring at *my* husband," Piper confirmed, her voice nearly as possessive as said husband's.

"From her drool?"

"Yeah, let's go with that, otherwise I might be tempted to make her choke on a cookie."

"Oh God, it was that bad?"

"Yes." With a sigh, she crossed her arms and tipped her head back to shake it at the ceiling. "On paper, she was perfect. Great skills. Great portfolio. A little older, more established, a home run. Then she showed up, took one look at me, and turned condescending. Like, how can you be condescending while standing in *my* bakery? I was willing to give her some leeway to adjust, but then Jake came in, and it was like I was invisible. Even after she realized he was *my* husband—" Her rant cut off, and she gave a self-deprecating smile. "*My, my, my*. I bet I sound like one of your kindergarteners."

"No, you're not using new slang words that make me feel a hundred years old."

"It starts that early?"

"Oh yeah."

Her expression was a mix between horror and surprise as she adjusted her shirt. With a shrug, she crumpled up what I assumed was the resume. "At least I have you and Sophie. Are mornings still going well?"

"Perfect. We mesh well and get a lot done. She's still a little reserved, but ya know. Pot. Kettle."

Of course, if there's one thing that can bring a girl outta her shell, it's working here. Next thing she knows, she'll be standing in the middle of the bakery, getting kissed by a man until her toes curl.

Like she could read my thoughts, a wry smile twisted Piper's lips. "I don't think you can claim to be the shy girl anymore after that kiss on Saturday. Now you're really one of us. Onc of us. One of us," she chanted.

"I don't think it's official until he carries me out over his shoulder," I pointed out, something Jake and Kase both did to their women on the regular.

"I give that two weeks. *Tops.*"

"Well, thanks for the lengthy anxiety attack courtesy of your vague text message and," I raised my nearly empty mug, "the anxiety extender."

Piper grimaced. "My bad. I meant to text you back, like, a million times but the day got away from me."

"Liar. You just like torturing me."

She rolled her eyes again before drawling, "Sooo, heading to Wicked for the first time since your date, huh? That should be interesting."

"See?" I stood. "Torture."

"C'mon, a little girl talk isn't torture."

It wasn't. Not really. Prying was her love language. It meant she cared about me and my life. If she didn't, she'd be friendly but not lovingly nosy.

What was torture, however, was the anticipation of seeing Lars. I couldn't wait. But at the same time, I was nervous it'd be awkward. *I'd* be awkward. He'd made me come, and then I was just supposed to go in and organize his filing cabinets?

That sounded like a bad innuendo.

Or maybe some bad porn.

The point was, I had zero experience with that kind of morning after. I didn't want to overthink it and make it weird.

Proving I had no poker face, Piper's expression softened as she reassured me. "It'll be fine. Like you said before, you barely see him."

"Uh, that wasn't exactly true."

Her brows rose but she wasn't pissy at my fib. "Well, he's still a workaholic, and so are you. It'll be business as usual, just with a lot of sexual tension." She glanced at the door that led to the Hyde waiting room. "You'll love it."

I hoped she was right.

Bagging up a snickerdoodle cookie—one of the few remaining treats—I went to Wicked. I expected to find him waiting at the back door, a cigarette hanging in that casually cool way as he watched me from the shadows. Just the memory of it was enough to send a tremor down my spine.

But he wasn't there. One of the bouncers, Killer, was.

Scary nickname and massive appearance aside, Killer was a softie. A big teddy bear. No one broadcasted that since it was counterproductive to doing his job, but all the Wicked employees knew the truth.

"Hey, Teach," he greeted me.

A few times, the bouncers had copied Lars and called me hotcakes before suddenly switching to Teach. That's the nickname that caught on, and I couldn't say I was mad about it.

Like being nosy at Sweets You Rock, a nickname at Wicked was their way of showing I belonged. I was one of them.

Kinda.

I was the back-office version of them.

Whatever. Point was, I liked it.

"How's it going, Killer?" I asked.

"Can't complain. Nicer to throw people out when the sun is shining. Not long before I'll be trudging them through the snow. That'll piss me off."

"Did you have to throw someone out today?"

"Not a workday without one dumbass."

Guess that was true of all jobs.

"Boss said to take you to the office. He's stuck behind the bar."

I forced a smile despite my disappointment.

And worry.

Maybe he's avoiding me.

I was being an idiot. Lars had been honest to the point of intimidatingly blunt about his intentions with me. He wasn't about to go from giving me orgasms to dodging me in less than twenty-four hours.

Killer froze and looked down at me. "You okay, Teach?"

His question made me realize I was glowering at my stupid insecurity.

Damn wounds.

Internally rolling my eyes at myself, I nodded. "I'm good. Long day."

He lifted his chin and unlocked the door, bringing me to the office.

Since I didn't trust myself alone with it any longer, I handed him the snickerdoodle. "As a thank you for waiting around for me."

His face split in a boyish smile. "Sweet. I'm gonna go eat this where he can see me."

I laughed. "You're playing with fire."

"Keeps shit interesting." Killer headed down to the end of the hall, standing in the open doorway as he dramatically unbagged the cookie and took a bite.

Laughing, I went into the office to get to work. Thanks to the stop at the bakery, I was already behind on the schedule I'd set for the night.

I'm going to have to work through dinner.

I sat at the desk and grabbed the pile of papers I'd been working on the week before. Sitting on top was a takeout menu to my favorite burger place and a note in thick, masculine scrawl.

Shit is crazy up front. Will explain over dinner. Text me your order, I'll call it in.

Miss you, hotcakes

-Lars

PS You say a single thing about paying, I'll bend you over that desk and spank your ass until you can't sit.

I switched between reading he missed me and that PS about a million times. I wasn't sure which I liked more.

Now I feel bad about giving away his cookie.

Wet, hungry, and, it was worth repeating, *wet*, I stuck the note in my purse and texted him my order before getting to work.

I didn't think I'd be able to concentrate on numbers, but before I knew it, the door was thrown open, startling me. Lars filled the doorway, holding a beer bottle, a Diet Coke, and a bag of takeout that smelled mouthwatering.

Or maybe it was Lars who was making my mouth water.

Never mind, it was both.

"Hey," I said when the silence was stretching to the point of middle school dance awkwardness.

That broke whatever trance he'd been in. Stalking across the room, he tossed the bag and unceremoniously slammed the drinks down, nearly knocking both over. I reached out to steady them just as he cupped my cheeks. It was a good thing I released them before he pulled me out of the chair, or I'd have been the one to dump the liquid all over the keyboard.

Although, with annoyance tightening his face, an electrical fire might've been what he was hoping for.

Taking my mouth, his tongue coaxed it open so he could deepen the kiss. There was no teasing. No playful dance. No fight for supremacy.

Lars dominated the kiss. Owned it.

Owned me.

I could do nothing more than clutch his shirt as he devoured my mouth like a starving man. Like it'd been years since he'd tasted me. Like I was his to kiss and hold.

After a minute, his touch softened. Slowed. I could actually feel his body loosen.

Well, most of it.

A certain part remained hard and pressed tight against me.

"Fuck, I missed you," he said as he pulled away, breathing hard. "Couldn't stop watching the damn clock today, then shit went to hell, and I wasn't able to see you when you got here."

"You're here now."

"Yeah, but not for as long as I wanna be. Gotta eat fast and get back out there." He sat and tugged me down onto his lap before unbagging the food.

It was hard enough to eat a loaded cheeseburger without making a mess. It was nearly impossible to do it perched on Lars' lap, with his arm around me, and my heart in my throat.

But I made it work because I got the feeling he needed me there just as much as I wanted to be there.

"What happened today?" I asked, using a sweet potato fry to point toward the door.

"Typical shit. Asshole customer. Flaky chicks. It happens."

I could tell there was more to it than that. But call me crazy, the empath in me was saying he didn't want to talk about it. Or maybe it was his clipped, two-word sentences. Whatever.

"Tell me about your day," he ordered, confirming my theory. "Shit okay at Hyde?"

"Piper had an interview today."

"And?"

"It was done before I even got there."

"Shit, that's bad." He grimaced. "Joys of being a business owner." There was humor in his tone, but a lot of frustration.

To distract him while he scarfed down his food, I told him about school. More specifically, the antics of the kids. They were all trying to learn some new dance the older kids kept doing.

Five-year-olds didn't have a lot of coordination. Or rhythm. Or attention to detail. That meant, rather than the precise arm movements, they were all flailing like fish out of water.

My description—complete with visual example—was enough to relax the tension lines near Lars' eyes as he grinned. "Gotta be hilarious as shit to watch."

"It is," I confirmed. "Not the most productive during story time or math circles, but I've added in some movement breaks."

His smile shrank, but not in a bad way. It was intimate and soft. "You're good with them."

Like the last time he'd complimented my teaching, warmth swirled through my stomach, settling into my bones. "I try."

"Sounds like you succeed." Lars crumpled his wrapper, and it was as if his body was connected to it. His muscles tightened and bunched like the paper in his fist. "Gotta get back."

"Hopefully the rest of the night is better."

"I'd say it can't get worse, but that's a challenge to the universe to fuck with me." He leaned down, but I turned my face so his lips hit my cheek. "The fuck?"

"I've got burger breath."

"Like I give a shit. If I'm getting through this night, it'll be 'cause of your lips." He gripped my chin and tilted my head toward his. "Kiss me, baby."

How could I argue with that?

Especially since his tight hold wasn't giving me much choice.

Even though he'd said he had to go, his kiss was deep yet leisurely. He took his time, licking and teasing and nipping until I was ready to turn around and straddle him. Or maybe push his hand to possessively cup me like he'd done against his motorcycle. Anything to ease the ache that he'd built.

"Text me when you're leaving," he ordered, his lips still grazing mine.

"Okay."

"Fuck, I wish I had time to make you come."

I wished that, too. Fervently. If I had a genie and three wishes, they'd be world peace, end hunger, and unlimited Lars supplied orgasms.

And not necessarily in that order.

Gripping my hips, he lifted me and stood. With another quick kiss —and a not-so-subtle adjustment of his hard-on—he left me alone to take my frustration out on invoices and math.

Stupid math.

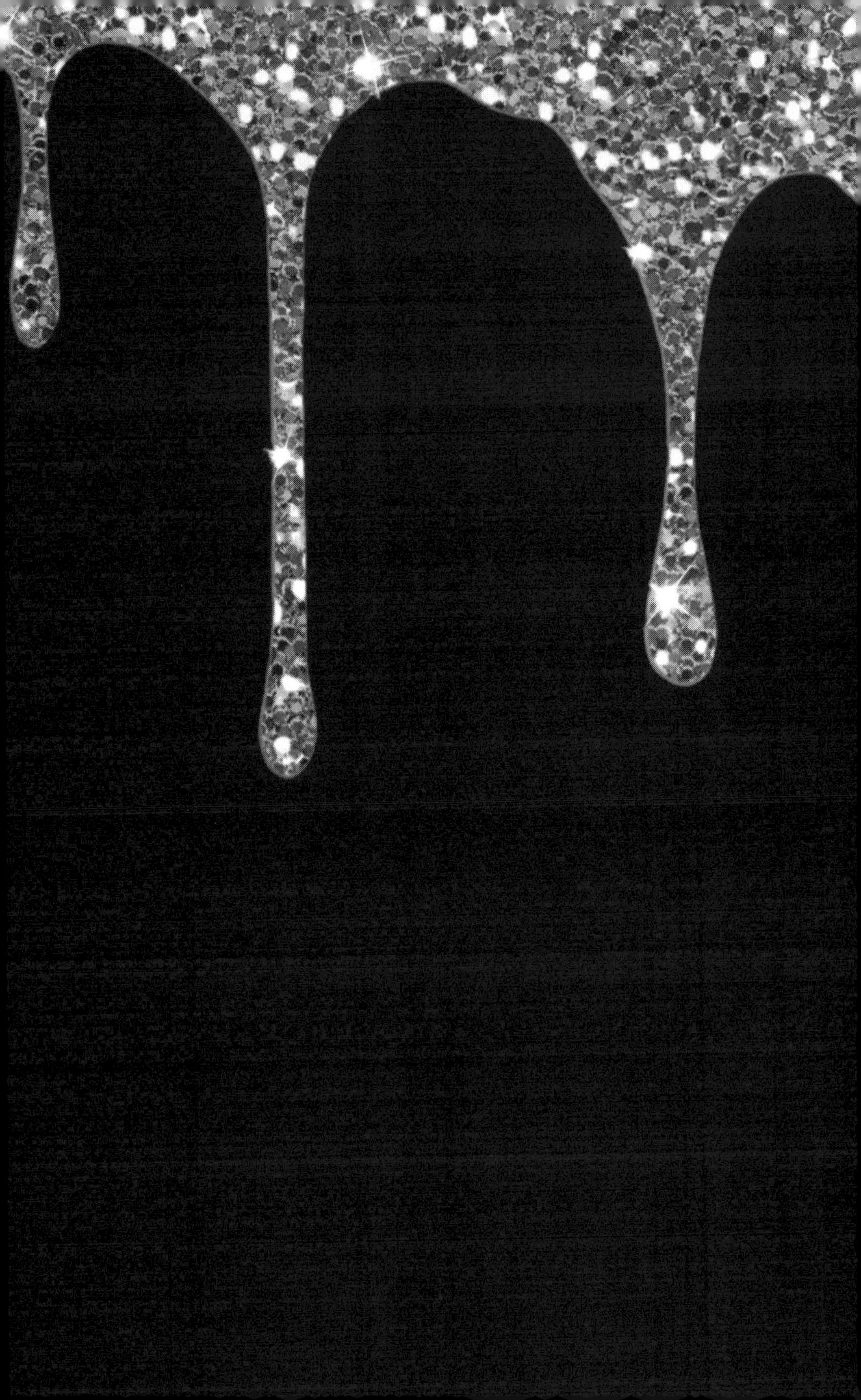

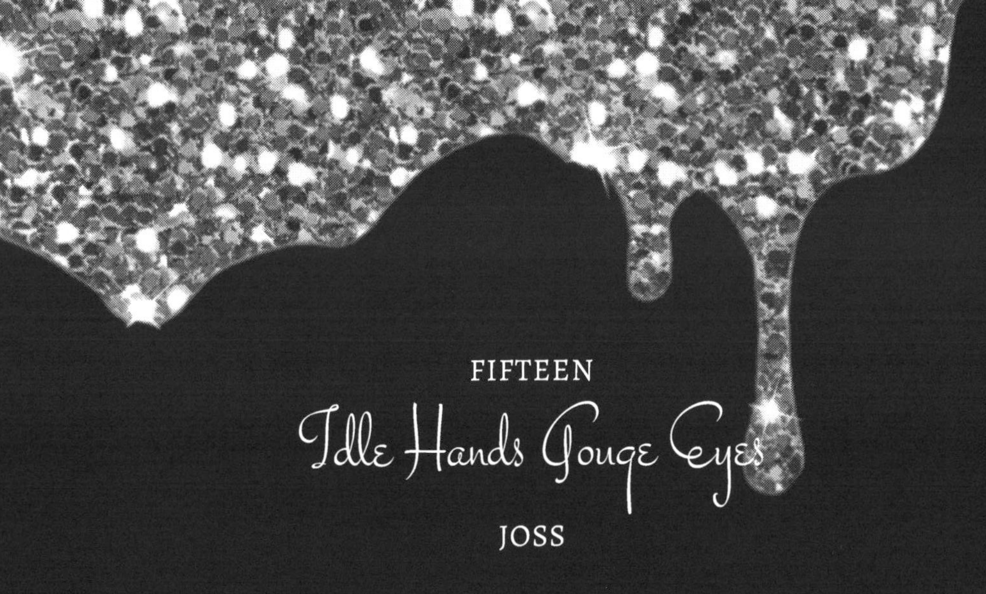

FIFTEEN
Idle Hands Gouge Eyes
JOSS

NO.

But seriously.

Stupid freakin' math.

On Wednesdays—the last day of Wicked's pay week—I liked to input the current numbers before time traveling to the past clusterfuck. Okay, maybe *like* was too strong of a word. But it'd been working well.

Again, *well* may also have been too strong of a word.

Whatever.

Point was, it was my routine, and it usually went smoothly. Lars, despite his claims otherwise, was good with numbers. More than that, he was a shrewd businessman. He got discounts and bulk pricing on everything from alcohol to bar snacks to soap—all incredibly important things to have at a strip club. From what I could tell, Wicked made an impressive profit even with the stellar wages he paid. Deep, deep, *deeeeeeeep* beneath the layers of chaos were surprisingly organized and methodical bookkeeping. It seemed like something had gone to hell along the way, office management wise.

Based on what he'd told me, that something was named Eddie.

Tapping my pen on the desk, I looked between the numbers on the screen and the array of papers spread in front of me. Something wasn't matching up. No matter how much I hunted, I couldn't find an invoice or receipt that lined up with the hidden recurring payment.

With a frustrated sigh, I stood and stretched before heading into the hallway.

The empty hallway.

Usually, there was a bouncer stationed at the dressing room, but he was missing. I went down to the swinging door that led to the main room, but there was no one there, either.

A little peek won't hurt.

I always came in through the back entrance. I worked in the office. I only ever used Lars' private bathroom. I never even went near the dressing room, much less the front room. But my stubborn mule brain wasn't letting me move on until I figured out what the hell that payment was for and where to categorize it in my spreadsheet.

So, really, I had no choice but to go into the *strip* part of the strip club. Not for my own curiosity, of course. It was in the name of science... Er, math.

The timing was perfect, the quiet music signaling it was between stage sets. I eased the door open, expecting to hit a wall of hired muscle, but it was unmanned on that side, too.

Huh.

Since there were scantily clad goddesses chatting up the few afternoon patrons, no one paid me any attention as I slipped into the room.

And froze.

Wow.

Lars—despite his frequent threats to burn the place down—took a lot of pride in his business. It showed in the exterior and the back of the place. I'd known the front wouldn't be faded carpets, tattered wallpaper, mystery stains, and flickering bare bulbs.

There were, of course, lots of other *bare* things, but that was kinda the point.

Even with my high expectations, I wasn't prepared for how *sexy* Wicked was. The bar, tables, and stage were made of matching black wood that gleamed almost as much as the poles. Dark blue cushioned booths lined one wall with coordinating tall tables and stools filling the space between the bar and stage. The chairs that lined the stage looked made for comfort rather than affordability.

Which made sense. They invited the occupant to relax. Stay a while. Spend a lot.

That wasn't to say it was an upscale place with chandeliers and crystal goblets. But it also wasn't the stereotypical dive. It was somewhere between. Cool yet comfortable. Nice yet unfussy.

Masculine yet so damn sexy—much like the owner himself.

Keeping an eye out for Lars, I made my way to the bar. If anyone knew where he was, it'd be Sasha. The former dancer was the bartender, fill-in supervisor, drama referee, and a million other things that made her the mother hen of Wicked.

I liked her. She had a charmingly crass sense of humor. She was also the only employee Lars seemed to trust, which said a lot.

"Hey, babe," she greeted. "You look like you need a cold Diet Coke almost as much as I need a hot man."

That wasn't what I'd come out there for, but once she mentioned it... "Please."

She grabbed a glass and the soda gun, scanning the room as she filled it. "How's it going in paper hell?"

"Hellish. Do you know where Lars is?"

"He's... uh... busy. Idle hands and all that." Her smile was wide. Maybe too wide. It had the same mischievous edge to it that Piper's did when she was up to something. Not that I knew Sasha well enough to tell for sure. "Why don't you wait here for him? I'm sure he'll be finished soon."

I was about to ask for clarification when a drunk at the far end of the bar started groaning. And then retching.

Ew.

Sasha rushed down the bar, and I averted my gaze as a sense of foreboding filled me. The refreshing and delicious soda was suddenly a brick sliding down my throat to churn in my uneasy stomach.

It had nothing to do with the heaving man or Sasha's evasive answer—no matter how easily it could've been twisted. And, trust me, there was a part of my brain that was doing its damnedest to twist it like a pretzel.

Or like a very naked and very agile dancer wrapping her body around Lars, his idle hands full of her wildness.

No, the warning bells going off like a broken grandfather clock were courtesy of a random guy who was suddenly all up in my space.

On the outside, he didn't look creepy. He was young. Kinda attractive, in that prep-tastic, spoiled way that said he was one minor inconvenience away from summoning his father's lawyer. There was just something... off about him. Date rape drifted from him as strong as the Drakkar Noir he'd bathed in.

I could've been wrong. He could've been a great guy, just coming over for a new beer or whatever.

I still wasn't setting my drink down near him.

My instincts were confirmed as he stared at my breasts, talking to them while he flashed a stack of bills. "Gorgeous, what time does your shift start? I don't wanna miss it."

"I'm not a dancer," I said, polite but not inviting any further conversation.

That didn't stop him from moving closer, as though I'd rolled out the red carpet and sent an invite via courier pigeon. "You are. Girl who looks like you doesn't just sit in a place like this unless she's a stripper. Don't worry, baby, I won't tell anyone I saw you before you're all done up. This is a treat just for me. I like my girls natural."

Oh barf.

I had years of that bull crap. As if a woman's value decreased as her eyeshadow increased. I may have resentfully put up with it from my ex, but I wasn't putting up with it from some random douche.

"Not a dancer," I gritted out firmly.

He was studying me way too intently before his lip curled. At odds with the disgust that coated his expression, there was naked lust in his heated bedroom eyes. At least, that's what I thought he was going for. He could've been holding in a sneeze.

Or a shart.

"Don't break my heart by telling me you swing *that* way. You just haven't had the right man." He licked his lips. "We'll watch the girls together and then I'll take you back to my place to give you what they never could."

An orgasm-less night, a lifetime of regret, and a venereal disease?

My retort burned on the tip of my tongue until I had to literally bite my cheek to keep the words inside. I wanted—no, I craved—to tell him where to stick his clichéd, condescending attitude. That the only reason any of these *women* would touch him was because it was their job and they were professionals who deserved respect. That there was literally no amount of Daddy's money he could pay me to shake his hand, much less his anything else.

I knew better. Mouthing off, no matter how accurately and well deserved, wasn't worth the risk. A man with a fragile ego was a dangerous thing. Sometimes emotionally, like with Peter. But, far too often, physically.

Opting for silence, I turned to check on Sasha and the drunk who was struggling to stay on the stool.

A hand wrapped around my upper arm and violently twisted me. The man's face was way too close to mine as he kept hold of me. Anger glittered in his eyes, his face tight and his expression thunderous. "Who the fuck do you think you are, bitch? No one ignores—"

One second he was there, the next he was sprawled on his ass with Lars looming over him.

Oh shit.

"Were you touching my fuckin' woman?"

"Whoa, bro, I didn't—"

"I'm not your fuckin' bro. Now answer me. Were you touching. *My*. Fuckin'. Woman?" Lars bit out, each word a rough staccato.

"Lars," I cut in, trying to defuse the situation before it went nuclear.

If the douche's expression was thunderous, Lars' was a freakin' hurricane mixed with a tsunami all in the middle of the tornado as his glare cut to me. "I'll deal with you after I finish killing this motherfucker."

Deal with me?

What the hell is there to deal with?

I returned his glare. "What'd I do?"

"Told you to stay in the back. Repeatedly. You don't belong out here."

You don't belong out here.

The words ricocheted around my brain on a loop, tearing at my heart. At my soul. Eviscerating me.

I didn't belong out with the wild and the wicked. I wasn't sexy. I wasn't technicolor. I wasn't capable of raising heart rates.

Lars had said it himself. To my freakin' face. I was pretty. He'd made it seem like a good thing, but I wasn't so sure anymore.

Because I didn't belong out there.

Then fuck it.

Fuck *out here.*

And fuck him.

Lars

What the fuck just happened?

I watched Joss storm away, but not before I'd seen the fire in her brown eyes.

Fire she'd aimed my way, which made not a lick of fuckin' sense.

If anyone deserved to be pissed, it was me. I'd told her to stay in the back. To use the bouncers if she needed to find me. Yet to my motherfucking surprise, I'd come back inside after dealing with an aggressive customer to find her fine ass sitting at the bar. Like a beacon of innocence in a den of wolves. A taste of heaven in a circle of hell.

So damn irresistibly pretty, every man in the place had been staring at her. And I wanted to kill them all for it. I'd known even before the bastard wrapped his hand around her arm that my afternoon of violence was far from done.

Breaking fingers for touching women without their consent was child's play compared to what I was gonna do to the bastard at my feet for touching *my* woman.

"Follow her and don't let her leave," I ordered Killer. The dumbass on the floor tried to scoot away, so I put my heavy boot on his chest. "Lock the door if you have to."

I waited until he was to the *unguarded* hallway before looking behind me. Seeing Frankie was expected. He'd been the one to drag the handsy asshole outside for me.

What wasn't expected was Gary's smirking face.

I didn't know him well. Newer bouncer, cocky as hell, and, thanks to his inability to follow simple directions, unemployed.

"You're fired," I bit out.

His smile fell. "What? Why?"

"Where were you supposed to be?" I demanded.

He puffed his chest out, lifting his chin. "You needed me outside."

I hadn't even noticed him out there, much less needed him.

I gave a humorless laugh. "The day I *need* three bouncers to break one asshole's fingers is the day I sell Wicked."

Hell, I didn't even need one bouncer. Sure, the backup was smart. And them doing retrieval and detainment until I got outside was convenient.

But I did my dirty work myself.

One of the perks of being the boss.

"Man, it's just a hallway," Gary whined, flinging a hand toward it. "Nothing was gonna happen."

My expression went to stone, and he went pale. Moving my eyes from him down to the man pinned below my shitkicker and back again, I rumbled, "Nothing, Gary?"

"It's not my fault you don't keep your bitch on a short leash."

"Fuckin' hell," Frankie said, moving his body to block Gary's. "Boss, he's an employee."

"I don't give a fuck," I growled, almost willing to let the bastard on the floor go. Almost. But why do that when I could have double the fun?

"Think of the paperwork."

Shit. If there was one thing I didn't need more of, it was paperwork. Explaining to the labor department why I beat the ass of my ex-employee would likely bring a stack of it.

"Get him outta here," I ordered, but Frankie was already frog-marching Gary toward the door.

Like he was a sad little puppy, I grabbed the man from the ground by the back of his shirt and dragged him outside while he yelled some threats about his dad and a lawyer. Or legal. Eagle? Beagle? I didn't fuckin' know, I wasn't paying attention.

He was someone important and his dad was a half-bird, half-dog lawyer.

Blah, blah, blah.

Didn't change a damn thing.

He tried to cling to the door as I used his face to slam through.

"This is just sad," I muttered. "You're embarrassing yourself."

Once I got him to the side of the building, in the hidden recess that would glow neon under a blacklight thanks to the blood I'd spilled there, I jacked him against the brick.

And he started crying.

Holy shit, the kid just fuckin' crumbled into hysterics. Blubbering an apology and bribe and other shit I couldn't understand even if I wanted to—which I didn't—he was a pathetic mess.

I almost felt bad for him until I remembered the way he'd touched Joss. The way he'd twisted her around. He'd been man enough to touch a woman half his size, he was man enough to take the consequences without threatening or buying his way out of them.

First damn time for everything, it seemed.

My fist flew fast, connecting with his jaw and cutting off his words.

Pinning him with one hand around his throat, I had to hold him standing as my next jab hit his nose. The satisfying crunch was felt *and* heard before blood gushed. His hands went up, but not to swing at me.

No, he just covered his nose and hissed. When he pulled them away, his eyes went wide and then rolled back.

And down he went.

Passed out cold at the sight of his own blood.

"That was the saddest shit I've ever seen," Frankie said with a tsk. "My seven-year-old niece coulda taken him down, and that was before she started karate."

He wasn't exaggerating.

"Put his face on the blacklist," I ordered. "Then get him outta here."

Frankie jacked the guy up by his collar, ready to smack him awake.

I left him to deal with the inevitable tears so I could face the fiery brunette.

Going through the front door so I could make sure there were no other disasters taking place, I stopped behind the bar to wash the speckles of blood from my hands. I was almost done when I heard, "You're a dumbass."

I turned a warning glare to Sasha. "I'm your boss."

"You're right." She shot me a saccharine smile that could kill. "You're a dumbass, *boss*."

"What the fuck did I do?"

"You told her she didn't belong here... you dumbass."

"She doesn't. Otherwise, I'm gonna have to stab the eyes out of every bastard in the place." I was vaguely aware of a couple of said bastards scooting from the bar to sit elsewhere.

Smart of them.

Sasha rolled her eyes and spoke slowly, as if talking to a child. Or a moron. Or a moronic child. Few people would attempt that and even fewer would get away with it. "You told your sweet girlfriend that she doesn't belong out here where all the women are sexy."

It took me longer than it should've to get what she was saying. 'Cause in my mind, none of them came close to Joss. No one did. She was perfection, wrapped in a fantasy, multiplied by my own personal wet dream.

But if she didn't know that, I could see how I'd fucked up.

I'd just have to make sure she knew it. Without a shadow of a damn doubt.

When I got into the hallway, Killer was standing across from my office, his arms crossed and his expression tight. "She's pissed, boss." Usually, my employees would be amused that someone was giving me grief. But Killer had a soft spot for Joss, and her being upset just upset him. Which meant he glared at me and continued. "Fix it."

I unlocked the office and went inside to find her all geared up. Hoodie. Bag. Wall of reinforced steel around her. "Finally. Tell your..." Her words trailed off when she saw it was me and not Killer, but only for a moment. Then her shoulders went back and the only emotion in her mostly blank expression was stubbornness.

Christ, it made me hard.

"I'm taking off early today," she stated, just daring me to argue.

I would 'cause there was no damn way I was letting her leave until I set things right.

Getting her taste back on my tongue would just be a bonus.

Before I lost my head, I asked the most important question. "Did he hurt you?"

She rolled her eyes. "Only because I was biting my tongue too hard."

My shoulders loosened. Out cold or not, I'd have killed the motherfucker if he'd hurt her.

I stalked toward her. "What did I tell you about going out front?"

"Not to do it unless I'm hiding my face behind a *Phantom of the Opera* mask," she muttered, adding snark to her stubbornness.

That snark would've made me harder. But beneath it, there was something more. Something worse.

Hurt.

Fuckin' hell.

I am *a dumbass.*

"You're outta your mind," I growled, moving in closer. Close enough that I could feel her. Close enough that she could feel the effect she had on me. "Spend my time fighting a hard-on just knowing you're in the building with me. You think I want you in the same room with any of those motherfuckers? They're lucky I don't gouge their damn eyes out for looking at you earlier."

"No one was looking at me." She believed that. There wasn't an ounce of false modesty or fishing-for-compliments bullshit in her insane statement.

"You think that, then you're blind *and* outta your mind. Every last one of them was looking, wishin' he was where I am, with your body against them and the memory of your taste haunting their fuckin' tongue. Fuck, Joss, I got back inside after breaking a bastard's fingers for putting hands on one of the dancers just to see some other prick touching *you*. I'd have broken every damn bone in that hand had he not passed out cold before I could."

"You broke someone's fingers?" she whispered, her face carefully blank.

She knew I wasn't a saint. That I liked to go knuckles with anyone who was stupid enough to push me. That I'd done time. That I was a strip club owner who had no business being so damn obsessed with the pretty kindergarten teacher who baked cookies and made cardboard cutouts and all the other wholesome shit she did to make the world a better place.

But she'd made the decision to slum it with me anyway, which meant she was getting me. All of me, exactly as I was, 'cause I was damn sure demanding the same of her.

"Wasn't the first time," I said honestly.

"Why'd the creep pass out?"

"Broke his nose."

"Just because he touched me?"

"No *just* about it. No one puts their hands on you but me."

She didn't respond, and my gut tightened as the silence stretched. After a long minute, she shook her head and sighed. "Now who's out of their mind?"

"When it comes to you?" I speared my fingers into her hair and fisted, yanking her head back. "Abso-fucking-lutely."

Before she could argue, I covered her mouth with mine. Her lips were pressed together, her body rigid.

Lucky for me, I'd never been afraid of a little hard work.

I didn't coax her lips to open for me. I didn't have the patience. I used my tongue and forced my way in. I took what I wanted. Needing the reassurance the filth in my world hadn't reached out to hurt her. Needing the reassurance that she was in *my* arms.

I took and took and fuckin' took what was mine.

Before long, Joss softened. Leaned into me. Clutched at me. Accepted me, exactly how I was. For who I was.

A greedy, undeserving bastard.

"You're still insane," she muttered when I dropped my mouth to tease her neck.

"Yeah," I agreed, going up to taste her lips again.

"You can't just break people's noses," she panted between kisses. "Or fingers. Or gouge their eyes out."

"Can." I nipped her full lower lip. "And will."

Cutting off any further questions, demands, or insults with my kiss, I took advantage of the moment by undoing her jeans and shoving them down her legs. Fuck, I wanted to bend her over my desk with the fabric holding her thighs together as I slammed into her so deep, she'd feel me long after we were done.

Fuck it.

That was exactly what I was gonna do, first time be damned. I'd make it up to her when we had hours to spend in bed.

My hand had just moved to cup her pussy, my middle finger sliding through her soaked lips, when someone knocked at the door.

Ever since Eddie had fucked up my life and business in a multitude of ways, I'd been tempted to torch the place often. But never more than I wanted to right then.

"Fuck off," I shouted, my voice gruff as I pressed my finger into her.

Her moan was muffled against my chest as she half-assedly tried to shift away.

"Sasha needs to leave, and her replacement isn't here yet," Killer called back.

Shit.

Need to start scheduling people an hour earlier just so they get here on time.

"Have Frankie hop behind the bar. I'll be out in five."

"Is that all it's going to take?" Joss whispered, all innocent doe eyes with a sinfully fuckable smirk. "I thought you needed *time.*"

"Got it, boss," Killer called.

I wanted to wipe the smirk off her face by teasing her until she was begging me and then fucking her until she couldn't speak. My finger curved, rubbing a spot that made her breath hitch as I gave it serious consideration. I could tune out the inevitable knocking and meltdowns, but I doubted she could.

And, in addition to that *time*, I wanted her focus. All of it.

I'd spent weeks obsessed with her. Wrapped up in her. When I finally sank into her tight pussy, I wanted her to feel the same.

That didn't mean I wasn't gonna get her off before I jumped behind the bar. It'd make my night a helluva lot better having her taste on my tongue.

Dropping to my knees, I soaked in the way her lids went heavy as her breathing hitched. Her hand moved to my head, and I braced for a fight. But rather than push me away, she pulled me toward her.

Greedy for me.

I shoved the bundle of fabric further down her legs and hitched them apart like I'd done when I'd eaten her against my bike. The heavy wooden desk could take a lot more than the Harley, so Joss gave it more of her weight as she leaned back.

Diving in like it'd been years since I'd tasted all her sweetness, I tongued her pussy the same way I'd kissed her. Not coaxing or teasing. I devoured. Taking.

Her palm rubbed across my hair as she shifted her hips. I took her cues, going where she needed me and increasing the pressure when she ground harder.

"You," she breathed out.

"What about me, baby?" I asked before going back to her clit.

"This is... second time... you haven't... want you to..." She made a noise, somewhere between a growl and a whimper. "It's hard to focus when you keep doing that."

I flicked my tongue faster. "That?"

"Yes," she hissed on an exhale.

"You want me to come, baby?" I slid a finger back in as my lips skimmed her clit.

She nodded like her life depended on it.

"Want to see how I stroke my cock while I think about you? While I picture how perfect your pussy is going to squeeze me when I *finally* get inside you?"

Another rapid nod as she rocked her hips, her pussy squeezing my finger in a way that was already better than my fantasies.

Christ, she's gonna kill me.

Tasting her, feeling her, fuckin' smelling all that sweetness...

There was no amount of cold water or baseball stats that were making my hard-on go away. If my woman wanted to see me get some relief, who was I to argue?

Releasing my cock with my free hand, I fisted it as I sucked her clit. My groan vibrated against her, making her grip my head tighter.

She leaned forward and to the side, trying her best to keep my mouth connected while still being able to see. I twisted my torso and knew she could see everything when she gasped, "Oh, God."

I could feel her get wetter at the sight of me. Because of me. It was enough to make my balls tighten, but I wouldn't come. Not until she did.

Even if it fuckin' killed me.

And that was a real possibility 'cause her eyes on me while I stroked my dick was enough to make me lose my damn mind.

Especially when her nails scratched across my head as she ground herself against me.

I pulled my finger free and gripped her hip, pulling her tighter. Giving her the pressure she sought. *Needed*. Because within seconds, she was coming, her taste flooding my tongue and her moans filling my head.

"Lars," she whimpered, shifting away when it became too much.

I wanted to keep going. To greedily force another orgasm. But my control was razor thin, and I couldn't hold out any longer.

Standing, I kept pumping my cock. Squeezing hard. Stroking faster and faster. Getting off on the way she watched me. "You come so good for me, baby. So beautiful."

Another whimper as Joss' gaze followed my motions, her thighs moving restlessly.

"You wanna be a good girl and let me come on you, baby?"

A frantic nod, her big eyes wide and unfocused. Filled with desire aimed at me.

"Spread your pussy open for me."

Me.

Me.

Only ever me.

She did as I ordered. My good girl, her finger stretched to rub her clit.

Fuck.

Fuck.

Fuuuuuck.

I fought to keep my eyes open as my come shot out in thick bursts, covering her hand. Her pussy. Her soft thigh. I watched, fuckin' entranced, as her finger gathered my come before bringing it to her clit, using it as lube as she hurriedly got herself off.

It was, by a long fuckin' mile, the sexiest thing I'd seen in my whole damn life. Better than any porn. Any chick shaking her tits out on the stage. Any of the practiced and purposeful shit women did because they thought it was what men wanted. It was real and raw and so damn hot, my spent cock jerked.

I could be an old man on my deathbed, and that memory would be the last thing I thought of. I'd die happy with a hard-on.

That said, since the universe had seen fit to gift my undeserving ass someone like Joss, I hoped like hell it saw fit to let me die with my cock buried deep inside her. Not any time soon. When we were both old, gray, and I was undoubtedly still just as fuckin' crazy about her.

Her tits rose and fell with each labored breath. There was no self-consciousness. No embarrassment. No scorn aimed my way—and my woman wasn't afraid to glare me down.

The pretty schoolteacher just lazily smiled up at me.

Happy.

I grabbed a tissue and wiped myself off before tucking my still semi-hard dick away and redoing my pants. She reached for one, too, but I wrapped my hand around her wrist to stop her.

Her questioning gaze went to mine before she read my intent and shook her head. "No way. I can't work like this."

"Why the hell not?"

"I'm all sticky and... *wet.*"

Fuck, she's gonna kill me.

Weaving my hand into her hair, I tilted her head back gently. "Don't ever think I'm not attracted to you. That you're not the prettiest, hottest, sexiest woman I've ever seen in my life. Told you, spend my days, nights, and everything in between fighting getting hard from just the thought of you." I fisted her hair, pulling it. "Consider this payback."

Her cheeks flushed, her expression softening even as her eyes stayed hooded. Bedroom eyes. She could give the dancers lessons, and their tips would triple.

Can't wait until I have her looking up at me like this while I'm balls deep in heaven.

"Gotta get out front. I'd bring you with me," I slid my hand from her hair to drag along her jaw, "but then you know what'd happen."

"Broken fingers, gouged eyes... same old, same old," she deadpanned, still without a hint of judgment.

Kissing her, I started for the door before stopping. "Why were you looking for me in the first place?"

"Oh, crap, I almost forgot." She flipped through a stack of papers we'd messed up, pulling one out and then tapping a few keys. "I found something... odd."

"If it's about how much I stalk your Instagram, there's a simple explanation," I half-joked—'cause I sure as shit did it, but on my phone, not my computer.

"Which is?" she asked, playing along.

"I'm stalking you."

She grinned for a moment, and fuck, it hit me in the gut. But then her lips turned down, and my gut soured. "There are some payments I can't make sense of."

I knew without even looking it was another of Eddie's messes I'd have to clean. "Who're they going to?"

Her brows were pulled together. "Controversy LLC. I tried googling, but nothing came up."

I shrugged 'cause I had no clue who or what that was.

"If it's, uh, something you're aware of and you don't want to share, I can just disregard—"

I knew what I looked like. What I did for a living. What I'd done in my life. And who I was. But the insinuation from Joss cut. Stung like a motherfucker.

Killed.

"Not stealing from my own damn company," I bit out, my shoulders bunching.

At my defensiveness, Joss didn't apologize or even double down. No, my woman rolled her eyes in my face, letting me know I was continuing to be a dumbass. "Yeah, embezzling from yourself would be kinda counterproductive. But maybe it's for tax purposes. Retirement. Hookers and blow. I don't know, there are a million explanations."

The side of my mouth curved into a smirk. "'Hookers and blow?'"

"Or retirement savings," she repeated slowly, fighting her own smile.

"No, hotcakes, nothing with a bogus LLC. Any chance it's only a couple bucks and we can forget about it?" The tension in her body told me the answer, but it was worth a shot so I didn't have to deal with the growing headache—literal and metaphorical.

She shook her head, not tearing her focus away from the computer as she scowled with frustration. I wasn't sure if it was on my behalf or 'cause my stubborn woman didn't like the mystery. Either way, she wasn't happy. "Each one is small-*ish*, but they add up fast. At first, I thought it was just typical variations, but your order was the same. That made me worry the suppliers were trying to bilk you, so I dug into it. And I mean *dug*."

Backtracking, I rounded the desk so I could see the target of her wrath. There were so many windows open on the computer, I wasn't sure what I was supposed to be seeing.

"From what I can tell," she clicked through the different screens, "when your software gets the prompt to autopay certain invoices, a good chunk of change is being added and then split off and sent elsewhere."

Yup, sounds like Eddie's bullshit.

"I *think*," she continued. "I might be wrong because this was all buried deep in really smart, sophisticated programming."

And that does not *sound like Eddie. No one would've called the bastard smart or sophisticated.*

Joss' thoughts followed mine. "Was Eddie good with technology?"

Caging her in with an arm on either side, I clicked the mouse and shook my head. "Unless it was checking Celtics scores to see how much he owed his bookie or watching porn, he didn't know RAM from Instagram."

She smiled, tilting her head to look back at me. "I'm not even sure what RAM is."

I closed the gap between our bodies, my hardening cock pressing against her rounded ass. "It's what I can't fuckin' wait to do to you."

Her eyes went huge, her lips parting. I took the invitation, gripping her chin and tilting her head further so I could cover her mouth with mine. My tongue wasn't what I wanted to shove in her mouth, but it was all we had time for.

Pulling away, I ordered, "Leave this window open when you go tonight."

"Got it."

"Thanks, baby. Don't stay too late."

Her face was soft and sweet and so damn pretty as she nodded, repeating, "Got it."

She didn't—yet—but I was damn sure looking forward to giving it to her.

As I worked behind the bar, my thoughts were on Eddie, how

much he'd cost me, and how he continued to make my life hell from beyond the grave. Since I didn't have perky tits, none of the customers were chatty. And since it was happy hour, everyone was ordering cheap domestic bottles. That left me a lot of time to think.

And nothing I came up with did anything to loosen my tense muscles, unclench my jaw, or calm the anger that was flowing through my veins like toxic waste.

When I got a break between slinging watered-down hops, I pulled out my phone and brought up my texts with my ex-neighbor—cell neighbor, that was. Killian Nox was part Scottish, part Irish, and all-around scary mother fucker. Unless he was in your corner—which, thank fuck, he was in mine. His exact job description fell somewhere in the gray, as did the man himself, but it involved finding… whatever. People. Bodies. Information.

Shady LLCs.

He was good with a computer. As were his guys, Beck and Matt.

But it was Wicked we were dealing with. It may have been a pain in the ass, but it was *my* pain in the ass. If anyone was gonna burn the place to the ground, it'd be me. That's why I didn't need good. I needed the best. Which was why I asked about his associate.

Me: Dair still in the states?

Nox: Nah, he's handling some shit back home. Why?

Me: Need his tech expertise.

Nox: He'll welcome the distraction. Send the info, I'll pass it along. Aye?

Me: Controversy LLC. Need to know everything about them. More specifically why the fuck I'm sending them money hidden inside other payments.

Nox: Paying off call girls and bookies?

And then, to my utter fuckin' surprise, another text came through. A winky emoji.

Holy shit. The bearded beast went from loathing texting a single word to sending emojis. Betting Gus is to thank for that since he can't go longer than an hour without checking on her.

Me: Joss already beat you to that joke with hookers and blow.

Nox: The sweet lass said that? Nah, don't believe it.

The *sweet lass* said that and a shit-ton of other sexy, sarcastic, or filthy things I'd never have expected when I first set eyes on the pretty teacher.

All of it, every damn thing about her, drove me wild.

Made me fall.

Nox: Sent the info to Dair. He said you owe him a scotch and a lap dance, but he'll figure it out.

Me: Have to clear it with Joss and see if I can find the right song, but I guess I can owe him a lap dance if he's insisting.

There was a couple minute break before another text came through.

Nox: Fook, you made me laugh and startle Nolan. Had to calm the lad down before he pissed on the rug.

Nolan was partially responsible for Nox and Gus' love connection, so he went from a spoiled dog to a worshiped one. A small startle was likely worth belly rubs and a handful of treats.

Could be worse—Dair was known to buy the damn dog porterhouse steaks.

Nox: Rumors true, then? You and the lass hooked tight enough you gotta clear things with her?

Me: Tight enough I'm never letting her go.

Nox: She know this?

Me: If she doesn't, she will.

Nox: Aye, that's what I like to hear. Don't fook it up, ya muppet.

Pocketing my phone, went back to slinging swill and thinking about the sweet lass in my office.

The one who was covered in my come.

I WAS CONTINUING my dumbass streak.

Standing outside of Joss' house later that night, I raised my fist and knocked harder.

Loud enough to wake the neighbor's dog if the barking was any indication.

I was about to give up when the peephole brightened then went dark. A moment later, the door swung open. Joss' panicked gaze scanned me even as she clutched the baseball bat she wielded.

Seeing her in her tiny PJ shorts and thin top, the bat was necessary if she wanted more sleep. 'Cause, dead on my feet or not, I'd summon some energy from somewhere unless she started swinging to keep me away.

Never mind. Doubted even the weapon would deter me.

How could I resist cute-as-fuck book themed PJs? I was only a man, dammit.

And the way she handled the bat...

My cock hardened faster than should've been humanly possible.

I'm a sick fucker.

"What's wrong?" she asked when I just stood there, staring at her pointed nipples.

"Nothing, hotcakes. Long, shitty night. Wanted to end it on a high note in bed with you."

My woman may have been as wiped as me, but that didn't stop her from perking up at the insinuation.

Fuck, she really will be the death of me.

"Sleeping," I added, not buying my own bullshit claim.

"Oh." She deflated, but she did it with a sleepy, sweet smile on her face as she stepped aside so I could enter. "You know I wake up at the asscrack of dawn, right?" At my chin lift, she gave a little shrug before setting down the bat and rearming her system.

I followed her up to her cute-as-fuck room that was filled with books, pictures, and a queen bed that was not big enough. Since I planned on having her pressed tight to me, though, it would work. I stopped to kick my boots off and pull my shirt over my head. Once the fabric cleared, I caught her gaze and growled a warning. "Keep looking at me like that, baby, not gonna be responsible for what I do."

She jolted like I'd startled her, but she didn't look away. She leaned forward on the bed and rested her chin in her hand, batting her lashes at me.

I'd have followed through with my threat, but before I could, she yawned, and I felt like an ass again for selfishly waking her. Not enough to leave or never do it again.

Since I wasn't wearing boxers, I kept my pants on and climbed into bed, pulling her mostly on me. Cupping the back of her head, I tucked her forehead tight against my neck.

For the first time since I'd left her in the office earlier, my muscles relaxed.

Something's wrong.

That was the only explanation for how I was somehow awake before I'd even fallen asleep.

"Sorry," a soft voice whispered from close to my ear, smelling like mint, chick soap, and heaven.

Never mind. Still sleeping 'cause that was a dream girl talking.

A wet-dream one.

But unless my dreams had turned into realistic 4K, I wasn't sleeping.

I was just a lucky bastard.

"I've got to go." I started to sit up, but she put a hand on my shoulder. "Stay and get some sleep." She brushed a kiss against my lips and moved away before my exhausted limbs could drag her back.

Closing one bleary eye, I focused the other on the clock. "I've only been here an hour."

"I told you I wake up early. Press brew on the coffee maker downstairs when you get up. Miss you." Like she knew those words were enough to make me throw her over my shoulder and tie her to the bed to keep her there, Joss hauled ass out the door.

Miss you.

Yeah, driving over had been the right choice.

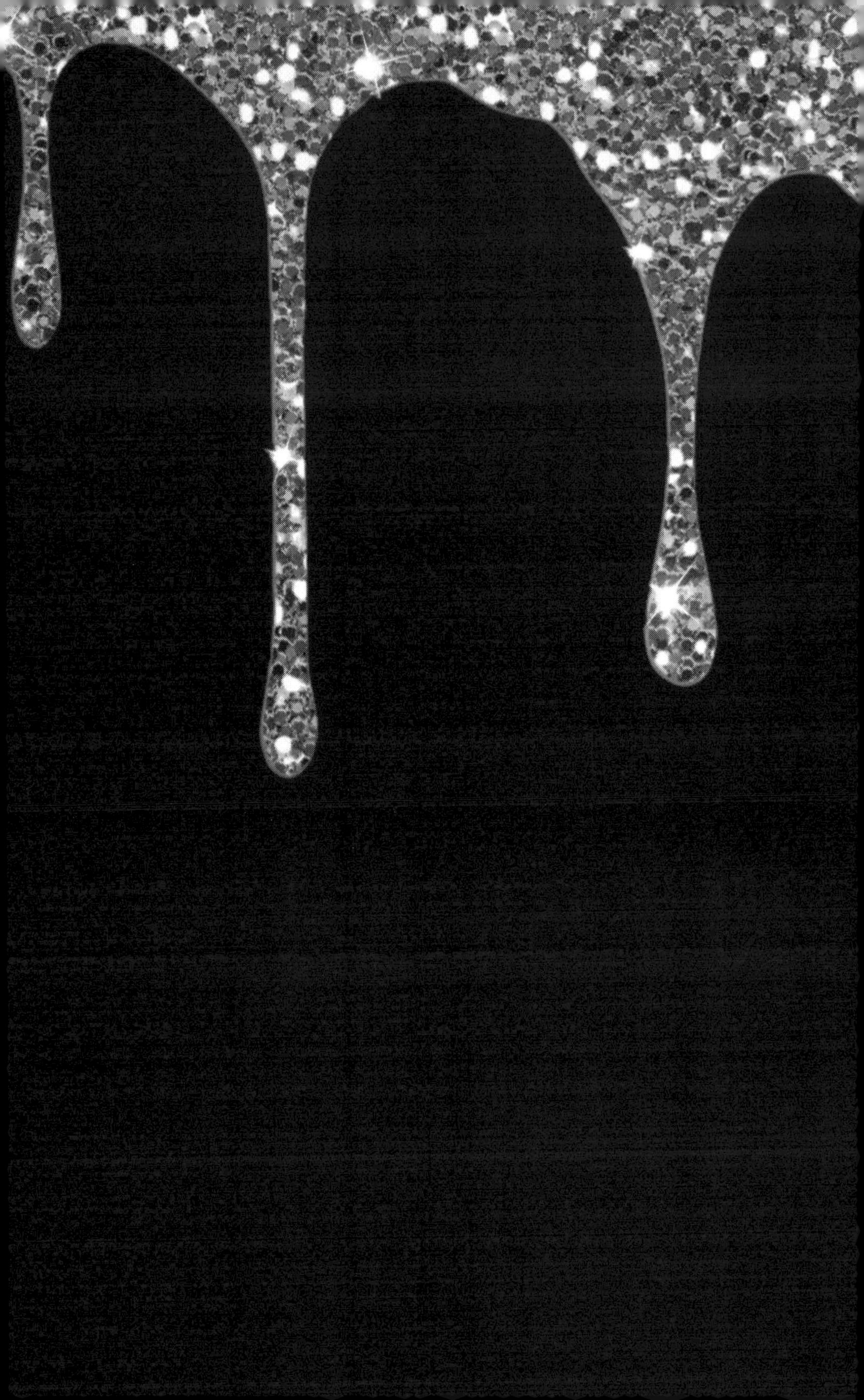

SIXTEEN

In Queso Emergency, Throw Axes

JOSS

"MR. HENRY IN?" I ASKED CLARA, THE MAIN OFFICE extraordinaire and world's nicest lady.

Giving me *a look* that said she was rolling her eyes without physically doing it, she tilted her head toward the office. "He may not be able to see you right now."

I'm so shocked.

I wasn't, of course. The only shocking part was that he was actually in his office. The man spent more time in meetings out of the school than he did inside it.

Which was fine. Whatever I couldn't handle, there was a teacher with seniority who could help. Or Clara. She was Wonder Woman.

But I'd drawn the short straw in the teacher's lounge—literally—so there I was, knocking on the principal's door.

"Come in." When I opened the door, he barely glanced up before adding, "I'm just on my way out, Miss... Miss."

Wow. Way to make a teacher feel valued.

"Of course." I forced a smile even as I ground my teeth to nubs. "The teachers were just wondering what the plan is for tomorrow."

"Tomorrow?"

"The teacher's appreciation dinner," I said slowly, dread filling me.

His slow blink and gaping mouth said a similar feeling was coursing through his veins.

We stood like that for a long, awkward moment. Staring. Waiting for the other to put us out of our misery with a *psych*, or *kidding*, or *my mistake*.

It didn't happen.

Mr. Henry cleared his throat and sat straighter. It may have worked to restore his air of authority had he not reached to adjust the tie he was *not* wearing. "Right, of course. That's tomorrow."

"It is, yes."

He held up a finger to me. "Clara!"

Not looking pleased with the panicked shout he'd used to summon her, Clara stepped into the office. "Yes?"

"What did we decide on for the teacher's appreciation dinner?"

"*We* did not decide on anything."

He didn't bother to internally roll his eyes. He just flat-out did it. "What did *you* decide?"

"Nothing."

The attitude he'd shot her way disappeared as a fresh rush of alarm made the color drain from his face. "What?"

"I made multiple suggestions, but you shot them down for budgetary reasons."

"Well, yes, there isn't much discretionary funding for parties."

It was hilarious to me that he said that behind his big, expensive desk with his shiny new computer perched on top, but okay. Sure.

He'd been the one to promise the event.

He'd claimed it would be a big show of gratitude for us busting our asses to make us the top ranked elementary school in the region.

And then he'd shot down any of Clara's ideas before promptly forgetting? That was so jacked.

We didn't get into our line of work for accolades. We sure as hell didn't do it for the money.

We did it because we loved teaching.

So while we never expected parties, being promised one was different. What he'd done wasn't an insult.

It was a slap in the face followed by a kick to the crotch.

And Mr. Henry knew that. I could practically see the gears on his brain spinning so fast, it was a wonder smoke wasn't coming out of his ears. Of course, he hadn't learned anything from the mistake and placed the blame on Clara. "Why didn't you remind me?"

She was unfazed by his ire, though I'd have expected God to smite him with a lightning bolt for talking to her that way. "I did. Multiple times. You said you'd handle it, Principal Henry."

Oh, I so want to be Ms. Clara when I grow up.

Her use of his title as a subtle reminder that it was his responsibility? It was *chef's kiss* perfection.

The tension in the room was so stifling, it reminded me why I preferred hanging with my kindergarten friends and not the adults in the building.

The planning wasn't my business. I hadn't dropped the ball. I wasn't the bad guy. I should've slowly backed out of the room to extricate myself, but I was frozen to the spot. I couldn't tear my eyes away. It was like a trainwreck in the making.

"That's fine." Mr. Henry once again attempted to straighten his nonexistent tie. "We'll have it in the gymnasium. Order pizza and—"

"No!" I interrupted, inserting myself in the very situation I'd been anxious to escape.

The only thing worse than no party at all would be a pizza party.

That was a slap in the face, a kick to the crotch, and a squirt of hand sanitizer in every papercut.

"Well," Mr. Henry started, failing to mask the hopefulness coating his expression, "what would you suggest, Miss Lennon?"

Ayyy, look at him. He finally remembered my name. Forgot to plan an entire event that was his idea, but he got a name right... eventually.

I wasn't trying to save him. I didn't want to. A lack of planning on his part didn't constitute an emergency on mine, and Mr. Henry deserved what karma was going to slap him with. But my fellow teachers didn't. And the students didn't deserve to have a handful of their teachers quit—something that was guaranteed to happen with that kind of insult.

Mentally, I ran through the options.

The bakery, although delicious, was not a party space. Pretty sure Hyde was out since having people around expensive car parts and dangerous equipment was a bad idea. There were some empty spaces in the building that had yet to be rented out, but bare drywall and unfinished floors didn't scream party.

Not unless the theme was industrial chic or serial killer hideout.

Wicked was an HR violation waiting to happen. Plus, overworked teachers got rowdy. I doubted even Killer could keep them in line.

The regular venues I knew of were probably long booked. Even if they weren't, they were likely beyond the *discretionary funding* available. I was beginning to think we'd have to settle for Mr. Henry's idea of pizza in the gym when it hit me.

I knew the perfect place *if* I was able to finagle it.

And, since the co-owner had spent a magical hour sleeping with me —in only the literal sense, dammit—I was betting I could.

"Hold on." I pulled my phone from my pocket and called, hoping he wasn't in the middle of something important.

Like beating someone up.

That'd be awkward.

"Hotcakes," he greeted, and I could hear it. Not the club noise. Or the music. Or sounds of violence.

It was his smile. I could literally hear it in his voice.

When my silence stretched, his tone was no longer happy as he went alert. "You okay?"

"Yeah, sorry. I just had a question."

"Anything."

"I know it's short notice, but can you ask Demetrius if I can book a few lanes at Bury the Hatchet tomorrow?"

"Got a hot date?" His words were meant to be playful, but his tone still wasn't happy.

"Yes. Whole parade of them." His possessive growl sent a thrill through me, but before he could start adding equally possessive and filthy words to it, I continued. "It's for a teacher's appreciation dinner. There was a... uh... snafu."

"Right," he said through a low chuckle, seeing right through the BS excuse. "How many?"

"How many?" I relayed to Mr. Henry.

"Uh, forty-five?"

"Eighty-three," Clara bit out, looking less annoyed and more angry at the incompetence and disregard.

"Got it." There was a brief pause. "Gimme a couple minutes."

When Lars clicked off, I didn't say a word. Neither did Ms. Clara. We let the heavy silence stretch until Mr. Henry was shifting and fidgeting.

We let him stew in the discomfort.

My ringtone cut through the room, and Mr. Henry nearly jumped out of his seat.

Barely holding in a smirk, I answered it. "Hey."

"All set," Lars told me, and I breathed a sigh of relief for the teachers. "Six until whenever. Assuming you're going?"

I pretty much had to at that point. If anyone deserved some appreciation, it was me.

"There'll be queso," I pointed out. "So, yes. Yes, I am."

"How much is this going to cost?" Mr. Henry asked loudly. No acknowledgment or appreciation or apology for me having to do his job.

"Gotta run, hotcakes." He clicked off but not before I heard the chuckle that said he did not, in fact, have to run. He wanted my principal to suffer.

I shared that same desire.

"As much as you teachers hate it and blame me, there is a budget for a reason. I can't blow the year's budget on one party." Mr. Henry gave a sad sigh, as if it pained him. "It's the children who will suffer."

I was about to put him out of his misery by texting Lars for an answer when Clara cut in. "Oh, get off it, Ted. They'll suffer a lot worse if half their teachers don't show up on Monday because their principal disrespected them."

Whoa.

Clara was still the world's nicest person.

She was also the world's nicest badass.

Mr. Henry took a moment before sitting back. "That's a good point. And why we should keep this... snafu, as you called it, to ourselves. There's no reason to needlessly upset anyone with the hows and whose. The only thing that matters is we're spending the evening together as a happy work family."

Oh barf.

I plastered on a smile as I rattled off the venue info. When he just stared at me, Clara sighed. "Come on, I'll send out the email."

"Oh right," Mr. Henry muttered, but Clara was already closing the door behind us.

I scrawled the name and time onto a sticky note before handing it over.

"Don't worry, I'll make sure everyone knows this was all you," she said.

"No, no, it's fine. Really. I'm just glad I could help."

There was a hint of malice in her gaze as she looked at Mr. Henry's door then back to me. "Well, if word gets out... Oops."

I so want to be her when I grow up.

With a headshake, I opened the door. Before I could step out, Ms. Clara called out, "*Hotcakes*, huh?"

I hadn't thought she was standing close enough to hear.

I'd been wrong.

Oh man.

The main office and teacher's lounge had nothing on Hyde, but that bit of juicy gossip was gonna spread.

And it was gonna happen *fast*.

"DON'T FUCKIN' PULL that shit again."

At odds with the anger vibrating through his voice, Lars' touch was gentle as he rolled me to him and covered us with my blanket.

Trying—and failing—to pry my eyes open, I nuzzled closer. "What shit?"

"Leaving the door unlocked."

"The alarm was on."

"Doesn't matter. Don't risk your safety like that."

"I didn't want to sleep through your banging."

"Trust me, baby." His large hand spanned my thigh and positioned my leg over him so I could feel his even larger something else. "You couldn't."

Truer words had likely never been spoken.

But that wasn't the kind I'd been referring to. "I meant your knocking. There was a passive-aggressive note from my neighbor stuck to my door when I got home tonight. He wasn't happy about the noise two nights in a row."

Lars tensed. "Scrawny guy? Looks like he cheats on his wife, his mistress, his taxes, and his yuppy IPA appreciation group?"

"Can someone cheat on a social club?" I mumbled, all while nodding because, yes, that was a spot-on description.

"Saw that fucker walking his dog when I left this morning. Funny he didn't have the balls to say shit to me."

"Might have something to do with your resting I'll-gouge-your-eyes-out face."

His chest rumbled with a low chuckle as he pressed his lips to my forehead. "Thanks, baby, that's the nicest compliment I've ever received."

I rolled my eyes, even though he couldn't see them. "Plus, technically, he didn't have the balls to say anything to me, either. Passive-aggressive note, remember?"

"Not talking to you in person is the only reason I'm not over there banging on his door till I wake up every dog, cat, and bird in the neighborhood." He pulled me tighter to him. "'Course, if he'd been stupid enough to get in your face, you'd have already fucked him up with kindness the way you do."

"Now who's giving flowery compliments?" Jokes aside, it really did warm my insides to chocolate fondue that he saw me like that. Not shy, boring Joss. Not the nice girl.

Not the goody two-shoes.

I may not be a biker badass, but he still saw me as strong in my own way. Maybe I really could be Ms. Clara when I grew up.

"Everyone have fun tonight?" he asked.

"Well, Demetrius had to order basically every Uber carpool in the city, so I think the answer is yes."

"That was me." His hand came up to tease the swell of my breast. "I know how wild teachers can get."

I warmed at his words, the touch, and everything he'd done to make that night a success.

No. That was an understatement.

Because it hadn't been a stale school function. It'd been a *party* with all the best things.

Food.

Drinks.

Projectiles.

And queso.

I was at least three-percent cheese by the end of the night.

Clara had spread the word I'd been the one to plan the event. Surprisingly, the teachers didn't seem to care. Not then, at least. They'd just wanted to feel valued by someone, and I'd arranged that. Then Demetrius had announced that the entire night was free, his way of showing appreciation for the thankless job teachers did. Either Mr. Henry hadn't caught the dig or he'd ignored it. My money was on the latter since he'd probably had a happy stroke at the word *free*.

"I'm everyone's favorite now," I said through a yawn.

"You're sure as fuck my favorite." He snuggled me closer. "Wish I coulda stayed longer."

At the height of the party, he'd blown in, kissed me like we were the only people in the world, and then turned around and left.

No exaggeration. It'd been that abrupt. And hot.

Seriously, so hot.

I didn't even care that it was far from appropriate and totally shattered my reserved, professional image.

I was sick of that image.

With a small smile pulling at my lips, I was nearly asleep when he spoke again.

"About the unlocked door." Lars gripped my ass and squeezed so hard, a jolt of pain went through me.

But not a bad one.

"This isn't over, hotcakes." Then, so quiet, I wasn't sure I hadn't dreamed it, he added, "Never will be."

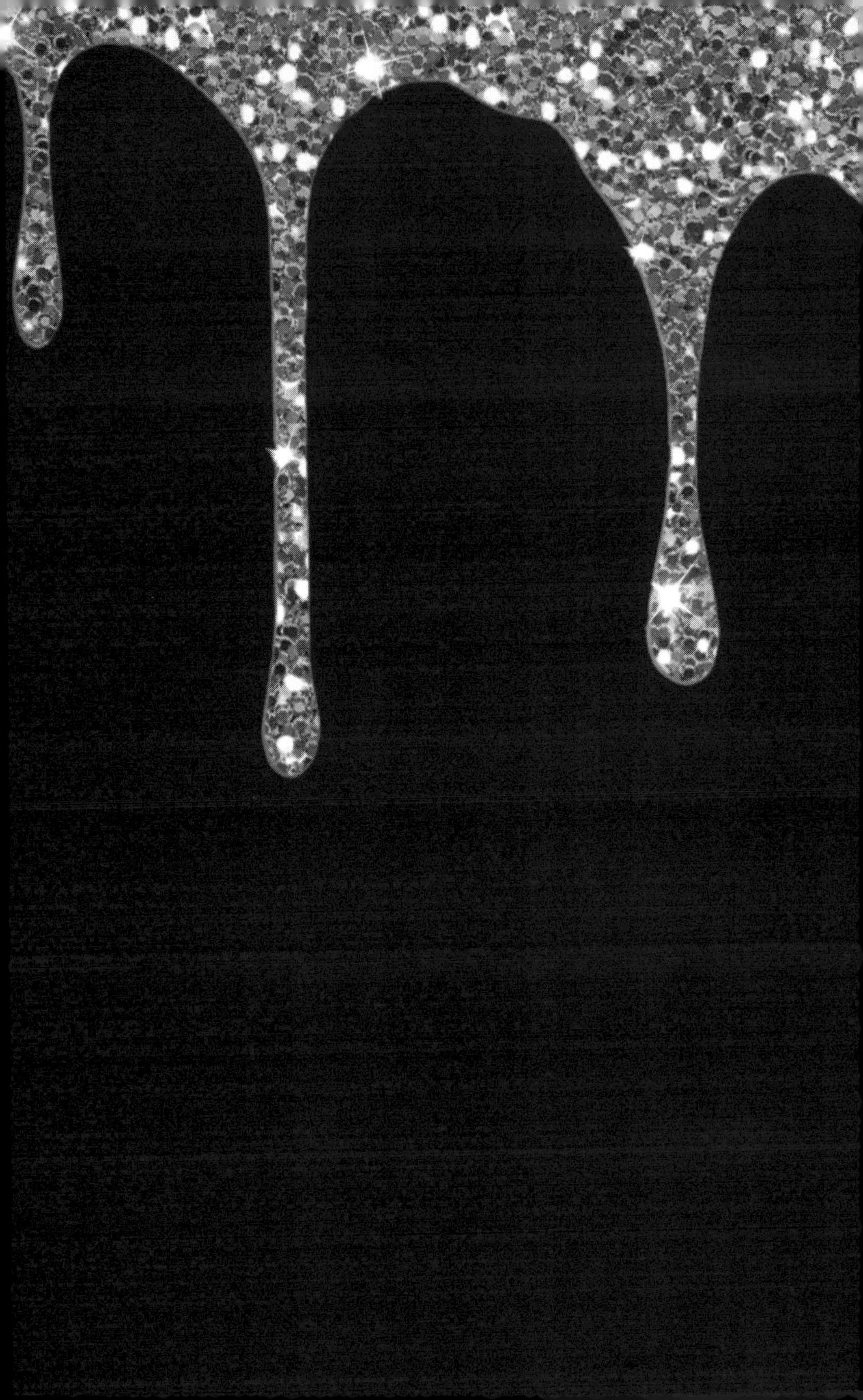

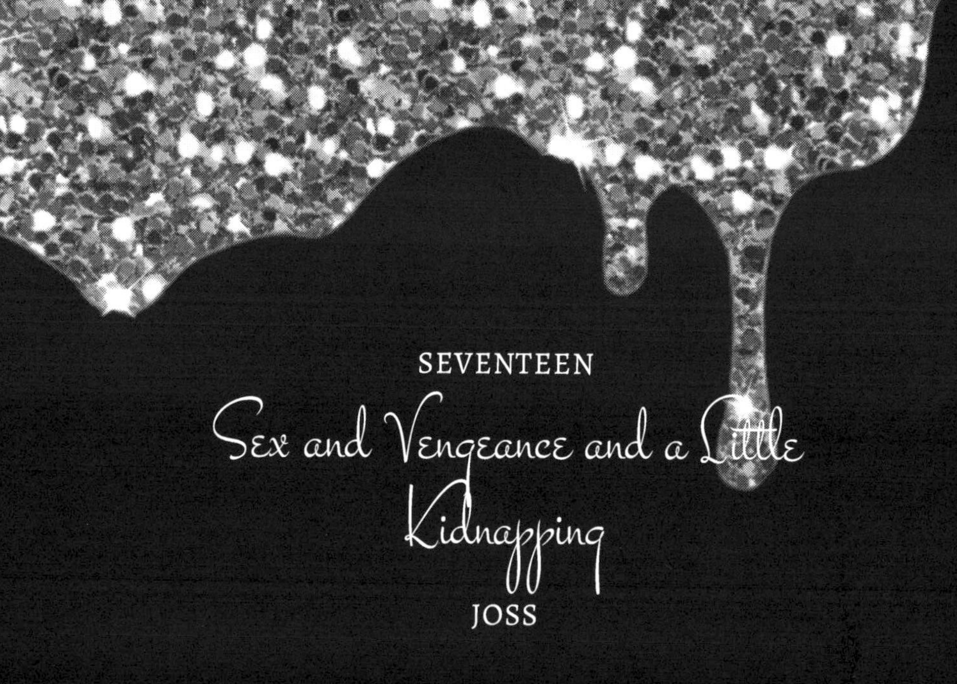

SEVENTEEN
Sex and Vengeance and a Little Kidnapping
JOSS

I'M GONNA EXPLODE.

No exaggeration. No dramatics. No… dick.

Hence the problem.

I hadn't even known female blue balls—blue clit?—were a thing, but I was definitely suffering from it.

Suffering.

It'd only been three days since Lars had brought me to orgasm on his desk. Not three weeks. Or three months. Three days shouldn't feel like an eternity where my neglected woman bits were concerned.

Shouldn't, yet it totally did.

It was Lars' fault. One hundred percent.

Every night, he climbed into bed with me even knowing we'd only have an hour or so. Then at Wicked, it'd be sweet words, hot kisses, and torment me thanks to all the praise he nonchalantly hit me with for whatever minimal progress I'd made.

I wanted to roll my eyes each time he said the room looked better when it did *not*, but the truth was, I lived for it. Something sparked inside me with each offhanded compliment.

I was beginning to worry for my sanity.

But, before that, I was worried for my poor, aching body.

Which was why I had a plan. An awkward one.

Like, a *really* awkward one.

So much so, I wasn't confident I could go through with the first part, much less scary second.

For the millionth time since I'd begun preparing the front counter at Sweets You Rock for Saturday morning chaos, my eyes darted across the room.

And Piper noticed. "Okay, spill."

I went for innocence. "What?"

"You keep looking at the tables."

"No, I don't."

"Yes, you do." She glanced at Sophie. "Back me up, dude."

Sophie gave a quick nod. "You do."

"Told you." Aiming her too sharp focus my way again, Piper said, "They're not going to come to life and jump you."

No, but maybe they'll make someone else come to life and jump me.

But I'll settle for a little payback.

I kept my voice low so only Piper could hear me. "I need your help with something."

Technically, I could do it myself, but it would be easier with another set of hands and eyes. Not to mention, it was crunch time if I wanted to do it that day. And I really did.

Lars' schedule was so packed, he'd already said he couldn't come in for his cookie—or a kiss. It was the perfect time to inflict a little retaliation torture. Turnabout's fair play and all that.

In true Piper form, her answer was instantaneous. "Anything."

"You might regret that," I warned. "It's for sex and vengeance."

"I love both!"

Leaning in close, I began to whisper my idea so Sophie couldn't hear.

Not because I didn't like her. I did. She was nice and a hard worker. Our weekday mornings ran so smoothly, we were barely aware of each other—a boon in my book. I had help without sacrificing my quiet mornings. Quiet that was needed before my kindergarten friends ensured my ears had constant stimuli.

But that didn't mean Sophie needed to be bombarded with the intimate details of my life while she was trying to do her job.

As I spoke, Piper's eyes lit with glee. I didn't even get through the whole thing before she cut me off to ask Sophie, "Can you take over frosting the sugar cookies in the kitchen and make sure none of the scavengers come in here?"

"On it." Sophie set down the napkins she'd been restocking and went into the back.

Once it was just the two of us, Piper grabbed my arm. "I love this idea. *Looooove* it. Can I do it, too, or would that be totally creepy?"

I tilted my head toward the wall she shared with her husband's garage. "I don't think you need the help, but go for it."

"Oh, this is gonna be fun. I won't send mine today, otherwise poor Sophie will have to man the... place... herself..." Her words slowly trailed off, and I could just see her plotting which Hyde man she'd rope into coming over, leaving Sophie in their charming hands.

As fast as the scheming look was there, it was gone again.

Piper may have been a romantic who wanted to matchmake until everyone was as loved up as she was, but she knew not everyone wanted that. Some were happier single and ready to mingle. Or single and ready to go home to cats and plants. All she wanted was for the people in her life to be happy, however that looked. She wouldn't push. Not until Sophie asked.

"What am I, chopped liver?" I asked. "Send it. Go crazy."

One of us should.

Piper shook her head. "You won't be here once you send that message. Lars—"

"Is in meetings all day and then he has, like, a million parties tonight."

"Bummer." Her small frown slowly twisted into an evil smile. "Never mind, I get the vengeance part now. This is way better. He'll spend the whole day going crazy."

That was my hope.

I moved into the storefront before stopping, doubt filling me as I scanned the big windows and the door that connected the waiting rooms.

I was about to chicken out when Piper said, "If we don't do this quick, customers are gonna start lining up outside and you'll have an audience."

Yikes.

Hoping I didn't look as awkwardly stupid as I felt, I got into position and Piper did her thing before we switched places. Once we were done, she grinned. "If this doesn't drive him wild, I'll eat my cupcake."

"Isn't the saying *eat my hat*?"

"Yeah, but who'd wanna do that when you could eat cupcakes? Point is, he's gonna come running. Do some stretches, you'll need it."

Sophie, of course, chose that moment to return with the frosted sprinkle cookies. She tried to hide it, but something flashed across her face as she slid the tray into the case before hauling ass back into the kitchen.

It was quick, but I knew that expression. I'd seen it on my kindergarten friends' faces often.

My attempt at professionalism had backfired with unintended repercussions.

"I made her feel left out," I told Piper.

"You think so?" Her head tilted to the side as she stared at the door Sophie had disappeared through. "I thought she looked offended. She told me she grew up in a small family and was sheltered. I don't think she's used to my brand of perviness, so I won't talk about dick appointments in earshot. And I should probably speak with Jake about his, uh, mild PDA."

Mild, my ass.

"I'd love to be a fly on the wall during that conversation."

Jake Hyde was going to lose his mind if he wasn't allowed to touch his wife whenever he wanted. He'd follow along with her request because he respected Piper and her business, but he wasn't going to be happy about it.

She looked disgruntled, showing it wasn't just Jake who'd suffer. "I might need you there for moral support because if he starts touching me and kissing me, I'll leave the office having begged him to *up* his PDA."

I patted my friend's arm. "You're getting ahead of yourself since neither of us even knows what she's feeling. She could've been thinking about her to-do list or a movie or something else in her life. Or maybe she wasn't thinking about anything at all, and her brain was just a cow in a grass skirt playing a ukulele on loop. Don't worry about it."

"That's true." Even so, the way Piper gnawed at her bottom showed she was literally all worry.

It was why she was a good boss and a better friend.

That, and her willingness to assist in plans of sex and/or vengeance.

"Did you do it yet?"

I glanced at my good boss, better friend, and annoying wing-woman, repeating the same answer I'd given her the last time she'd asked—a whole five minutes before. "No."

"Come on. It's died down. Perfect timing."

It had died down, but it wouldn't last. The way-too-early crowd had come, but there was still the regular morning rush and then the stragglers. Since Harlow was busy at some wedding expo with her mom, it was just Piper, Soph, and me. I didn't have time to stop and text.

Plus, Lars was likely super busy. I didn't want to bother him.

And there was also the fact I was a big coward.

"I'm not even sure I'm going to do it today. Maybe I'll wait." I was partially messing with Piper, but it was mostly the being-a-wuss thing.

I knew Lars wanted me. Oh God, did I know it. I'd felt the proof. Seen the proof. Spent a wet, sticky, needy night at Wicked covered in the proof.

I wasn't scared of his rejection, per se. I just wasn't great with being vulnerable, especially when it came to matters of desirability.

"Don't you dare back out now," Piper hissed, garnering attention from the few customers hanging out. "You are an ultra-babe, and you know it. Now rub his face in it. He deserves to feel your sexy wrath... or something."

"No, no, keep going," Eli said from the doorway as he clutched a cup of coffee. "This is the most empowered I've felt in a while. I am woman, hear me roar. I don't need no man. I just need a girl with big—"

"Eli," Piper warned.

"Big dreams, Piper. Big dreams." He blinked his eyes innocently at her, giving off tattooed-boy-next-door vibes. "What did you think I was gonna say?"

She just rolled her own eyes back at him. "You know exactly what."

"You know I'm a very motivated person, especially after one of these pep talks. I need her to have that same drive." In a blink, that wholesome act was gone, leaving nothing but trouble. "And a thick ass and soft everything wouldn't hurt, either."

"Watch your mouth. This is a place of business," Piper called to Eli as he walked back into the kitchen, chuckling as he went.

"You can cross him off your matchmaking list for Sophie," I pointed out as I did busywork—all in an attempt to ignore my phone and distract my impatient boss.

"Not doing a good job playing it cool, am I?" She shot me a wry smile and shrugged. "He was never on it. They aren't each other's type. Soph is so sweet and quiet and should be protected. Which means she needs someone rough and protective and, oh, I dunno.... on the *bossy* side."

That described most of the Hyde men *and* their extending factions of friends. But the emphasis she'd put on the word bossy gave me a solid inkling who she had in mind.

"Scheduling a girls' night at Rye soon?" I asked.

Dropping her jaw and widening her eyes in faux surprise, Piper gasped, "How'd you know?"

"Wild guess."

"Honestly, that's just a coincidence. We could do it at someone's house, a club, a restaurant, a Target parking lot. I'm tempted to sign us all up for a Freedom Trail walking tour just to get my girls together. It's long overdue." Using that segue, she fluttered her lashes. "You know what else is overdue? Sending a certain text." When I just blinked at her, my face blank, she threw her hands up in the air. "This was supposed to be payback against him, not me."

"Payback?" Sophie asked as she came through with a muffin restock.

"The ultimate payback for someone who left her high and dry," Piper said, laughing before turning to whisper, "Or *not* dry, in this case."

I whacked her arm, which just made her laugh more. "Keep this up, I'll tell your husband about your picture."

She gasped, playfully affronted that I would threaten to get her laid sooner rather than later. "Killjoy."

I wasn't a killjoy, but I was evil enough to extend Piper's impatient misery while ending my own anticipatory anxiety. Not telling her I was finally doing it, I waited until she was otherwise occupied to take out my phone.

No text. No cute flirty message. I just added the picture to my text thread with Lars and hit send before I changed my mind. Shoving my phone in my pocket, I tried to ignore it while being painfully aware of every non-existent vibration.

He's just busy.

I know this.

I kept telling myself that as the crickets from my phone stretched. The second wave of customers filled the bakery, and I threw myself into making sure each one had the best damn service of their life.

Damn it.

I was boxing up the millionth cupcake of the morning—or so it seemed—when my stomach tightened. The hairs on the back of my neck stood. The familiar rumble sounded in my ears, ricocheting down my body until I could almost feel the vibrations. In my chest. My stomach. Between my legs.

Everywhere.

Lars wasn't a chatty texter, so I hadn't expected a lengthy paragraph or a heart-eye emoji or anything like that in response to my picture. I'd figured he'd send something short, sweet, and filthy. He was good at that. Riling me up with minimal gruff words.

I certainly hadn't anticipated him showing up on a day when he'd said his schedule was so loaded, there were overlaps.

"You sent the picture," Piper gasped, excitement in her voice as she stood beside me.

It wasn't a question, but I answered her anyway, not tearing my gaze from the large windows. "Yes."

A buzz of anticipation zipped through my veins like a live current as I watched him approach the door, cutting through the waiting line.

No one said anything to him. It'd be insane to argue with a man with thunder on his face and fire in his eyes.

As his large frame filled the doorway, even my instincts were telling me it was flight not fight time. But I knew better. Because it wasn't anger in his expression.

It was lust.

It was want.

It was *need*.

It was the same way he'd looked at me while he'd gone down on me against his bike. And against his desk. It was the way he'd watched me while he'd shot his come on me, marking me as his before he'd even been inside me.

It was all that and so much more. Tenfold. A millionfold.

My brain yelled at me to move, to meet him halfway. But I was frozen, entranced by his lust-filled stare.

High off it.

His single-minded focus stayed on me as his powerful strides ate up the distance, giving no thought or regard to the other people in the room. I thought he was going to kiss me like the week before. I hoped he would. My brain kept up its demands, telling my body to move, to lean into him, to climb him like a tree, and kiss him.

I was a strong, independent woman. I didn't need to wait for him to do it.

Before I had the chance, Lars was bending down. Then I was soaring through the air before ending upside down with his shoulder in my gut.

He didn't say a word, just turned and strode back toward the exit, carrying me with him.

"Wait!" But he didn't slow, even as I shifted in his hold, trying to clear my hair from my face. I was able to catch a glimpse of Piper and Soph watching us. Rather than being upset at being ditched, the smiles plastered on their faces made it clear they were unbothered by Lars stealing me away. Basically kidnapping me.

I mean, I was also unbothered by it, but still. They didn't know that. A little concern for me would've been nice.

That brief glimpse was all I got before Lars' free hand came down on my ass—and not gently. It slid down to span my thigh, holding me in place so I'd stop wiggling. Unfortunately for him, his fingers had ended up pressed against my pussy. I didn't stop moving.

Couldn't.

I did it more.

Lars remained silent, his fingertips digging in was his only reaction. Once we reached his bike, he swung his leg over and settled me straddling him. I didn't have the chance to say anything as he quickly grabbed the helmet—*my* helmet—waiting on the handlebar and fastened it on me before pulling his on. He didn't bother with the clip, as if the extra ten seconds to secure it would be too long. I grabbed the straps and was about to lecture him on safety when he clutched my ass and shifted. The bike roared to life beneath us, and he eased out of the spot.

I let out a squeal, spider monkey clutching at him. Even as close as I was, he used his grip on my ass to press me tighter still. It was hot.

It was also terrifying.

I wasn't confident on a bike to begin with. Riding backward, unable to see where we were going, made my chest tighten. The rush of adrenaline that already tingled through my body and made my head spin was more than enough.

I'd rather not die of a heart attack before we got to the fun part.

Leaning back, I frantically shook my head at Lars.

He rolled to a stop in the middle of the lot and practically flung me around his body. Okay, not really. He was cautious with me—always—but there was urgency in his movements. Once my front was to his back and I was securely gripping him, he took off.

The chilled wind whipped my sensitive skin even as the sun overhead warmed it, causing goosebumps to spread. The vibration from the bike rumbled between my thighs, traveling up. Lars continuously dropped his hand from the bar, making my heart race and my panties melt as he touched me. Often. My hands. My calves. My knees.

I was hyperaware of every sensation. Every touch. Every rush.

When we slowed for a red light, I stretched to look over his shoulder and realized we weren't heading to my place. Gripping his shirt, I shouted, "My house."

"Mine is closer," he called back, once again using the brief break to touch me to stoke my desire higher.

At the rate we were going, I'd combust before we arrived.

That didn't stop me from repeating, "My house."

With my body pressed to his, I could feel his already hard body go to marble before he gave a chin lift, checked traffic, and hung a uey.

I knew how he'd taken my request. That I wanted to go home because I'd changed my mind. Or was undecided. That I was doubtful. It wasn't any of that. I'd never been more sure of anything in my life. It was just...

I wanted our first time to be at my place. In the home I loved so much. I wanted that memory. Of something good. Something wild. Not settling and cheating and toxic resentment.

Since the motor was too loud for me to even attempt to explain what I didn't fully understand, I let my hands do the reassuring. I ran one of them down from his abs. Down. Down.

Landing on his cock, I savored the feel of it hardening from just that slight touch. And then I cupped his thick length as best as I could with the pesky denim in the way. It hardened further under my palm while my other one felt the groan that rolled up his chest.

I released my grip only for him to harshly encircle my wrist and shove my hand harder against him.

Biting my bottom lip, I waited until he returned his hold to the handlebar before moving back to his abs. Then down to his thigh. Then his cock. Then thigh again. Teasing him with light grazes and firm grasps.

His muscles bunched tighter the more I played. Our speed crept higher. Not enough to be dangerous, but I wasn't sure I'd have cared if it were. The heady power of his reaction made me reckless. I wanted more of it.

I wanted to ride the wild wave that'd overtaken me. Drowned me.

I wanted to ride the high of his lust. His desire.

I wanted to ride... him.

My plans for vengeance and torment backfired.

Majorly.

With each stretching, never-ending mile, I regretted my choice more and more. I should've gone with the closer destination. His place, mine, off a dirt path, a dark alley. It didn't matter. I just wanted him. Badly. Right then, I'd have settled for the nearest large shrub. But when

I looked to the side to see what my hypothetical options were, I saw the unmistakable hedgerow belonging to my neighbor, Mrs. Jordan.

Considering she'd been known to call the cops, mayor, neighborhood watch, and any other point of authority to complain about the pesky squirrels daring to ruin her meticulous horticulture, I doubted she'd be cool with two adults planting a different kind of nut. So to speak.

If my house wasn't two doors down, I may have been tempted to risk it. I was that worked up. Beyond ready.

I wasn't the only one.

Because as soon as we pulled into my driveway, Lars killed the engine and dismounted. I didn't have time to stand or pull off my helmet before I was in his arms, my limbs wrapped around him. Taking the porch steps two at a time, he paused for me to unlock the door and punch in the alarm code, his busy hands distracting me the whole time.

Teasing up my throat to unclip and remove my helmet.

Running down the curve of my breast.

My side.

My hip.

Tightening his grip and lowering me just enough that his hardness was pressed between my legs.

It took more focus and effort than it should've, but I managed to unarm the alarm before the security company sent out the cavalry. The confirmation beep had barely sounded when what limited control Lars had been exercising was gone. He snapped.

Fisting my hair, his mouth crashed down on mine. His tongue pressed in, battling for supremacy. Possession.

It was an easy battle.

Or maybe an easy surrender on my part.

Either way, I clutched his shirt and opened wider, giving him the access he demanded.

The ownership.

Of the kiss. My body. *Me.*

He turned us until I slammed into the side of a banister, and not gently. Not that I cared, I just wanted more contact. More pressure. More friction. But Lars must've cared because he tore his mouth away and scanned my face. He didn't see pain there, but what he saw was enough to make him release a pained groan of his own before he took the stairs two at a time. I barely held in a moan, my core bouncing against him. Instead, I put my mouth to better use. Licking his neck. Dragging my lips across the scruff. Nipping his biteable jaw.

I didn't realize we'd made it to the top of the steps until my back hit a wall, the pictures rattling.

"Christ, you're gonna be the fuckin' death of me," Lars bit out between hard kisses.

"You can die later." I arched my back into his touch as he palmed my breast. "Much later."

"Dare the devil himself to fuckin' try dragging me away." With that growled challenge, Lars twisted away from the wall and lowered me to stand before his mouth crashed back to mine.

And everything went *wild*.

Shoes were kicked off.

Shirts were frantically tugged off and tossed to land wherever.

Every inch of accessible skin was kissed.

Bit.

Caressed.

Scratched.

The short distance from the hallway to my room took longer because neither of us were capable of keeping our hands—and mouths—off each other. When my legs hit something, I pried my eyes open to see we'd managed to make it over to my bed.

With deft fingers, Lars undid my bra and slid it down my arms. The fabric had barely cleared my nipples when he bent to take one in his mouth. Holding it between his teeth, he rapidly flicked his tongue across the hardened peak before sucking. My hips rocked. I needed relief. Pressure. *Something*.

But all I found was air.

I'm in danger of imploding, I'm sure of it.

Death by arousal.

My fingers shook as I gripped his jeans—not with nerves, but intense desire.

Okay, and maybe a bit of nerves.

Unfastening the button, I slid the zipper down carefully, expecting to feel boxers. Instead, it was hot, veined skin that met my fingers. I pulled back, his teeth dragging across my nipple as I moved. A tremble and a moan shot through me, and I was torn between needing to see him and needing him to do that again.

Seeing him won.

With his zipper down, I'd thought his cock would spring free. But the long length of him was still held by his jeans, curved across his pelvis in a way that didn't seem real... or real comfortable, for that matter.

How is that going to fit inside me?

Logically, I knew the human body was capable of such amazing feats, but the longer I looked, the more my nerves grew.

My wetness, too.

"Fuck, I'm already dead. Only explanation."

My gaze darted up to Lars' hooded eyes, the dark blue nearly black, even in the bright morning sun that streamed through my windows. "Explanation of what?"

"How a bastard like me got so fuckin' lucky." His voice was rough when he ordered, "Take it out."

My brain hadn't even communicated with my hand before it automatically moved to do as he'd demanded. Shoving the denim away, I finally got an unobstructed view of him—no fabric or rough stroking fist in the way.

My mouth watered.

I'd never been big on oral—receiving or giving. I wasn't even any good at it. But everything was different with Lars. I'd loved when he'd gone down on me, easily coming from his skilled mouth. It was my turn to try. To taste him. To feel the thick veins against my tongue.

Desperate enough to not overthink, I started to sink to my knees. Before I could, he gripped me under my arms and tossed me to the mattress.

"I want to—"

"Know what you want to do, baby. And I want it, too. Aching for it. But if I get that fuckin' mouth around me, I'm not gonna be able to stop myself from coming. And, right now, I *need* to be inside you." Gripping the waistband of my leggings, he gave me a smirk. "We'll get to the rest later."

"Because we've got time?"

The smile died on his face. Unguarded. Real. Raw. There was nothing but hunger and intensity as his gaze seared me until I lost my breath. "Fuck yeah, we *do*."

In a blink, my pants and panties were gone, and Lars was settled between my spread thighs. His lips were on mine, putting even more... *everything* into it. Overwhelming me. Devouring me. Owning me.

I'd never been kissed like that, and, even if I lived to be two hundred, I knew I'd never be kissed like that again.

Not by anyone else, at least.

His hard cock was trapped between us, sliding between my lower lips to grind against my clit and tease my entrance. So close. So damn close to where I needed him, yet so frustratingly far.

His palm cupped the back of my head while his other dipped between us. Knuckles grazing in a maddening way, he moved with the same urgency I felt as he adjusted himself. Lining himself up. Just his thick head was enough to stretch me, causing a blissful pleasure-pain to radiate.

Pulling away just as much as he had to, his lips brushed mine. "Condom."

"Pill. Clean," I shot back with no thought or hesitation.

"Fuckin' *Jesus*," he bit out as he slammed into me in one violent thrust. Filling me so fully. So completely.

And then he stopped, planting himself deep.

Resting his forehead to mine, his rough breath warmed my face as his body stayed rigid. After a long moment, he lifted his head so he was looking down at me. He fisted my hair in one hand, angling my face up. His other thumb skimmed the side of my arched neck and along my jaw to land on my mouth. "Hasn't been anyone since the day I walked into the bakery and saw you behind the counter. Not in real life and not in my head." His calloused thumb dragged across my lower lip, his eyes heating as he raptly followed the motion. "Obsessed after one pretty smile."

With that stunning proclamation dropped like it was nothing, he rocked his hips.

But it was my turn to stop him with a hand to his shoulder.

He froze, his questioning gaze on me.

I'd never be able to see that spot in the hallway without thinking of him having me against the wall. I'd never be able to look at my bed without remembering the way his thick cock filled me to bursting.

If I was making memories with a man straight out of my wildest fantasies, I was gonna go all out.

Leaning up, I kissed him, running my hand from his shoulder to rub across his head. I loved his hair. The way the short buzz felt under my palms. The way he always leaned into my touch. "Never change your hair."

"Never," he agreed between harsh kisses, his pelvis grinding against me, pushing him somehow deeper still.

The sensory overload was so good, I nearly forgot why I'd made him stop. I returned my hand to his shoulder and pushed again, shimmying up and up and *up* until his cock slipped free. "On your back."

Lars didn't say anything, but a hint of amusement infused the heat in his eyes, as if he were humoring me. Once he rolled to his back, I threw a leg over his torso, my sex pressed to his thighs.

It reminded me of how it felt to straddle his motorcycle. To have my thighs pressed tight against something so powerful. Something so exciting. It was a rush. Not because it was new or different—though it was both—but because it just was. I was willing to bet it always would be.

And, for the time being at least, it was all mine.

He was all mine.

Fisting his hard-on, I went up onto my knees and paused. In theory, my idea had been a good one. A brilliant one, even. But I hadn't thought out the logistics and apprehension set in. Rather than being filled by Lars, it was self-doubt that churned in my stomach.

My old wounds, telling me I'd never be enough. I'd never do enough. That there was a reason I'd never gotten to be on top.

Because I wasn't good enough.

Despite how quickly my thoughts had been able to race, trying their hardest to undo all the anticipation of the moment, I'd only hesitated a few seconds. That'd been a few seconds too long for Lars. His large hand encircled my throat, barely squeezing the sides as he yanked me down to him.

Kissing me until the shadowed memories in my brain cleared, he gruffly whispered, "Not a patient man, baby. Been waiting for this too damn long for you to tease me." After another hard kiss, he used his hold to lift me back up. "Now give me what I need before I gotta take it."

A hard tremble coursed through me, and I put my hand on his chest to support myself before I fell.

His words.

The look in his eyes—like a wildfire and a thunderstorm mixing in a midnight sky.

The feel of his hard length trapped between us, stretching up his stomach.

But the thing that worked to heal my old wounds was his heart beating under my palm.

Racing.

Pounding.

I did that.

I made a man like Lars' heart rate skyrocket. It was enough to shut my thoughts up. Turn them off.

Turn me on.

Rearranging myself, I lined him up and slid down. Slowly. Agonizingly slow. Partially to watch him battle to keep control, his fingers gripping my hips to that point of pleasure-pain. But mostly it was because my body needed to adjust to his size, the angle, and my movements.

"You can take it," Lars bit out between clenched teeth. I dropped a little farther, both of us moaning at the sensation. "That's my good girl."

God.

I wanted to hear him say that on repeat. Make it my ringtone. My personal motivational soundtrack.

I sank down suddenly, filling myself with him until I was sure I'd burst if I moved. Or go mad if I didn't move.

I wasn't sure which, but my body decided for me.

My hips rocked slowly before circling. The way Lars' coarse hair rubbed my clit was good. Amazing. But I needed more.

Rising and falling, I found my rhythm. Gained my confidence. I moved faster, spurred on by Lars' low groans and rasped praise.

Not to mention, my own growing pleasure.

Lars moved, and my hands shot to his shoulders so I didn't fall—and so I could push him back down if needed. But he just leaned up, his abs bunching deliciously as his gaze locked onto our connection.

"Look how beautifully you take me." His hands dropped lower on my hips so his thumbs could hold my pussy lips apart. Letting him see all of us. All of me. The way he stretched me. "Perfect. Fuckin' perfect, baby. Made for me."

My speed and desperation grew with each touch. Each rumbled word. I wasn't the only one. Lars' pelvis rose to meet mine, slamming up into me as I dropped down. His grip turned rougher, his words filthier.

No thoughts.

No doubts.

No wounds.

It was just Lars and me.

The coil in my lower stomach twisted. Tightened to the point of frustration. I was so close, but every time it nearly came undone, I lost my rhythm and was flung further from release. My orgasm, desire, and fervor heightened until I worried it would break me.

Shatter me.

Reading me as easily as always, Lars stretched a thumb to stroke my clit while his other hand used his hold on my hip to move me up and down his length.

Harder.

Faster.

Savage thrusts until we were coated in a thin layer of sweat, our breaths coming in harsh pants.

The steady, forceful pace was what I needed. My body didn't stop moving—couldn't stop moving. Every tiny atom exploded with pleasure that radiated out from my sex, as if the blood in my veins had been replaced by effervescent bubbles and electricity.

"Hold tight, baby," Lars ordered.

I expected him to flip me, and although I loved riding him, I'd take anything he gave. Over, under, side, front. I'd have twisted like a pretzel if it meant he stayed deep inside me.

He didn't roll, though.

But that didn't mean he hadn't taken over. Taken control.

Gripping me tight, his upward thrusts slammed into me as he pulled me down to meet each one. His hooded gaze moved between our connection, my bouncing breasts, my face, and back again. Each look urged him on until his movements were wild and frantic.

Brutal.

The tension in my body didn't slowly build. There was no working to find it. No chasing. It snuck up on me fast, yet no less powerful than the first time. When I came apart again, Lars' own grunts filled my head, mixing with claiming words that made my orgasm stretch and stretch and stretch.

When Lars stilled, planted deep, I flopped forward into a graceless heap. My face pressed to his chest, my lips skimming the skin there as I caught my breath. "I've never done that before."

At my murmured words, Lars' body under me froze. I could literally feel the tension infusing his muscles. I could almost hear his thoughts.

"I've done... *it*," I amended. "Just never that way. Or that good. I didn't know it could be that good. I've just only... we only... He didn't like—"

"Don't fuckin' wanna hear the specifics, Joss," he bit out, cutting off my awkward rambling.

Oh shit.

He used my real name.

I sat up so I could see him. And then instantly regretted it. Kinda. He was pissed, but it was still hot.

His expression and voice softened, but his grip on my hips didn't. "Don't need to hear what that bastard didn't like. Just wanna know what you like."

"It's a short list," I admitted quietly.

"Okay, then I wanna know what you wanna try."

"That's a much longer list."

His lips tipped in a smirk, but like the rest of him, it dripped with fire and sex.

Moving carefully, Lars slid free and rolled me to my back before going onto his elbow at my side. His gaze stayed locked on mine, intense and sweet and hot and a million other emotions I couldn't decipher. "My woman was tired of waiting."

He was right. I had been. It'd been *so* worth it, though.

I didn't get the chance to respond when he stretched an arm down so his finger could run between my legs.

Teasing across my swollen clit.

Rekindling the ache he'd just eased.

Running his finger through our mixed releases.

My lids closed on their own as my hips shot off the bed. It should've been weird. Gross, even. Instead, it was one of the sexiest things I'd ever experienced.

I wasn't the only one to think so.

Because pushed against my side, Lars' still semi-hard cock jerked.

Before I could reach for him, he rolled to stand.

My heart sank.

I knew he had a full day of meetings followed by the usual crazy Saturday night at Wicked. That he'd pushed things off for me wasn't just a big deal.

It was a huge one.

All good things must come to an end and blah blah blah. I got it. But that didn't mean I was happy about it.

I assumed he'd grab his clothes from where they were scattered, but he moved out of the room, naked and unashamed.

I didn't blame him.

His body was an absolute work of art. Etched lines, thick muscles, a mix of monotone and colorful tattoos covered much of his tanned skin, that mouthwatering hip indent that led to an impressive... everything. If I were him, I'd never wear a shirt.

Or pants for that matter.

I was curious what he was up to, but not enough to get out of bed. Instead, I closed my eyes, flopped back, and smiled. I'd finally had sex with Lars. After months of wondering. Of wanting. Of thinking there was no way and then being so close, only to get interrupted when we got close.

And it'd been even better than my many fantasies.

Being on top had surpassed them, too. I was woefully out of shape for it, but I'd do it again in a heartbeat. Well, once my thighs stopped burning and twitching.

I shouldn't have skipped leg day the last... twenty-four years.

Whatever, totally worth the strain.

And worth going for what I wanted.

My lids popped open to stare at my ceiling—a different section than usual. I leaned up and, for the first time, realized we hadn't even made it to the middle of the mattress. We'd been at the bottom.

To make it even better, the sun had been shining through my window.

No subpar sex, always in the same position, always in the dark.

I wasn't comparing Lars to Peter since that was an insult and a waste of time. I was comparing myself with my old self. With what I'd convinced myself was normal. With what I'd felt I deserved. With all the many hang-ups and wounds that'd festered over the years before becoming so unbearably deep once I was single. I'd been so bitter and hurt, I hadn't thought I'd ever heal.

But I had, more than I realized.

I'd spoken up about what I wanted. I'd trusted Lars. I hadn't thought about our positions or the brightness of the room. And once he filled me, I hadn't been even a tiny bit self-conscious while riding him.

Progress.

Lars returning to the room was the only thing that could get me to move. I was spent, but I couldn't resist the view.

The disgruntled look he aimed my way wasn't what I'd expected, but it was still worth tilting my head to see. "Got shit for food, hotcakes."

My body may have been capable of minimal effort, but my brain wasn't, so my witty reply was, "Do not."

"Fruits and vegetables and grains and shit."

"That's a balanced diet," I pointed out.

"Yeah, for a fuckin' gerbil."

He had a point. Since I spent my mornings surrounded by sinful baked goods and most nights eating dinner with him at Wicked, I needed some semblance of balance in my diet.

My brain decided to catch up to the conversation, and my brows furrowed. "Why were you in my kitchen?"

"Your stomach growled."

"It did?"

With a chin lift, he prowled toward me, dipping to grab his phone from his jeans without missing a step. It was surprisingly graceful for such a large man. I admired the way he moved with such control over his body.

But I was also a woman.

And he was also naked.

Which meant my eyes kept dropping to admire something else about him.

His knees went to the mattress, and he dropped, half his body hovering over me so his face was close to mine. "Keep looking at me like that, baby, I'm not gonna be able to feed you." He leaned down farther, running his nose along mine before adding, "And you're gonna need the energy for what I have planned."

My brain automatically started flipping through local restaurants like a mental Yelp because I really freakin' wanted to know what that plan was.

Plus, I hadn't noticed or cared that I was hungry, but once he mentioned it...

"You're not leaving?" I asked at his implication that he'd be there a while. "I know you're busy today, so I totally get it—"

"Fuck," he kissed me, hard but quick, "no. Put Sasha in charge of some shit she could handle, told the rest to fuck off."

He hadn't just made time for me.

He'd made *time*.

"Finally have you," he whispered, his gaze traveling over my face like he couldn't believe it. Like he was the one in awe. "Have to pry me off with a crowbar and shove me out the door to get rid of me."

I had no intention of doing either.

Before I could say as much, he sat back up and unlocked his phone.

His lock screen was the generic factory setting one.

His home screen, though?

It was me.

More specifically, the picture I'd sent.

Bent over the table at Sweets You Rock.

I may have been fully clothed, but that didn't stop it from being overtly sexy. Especially to him. He'd mentioned more than once how much he'd enjoyed my 'fine ass' in that position.

"You set it as your background?" I was horrified yet amused.

"Fuck yeah I did. Would wallpaper every damn room in my condo with it if I could. But then I'd have to gouge out the HOA's eyes when they come to bitch about the view through the bay window." He dragged a knuckle down my breast, skimming it around my nipple. "Or I'd die from lack of blood flow from being constantly hard."

I shook my head, not laughing because... well, I wasn't sure he was completely joking. "What about when someone sees your phone?"

"No one but me does."

"And me," I pointed out, realizing he hadn't attempted to hide his screen. I'd had a full view of it *and* his passcode.

"And you," he agreed, still unfazed that I looked at his screen. No dodginess. No tension. Not poised and ready to swipe at *junk* notifications that popped up before I could see what it was. "What's my woman want for lunch?"

"I can make something," I offered.

He didn't respond verbally, but the taciturn look he gave said it all.

"Sandwich," I said, choosing something fast, easy, and that wouldn't leave me feeling too bloated to move.

Like Lars had said...

He had plans.

"ON YOUR BACK, BABY."

Plans hadn't been a figure of speech.

It also hadn't been an exaggeration.

If anything, it was an understatement.

After eating sandwiches naked, we'd showered while Lars had thoroughly soaped me up. I'd assumed we were going to relax or talk. Instead, he'd carried me back to bed and made me ride his face.

I'd barely finished coming before he'd ordered me to my back. My body was sated goo as I gracelessly flopped to the side, hoping it looked sexier than it felt.

He must've thought so because Lars' cock jerked as he looked down at me. His large hands went to my thighs, his fingertips digging in as he spread them wider. "So fuckin' pretty."

Positioning himself between my legs, he filled me but didn't thrust. He stayed planted deep until I was rocking my hips, greedy for the little bit of friction I could get. It wasn't enough, though. It was even less when he pinned my hips with his own until I wanted to weep and beg.

A sinister smirk curved his lips as his gaze grew hooded while he watched me fight to move. To rock. To create some sort of motion. He was getting off on the torture he was inflicting.

The bastard.

Before I could curse him to hell and back, he shifted forward, the coarse hair grinding against my clit, making me sharply inhale as my hips rose. Once my brain stopped short-circuiting, I tilted my head to watch helplessly as he opened a bedside table drawer.

The drawer.

Theeeee drawer.

My irrational panic grew to an irrational horror as he produced my vibrator. Not my simple one. Nor my wand. Not even the rabbit.

No. Like the sword in the stone, he pulled out my Excalibur. Bright pink, it had a curved shaft on one end and clit suction on the other.

Unlike my ex, Lars wouldn't judge me. He literally owned a strip club. His job was sex, even if he was professional about it. Professional *and* sex positive, never shaming the dancers.

I was *not* as comfortable as he was. Seeing him hold my silicone ol' reliable made me want to shrivel up and perish on the spot.

"How'd—" I started, but it came out about fifty octaves too high. I cleared my throat and tried again. "How'd you know what was in there?"

"Looked when you were in the bathroom," he said with not an ounce of shame. Totally unabashed in his snooping.

I'll remember that. Turnabout being fair play and all.

"Thought about this the whole shower," he continued, his voice rougher and his cock somehow harder inside me.

Centimeter by so many centimeters, he slowly slid out of me before replacing his cock with the fake one. The one that'd, up until that day, seemed so sufficient.

Right then, even with it seated fully inside me, it was lacking.

"Show me," he ordered.

He can't possibly mean...

Can he?

I froze, even as anticipation and anxiety and arousal filled me in equal measures until I was vibrating with it. "Why?"

"Want to see."

"*Why*?" The one word was packed with so much repression and horror, a puritan would call me a prude.

"Curious."

I blinked at him. "You don't think it's insulting?"

It wasn't the right word, but I couldn't think of how to explain it. In my limited experience, certain men thought of vibrators as substitutes.

Or replacements.

Certain men were also right about that, but still.

Lars gave me another smirk, that one loaded with fire and humor and, thank God, tenderness. "Fuck no. It's my..." He tilted his head. "My coworker, not my competition." He wiggled the *coworker* in question, letting out a groan as if he were the one being tormented. "Show me, baby."

No.

I could *not* do that.

The excitement that filled his eyes as his gaze ran over me was enough to make me drunk on it. On him. That rush skyrocketed as he sat back and fisted his cock.

Okay. I could do that.

I could *so* do that.

Licking my lips, I pulled the bottom one between my teeth as I pushed the two buttons, making the shaft vibrate as the other part gently suctioned my clit.

The buildup.

What Lars was doing.

What I was doing.

It all worked together to make my skin flush, sweat breaking out. I was overwhelmed and overthinking, wondering if I looked good. If it was what he expected. If he liked it.

He stopped stroking, and my heart fell. It wasn't good. I wasn't turning him on.

But when I risked a peek down, his cock was still hard. It twitched and my gaze darted back up to Lars' face.

"Fuckin' love the way you look at me, baby," he rumbled, reaching out to pluck my nipple. He teased it between his deft fingers.

I knew he was creating a distraction.

And it worked.

I pressed the button and increased the vibration.

"Wanna know why I want to watch?"

I gave a quick, jerking nod.

Rather than answering, he asked another question. "Do you think of me when you play with this perfect pussy?"

God.

I increased the suction.

His hand went back to his cock. He squeezed it tight, dragging his fist up. "While I'm in my bed or my shower or my damn office picturing you while I stroke my cock, are you here playing with yourself and thinking of me?"

I increased the vibration a couple more times.

"Do you make yourself come, imagining it's my dick filling you?"

I increased the suction until it was a hair away from too much. Gripping the base, I rocked it up and down so it stroked my clit the way I liked. I spread my legs wider, showing Lars what he wanted to see.

"Tell me," he ordered, stroking faster.

My eyes closed. My back arched. My thoughts went wild, a vortex of depravity. Before I exploded into a billion pieces of nothing, I held it off long enough to force out two words.

"Every. Time."

A million miles away, I heard his grunt, but it was mostly lost in the blood rushing through my ears and the voltage sparking in every atom of my body.

It'd just started to ebb when the toy was pulled free, replaced by something better.

Lars' unhinged thrusts shifted my body up the bed as he prolonged my orgasm before launching me toward the next. He lowered himself so our bodies were tight together, each thrust clipped and brutal as he ground deeper. "Since the first time you smiled at me, it's always been your pussy. Always been you."

I couldn't breathe. Couldn't think. Couldn't move.

Taking him over and over, my head swam and I saw stars as my orgasm ripped through me.

Ripped me apart.

Lars' primal groan cut through the haze as he came, filling me until I could feel it dripping out around his thickness.

Slowly, my brain returned to my body and my heart slowed to a human pace rather than a hummingbird one.

Lars gave me his weight, his breathing harsh as he buried his face in my neck. In that moment, I knew one thing to my very used and tender core.

His coworker was good...

But Lars was irreplaceable.

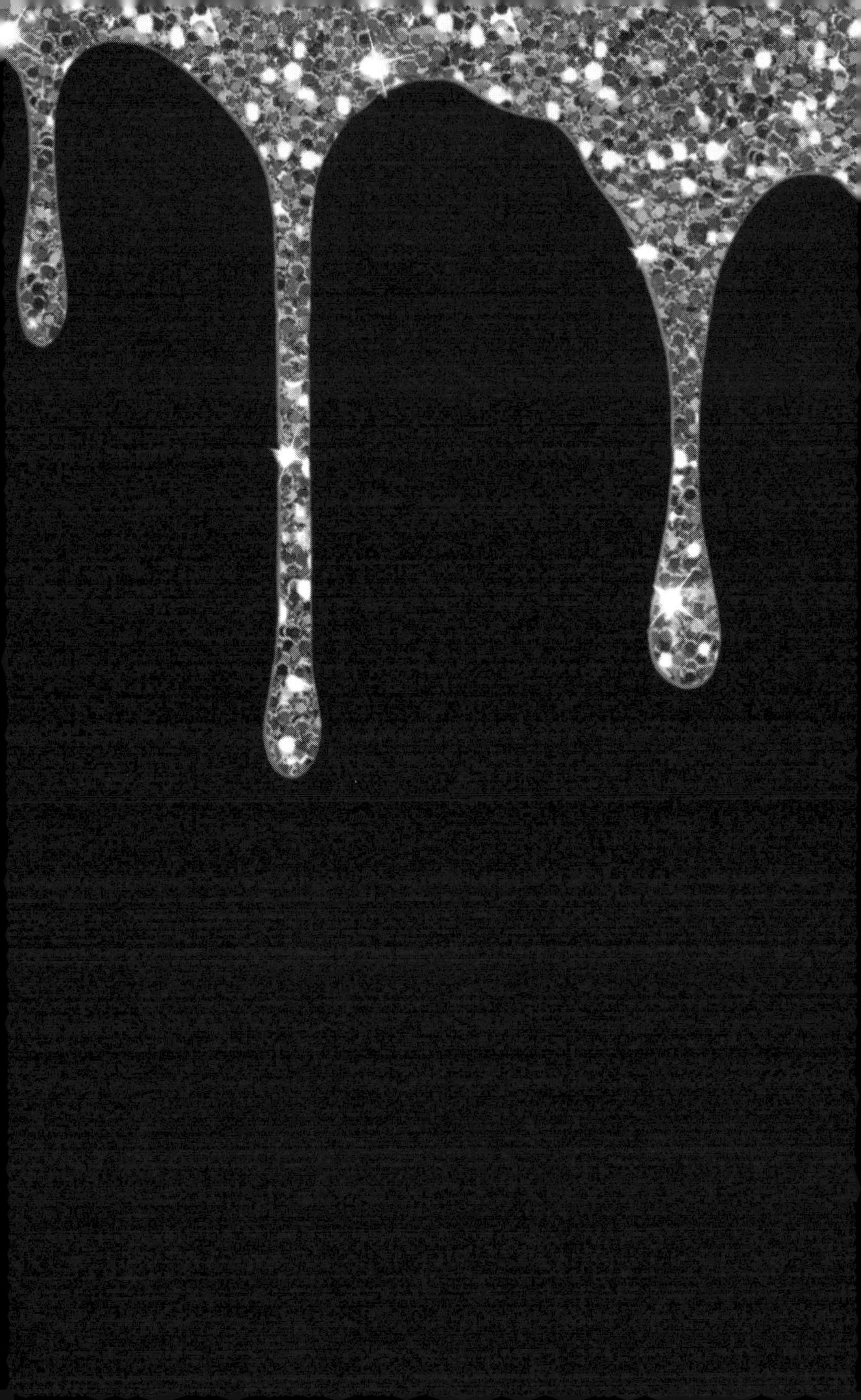

EIGHTEEN
Tentacles and Crabs

JOSS

I WAS SORE.

Exhausted.

Likely dehydrated.

Definitely satisfied.

Happy.

More than twenty-four hours of sex, delivery food, and movies interrupted by more sex does that to a woman.

I hadn't thought it was possible for a man to go more than once every few days. At least not without popping little blue pills like they were Pez candy coming out of a penis shaped dispenser. It reaffirmed something I'd already known.

I'd been with the wrong man.

We'd slept in—something I was rarely capable of doing—before Lars had woken me with his mouth between my legs. After I'd come, we'd hopped in the shower where my greedy mouth had returned the favor, and then he'd fixed me breakfast.

He'd grumbled about gerbil food the whole time even as he'd made a week's worth of eggs, turkey sausage, and pancakes.

The man could eat—in every sense of the word.

It also seemed he was a bottomless pit because he'd just pulled me onto his lap, kissed me stupid, and then asked if I was hungry.

"We had breakfast a couple hours ago," I pointed out.

He lifted the remote, muting the loud announcers who were arguing over their biased picks for the day's football games before gripping my hips. He ground me down into his hardening cock. Since he was only wearing his jeans and I was in a pair of thin PJ shorts, it would be easy to move two layers of fabric out of the way.

I may have been sore and tired, but I wasn't dead.

"Gotta keep my energy up," he rumbled, his gaze dropping to zero in on my nipples pressing against my tank top.

"You don't have to leave?"

I hated to ask. I didn't want to think about the outside world. I loved the bubble we were in, just the two of us. Enjoying each other.

Taking our time.

But we both had responsibilities, so I was surprised.

Surprised, but pleased.

And by pleased, I meant happy as hell.

"Told you, hotcakes, you'll have to pry me off with a crowbar."

I grinned up at him. "I'll cancel Sunday dinner with my family then."

"Don't gotta do that."

A Sunday of Lars, more sex, and no *family dinner? Trust me, not a hardship.*

"It's okay," I rushed out, a little eagerly. Not wanting to scare him away with tales of my crazy family, I left it at that.

He lifted his chin in acknowledgement, but he wasn't looking at me. When his jaw clenched until a muscle ticked, I was about to ask what was wrong before I followed his gaze over my shoulder and saw injury reports sprawled across the pregame screen.

The starting defense had more holes than Swiss cheese. It was enough to make any fan worried. It was also enough to make me glad I was canceling out on family dinner. My dad would likely spend the day yelling at the TV until my mom lost her shit at him.

"What do you want for lunch?" I leaned up to kiss his tight jaw before adding, "You're going to need the energy for what I have planned."

I didn't have anything planned, but I couldn't resist the chance to use his own words from the day before against him.

Game tension forgotten, his body softened. Well, parts of it. He twisted a lock of my hair around his finger. “You want tacos?”

“What kinda psychopath doesn’t want tacos?”

The side of his lip curved up, and he started shifting me off him.

Without thought, I reached out and gripped his shoulders. I didn’t want to move. Ever.

Tenderness and molten heat infused his expression in equal measure. “Gotta grab my phone from your room.”

“I’ll order on my phone,” I said, grabbing it from the couch and opening the delivery service app.

“Your app linked to my bank account?” he asked.

“No.”

My cell was plucked from my hands before being tossed to the table behind me. “Then you’re not ordering till it is.”

“That’s not fair.”

“Sure, it is. I’m the one who wants something other than gerbil food.”

“So if I suggest dinner, I can pay?”

“If I’m not around, have at it. But if you’re eating with me, I’m paying.”

“That’s archaic and stupid.”

“You think that now, just wait till we live together.”

The retort I had queued up fritzed out, along with my brain.

Lars took advantage of my catatonic state and slid me off to the side, not bothering to hide his smirk.

I knew I needed to move. If I didn’t send a text that I wouldn’t be at Sunday dinner, someone—or *someones*—would show up to see if I’d been kidnapped, murdered, or, worse, if I really had rudely ditched dinner without notice.

I didn’t want to subject Lars to that kind of invasive visit—especially since he’d consistently been in some state of undress since we’d arrived.

But all I could think about were his words.

Just wait till we live together.

Till.

As in until.

Not *if.* Not *maybe.*

Till.

Usually when his words left me speechless, it was because they were filthy. Or phrased in such a way that my brain could twist to make them filthy.

But if he was going to start adding nonchalant declarations about our future, there was no way I'd survive.

I'm so screwed.

Shaking myself out of my stupor, I grabbed my phone. Before I could open my texts with Ruth—the safest and easiest family member to message—Lars jogged down the stairs.

He was dressed.

Pants, shirt, boots—*dressed*.

It was a crime to cover all his rough male beauty with clothes, but that wasn't what made my heart sink.

It was the look on his face.

"You've got to go," I surmised.

Sasha must've done a good job holding down the fort at Wicked because Lars hadn't gotten a single call the night before. He hadn't had to run out to deal with any drama.

Or break any fingers.

I hadn't been surprised it'd gone smoothly. Lars emanated power, fear, and a demand for respect, and almost everyone heeded the nonverbal warning. Sasha had an air of fuck-around-and-find-out. Not as scary, but still pretty damn effective because no one wanted to be publicly eviscerated by her cutting insults.

But all good things had to come to an end and whatnot. Our bubble couldn't last forever.

"Sorry, hotcakes, something came up I gotta deal with." He ran a hand over the top of his head. "Wish I could say it'll be fast, but..."

"I get it."

Pulling his phone from his pocket, he unlocked it and held it out to me. "Order your tacos. Just 'cause I gotta deal with bullshit doesn't mean you should have to eat gerbil food."

I smiled but shook my head. "If you're leaving, I might as well go to my family dinner."

Before he could respond, his phone rang. Jaw clenched, he swiped to silence the noise as he stalked toward me. "We'll talk about this later."

I didn't know what *this* was referring to, and I didn't have the chance to ask for clarification.

His mouth pressed against mine. I knew he had to go. I knew he meant it to be a quick kiss.

But I also knew he was pissed at the *bullshit* he had to deal with.

Which meant I wanted to make it better. Just a little. For just a moment.

Gripping his shirt, I pushed up on my toes and ran my tongue across his lips. That was all it took. The only prompting he needed.

He took over, fisting my hair and leaning down to palm my ass. His body was still tight, but not with anger.

With need—the long, hard evidence of it pushed against my stomach.

"Fuck," he murmured, dropping his forehead to mine. "Always keeping me on my toes, hotcakes."

I wasn't sure if that was a compliment. It was the same thing I told parents when their kindergartener was... mischievous. But since Lars was still holding me tight while he said it, I was going with yes.

"Probably won't be able to respond, but text when you leave and arrive."

My belly warmed at the protective request. Well, the order. "I can do that."

"Good girl." Releasing me, he opened the door and paused. "Need a key ASA-fuckin'-P, baby."

With *that*, Lars jogged down my porch and climbed onto his bike before taking off like a bat out of hell.

Or a badass out of the suburbs.

Lars

"Fook, I can smell the crabs in the air."

I wished like hell Nox was talking about the crustacean. But since we were standing outside of a strip club and not a seafood restaurant, that wasn't the case.

"Fuckin' hell," Beck—one of Nox's boys—bit out with a shake of the head as he climbed from behind the wheel of a Land Rover.

"What can I say?" Nox said. "I've got a way with words."

The thing was, he likely wasn't wrong. It wasn't just asbestos and lead paint to watch out for in the shitty building across the street.

My lip curled as I looked from the rundown exterior of the cheap club to the man sitting on a stool, scrolling his phone. "You'd think with all the money I've been paying him, he'd hire better security."

It'd taken *two* of Nox's guys to electronically track down the owner of Controversy LLC. And, 'cause Eddie hadn't left me with enough headaches, that owner had been Elliot Nash.

If life were a movie, Elliot Nash would be our nemesis—and not the easy-to-defeat villain who was created just to make the heroes look good. Since it wasn't a movie, he was our pain in the ass. Greedy and evil, but smart, too.

He'd fucked with Nox by stealing from him and dragging his name through filth. He'd placed the blame elsewhere, but I didn't buy it.

He'd fucked with the Hyde group by setting his sights on Harlow when she'd become collateral damage for someone else's debts.

I hadn't given a shit when Nash got his hooks into my cousin—Eddie had made his bed of garbage, and he could rot in it *and* his unmarked grave. But I drew the line at him fuckin' with Wicked.

Unlike me, Nash *did* have business envy. He wanted my building. My dancers. My customers. The business I'd built from the ground up.

Most of all, he wanted my reputation and the power that came with it.

The loyalty.

"You got a plan?" Nox pulled out a cigar, put it in his mouth, and then immediately shoved it back in his pocket.

Ignoring his question, I asked the more pressing one. "You forget how to light that?"

"No, you fookin' muppet. Trying to quit."

"How's that going for ya?" 'Cause I knew it was shit for me. Joss had never asked me to quit smoking, but I knew she didn't like the smell. And since I wanted her in my space, I'd cut way the fuck back. But I hadn't been able to fully kick it.

He didn't respond verbally, but the glare he shot me said more than enough.

Wasn't sure why he was quitting, but I bet it had something to do with his woman, too. "Is Gus pregnant?"

They hadn't been engaged long, but they also hadn't known each other long before he'd put his ring on her finger. Hell, they hadn't known each other more than a few minutes before she'd moved in. Nox wasn't a patient man.

He confirmed that by grumbling, "Fookin' wish. I'm tempted to just toss her pills off the balcony."

Knew Joss was on the pill, too.

Knew we'd just started being *us* and it'd be a while before I could convince her to go off the pill.

But that hadn't stopped me from gathering my come and pushing it back into her when we were done fucking. The sight of her like that —so tight, wet, and filled with me—was seared into my brain. It was better than porn. Better than any of my fantasies of her. Like a junkie, I was already craving it. If I hadn't been trying to go easy, I'd have had her again and again until there was no more room in her.

Until she was stretched and filled and dripping.

"The plan?" Nox prompted, dragging my focus back where it needed to be.

"Just having a chat with a fellow business owner."

"Aye, fair enough," he said, his smile holding a sharp edge.

I wanted to get back to Joss. Safe bet Nox wanted to get home to Gus. And Beck...

Hell, he likely had romantic plans with a flamethrower and a fleshlight.

But if my friendly chat were to go south, none of us would be averse to dealing with it in our own fun way.

Which was why I knew that same edge was mirrored on my face. "Your boys ready?"

He glanced at his phone and lifted his chin.

Matt was back at Nox's warehouse headquarters, sitting in front of a computer, ready to do his *Matrix* shit I didn't understand. Dair was halfway around the world, doing the same. Between the two of them, they'd managed to pull apart a labyrinth of misdirection to find Nash. I had no doubt they could complete their assignment.

"Then let's get this shit over with."

The three of us walked toward the club with purpose. It wasn't until we were walking in that the bouncer pulled his focus from his phone. My gaze automatically dropped to see what had his rapt attention.

I immediately regretted that decision.

Didn't need to know the dude had been watching porn. Definitely didn't need to know it involved tentacles.

"Hey, I recognize you from your picture. You aren't allowed in here," he said, narrowing his eyes at me as he fumbled to hide his screen.

Too little, too late, man.

I was already palming a hundred-dollar bill in case I needed to subtly bribe the guy. There'd be no subtle 'cause there was no way in hell I was shaking his hand. Instead, I gripped the very edge of it as I handed it off with no contact.

He took it, his gaze darting to the metal detector wand. "I have to at least scan you."

Since all three of us were carrying, I grabbed another hundred I had waiting in my pocket and handed it over the same way.

"Never mind," he said with a conspiratorial grin before returning to his cartoon kinkfest.

With no loyalty, it was that easy.

"I'm on the banned list," I said, pressing a hand to my chest. "I'm fuckin' honored."

"Guessing I am, too, but you bribed him before I could find out," Nox said. He may have been joking, but there was a vein of resentment in his tone that I stole his fun.

"My bad. I'll keep an eye out for your photo on a wall-o-shame."

"Aye, I'll snap a pic. Gus would love it," he said, grinning as he rubbed his beard.

Beck just shook his head, leading the way into the main room like a silent enforcer.

Once we pushed through the saloon doors, I paused as my senses were assaulted.

It wasn't bad.

It was worse.

One side of the room was cliché wild west, covered in a sticky layer of muck, filmed in grime, coated by dust. The other side was gaudy chairs that resembled thrones, dark wood, velvet curtains, and ropes.

Apparently early Sunday evenings aren't big for VIPs.

It was like the place couldn't decide if it was a country bar or a gentleman's cigar club. I got the need for a VIP section, but it clashed so damn bad, I almost wanted to give him my contractor's number.

"Nothing's changed since he teamed up with Rick," Nox noted, looking around with a grimace. "He's still only employing the A-team."

It wasn't just the distracted and bribable bouncer. There wasn't a security guard in the large room. The girls behind the bar looked like they'd been knocking back shots and saving the watered down booze for the customers. The dancers on stage moved robotically, their eyes glazed over like they were picturing being anywhere else, doing anything else. Some of the ones working the room had the same expression, not even flinching when they were groped.

I hadn't even realized I'd taken a step toward one of them until Beck put his hand on my chest to stop me. "She's got no interest in a rescue. You'll only make it worse for her."

I wanted like hell for him to be wrong, but I knew he wasn't. It fuckin' burned in my gut. The whole scene did.

The stagnant air. The desperation. The undercurrent of violence and depravity. It wasn't fun. It wasn't a chill place to hang out and enjoy the views.

It was toxic.

It was everything I hated and everything I'd worked my ass off to *not* be.

"No sign of Nash," I said.

"Not surprised," Nox said, his own jaw clenched tight. "He doesn't get his hands dirty helping out."

A short but beefy motherfucker stormed through the crowd, knocking into already wobbly dancers without a single apology or acknowledgment. Meeting my gaze, he crooked a finger.

Fuck.

That.

Realizing there was no way in hell I was being beckoned, he continued walking, his face growing redder when I didn't meet him halfway. When he reached us, he puffed his chest and snarled, "Follow me."

Aw, the big boy wants to be a big man.

I was tempted to tell him to fuck off. If Nox, Beck, and I took up space at the bar, it'd be easy to scare off the customers and cut his alcohol sales by a wide chunk. Easier still to take the dancers away, too. All the fragile masculinity in the room wouldn't take well to the insult. To the fact that they couldn't even pay for women's attention. I could just imagine the way they'd storm back to their mother's basements to leave nasty online reviews.

But doing any of that would require touching the stools. Drinking from the bottles. Talking to people.

Spending more time than needed in a room that had more bacterial growths than a petri dish.

I wanted to get in, make my point to Nash, and get the fuck out so I could shower before touching Joss.

We followed through a door with no security to a long, curved hallway. We continued past a dressing room with wide open doors and also no security. Past closed ones with over the top, fake moaning coming from behind them but, surprise, surprise, no security. Down to the end to land at a heavy wooden door.

That, unsurprisingly, did have security.

Always worried about himself.

The short security guy knocked, but no one answered.

It was a powerplay—and not a good one since the only one who looked insulted was the guy.

After a wait that reeked of ego, Nash called out, "Come in."

The guy opened the door, chest somehow going more puffed until I wondered if he had a bike pump under his shirt. With a scowl, he stared me down.

And I stared right back at him.

Nash was saying some bullshit greeting to Nox, even though their last interaction had been far from friendly.

It had, however, been intimate since Nox had broken into his Fortress of Fuckery to aim a gun at *little Nash*.

I didn't give him my attention yet. I kept my gaze locked on the man with a chip on his shoulder. There was something unsettling about him. He was too angry, like it was nothing but poison down in his bones.

But he was also a coward. It was clear in his disregard of the women he'd run into like they were nothing, and it was clear in the way he looked away first, disguising it as him responding to Nash. "You say something, sir?"

Nash didn't even glance at him. "No. Leave."

Without looking my way, he mumbled something inaudible and left.

We weren't alone with Nash, though. Locked away safely in his Office of Fuckery, he had three girls sprawled on a couch together, each higher than the last. It was his thing. His kink.

My gut soured and roiled.

"What can I do for you, *boys*?" The condescension dripped from the last word even though he was only a handful of years older.

"Here to talk to you about your business," I said.

Nox was positioned to my right, leaning against the wall with his hands in his pockets, exposing the piece at his hip. Beck stood statue still on the other side of me, and though his suit covered it, it was still somehow obvious he was armed to the teeth.

A look of fuckin' glee lit Nash's expression. Taking a note from his dismissed guard, his chest puffed up like a fuckin' peacock. "Are things that bad at Wicked? You didn't have to bring your buddies to try to intimidate me. I already told you I'd buy you out." He leaned back and laced his fingers behind his head. "And since I'm such a generous guy, I won't take advantage of your misfortune." He smirked. "Not much, anyway."

I barely held in a laugh. Even if I was a day from closing, I'd never sell to him. I'd follow through with my threat to torch the place before I handed over my life's work. But mostly, it was hilarious that he assumed I'd deal with my setbacks using threats and intimidation.

It was just like a narcissist to expect that everyone dealt with problems the way they did.

"Not NashVille," I said. "Controversy LLC."

He worked to hide his reaction, but he failed. His eyes widened in surprise. A hint of fear. The stoned dancers could've seen it from the hallway, so we sure as shit saw it standing just feet away. That didn't stop him from doing what he did best. Lying. "I don't know—"

"Bullshit. Traced it back to you." I glanced at the clock behind him. "As we're speaking, every cent you pilfered from me with my cousin's help is being taken back."

The always present cockiness on his face disappeared, replaced with outrage.

But I wasn't done.

"And a tracer is being hidden deep, deep, *deep* in that account. Hidden so well, it's basically on a beach in Little Cayman."

He didn't even try to stop the way his brows shot up at the mention of where his offshore account was located. Rage tightened his features, and he jolted forward like he was gonna stand. Gonna come at me.

I wished the motherfucker would.

At his movement, I braced in anticipation. The men to the sides of me did the same, standing upright and losing any hint of casualness they'd had.

It was enough for Nash to sink his cowardly ass back in the seat, shifting to try to make it seem like he'd just been readjusting.

I let it go. The sooner we got out of there, the less likely we were to catch a disease that was hanging in the air with the body odor and sadness. "Move the money, I'll know where. Make a purchase, I'll know what you bought. Come after my club or money again, I won't stop at retrieving my stolen losses. I'll take every last cent. We clear?"

I was shocked his teeth didn't crack with as tight as he clenched them. After a long, glare-filled moment, he jerked his chin up.

"Shit's gotta stop, man," I said, my voice low and calm yet lined with barbed wire. "It's a big fuckin' city. Plenty of clubs, no shortage of sad bastards to fill 'em. Focus on your own businesses and stay the fuck outta mine."

His gaze narrowed even as his chest puffed out with trumped up ego. "I don't give a shit about your club." That was a lie. No one expended that much time and energy on something they didn't care about. "It's not like mine are hurting."

That much was true. But it wasn't enough for the greedy fucker. He'd already proven as much, and I was done dealing with his bullshit.

"Not coming back here," I said. "No more talking. You keep this shit up, you fuck with my friends, business, or life again, I won't let it roll off my back. I won't ignore you like the annoying gnat you are. Instead, I will return the favor. And I'll call in every marker I have to make sure your life is hell. Not an annoyance. Not an inconvenience. Not a frustration. *Hell.* You get me?"

Loathing coated his expression as thick as the layer of stank in the club. I didn't care. It made no difference to me so long as he hated me in his own space.

But there was something behind the hatred.

Fear.

Panic.

Seeing it made me wonder if his clubs weren't doing well. He had drugs. Women. Whatever else he ran in his quest for power and money. I didn't know the logistics since I wasn't a scumbag, but I figured he needed those legit businesses as a front. Made sense he'd lose his mind at the possibility of them sinking.

Also made sense that I didn't give a fuck.

There was a rustle from the couch, and the disruption was enough for him to lock down that alarm. Un-fuckin'-fortunately, he didn't lock down the anticipatory lust that bled into his expression.

"If we're done," he said, pushing his chair back, "I've got better things to focus on."

The dismissal may have been meant as disrespect, but I wasn't sticking around to prove a point. Not with the risk of seeing something far worse than tentacle porn.

Without another word, Nox, Beck, and I got the hell out of there. We were almost to the exit when movement from the side caught my attention.

I looked over to see the side profile of a dancer standing near the bar, forcing a smile as the asshole security guard talked at her tits. He reached out, running a finger along her top—and her tits. She tried to step away, but he had her boxed in. At her flinch, he smiled.

Cruelly.

That time when I moved, Beck didn't try to stop me. I pulled my wallet out as I walked, grabbing a hundred-dollar bill, and wrapping it around one of my business cards.

When I was next to the fragile fucker and his prey, his glare cut to me. "Ya mind? I'm in the middle of something here."

If this is the middle, at least it'll be quick for her.

Which doesn't surprise me.

He seems like he has to clean his jeans out once a shift.

I didn't say jack shit to him, my focus going to the terrified stripper.

And fuck if she didn't shift closer to the devil she knew in the face of the devil she didn't.

I should've softened my expression to put her at ease, but I couldn't risk the guard getting suspicious. Could've bought a private dance to get her alone, but there was no fuckin' way I was doing that shit.

Remaining silent, I slid the folded cash into her g-string with the same barely there hold I used to pass the bouncer cash. I tilted my body away from security, blocking out his huffing and whining. It was hot air, he wasn't going to do a thing about it.

"For your help earlier." I raised a brow.

She looked confused, but she rolled with my lie—proving she wasn't as far gone as the dancer earlier. "Thanks, baby."

Don't like that.

There was only one woman I wanted to call me baby, and with the way shit was going, I'd have to bathe in bleach before I could touch her.

Didn't know if I'd hear from her, but I'd done my part. I returned to where Nox and Beck were watching.

"Ya big fookin' softie," Nox said, gaining attention none of us wanted. Like his booming Irish-Scottish accent had been a beacon, the dancers in the area perked up. The few that weren't already occupied started making their way toward us.

Fresh meat.

"Let's get the hell out of here," Beck said, backing away like we were about to be attacked by zombies.

"Aye," Nox agreed.

None of us said another word until we were to our rides—again breezing by the bouncer.

"Tell me again why I shouldn't just kill the thick bastard," Nox said, pulling out his unlit cigar to bite it.

"Didn't you promise Gus you'd tone down the murders?" Beck reminded him.

I had blood on my hands. I would wound. Maim. Break fingers. Even gouge eyes when it came to Joss. And I'd do that all with a fuckin' gleeful smile. But I'd never taken a life.

Nox had. Not without reason. Not anyone who hadn't deserved it and worse.

Gus knew all about Nox's *work*. Or at least knew as much as she wanted to know. Which was how I knew Beck's question wasn't a joke.

It was fucked in the head, but that didn't stop it from giving me hope that sweet women really could love fucked up men.

"Aye, but she'd understand." Even as he said it, though, there was no hardness in his voice. He'd do a lot of shady shit in the shadows, but nothing that would risk taking him away from Gus.

And everyone with a brain in their skull knew killing Elliot Nash was a risk. A big one. He was known for being paranoid, protecting himself with bodyguards, constant camera surveillance, and other fail-safes he had in place. The world would be a better place without him in it, but it was almost guaranteed that whoever took him out would be taken out, too.

Or worse.

They'd get caught and do time.

Nash was a pain in the ass, but that's all he was. A pain. An annoyance. A gnat. He wasn't worth adding life's blood to the stained hands I touched Joss with.

And he sure as shit wasn't worth the risk of losing her.

"Giving up cigars and murder?" I gave a low whistle. "You really are changing for her."

"Fook off," Nox bit out around the cigar, but he did it smiling. Proud. "Like you got room to talk. Never seen you away from Wicked so much. Thinking you've taken more time off since you met the sweet lass than in the last five years combined. Amirite, lad?"

"Fook off," I shot back, exaggerating his accent.

"That's what I thought." Taking the cigar out of his mouth, he rubbed a hand across his beard and jerked his head to the side. "Ya think the thick bastard got the message?"

Looking at the building, I thought about the fear on Nash's face. The panic. I wasn't sure what it was from, but it'd been there. That didn't change the fact he was greedy and stupid as hell, which was why I shrugged. "Who fuckin' knows. How'd Matt and Dair do with the transfer?"

Nox pulled his phone out. "Done."

I lifted my chin. It wasn't millions, and it wasn't like Wicked was gonna tank without it. But that wasn't the point. "Wonder if we should've kept the tracker part to ourselves."

"Nah, this is better. Far as Matt could tell, Nash deposits to that account but spends. Now he'll be afraid to touch all that money he's been growing. That'll be real torture."

He had a point.

His phone beeped in his hand, and he looked at Beck. "Matt says he'll meet you at dinner."

Beck grimaced. "I'll text him a new place." With a sigh, he explained, "We were supposed to eat at one of the seafood shacks on the water. After Nox's description of the smell earlier, I'm not feeling crabs right now." He looked green. "Or ever."

"Fook, sorry, lad," Nox said through his laughter. "Clams are probably out, too, huh?"

"Now you're killing my appetite," I said.

Joss had texted a while ago to say she was at family dinner, but since I was done, I hoped she'd ditch out early.

I didn't give a shit about the taco lunch I'd missed out on. I wanted to eat her.

I was pulling out my phone to text her to get her fine ass home when my cell started ringing.

Fuckin' cursed.

"Hey," I answered.

"Sorry to bother you, sir," Killer started, even though I'd told him repeatedly the formal shit wasn't necessary. "We've got a situation here."

"Dancer or customer?"

"Uh… both? Neither?"

I had no clue what that meant, but it didn't matter. "Be right there."

"Sorry again, sir."

"Killer, I—" But he'd already hung up.

"Everything okay?" Nox asked.

I lifted a shoulder. "Guess I'll see when I get there."

Saying my goodbyes, I hopped on my bike and went from one strip club to another. If nothing else, Nash had given me a new appreciation for Wicked and how I ran it. I wasn't happy about the delay in getting to eat Joss, but I also hadn't told Beck to torch the place for insurance money.

My positive outlook lasted right until I saw the flashing lights of cop cars in Wicked's parking lot.

What the hell?

Maybe I should've had Beck take a flamethrower to it after all.

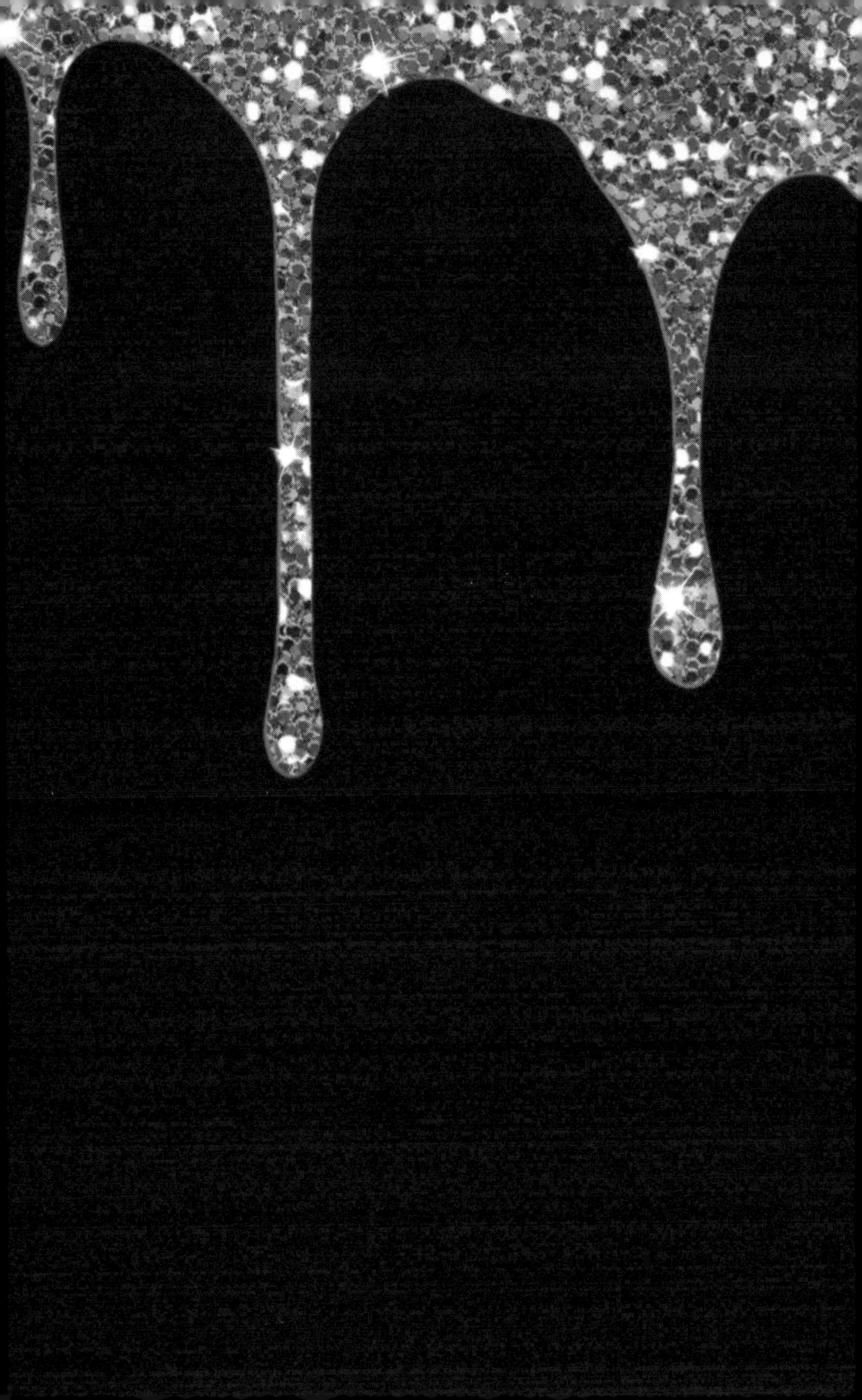

NINETEEN

Brace for Fun-ishment

JOSS

I'M HOT. BURNING.

Like I was sitting in a clear, blue lagoon under the tropical sun, making goosebumps spread across my body.

Not in a bad way. Just at odds.

Relaxed, but tense.

Oversensitive.

Exposed.

Another rush, sluicing through me like a cool waterfall down my spine. Waking me to find I was already moving.

And I wasn't in a tropical paradise.

I was somewhere far better.

My hand, which was already holding Lars' head between my thighs, rubbed across his short hair. "Time is it?"

"Late," he murmured between long licks up my slit, his voice clipped. "Or early."

I was guessing that meant it was approaching the time my alarm would go off, but I'd take what he was giving over a little more sleep any day.

"Everything okay?" I raised my hips.

When he'd left to handle his situation, I'd figured he'd be gone for most of the night. Then he'd texted to say something else had come up, so I hadn't expected to see him until the next afternoon at Wicked.

But that hadn't stopped me from leaving the door unlocked, just in case.

With his head buried between my thighs and his tongue driving me wild, it was a decision I stood by.

"Couldn't get you outta my damn head," Lars said roughly, his finger spearing into me while he talked. Like he couldn't go without touching me.

Which was good by me because I couldn't go without his touch.

"Home with you, got your taste on my tongue, your pussy squeezing my finger. Don't wanna talk about any other bullshit."

That was also good by me.

I relayed that fact by putting a little pressure on the back of his head. His deep chuckle vibrated against my core before his lips latched onto my clit.

He sucked.

Nipped.

Lapped at the bundle of nerves before flicking it with the strong, firm tip.

All while his finger worked me, stroking and teasing and thrusting.

He built and built then pulled away.

Built and built.

Pulled away.

Built.

Pulled.

I was losing my ever-loving mind. My body was strung so tight, I wasn't even sure my hips were touching the mattress.

That time after he built, getting me right at the edge where my thighs shook and I could no longer form words, he pulled away completely. I opened my mouth to release a nonsense disgruntled pelican noise when he covered my body with his.

My sleep shorts had already disappeared, but my shirt was still on. Lars, however, was completely naked. As he should be.

It was a crime to cover such pure male beauty.

Unless, of course, anyone else was seeing him. That view was just for me.

His hard cock slid between my lower lips, gliding through the wetness to tease my clit with every rock of his hips. Lowering his body, he tormented me as he took my mouth in a bruising kiss, his tongue dominating mine.

And then he pulled away.

He.

Fucking.

Pulled.

Away.

His mouth. His dick. His muscular body.

He went onto his knees, taking it all away.

One second, I was on my back, the next, I was on my knees with my ass in the air. His muscular legs were on the outside of mine, holding them tightly closed as he pushed between my shoulder blades until my cheek hit the mattress.

The blunt head of his thick cock rubbed my sex, tormenting me as he coated himself in my wetness. His hand went up my shirt to tease along my spine. He shifted, and I thought he was finally releasing the hold he had on my legs. I started to spread them so he could *finally* take me from behind, a sigh of relief hissing out.

A sigh that froze, along with all the air in my lungs, when he surged forward, burying himself to the hilt.

With my legs still *closed*.

Lars was big. Beyond big.

But with my thighs tight together, he wasn't big.

He was massive.

I felt like I was being split in two. Torn apart. Eviscerated.

In the most insane, overwhelming, amazing way.

Lars didn't lessen the force in his thrusts. He wasn't gentle. His fingers dug into my hips as he slammed into me over and over again from behind. He took my knees off the bed and still he didn't slow. The coil of need he'd started with his head between my legs tightened until it hurt. Until I was about to shatter.

And then that bastard stopped.

Cock planted deep, at least he had the good grace to verbalize the frustration I felt to my soul with rough curses.

Though, honestly, I didn't know what he was cursing about. *He* was the one torturing *me.*

"What's—" I started just as he began moving again.

Another fast build as he fucked me roughly.

As amazing as it felt—and it was otherworldly levels of amazing—there was something going on I didn't understand. It started small, a tiny tightness in my chest, but kept growing.

When he stopped again, realization hit me, making stupid tears fill my eyes. "You're mad at me. This is..." I gasped as he reached around to rub my clit. "You're... This... It's sexual fun-ishment!"

"Yup," he admitted without a hint of guilt. There was, however, a lot of pain in his gruff voice.

At least he's suffering, too.

"Why?"

"The," he pulled back slow and slammed in fast, "door."

Shit.

He stopped thrusting, but he slid his hands under my shirt to caress me. I wasn't even sure he was aware he was doing it. There was something frenzied about the way he stroked my skin, a desperation to touch me everywhere he could reach. My back. My sides. My thighs. My ass cheeks. His thumb moved between to stroke at our connection, a low groan rumbling through him. "What'd I tell you about leaving your door unlocked?"

"How else would you have gotten in?" I asked, not answering his question.

"Hotcakes, I'll huff and puff and blow the damn thing down before I let it keep me from your bed."

"You're the big, bad wolf now?"

"Better fuckin' believe it. Except *my* Little Red likes to be eaten." Grinding against me, he pushed in as deep as he could before freezing. "Never, Joss. Never do that again. Bad shit happens to good people. Bad shit happens in good neighborhoods. Bad shit happens at random. Finally got you, don't fuckin' take that risk with what's mine."

His concern.

His possessive words.

His *everything.*

It made the tightness in my chest unbearable.

I hated it.

I hated that he was mad at me. Not because he was withholding the orgasm I needed more than my next breath—although that wasn't fun. It wasn't even because I felt guilty for taking a stupid risk—although, again, that wasn't fun. It was just because it felt so wrong. I wanted to hear him tell me how good it felt. How good *I* was.

I was desperate for it.

As he started slowly gliding in and out, my forehead pressed to the mattress and my eyes closed. Words tumbled from my mouth in a mindless babble. "I'm sorry I left the door unlocked, but I didn't like the idea that I'd sleep the whole night without you next to me. Which is stupid, but it's also the truth. And I have a key for you on my kitchen counter so you can come over whenever you want after work. Even just to sleep. But I hope sometimes you wake me up with your mouth and tongue because that was the best wakeup call I've ever gotten. And I'm sorry."

Somewhere in my gibberish, Lars had stopped moving. Even once I was finished, he stayed still for a long moment before speaking. "You serious, baby?"

"About being sorry? Yes. Or about your mouth on me? Because also yes. You're very, uh, skilled at that."

"Glad you think so 'cause I plan on doing it until your taste is permanently on my tongue. Not what I'm talking about, though." Moving a hand to my shoulder, he lifted me before gripping my chin and turning my head so I was looking at him as best as I could. "You got a key for me."

It wasn't a question, but I answered anyway. "You said you wanted one."

"You got a key for me," he repeated.

Giving someone a key was a big deal. I knew that. I was inexperienced, not a moron. But still, I hadn't expected Lars to be so… touched? Moved? Possessively happy and alpha-y?

Yeah, that was the one.

Releasing my chin, he palmed my ass cheeks before squeezing. He used that hold to rock me back and forth on his length. No control. No teasing. No stopping.

It was savage and brutal.

Primal.

It was too much.

I tried to twist, but his hold was too firm. When I jolted forward to get away, his hands moved from my hips to my shirt. He clutched the fabric, using it to keep me in place so he could have me how he wanted.

Use me how he wanted.

I was going to explode and die from pleasure, but I had no choice but to take it. To take all of him.

I'd never felt more restrained yet free.

No expectations to be perfect. To do what someone else wanted. To be who others wanted.

I didn't have to worry I wasn't doing something correctly.

Lars wanted me exactly as I was.

And he took me exactly as I needed.

I cried out as my orgasm hit, waves of electric pleasure crashing over me until I saw static. It wasn't enough for Lars. Shoving a hand under me, he stroked my clit, wringing more from me. His thrusts were relentless.

"Wish you could see how perfectly your pussy takes my cock. Fuck. So pretty, baby." He lost his rhythm, nothing but power and need in his movements. "You take me so good. Made for me."

God.

God.

My pussy was still trembling with aftershocks when his words and the reverence in his gruff voice sent me over the edge again. I'd drown in pleasure. In Lars.

But I'd die happier than I'd ever been.

When he groaned, his come filling me, it was my turn to keep moving. I rocked back and forth, greedy for it. For him.

Raw and used in the best way, I collapsed forward, wincing as his still semi-hard cock slid from my oversensitive body. My brain was dead, a gooey lump of nothing. That was the only explanation for why I muttered, "I like when you do that."

When Lars chuckled, I heard and felt it as his body lowered to cover mine and his lips grazed up my neck. "Noticed."

"Not that," I said, even as I wiggled my ass against him because I did, in fact, like that, too. "When you say stuff like that."

"'Course you do. Good girls like to know they're doing good. And you, baby," another brush of his lips in the crook of my neck, "are the fuckin' best."

The orgasm he'd given me had undone the tightness in my lower belly. His words undid the tightness in my chest.

But they also sent a new surge of need through me. A surge my exhausted body was not equipped to handle.

"Don't get me hot when I'm wiped out and tender from being so full."

"Don't get me hard by saying you're full and making me picture stretching you out again."

Maybe I'm not too spent after all...

That wasn't the case. Because wrapped up in Lars, drowning in him, I fell asleep.

For a whole twenty minutes until my alarm went off.

Worth it.

Lars

After the night I'd had, I hadn't thought it was possible. But as Joss fell asleep, in my arms, filled with my come, I smiled.

A taste of good in the midst of fuckin' gutter shit.

Someone was fuckin' with me. Bad.

They'd called the cops, claiming a *young* dancer was physically fighting with a customer. There'd been too much emphasis on that word. Young. Like I was hiring underage kids. Like I was a scumbag.

With no complaining witness, dancer, or customer to be found, the police had moved on to deal with the other bullshit their night would bring. Leaving me to deal with my own. I'd parked my ass at my desk to review every inch of footage from every camera in the place.

And then I'd fired two dancers for doing blow with customers.

I didn't fuck around with that shit.

Other than that, though, nothing popped up. No fight. Not even an argument.

But it wasn't the first anonymous complaint we'd had. And the timing, right after I'd visited Nash? Suspect as shit. But I wasn't convinced.

My gut said something else was going on.

And my gut was never wrong.

Whatever was happening, I'd figure it out. And then I'd make them pay for the inconvenience.

Until then, I'd hold my girl and try to figure out how long I had to wait before filling her with my come again.

And before I could toss her birth control pills out of a window.

Joss

"You okay, Joss?"

I jolted at the voice behind me and spun around. "Sophie, hi." I pulled my ear bud out and held it up. "Sorry, I was listening to..." My words trailed off when I realized I'd forgotten to start my music. "Did you just get in?"

"A couple minutes ago."

Not noticing the lack of music was bad enough. Not noticing a whole-ass other person for minutes was embarrassing.

Her expression pinched as she continued. "I already texted Piper I was going to be late. She said she was going to let you know."

Shit, she thinks I'm gonna narc on her.

"She may have, but I'm obviously still half-asleep."

Her face softened and her cheeks went pink as she touched her sleek hair that was left down instead of pulled back in her usual bun. "I, uh, tried something new, but it took longer to blow dry than I expected."

"I was gonna say, it looks great," I told her honestly.

Her shoulders loosened as she beamed. "Thanks. Except I forgot a headband or something, so now I've got to put it in a ponytail anyway."

I grabbed my purse and dug around for the spare claw so she didn't undo all her hard work.

"You're a lifesaver." She secured her hair. "Now I just need to get faster. Otherwise, I'll have to wake up at four, and no one wants that."

I would if Lars is eating me out before taking me from behind.

Waking up that early may have been worth it, but it wasn't helping my productivity. I kept switching between exhausted and distracted by the memory replaying on a loop.

"Do you have any tips?"

I slow blinked at her before realizing she meant *hair* tips.

I also realized I needed to drag my head out of Lars' pants, or it was going to be a long day.

"I use heat protector, a round brush, and then pray to the hair gods and the humidity gods that things cooperate."

"Crap, I was hoping you had some secret method since your hair always looks perfect."

"You should see it at the end of the school day. I swear, there's still glitter in there somewhere from three weeks ago."

We talked for a few more minutes about hair techniques, color, and disastrous cuts—like my six-year-old self's bowl cut. It had been my only option after Ruth and Nora had roped me into playing hair salon with them.

Once we fell into our usual silent morning routine, I grabbed my phone to actually start my music only to find three waiting texts.

Piper: Soph is gonna be a little late. I may be, too. Gotta go...

The winky emoji left little doubt what she had to do.

Or *who*.

The next two were reminders of why *I* was almost late.

Lars: Your tiny bed feels less tiny without you.

I rolled my eyes. My queen mattress was plenty big. It wasn't its fault Lars was giant.

Lars: Thanks for the key, baby. Can't wait to use it tonight.

That one made me flush all over.

After sending him a picture of me bent over—and seeing how well that'd worked out for me—a little dirty flirting wasn't a big deal.

Me: And use me too?

Lars: Fuck waiting. Be there in ten.

I pressed my lips together to keep the giddy laugh that bubbled in my chest from escaping. I knew he'd do it. He'd already proven as much when he'd blown off a weekend of meetings and work.

Me: I can't go to school smelling like sex. You'll have to wait.

Lars: Counting down the damn minutes.

Guiltily, my gaze shot to Soph to make sure she wasn't close. She was oblivious to my mild sexting because her attention kept darting between the tray of muffins in front of her and the door.

Duh.

The hair.

I hadn't asked Sophie what the occasion was or who she was trying to impress with her new hairstyle. I'd just assumed she wanted to try something different. Not every decision was driven by approval from the opposite sex. Actually, it was rare. A compliment from a random guy was nothing compared to the high of one from a random girl.

But, based on the way she was eyeing the door, maybe her decision *was* driven by a man.

A Hyde Garage man.

I wasn't going to pry—though I wanted to. I would just watch from the sidelines.

And die of curiosity, but whatever.

When Lars had said he couldn't wait to use the key, he hadn't been exaggerating. He'd cut out of Wicked at the same time as me, following me home. He'd insisted on using his key to unlock the door before carrying me upstairs to show me exactly how much he liked having it.

And me.

"How come we never go to your place?" I blurted once I could breathe again, still wrapped in Lars' arms in a post-sex haze.

It wasn't that I thought Lars had a secret family or was a slob or neat freak or something. There was likely no nefarious reason for keeping me away from his house.

I was just curious.

"Your place is closer to the bakery. If we stayed at my place, you'd have to wake up even earlier."

"It's a longer drive for you at night, though."

"Don't give a shit. As long as I get time with you, I'll drive across the damn country."

That soaked into my soul.

"If we went to your place, you would be climbing into bed with me sooner," I pointed out.

"Christ, you kill me." He pulled away, and I watched his bare ass as he padded out in the hall, likely to use the bathroom.

I rolled onto my back and stretched, closing my eyes. There was some rustling, and when I opened them a minute later, Lars was standing over me, fully clothed. "Get dressed and pack a bag. We'll go to my place."

"It was just a question," I said even as I stood to do as he said.

I really was curious.

"Yeah, but I've been wanting to fuck you in my bed since before we were together."

How was I supposed to argue with that?

I got ready and followed in my car to a nice condo in the city. A really, really, *really* nice condo. If I hadn't already known the kind of revenue Wicked made, that place would've made it clear.

Stepping inside while he dealt with the alarm system, my gaze darted around, trying to take it all in.

I quickly realized I'd been wrong with one of my assumptions.

Lars may not have been a slob, but he was, indeed, a neat freak.

His place wasn't tidy. It was spotless. It was also modern. Masculine. Cool as hell.

It was just like him.

I jolted when he wrapped his arms around me from behind. His lips grazed my neck when he asked, "Thoughts?"

"Well, there's no secret family. No porn shrine. No dude-bro display of empty beer bottles. No leftover containers growing a new universe in the bacteria spores." I shrugged. "But it's still okay. I guess."

He laughed as he spun me around. "Were any of those concerns?"

"Maybe the porn shrine," I lied.

"Baby, if I'm making a shrine to anyone, it's you." The humor left his face, snuffed out by nothing but lust and love. "And I'll fuckin' worship at it till I take my last breath."

Before I could respond, I was in his arms with his mouth on mine.

I didn't end up seeing as much of his place as I'd anticipated.

There was always another time.

We had lots of it.

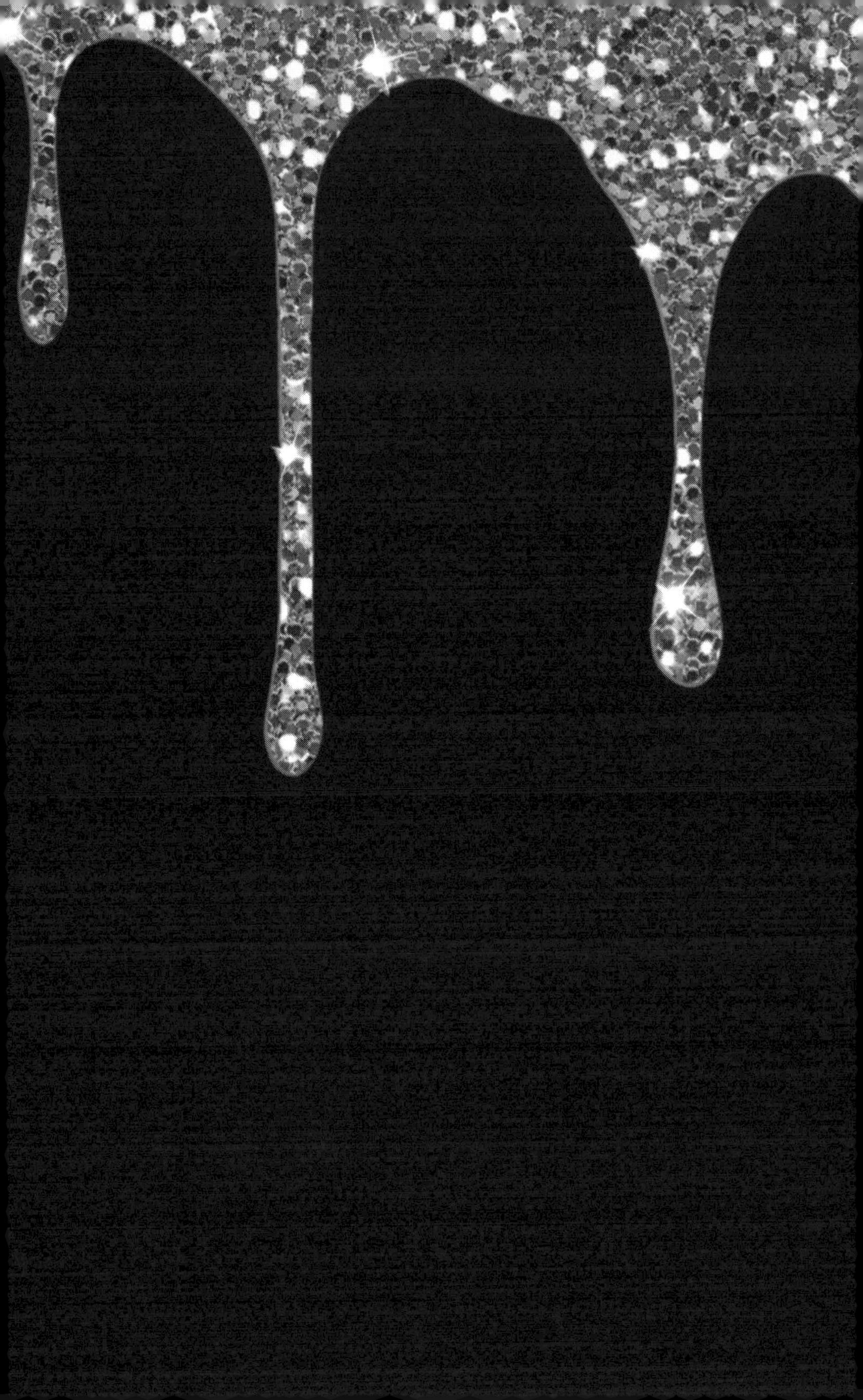

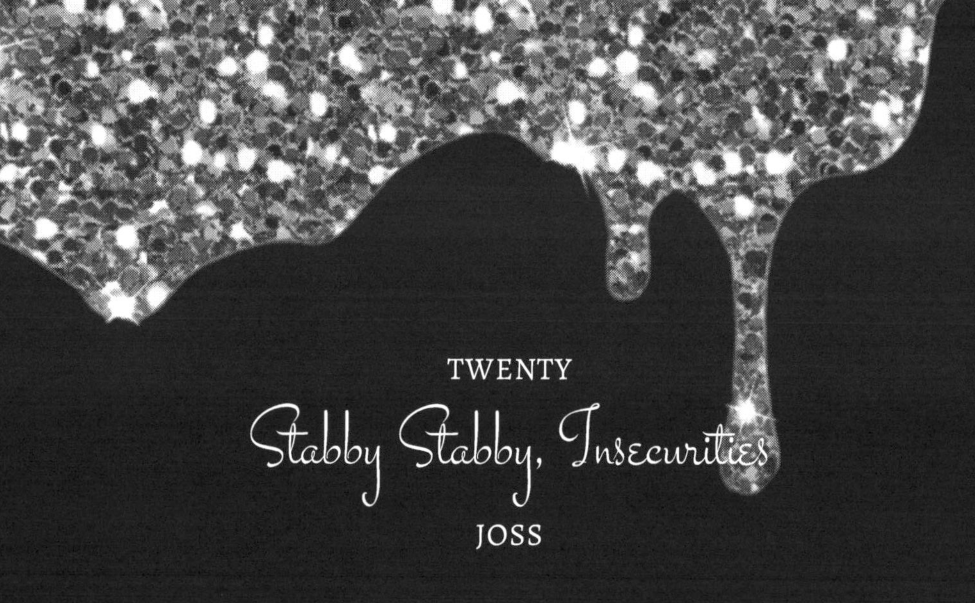

TWENTY

Stabby Stabby, Insecurities

JOSS

SOMETHING WAS WRONG.

Way wrong.

Once the excitement of Halloween festivities at school, Wicked, *and* Sweets You Rock were over, things had been uneventful. Calm, even.

Ever since the axes event, I'd been a rock star in the teacher's lounge. Everyone smiled at me. Chatted with me. They did it while trying to get the gossip about the hot man who called me *hotcakes*, but whatever. Even Mr. Henry still remembered my name, which was as close to a win as I could get.

Minus their weeklong fun-sized sugar bender, my little kindergarten friends were fully into the swing of things. No more lunchtime meltdowns about forgotten student codes, sandwiches served *with* the evil crust, or the inability to place an order for chicken nuggets every single day. There were still tiffs over who was doing what center, who was sitting on what circle, and who was standing too close, too far, or too just right. But that was expected until, oh, I dunno... senior year, maybe?

My family was... well, my family. Apparently, I'd been a little too happy and a little too distracted. Ruth was suspicious there was a male reason for that, and she'd so kindly shared that theory with Nora and my mom. All three were doing their best detective work. Thankfully, none were exactly Sherlock Holmes, so my secret was safe.

Wicked was smoothing out. Kinda. Okay, not really. All my previous experience with old school bookkeeping at Lennon Family Hardware had finally come in handy, and I'd been able to make decent headway with the backlog of chaos. But I was still spinning my wheels at implementing a new system. There was a lot more revenue than I'd have ever guessed, and there were more disbursements than dancers, booze, and pole polish. I'd yet to piece together a way to streamline it. It was frustrating, yes, but it also made it all the more impressive how much Lars had managed himself—pre-Eddie's dumpster fire. I could technically leave him to do it his previous way. It wasn't like there was anything wrong with it, per se. But he was the only one who saw the way the pieces fit together. If I wanted him to have more flexibility to see me, I'd need to make it something Sasha could do.

And I sure as hell wanted him to see me because Lars was...

Everything.

It didn't matter that we worked opposite schedules, he made the most of what time we had together. After I'd mentioned in passing that the teacher's lounge coffee tasted like lighter fluid, he'd started bringing me the good stuff when he knew I had a break. He took his dinner with me in his office, though we usually just made out before he shoved fries or whatever in his mouth on the way out the door. Most of the time, we went to my place, but since he'd reciprocated by giving me a key, I'd used it to wait in his bed a couple times.

His *wet dream*, according to him.

My dream, period, according to me.

It didn't matter which house I slept in, he always ended the night by climbing into bed next to me and holding me close before waking me up with his fingers, mouth, cock, or some delicious combination of the three.

Was it enough time? No. No, it was not.

But was it still perfect?

Also, no.

No, it was not.

I missed him, and he'd been pretty damn vocal—in his gruff yet filthy way—that it was mutual. Other than that, though, it *was* perfect. Way better than I'd ever known it could be.

Where it all fell apart was, surprisingly, Sweets You Rock. My fun and, pun intended, sweet job. Because something was up with Piper.

She'd started working a lot. Like, a whole lot. She'd claimed it was to test new recipes, and maybe that was true. But it wasn't the *whole* truth. She was quiet. Distracted. Withdrawn. And it'd just gotten worse and worse.

And it wasn't just her. Jake was acting weird, too. He was always quiet, but it was a different kind of quiet. He still popped over to see her. Still touched her ass and was bossy. But there was something more to it. Concern that etched his face when she wasn't looking. Guilt, maybe?

If they were any other couple, my scarred heart would wonder if he'd cheated. If that's why she'd pulled away and why he'd become so cautiously attentive. But there was no way. Jake was obsessed with Piper. He'd sooner cut off his hand with a rusty hubcap than hurt her.

Even though Piper was just as crazy about Jake, she wouldn't be silently sullen if he ever lost his mind and cheated. She'd be telling him where he could stick his mechanic creeper—sideways—rather than leaning into his gentle touches.

So, no, definitely no infidelity.

Long before I'd started at Sweets You Rock, before it was even an official bakery, some awful stuff had gone down with one of Jake's employees. He'd betrayed him and had tried to hurt Piper in the absolute worst, most poisonous way.

I'd briefly wondered if it was something to do with him, but Jake would've put security outside of the bakery like it was a nightclub. He also wouldn't have stepped more than a foot from Piper. So it wasn't the ex-employee.

But there was something.

Worry for my friend tightened in my chest as I watched her come from the back with yet another tray of cookies. She moved to the display case and opened it before freezing when she realized there was no room.

Our Saturday morning customers were delighted with all the extras she'd baked after being in the kitchen since God knew when. We'd yet to run out of anything—which was unheard of. But I knew she wasn't overbaking for customer satisfaction.

It was for a distraction.

Holding up a finger to the waiting line at the register, I moved to Piper and took the tray. "I think we're good for a while."

She smiled, but it was brittle. "I may have gotten carried away."

"Just a smidge."

With the bakery in full chaos, it wasn't the time to push her. I set the tray down on the counter and handed her a cookie. "I bet Jake could use one."

She scanned the crowd. "Later."

Nudging her, I tilted my head to where Sophie was grabbing a couple muffins.

Muffins for Xavier and Key.

Not only that, but her cheeks were also adorably flushed as she smiled at them.

Smiled.

That would've filled me with more joy—and gossip—had I not been so concerned for Piper.

"We've got it," I insisted. "Go take a breather."

"Fine," she drawled dramatically, but she couldn't hide the smile pulling at her red lips. "I'll be back in five."

"Got it. See you in thirty."

She laughed as she and the cookie left, and it was the first real one I'd heard from her all week.

Less than a minute after she went, my focus was pulled away again. That time, though, it was by something good. So good.

A buzz of excitement went through me, leaving me giddy. Like my veins were filled with Diet Coke and mentos *and* rum.

I finished the order I was working on before holding up a finger and giving the next customer one of those awkward, apologetic smiles. I didn't see if they responded because by that time, there was only one person I could see.

Lars.

He'd bypassed the line, the counter, and any semblance of professional or personal space. I'd just left him in my bed a handful of hours earlier, but he kissed me like it'd been months.

Years.

Far too soon, he lifted his head. "Gonna be a late night."

Since staying up until ten was a crazy time for me, all his nights were late nights in my world. He must've meant really, really, *really* late. It made more sense for him to sleep at his place since it was closer to Wicked.

Pasting on a smile, I offered him a platitude I didn't feel. "That's okay. We'll see each other tomorrow."

He gave me a flat stare before continuing like I hadn't spoken. "Gonna be a late night, but I'm ending it in bed with you."

That sounds like a much better idea.

My smile must've said as much because his gaze dropped to my mouth and heated even as he smirked. "Don't know that I can wait till tonight. You made it clear my office is off limits, but you think Jake will let us use his for a quickie?"

A tremor went through me, and he felt it. Whatever mask of humor he'd been trying to force dropped, leaving nothing but intensity and fire and raw desire. "My girl likes that idea."

His girl seriously did. It may have only been a day since I'd had his cock, but it may as well have been forever. Unfortunately… "I'm pretty sure the office is already in use for that purpose."

"Bastard." He stood fully and moved his hands from my ass to grip my chin in a tender yet firm hold. "Gotta drop the office rule eventually, hotcakes."

Yeah, probably.

With another kiss, he left. No bike part. No cookie. No farce of visiting for any purpose other than seeing me. Driving out of his way just to kiss me.

"He's got it bad," Soph said from behind me, popping my Lars-bubble as my chaotic surroundings rushed back.

I couldn't help it. I grinned at her assessment and because it was her who made it. She never commented on personal stuff.

She's warming up to us and our nonsense.

Maybe it'll be her and Key next.

Or Xavier.

I was about to fish around, but my banter died on my tongue as I watched Piper push through the swinging door. It hadn't even been the five minutes she'd said, much less the thirty I'd predicted.

There was a smile on her face, but it was faker than the imitation vanilla she'd banned.

This has gone on long enough. Everyone else can wait.

I snagged her wrist and backed her into the kitchen. Once we were closed in, I leveled her with what I hoped was a loving yet intimidating stare. "Something is going on." She opened her mouth to argue, but I held up my hand. "I'm not going to make you talk about it here for," I gestured toward the front of the bakery and then to the Hyde side, "obvious and gossipy reasons. But we *are* going out tonight."

I thought she would argue. Based on the lift of her chin, she was gearing up to. But then her shoulders deflated like a popped balloon animal. "I totally freakin' need that."

"Good, because you don't have a choice in the matter," I blustered with a solemn nod. "Rye?"

"Are you going to force me to talk?"

"I am."

"Then no. It's too loud, too hectic, too likely Harlow will be behind the bar before we even get there. Plus," she gestured to the Hyde side like I had, "too gossipy. I'll have Ray get us a VIP area at Voodoo."

Ray, short for Rayna, was Piper's friend who owned a tattoo parlor. I'd only met her a couple times in passing at the bakery, but she seemed awesome. And since Piper had unequivocally pulled me into her fold, I was excited to get to know some of the other people in it.

Okay, fine. I also needed friends. Ones who weren't sexy strip club owners or five-year-olds who only wanted to talk about YouTube videos of other kids playing games until my eyes glazed over.

Even still, it was Saturday morning already, so I asked, "Is there going to be a VIP room available?"

"Ray has her own," Piper said. "Even if she didn't, Edge would physically throw an A-list celebrity out on their literal ass to make Ray happy."

Apparently, I'm not the only one who likes my man on the dangerous side.

With that decided, we each grabbed a restock from her emotional support baking and went to rescue Sophie.

"You're coming out tonight," Piper declared with a stone-cold expression.

Soph looked at me expectantly.

It took me a moment to get why. When I did, I clued her in, too. "She's talking to you."

Soph's brows raised. "What?"

That was the extent of Piper's firmness, and she softened like a gooey underbaked cookie—in the best way, because those were the best kind. "If you're available. And if you want to. But I'd love it if you could. And did." Her lips turned down and she shook her head at herself. "You get what I'm saying."

Sophie's expression lit like she'd gotten invited to sit at the cool table but was also filled with wariness like... well, like she'd gotten invited to sit at the cool table.

Like she was expecting there to be a catch or a *psych* or a bucket of pig's blood at prom.

I easily recognized it because I felt the same thing before realizing that Piper was actually as sweet and funny as she seemed. And Harlow was just as caring and endearingly nerdy as she had been in high school.

After a long moment, Sophie seemed to have reached the conclusion that we weren't pranking her, and a smile lit her face. "Where?"

"Voodoo. It's a club downtown."

She began to nod before pausing. Something flashed across her face, and just as fast as it'd arrived, her smile left. "I, uh, don't really have anything to wear to a club."

"You can borrow something of mine," I offered. "I promise I have more than durable teacher wear, even though we know it's totally high fashion."

We weren't the same size or figure. She was a couple inches taller than me—inches I was envious of—which gave her a leaner frame. Again, which I was envious of. Even still, I had a couple dresses that would work perfectly.

Sophie seemed to be mulling it over, hesitancy splashed across her pinched features.

"It'll just be the girls," I added, wondering if that knowledge would ease her mind. Dealing with the Hyde men could be overwhelming and intimidating. Especially if she was crushing on one.

Or more than one. Who could blame her?

Not wanting to be pushy, I let it drop and got back to work.

It wasn't long before she made her way to me, her voice low. "Can I ask you a favor?" At my nod, her gaze darted to the side and her cheeks flushed. "I've been wanting to update my wardrobe for a while. It's all office neutrals and casual stuff. If we're going out tonight anyway..."

"You want to go shopping?"

She nodded. "If you have time. And it doesn't have to be today. Or you could just tell me where you shop. I love Piper's style, but it's a little too bold and wild for me. I could never pull it off. But yours is more... simple."

Ouch.

She might as well have picked up an icing spatula and stabbed the dull edge between the cracks in my confidence to hit my biggest insecurity. I knew she hadn't meant it as an insult, but it still stung.

Knowing it was unintentional, I pushed the pain away and forced a smile. "I've got time today. Honestly, this is doing me a favor. We had a food coloring incident at school when we were making dough, so I need to replace some items."

"I really don't want to put you out if you have plans."

My plans revolved around trying to stay awake long enough to go out at night. A real riveting day. "We can get ready for Voodoo at my place after, if you want."

The excitement that brightened her face made it seem like I'd invited her to Buckingham Palace, not my house. "Really?"

"Yeah, then we'll Uber to Voodoo since we'll be drinking?" I ended it as a question because it occurred to me part way through speaking that I wasn't sure if she drank.

"I'm so excited," she said.

Her enthusiasm—not to mention the fact I hadn't stepped foot in a mall in ages—made me just as excited. "Me, too."

And I meant it. It'd be cool to get to know Sophie outside of the bakery. And if, oh, I dunno, she felt the urge to share who she was crushing on, that'd be cool, too.

"You really are so nice," she said as she turned away.

I let that softly spoken compliment dissipate her unintentional jab from earlier.

Kinda.

Whatever. It lessened it.

But I still made a mental note to step outside my comfort zone when I was looking at clothes.

It was time.

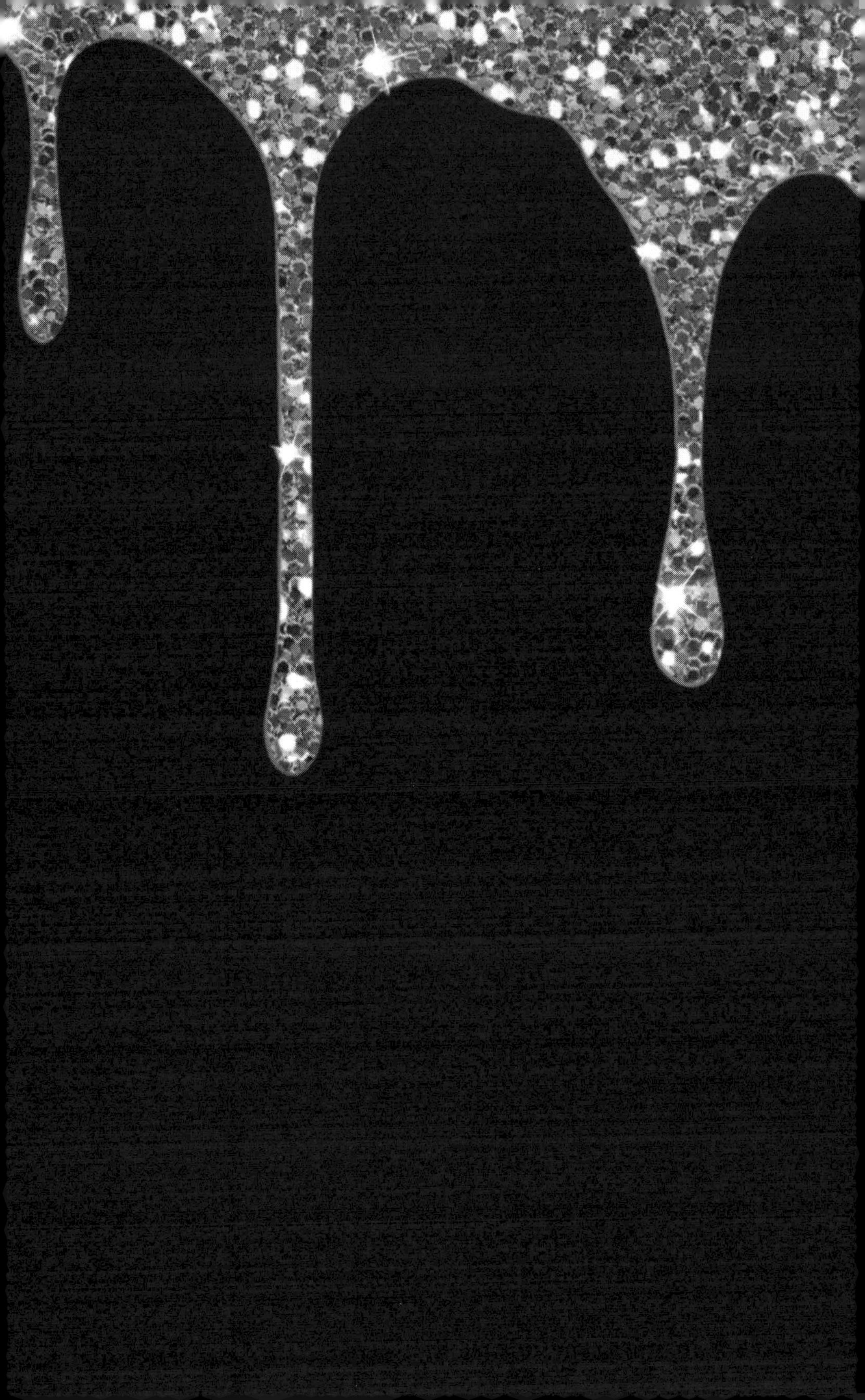

TWENTY-ONE
VIP, MVP, BFF, and BDE

JOSS

THERE WAS OUTSIDE MY COMFORT ZONE.

Then there was the dress.

My new dress.

I'd been right that hanging out with Sophie would be fun. It'd been a relaxing day but *long*. She hadn't been kidding when she'd said she wanted to revamp her wardrobe. Since it'd been forever since I'd had the extra funds to indulge in any retail therapy, I went a little crazy, too. We'd filled our cars with bags upon bags before she'd met me at my house.

I'd spent so much time getting ready for a night out, I was almost too tired to actually go.

But even if I was half-asleep, I would push through for Piper.

And, less importantly, for the new dress I'd splurged. I couldn't let it sit in my closet, collecting dust. It wasn't one I could wear at the bakery or to parent-teacher conferences, that was for sure.

Shimmery and black, there were thick shoulder straps and a high neckline but no back. The skirt started right above my ass, and I was worried about a plumber's crack situation. Or an accidental crotch flash because it was *short*. Like, if I was as tall as Soph, it would've been a tank top, not a dress.

Add in my matching heels with a delicate ankle strap, tousled curls, and more makeup than I usually wore, I didn't feel like sweet, shy Joss. I didn't feel like Miss Lennon. I didn't feel settled and plain and girl-next-door. I felt like...

Me.

Me after a major glow-up.

But still, *me*.

Something about that poked at my brain and warmed my insides. Before I could dig into it, our Uber pulled in front of Voodoo.

"Do I look okay?" Soph fidgeted with her dress. "My skirt isn't tucked into my panties or anything, right?"

Despite having bought a new dress, Sophie ended up wearing one of my wrap dresses anyway. It was a deep blue—reminding me of Lars' eyes—and totally flattering, just as I'd predicted.

"Gorgeous and with no wardrobe malfunctions at all."

"Good." She inhaled before admitting quietly, "I've never been to a club. My parents were strict, and then once I was on my own, I just worked a lot. I'm a little nervous."

"It'll be amazing," I reassured her. "And we're in a VIP area, so it'll be calmer."

She began to smile, but it faltered when she looked over my shoulder. "Oh shit. I should've brought a coat. We'll be waiting a while."

"Not when you know a guy," I said before shrugging. "Okay, not when you know a gal who knows a gal who's married to a guy." At the look on her face, I laughed. "See? Not as catchy."

We bypassed the line and went straight to the door, Sophie whispering the occasional doubtful commentary. Usually, I'd be right there with her. Like I told my kindergarten friends, no buts, no cuts, no coconuts.

But we were on the list. I didn't know if that was a literal thing, but it was still cool.

When we neared the door, I expected a bored, intimidating bouncer. And there was one. Right until he looked up and saw me. Then he was all smiles.

"Teach!"

"Killer! What're you doing here?"

He smirked. "Unlike with his woman, Boss Man isn't possessive of his bouncers. I split my time between here and Wicked."

"That must be fun."

"Pretty much the same shit, different place. Just less puss—" He cleared his throat. "Less pussyfooting around."

I patted his massive bicep. "Good cover."

He flashed me a bashful smile. "Anyway, what're you doing here? Boss Man know you're stepping out on Wicked?"

"Not here to do paperwork, so I don't think it counts as cheating. And he knows."

Probably.

Maybe.

I'd texted him earlier that it was girls' night, but I hadn't heard back. Multiple bachelor parties, including a big one for some VIP, meant he was likely dealing with *clusterfucks*, *shitshows*, and *dumbass bastards*—his words.

Someone behind us started complaining that we'd cut the line *and* were chatting. Killer glared over my head, his face hardened to scary-as-hell. I knew he was a teddy bear, but even I had to lock my knees to stop from retreating. By the time he looked back to me, his expression was friendly again. "Gimme a minute, Teach, I'll see if we've got a private area available tonight."

I shook my head, and he looked ready to argue before I added, "I'm on Ray's list."

His brows rose at the mention of Ray.

I couldn't say I blamed him for being surprised the tattoo-less teacher was hanging with the tattoo artist. Of course, I knew him from Wicked where the tattoo-less teacher was dating the strip club owner, so maybe the look was for something else.

"Good," he said, his shoulders visibly relaxing. "Drama-free."

I had no clue what drama he'd been worried about, and I didn't get the chance to ask—or reassure him that I was as boring as beige paint—before the complainer from behind me started up again. That time, he wasn't even pretending to be subtle about it.

Ignoring him, Killer turned to one of the other bouncers. "Take them back to Ray's area. And she's Lars', so if something happens to her, no more going to drool over Jade for you."

The man perked up at the mention of the Wicked dancer.

And I went all gooey and warm at his proclamation that I was Lars'. Not his friend, his girlfriend, or even his woman.

Just his.

With a chin lift, the man opened the door and gestured for us to enter. As I walked past, Killer called, "Sorry, man, club's at capacity."

The bitcher kept running his mouth, growing more outraged when Killer called for whoever was behind him to enter. "You just said it was at capacity."

"For you, it'll always be at capacity."

The guy's comeback was cut off when the door closed behind us.

Even though we were still a couple hours away from peak clubbing time, Voodoo was packed. Maybe not at capacity, but it had to be close. The long bar was four people deep in some spots. We bypassed all of it, the silent bouncer weaving through the cocktail tables until we reached a set of steps that led into the VIP-est of the VIP area.

It was gorgeous.

Overlooking the rest of the club, the space had high tables and chairs, a couple oversized and plush benches, and a bouncer standing right outside. Unlike the other sections that were connected, Ray's was separate. All that was missing were some chaise lounges and a Grecian hunk to feed us grapes.

"You're here." Piper stood from where she'd been sitting between Ray and Harlow. Her pretty face lit with so much genuine happiness, it made me wonder how I'd gotten so lucky to find a friend like her.

And how I'd let Peter wheedle away all my old friends until only his were left. I'd convinced myself they were my friends, too, right up until they'd helped him cheat on me.

There was a jumble of hellos and hugs before drinks were thrust into our empty hands.

Plus, compliments. A lot of compliments. It was proof a good group of friends could hype a girl up until she felt like a Victoria's Secret angel.

I wasn't sure if Piper would invite any of her other friends, but when no one else showed, it became clear she'd kept it to her small inner circle. I ignored my urge to question her. It was too early in the night, and we were too sober. Like she knew where my mind was at—or because I was staring—Piper reached over and squeezed my hand.

Or maybe it was a warning, because a moment later, Ray ran a hand through her aqua and lavender hair, going for casual. "So... you and Lars? How's that going?"

I couldn't even blame the vodka concoction I held since I'd barely sipped at it. My smile was entirely because of Lars.

Before I had the chance to verbally answer, Ray gave a low whistle. "The dickin' down is that good, huh? Didn't know if his BDE was just 'cause he's a big, bad business owner."

Nope, his big dick energy is all thanks to, well, his big dick.

"I was surprised when Edge told me you and Lars had hooked up," Ray continued.

"Edge told you?" My gaze went to Piper because I'd assumed it was her.

Piper crossed her arms and huffed her disgruntlement. "He stole my gossip thunder."

I bristled a little at Ray's surprise, my insecurities itching beneath my thin skin. "Am I not his type?"

Ray shrugged. "If he has a type, I don't know it. That man is married to his job. I just didn't think he was *your* type. But you chose well." She shared a conspiratorial smile and lowered her voice so no one else could hear. "The semi-psycho men do it best. Obsessive love is where it's at."

I opened my mouth to correct her. Not about the psycho thing because she had a point with that. About the *love* thing.

It's too soon in our relationship. Way too soon. But in the future?

Warmth filled me. A heady rush made me drunk despite the barely consumed alcohol.

Ray gave a knowing nod and clinked her cup with mine before peering in. "Not a vodka fan?"

"I'm a rum and Diet Coke girl," I shared.

She grimaced, muttering something about the fake sweetener ruining good liquor, but she did it while texting someone. Less than a minute later, a pretty cocktail waitress was at the entrance with a big glass of my preferred beverage. I thought the speedy service at Rye was good, but Voodoo was elite.

There are perks to the VIP life.

For a while, we split our time between chatting about lighthearted topics, people watching, and dancing with each other on our little private dais. And drinking, though no one was splitting their time with that. There was a steady flow of alcohol brought directly to us.

Once we were buzzed, I wanted to ask Piper about what was up but hesitated. It may have been the reason we were out, but she was having fun.

I didn't want to rain on her parade.

During a lull in the conversation, though, she decided to bust open the storm clouds herself. Her eyes scanned us, and she gave a small smile. "I haven't been hiding my bad mood as well as I thought, huh?"

"Sorry, doll, but no," Harlow said from next to her.

"I've barely seen you in person," she pointed out.

"I could tell something was up by your texts." Harlow wrapped an arm around her shoulders. "There was a distinct lack of dick jokes."

"Well, there goes my dream of being an Academy Award winning actress."

"What's going on?" I asked gently.

"You know how Jake has been, uh, gently insinuating he wants to start trying for a baby?"

There was no gentle or insinuating about it. The number of times I'd accidentally overheard him outright say he was gonna put his baby in her was ridiculous.

Sweet. Kinda hot. But also ridiculous.

She inhaled deeply. "I might not be able to have babies." Despite the wince from saying the words out loud, Piper's body visibly relaxed. Like she was relieved to get the secret off her chest. "I went to my doctor for testing, and they found a lot of cysts. Like, a lot. My ovaries look like they're wearing pearls." She gave a small laugh, the sound tinged with sadness. "I've always loved my accessories, but I didn't mean to take it that far."

"Did they say why?" Harlow asked.

"I've got polycystic ovarian syndrome." She sighed and sat back, chugging her drink. "It explains a lot, even if it sucks."

"There's no rush since you're still young," Soph said with an encouraging smile, and I fought hard to internalize my wince.

As evidenced by my rambunctious nephews, Nora and Ruth didn't have fertility issues. Even so, each month they were trying was filled with anticipation followed by heartbreak if their periods showed. I couldn't imagine how Piper felt to want it so bad, and to know that there was a chance it would never happen.

That cycle of pain was why Sophie's well-meaning sentiment wasn't as encouraging as she thought. And why she was digging a rude grave when she added, "I'm sure if you relax, it'll happen."

Piper had the patience of a goddess because she just smiled. "Maybe."

Sophie opened her mouth, but before she could make it worse, I interrupted. "Hold on, we need more alcohol for this."

Ray sent off a text, and refills were promptly brought over. When it was just us again, Piper gave the full, in-depth rundown of her appointment and lab work. She held it together through our medical questioning, using the detached and matter-of-fact tone of a doctor. But once it got to discussing her feelings, that mental barrier she'd built crumbled.

"All the possible symptoms are shitty, and my anxiety is being an asshole. I mean, Jake loves me. He'll always love me, no matter what happens. Logically, I know that. But in the middle of the night, when my brain is being a dick?" She shook her head. "He didn't even want kids, but now he does, and I can't... I can't..." She let out a hard sob as she fought for control. "I feel like a failure."

Ray, Harlow, and I all inhaled so hard, it was a miracle there was any oxygen left in the room. We spoke over each other, apologizing just to do it some more.

The gist of our firm reassurance was the same.

A woman's worth wasn't dependent on her ability or willingness to have children.

"I know, I know." Piper held up her hands in a defensive position, but she did it with a tender expression. "And I love you guys. I do. But I've spent all week switching between wallowing in pity and being fuckin' pissed. My body is being stupid. It's literally made to birth children, and it's... I'm..."

At her faltering words, I drew on my sideline experience with Ruth and Nora. "I get what you're saying. Well, I don't get it, but I get it." I shook my head, which just jumbled my thoughts more. "You feel like your body is betraying you."

She threw her arms out, her drink sloshing onto the floor. "Exactly.

That's exactly it." It was nearly imperceptible, but her gaze darted to Soph quickly and her smile tightened. "I know there are other options. And it isn't the end of the world. But I want to have babies. I want that so bad. The possibility that might not be in the cards for Jake and me? It hurts."

Ray jerked her head to the side. "What's he think of all this?"

Tears welled in Piper's eyes again, but they weren't from sadness. The lovesick smile on her face said as much before she spoke to confirm it. "He's more concerned about my wellbeing and made it known I come first." A blush hit her cheeks, and I was betting that statement was true in multiple ways. "For now, he's just being my support while I talk in circles and feel my feelings."

"I'm impressed," Ray said.

If it were anyone else, Jake's response may not have seemed like much, but we all knew how he was. It said a lot that he was showing restraint by not trying to fix things for Piper.

"Oh, I'm sure he's got a million plans behind the scenes," Piper said with a laugh. "Once I decide what I want to do, he'll likely take control. But I'm cool with that."

"What do you want to do?" Harlow asked.

"My doc referred me to a fertility specialist. Usually, we'd have to try for at least a year," she gestured to her bracelet and then her stomach, "but my stylish ovaries got me fast-tracked. Until then, it's just a lot of research and coming to terms with having an actual, official diagnosis of an actual, official syndrome. Honestly, I've compartmentalized everything else to focus on the fertility part. Because, right now, that's the part that hurts the most."

"Piper," Ray started, her voice loaded with so much love for her friend.

"I'm fine," Piper interrupted. "I'm lucky. I have the best life. And the best people in my life. It's just all fresh, so I'm still in the dramatic-wallowing phase." Shimmying in her seat, she steeled her spine, and wiped her tears. Then she demolished the solemn mood by looking at me and ordering, "Tell us about the dicking down you've been getting from Lars."

I didn't answer because I was too busy laughing, but we took her hint and moved back to lighter conversation.

For a few minutes.

"I don't have a lot of friends," Sophie confessed suddenly, making it heavy again—but not in a bad way. "I've always been quiet. Not talking kinda makes it hard to find friends." She gave a wry smile that grew into a huge one. "But not with you guys. You've shown me everything I could have." Standing near the entryway, she raised her cup. "To my new life."

Gah, I feel that in my heart.

Sophie's unintentional gaffe earlier was forgotten. Everyone clinked glasses and hugged and rode the high that her toast had sent us on.

As the night continued, Harlow, Ray, and Sophie kept surreptitiously checking on Piper when she wasn't looking. I was sure they saw me do the same. It was all for nothing, though. The night out had already helped. Getting to share her feelings seemed to do even better. Listening to Sophie's confession was basically the best.

And the booze.

The booze was the MVP of our VIP night.

A while later, Piper leaned close to whisper, "Thank you for demanding we go out." She pulled back to flash me a drunken smile. One that turned playful. "Do you think Lars will let us go to Wicked?"

"No. He already broke someone's fingers for touching me and the threat of eye gouging has been thrown down. If I brought you there, Jake would lose his shit, Lars would lose his shit, the building would get torched to the ground, and a bunch of eyeless and fingerless people would be left in the rubble."

As I spoke, I watched in real-time as her emotions flashed unbridled across her face. Humor. Disappointment. Shock. Horror. Awe. "He didn't really… Did he?"

I nodded, but not in an embarrassed way. Or a horrified way. I did it with a smile, my stomach flipping with a butterfly rave.

It said something about me that I was unbothered by the knowledge that he'd broken someone's fingers for me. And it really said something that I found it hot.

Arousingly so.

I didn't share that part.

"You guys are a match made in badass heaven," she said.

I laughed so hard, I was worried rum would shoot out of my nose. "He's the badass. I'm the—"

"One who demanded we go out, wouldn't take no for an answer, is dating a bad-boy hottie, saved the teacher's appreciation night, can ride a—"

"I get it," I squeaked.

"You can ride a Harley with ease." There was a twinkle in her eyes as she played innocent. "Why, what did you think I was gonna say?"

"Right," I drawled, but the rest of her words echoed through my head like the beat pulsing through the speakers.

Maybe it was the rum talking, but I *was* kind of a badass. Not Lars level because there'd be no doling out violent retribution in my future. And I was still on the quiet and shy side, but not because I was afraid of making waves. It was just who I was—and there was nothing wrong with that.

The feeling from earlier in the Uber returned. The prickle of awareness that started in my thoughts but traveled through my body. Somewhere in the chaos that was my life, surrounded by people like Lars and Piper and Harlow, I was becoming comfortable being... myself. Not the dutiful daughter. Not the perfect fiancée someone had molded me to be.

Just me.

I wasn't riding in the passenger seat of my own life. I wasn't making myself small, going with the flow so I was more palatable.

If people didn't want me as I was, they could choke for all I cared.

Because doing what I wanted was worth the fight.

Gathering my newly discovered badassery, I turned toward Ray suddenly. And nearly kept going. I steadied my body, though the spinning room may have been a lost cause. "I want a tattoo."

Her gaze scanned the expanse of my exposed skin before she confirmed. "Do you have any?"

"Nope. No technicolor for this girl." Even as I said it, the usual toxicity didn't flood my heart.

It was just rum flooding my liver.

"Virgin flesh sacrifice. My favorite." She grinned wide, her hands wringing in a maniacal way that was terrifying and amusing. "You drunk?"

I paused and took stock before giving a single nod. "I am."

Her grin slipped to a smile. "Okay, we won't do it now then. Don't want you waking up with regret." She cast a sidelong gaze to Harlow. "Or passing out."

Harlow threw her arms up. "I don't like needles."

"You have a tattoo?" Sophie asked her.

Harlow tossed her red hair over her shoulder and lifted her chin in the air. It would've been haughty and elegant, had it not been for the loud hiccup she let out. "I have an artistic representation of how short life is in the grand scheme of the infinite universe."

Ray grabbed Harlow's arm and pulled it under one of the lights. "See?"

No.

No, I did not.

Ray had to point out the very small, very faint blue line or none of us would've seen it. I wasn't even sure I *had* seen it. It could've been a pen smudge.

Harlow scowled and pulled her arm back. "I said I'd try again eventually, but if you keep this up, I'm having someone else do it."

With a hand to her heart, Ray let out a wounded groan. "Mean. You're mean." Her gaze moved to me. "Good thing I have a replacement virgin."

Oh crap, what've I started?

"If you still want one in the cold, sober light of day, get my number from Piper and text me."

"I will." Blurting it out may have been a whim, but the desire for a tattoo wasn't.

She didn't look convinced, but that was okay. "If you change your mind on ink, we could always start with some hardware."

My drunken mind filled with images of nuts, bolts, car jacks, and power tools. I was about to ask what the hell she meant, but the pointed look she gave my chest and lower region cleared it up.

"Oh." I'd never thought about piercings, but once she mentioned them... "*Ohhhhh.*"

"Don't give her any ideas," Piper told me. "You'll leave with a sleeve and so many piercings, you'll set off every metal detector in the area."

Sophie handed me the new drink a server brought over and took one for herself. I almost waved her off until I saw it was water.

The rum and Diet Coke went down easy.

The water was like the nectar of the gods.

I chugged half in one go, only tuning in to catch the last part of what Soph was saying.

"Too forever."

Using the back of my hand to wipe my mouth in a very ladylike way, I asked, "What?"

"Tattoos. They're so permanent. Pretty. But permanent."

That was true, but not really a deterrent. "So you don't have any either?"

She shook her head. "I've thought about it, but then—" Her words cut off abruptly as her eyes went saucer big. Before I could pry, she shrugged. "Like I said, they're forever."

There were worse things to be saddled with than beautiful art. And since I'd seen a lot of Ray's work, I knew it'd be nothing short of breathtaking.

Once I decided what I wanted, that was.

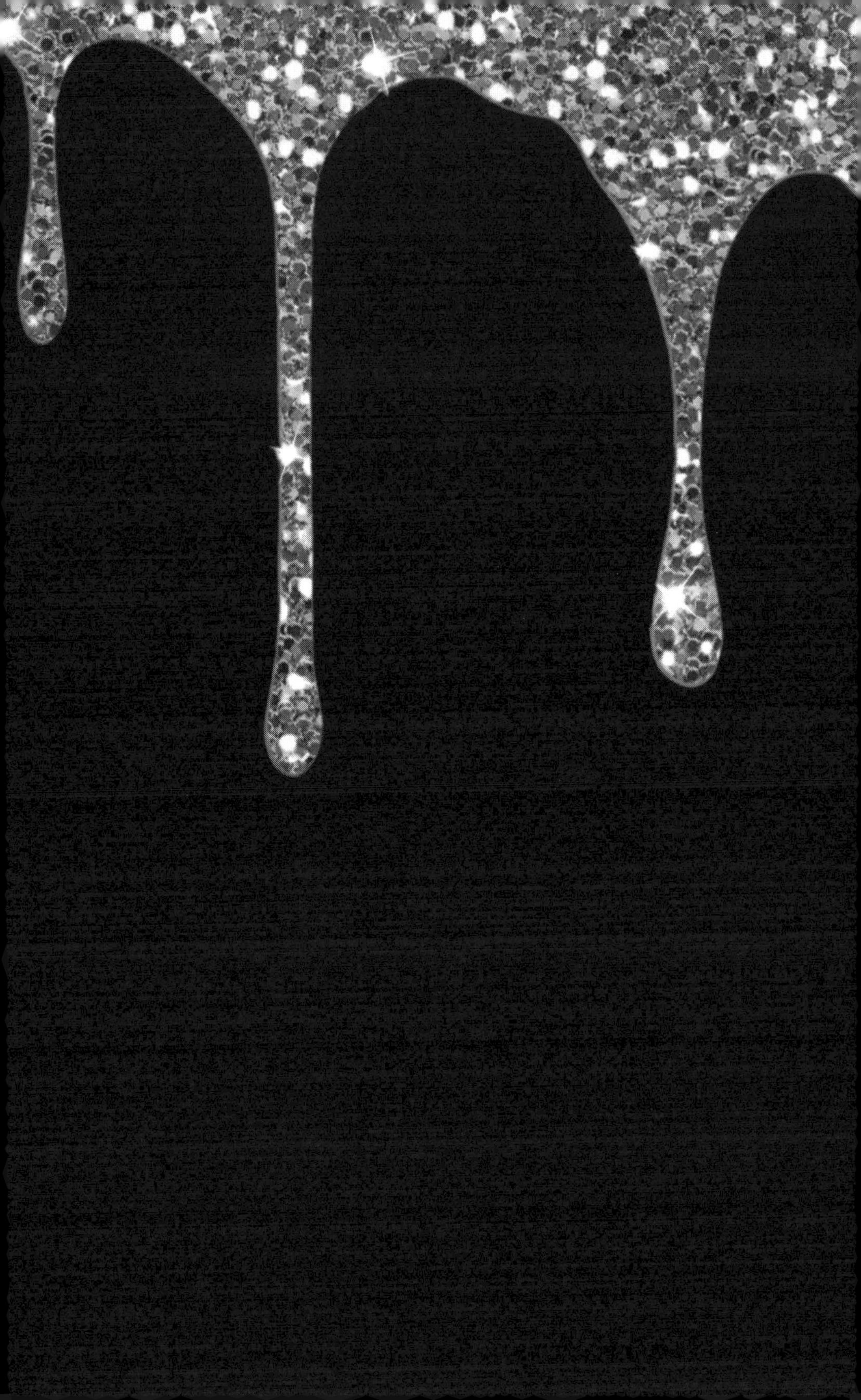

TWENTY-TWO
Welcome to Camp Serial Killer
JOSS

A COUPLE HOURS LATER, VOODOO WAS STILL IN FULL swing.

Us?

Yeah, not so much.

We were drunk. Not sloppy drunk, just fun drunk. The kind where everything was the height of hilarity.

We were also exhausted. Well, all of us except Ray. Unlike Sweets You Rock, her shop didn't open until two in the afternoon, so she hadn't been up since before dawn.

After the fiftieth yawn between us, Piper said, "Apparently I'm calling it a night."

Another lovesick smile covered her face and sugary sweetness practically oozed from her pores as she looked past me. I turned to see Jake standing by the entryway. As if she were the only other person in the world, the entirety of his focus was on her.

"Does he have ES-Piper to know when to come get you?" I asked in a not-so-quiet whisper.

"He's been at the bar."

"All night?"

He pointed a finger at her and crooked his finger.

"All night," she confirmed as she rolled her eyes at him. But she did it while closing the distance between them in order to get kissed into next week.

Some might say that was overprotective. Borderline codependent. Maybe even dysfunctional.

I said it was sweet and romantic.

That feeling of warmth for my friend expanded when I saw Jake wasn't the only man waiting. Kase didn't pause at the entryway. He went straight for Harlow, kissing her until I had to avert my gaze.

"Good night, ipo?" he asked when they unsuctioned their faces. I looked back to see him shoot a quick but pointed glance in Piper's direction.

"The best," she said through a yawn.

With a hold on her ass, he pulled her closer. "Too tired for what you promised?"

I didn't know what he was talking about, but her pinkened face said all I needed to know. I tuned them out while I ordered an Uber.

"We're giving you a ride."

I jolted at the gruff voice and glanced over at Jake.

He was a nice guy. Surprisingly sweet and super romantic to Piper.

But he still intimidated the hell out of me. I didn't want him to have to drive all over the city like a chauffeur. Plus, I was already set.

I hooked a thumb over my shoulder. "I already ordered Soph and me an Uber."

"Lars—"

"Is my boyfriend, but I'm still a fully-functioning adult. I've taken Ubers later at night from crazier parts of the city."

It'd been from the library to my dorm in college, but still. They didn't need to know that. Let them think I was cool and partied.

He looked like he was about to argue, but he just lifted his chin. His quick capitulation may have had something to do with Piper's hand unsubtly roaming from his back down to his ass.

I watched as both couples left, lost in their own world amongst the packed crowd. My heart squeezed. Partially because I was so freakin' happy for them. But mostly, I missed Lars. It was selfish. I couldn't expect him to keep missing work. He had a business to run. Just like he couldn't expect me to stay up as late as he did when I had the bakery and school every morning. We'd find a groove.

Probably.

Hopefully.

Soph looped her arm through mine. "Ready?"

"Yup."

Ray, along with security, walked us to the door, pointing out cool details we'd missed on our entry with the oh-so-chatty bouncer.

The beep on my phone indicated our Uber pulling up as we stepped outside. Unlike earlier when the short walk from curb to door had left me shivering, the cold night air felt amazing on my overheated skin.

Silently, the bouncer plucked my cell from my hand and walked around the car to confirm the details matched as we said our goodbye to Ray. A drunken goodbye that involved hugs, promises to return sooner rather than later, and vows of epic tattoos. Once he was satisfied, he handed my phone back and opened the door.

I'd set the route to drop her off first, but as we began driving away, I was tempted to invite her over for an old-fashioned sleepover—with less prank calls and more rum. Her car was parked in front of my house, so it made sense. At the last minute, my mind caught up with my drunken impulses as Lars' words from earlier ricocheted through my head and down my body to tighten my nipples in anticipation.

He'd be ending the night in bed with me.

Sophie and I were no longer just coworkers. We were friends, and I desperately needed those. I didn't want to ruin that newfound friendship with awkwardness if she heard Lars and me having sex.

And, unless she slept like the dead, she would hear.

There was no *if* about that.

After the driver dropped Soph off, I split my attention between scrolling my phone and covertly checking our surroundings. My life was nearly perfect. I wasn't messing it up by being drunk and stupid and ending up a *Dateline* special.

I was a badass, after all.

My vigilance was for nothing since he pulled in front of my house a short time later. We spoke for the first time since I'd climbed in—a guaranteed five-star rating from me—to say goodbye. I opened the door and climbed out, but before I could close it behind me, the hairs on the back of my neck stood.

A rush of awareness cut through my drunken fog, and I looked for the familiar bike or muscle car.

My car was the only one in the driveway.

Someone was there, though.

Straining my eyes, I could make out a shadowy form sitting on my porch swing.

Waiting.

Still and silent.

"Who's there?"

"Miss?" the driver asked, likely wondering if I was high, drunk, crazy, or all of the above.

Whoever it was stood, all tall and shadowy and dramatic. Pictures of chainsaws and summer camp serial killers and masked murderers went through my head.

I may not be a teenager at make-out point, but I am horny and drunk. That puts me at the top of the to-be-slaughtered probability scale.

But it wasn't a horror movie villain.

It was something worse.

Way worse.

Stepping into the light, a handsome face looked down at me. "It's just me, Jossy Bean."

Oh fuck.

Fuck *no.*

I climbed my ass right back into the Uber and closed the door. "I'll order a new ride. Just, for the love of rum, get me away from here."

I hadn't even finished when the driver pulled away from the curb and began driving. "Are you okay? Do you want me to call the cops?"

"No, no, nothing that severe. My ex is a moron but not dangerous." I brought up the app and ordered my escape ride to Wicked.

So much for being a badass.

The man's phone pinged since he was, of course, the closest driver. He glanced at it before meeting my gaze in the rearview mirror. "You sure about this, Miss?"

"Yeah, my boyfriend's there."

He didn't blink at that. A drunk chick running from her ex to her current boyfriend at a strip club likely didn't rank in his top hundred weirdest fares. Or maybe it did, and he just had a good poker face because he worked for tips.

Whatever.

I texted Lars to give him a heads-up, but like the entire day, I got nothing back. Going to Wicked had seemed like the smart choice, but by the time we neared the club, unease and second thoughts filled my head.

Lars had been clear about me not working at Wicked on the weekends because it was too chaotic. He wasn't going to be happy if I waltzed my drunk ass through the front door. There'd be broken fingers all over the place.

The driver followed my directions to the back lot, and my stomach erupted in a rush of electric butterflies when I saw Lars outside.

Then they fell like lead when I saw he was *not* alone

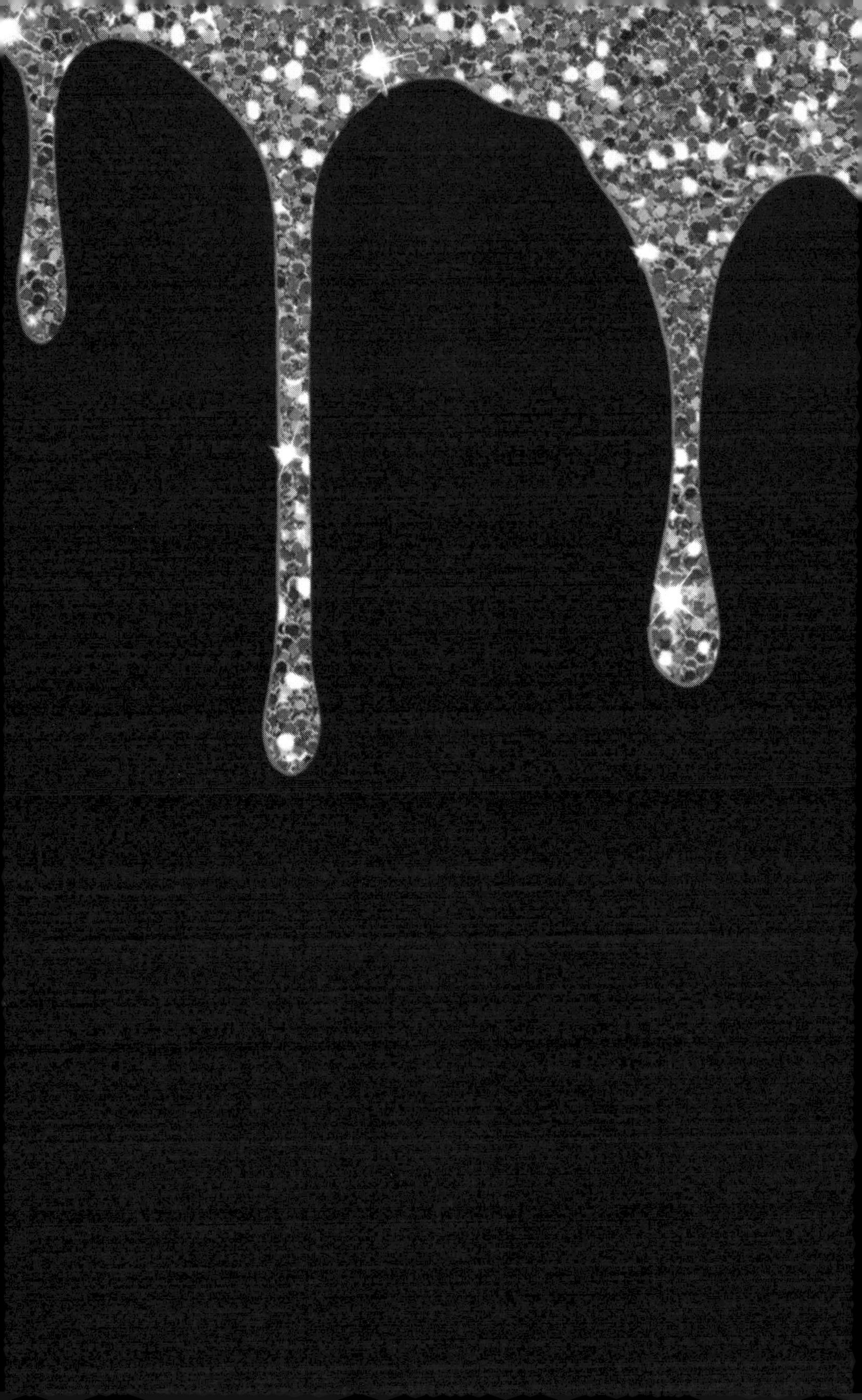

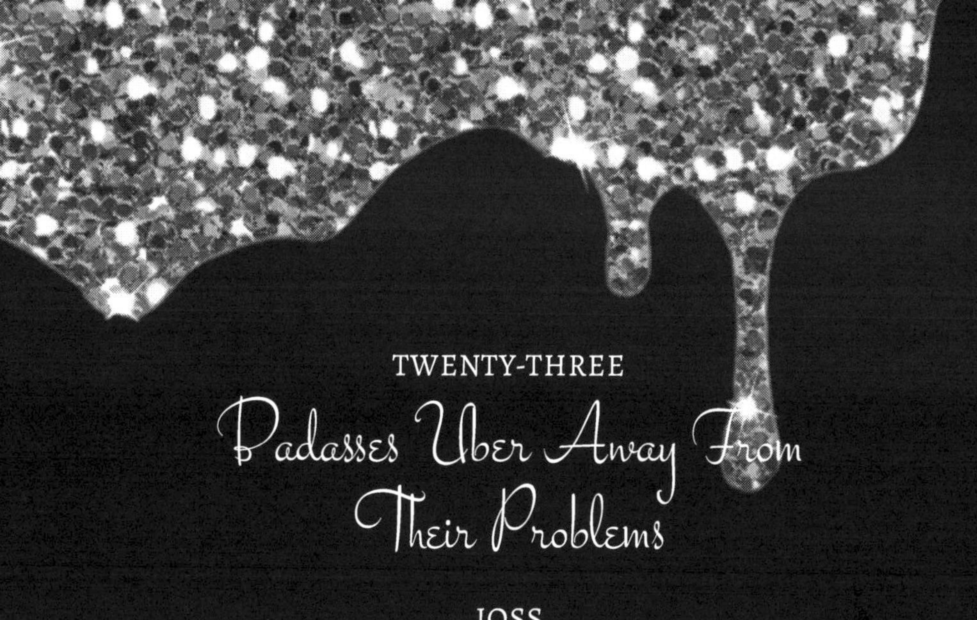

TWENTY-THREE

Badasses Uber Away From Their Problems

JOSS

THE LAST THING I'D EXPECTED TO SEE IN WICKED'S parking lot was a patrol car. Thankfully, the flashing lights weren't on, but the headlights perfectly illuminated two cops talking to a hot man.

My hot man.

Oh shit.

His violent streak caught up to him, and now he's getting arrested.

He wasn't, of course. Leaning against the wall with an unlit cigarette hanging from his mouth, he looked almost casual.

Almost.

But I knew him well enough to read his body. The tension in his bunched shoulders. The defensive way his arms were crossed. The simmering anger that filled his scowl.

Or maybe I was drunk and imagining it all.

That was also a distinct possibility.

I hesitated, unsure what to do. I'd already made the driver bounce all over the city. I mean, it was his job, and I was going to give him a crazy tip, but still. It was late. He likely wanted to get home.

Whereas I did *not*.

Not until I knew Peter was banished to hell where he belonged. Or the modern eyesore apartment he was likely renting for way too much because it fit his image.

Like I said… hell.

The choice was taken out of my hands when my gaze moved back up Lars' taut body to see his eyes were aimed at me with laser focus. He crooked his finger, and I could almost feel the strength and dignity flee my body. He summoned, and I was powerless to refuse.

With a thank you to the patient—or simply unfazed and jaded—driver, I climbed out. I did my best to project soberness as I beelined for Lars. I didn't want to escape Peter just to end up in cuffs for being drunk in public.

Maybe for other reasons…

"We done here?" Lars tucked my front tight to his side. His hand rubbed low on my bare back, and I heard a quiet growl rumble through him. Unlike his usual groans and low curses of desire, that noise hadn't sounded like a happy one.

I'd have rolled my eyes at the animalistic alpha nonsense, but it was too hot. He was too hot.

Since I'd missed him, I didn't care that we had an audience. I wrapped one arm around his back and placed the other hand on his abs. Pressed so close, I felt his muscles relax a fraction.

"We're good on our end," one of the officers said. "Reach out if there are any other issues."

Continuing with his stellar manners, Lars lifted his chin in an obvious dismissal. He remained silent as the cops got into the cruiser, so I did the same. Once they were out of view, I expected the rest of the tension in his body to loosen.

It didn't.

"I thought you were getting arrested."

He held out his arms. His sleeves were rolled to show off his tanned forearms, colorful tattoos, and lack of handcuffs. "No need to plan any conjugal visits yet."

I'd never thought of forearms… ever, really. But I'd especially never thought about a veiny forearm as sexy. Not until Lars, that was.

It took me a long moment to drag my attention away from his exposed skin. "Everything okay?"

"Fuck no."

"What happened?"

"Bullshit. Again." With that non-answer, he flicked his cigarette to the ground.

"It must've been bad," I started, gesturing to the litter, "it made you forget to smoke that before you threw it."

"Don't smoke," he rumbled, holding me tighter.

"Yes, you..." My words trailed off as I thought about it.

One of the few times I'd seen him smoke, I'd been the boring good girl who pointed out it was bad for him. Clearly, he hadn't minded since he'd still made me *his* good girl. Since then, though, I'd rarely seen him smoke. I'd only smelled it on him.

But not for a while.

I actually couldn't remember the last time.

My eyebrows were practically in my hairline. "You quit?"

"Yup."

"Why?"

"You don't like it."

My stomach warmed even as niggling anxiety poked at my brain. I liked him for him. Exactly as he was. I didn't want him to think he had to change. I didn't *want* him to change.

I gripped his button-down, wrinkling the fabric at his abs as I tipped my head back. "Baby—"

"Fuckin' love that," he murmured, tightening his arm around me until I could barely breathe.

Or maybe it was just his closeness and the intensity in his eyes that left me breathless.

Doing my best to not get distracted by all that was him, I said, "You don't have to quit."

"Know that. But also know I want you to want to be pressed up against me like this." I opened my mouth, but he didn't give me the chance to speak when he added, "Without your cute as fuck nose being crinkled from the smell." His hand moved to my ass, and he palmed one cheek. Hard. So hard, it took me onto my toes. "Even on shitty nights like this, it's an easy choice."

Using his hold, he lifted me, and I automatically wrapped my legs around him. Tight. His stomach wasn't the hard part of his body I wanted pressed between my legs, but I'd take what I could get. Anything to ease the ache.

He opened the door and broke the kiss long enough to bark an order at whatever security guard was behind me. "Turn the fuck around."

I hadn't even thought about how much my skirt had ridden up. And, right then, I didn't care. It was a strip club. There was far more skin on display.

Lars didn't share that sentiment. His glare was aimed over my shoulder until we were in his office.

The click of the lock seemed to echo around us as he closed off the rest of the world. Backing me against a wall, his kiss was hard and insistent. Desperate. He kept the connection as he lowered my body until his hard-on was pressed to my core. Pushing in to pin me against the wall, he moved his free hand up my thigh. My side. Along the curve of my breast, the backless dress allowed his thumb to slip in and tease the sensitive skin before continuing. He wrapped his tattooed fingers around my throat and tilted my head up.

His midnight-blue eyes were all I could see. They burned into me, like they were branding my soul with his name. His ownership. "Don't wear shit like this when I'm not around."

"Or what?" I raised my chin defiantly because there was no way I was agreeing to that. I'd spent far too much on the dress. I'd wear it grocery shopping to get my money's worth.

"We talked about this, baby." He lowered his head, his lips grazing mine as he menacingly whispered, "Gouged eyes. Every motherfucker who looks at what's mine. Who wants what's mine. Who jerks their sad little prick, wishing they were in my place."

I'd like to say his violent words were simply bravado, but I wasn't sure. And that was the messed-up part. Because I didn't mind.

In fact, if the tremor that rippled through me to painfully tighten my nipples was any indication, I *liked* his supercharged possessiveness.

"Oh," I breathed.

Lars read the arousal practically dripping from the one word. Or maybe he felt the arousal literally dripping from a lower region of my body. Whatever the case, he gave a low groan before taking my mouth again.

By the time he peeled himself away, I was vibrating with need.

He squeezed the side of my throat. Not enough to cut off my

breathing, but just enough to be good. So good. "Know you've got a rule—"

"Fuck my rule," I gasped when he loosened his hold. "Fuck me."

"*Jesus*." That was all he said before hiking me up his body so he could free himself. A moment later, he pulled my panties to the side and filled me to the hilt. No gentleness. No easing in. No chance for me to change my mind—not that I would. He needed it. *I* needed it. And rules were stupid. They were for the boring good girls, not Lars' drunk good girl.

Using the wall as support, he gripped my hips and moved me up and down his length. Building that pleasure inside me until I had to bite his shoulder to keep from screaming.

And then it burst. Lighting up my nerve endings until every atom was in euphoric bliss. All-encompassing. Earth-shattering.

An involuntary whimper slipped from my mouth when Lars pulled free and began walking. He lowered me onto wobbling legs before spinning me and putting a firm hand between my shoulders to forcefully bend me over his desk. Tugging my panties down my legs, I caught a brief glimpse of the lace flying to the side before he slammed in so hard, the desk skidded forward. Each time he filled me, it creaked its protest while I moaned my approval.

"Tempted to cut this fuckin' dress off you." Slowing down, he ran his hands up the back of my thighs, pushing the short skirt up. He palmed my ass cheeks and squeezed hard enough to leave marks.

Little love reminders for the next day.

He continued, putting more power behind every long thrust. "But my girl is drunk, happy, and horny. Called me *baby*. Not dumb enough to piss her off."

I wasn't sure if mini-orgasms were a thing, but at the filthy tenderness in his voice, I was positive I'd experienced one.

"Even if she's fuckin' killing me right now."

I didn't have the chance to point out that he was the one going slow because I lost the ability to speak—think, move, exist—when he snaked an arm under me to touch my clit.

God.

One time.

It'd taken one time together for Lars to learn what I liked. To read my body and my cues and my outright begging. He might tease. He might take his time to build up to it. But when I was ready, he knew exactly how I needed it.

He knew me.

So when he stroked the pad of his middle finger up and down my clit the way I loved, my hips came off the desk, and my soul nearly left my mortal body. I'd already come apart so completely, I hadn't thought there was anything left.

I'd been wrong.

I was skating on the edge when Lars curled his body over mine. The feel of his slacks on my bare legs. His shirt on my bare back. The reminder that we hadn't bothered to strip before he'd freed his cock just enough to take me. Our impatience.

Urgency.

Desperation.

It sent a heady rush through me that was nearly enough to send me plummeting, but his finger was going just a little too slow. A little too light. I was under no illusion this was accidental. He knew what he was doing.

Torturing me.

"No shoulder to bite, baby. Nothing to muffle your scream. They're going to hear you out there. They'll know who makes you come. Who you belong to."

My inhibitions were gone. Commonsense had been tossed aside like my panties. I'd given him an inch by breaking my own rule, and he was going to take...

Everything.

All of me.

And I didn't give a damn. I'd scream his name all through the club because it didn't just mean I was his... "They'll know you're mine, too."

His movements faltered for a moment, like I'd taken him off-guard. "Fuck yes, they will." He kept his body pressed to mine, driving in deeper. Filling me fuller. Taking me with vicious force.

It was completely unhinged. Savage. Brutal.

I loved it.

Whatever tender and filthy words he whispered were lost in the blood rushing in my ears. In the pleasure rippling through my molecules. That time when I exploded, he did, too, emptying into me.

He stayed planted, his harsh breath in my ear as he whispered, "Fuckin' *killing* me right now, baby."

I gave a soft laugh and wiggled my ass, making him groan as he slid free. My laughter switched to a pained gasp when the head of his cock grazed against my swollen and oversensitive clit.

One of his hands went next to my head, his body still curved around mine. Protective and overwhelming and calming. "Why would I smoke when I can release my stress deep inside this perfect pussy?"

It was a very fair point.

He dragged his fingertips up my thigh before teasing along my slit and our shared releases. I jerked as he roughly filled me with his thick fingers, but I locked my knees to stay where I was, even as his thumb brushed across my clit and stole the breath from my lungs. The room. The entire atmosphere.

Once he'd played long enough to set me on edge all over again, he pulled his hand away and tugged my skirt into place before redoing his slacks.

I was wiped. I could've easily closed my eyes and fallen asleep with my ass in the air. But since that might've made it a little tricky for Lars to do his end of night stuff, I summoned the energy to stand just as he snagged my discarded panties. I thought he was going to help me into them, or at least hand them to me so I could do it myself, but he pocketed the pretty lace.

"I need those."

"No, you don't."

"I can't just be pantieless."

"Sure, you can."

I sighed, but there was no real irritation in it.

He closed the distance between us. "Have fun at Voodoo?"

"Too much." My yawn proved as much. "I wasn't sure you got my texts."

"Didn't. Phone broke."

"Oh no."

He lifted a shoulder. "Kinda what happens when I launch it at the wall."

"They just don't make phones like they used to." My sad head shake was slow and dramatic. "What happened?"

"Beer distributor called out of the fuckin' blue to say they were dropping Wicked. No excuses. No bullshit. Just said it, hung up, and blocked my number. They've been late the last few times, and I've been patient. Then they completely fucked me over by giving me no notice the day before delivery. Fuckers."

"Which one?" I asked, but the amount of anger he was emanating clued me in.

Lars used multiple distributors. One for liquor, a couple who worked with the small batch breweries he featured on tap, and one who worked with the big dog domestics—the top-selling drinks.

Not having them was like cutting off Wicked's arm. Still had the breasts and ass, but that cheap beer did a lot of heavy lifting.

"InMug," he said, confirming my dread.

"Shit. And the cops?"

"Some punk called in a code violation. Said we were over occupancy. Which we sure as fuck were not. Had two huge parties, so we counted heads carefully and had a line down the damn block. One of the pricks we turned away must've decided to be a petty bitch. It could've been a shitstorm if they'd closed us down on a huge night." He ran a hand over his shaved head, and I may have drooled a little. "Thank fuck, Levar, the cop I was talking to, is a friend of Nox's. And a frequent customer. He knows how I run shit, so he waited until the end of the night and didn't even come inside."

I thought about Voodoo's line from earlier and smiled. I was proud of my man for running an equally successful—albeit vastly different—club that people would wait out in the cold for.

His narrowed eyes dropped to my smile. "Just told you that the cops were called and you're smiling, hotcakes?"

"You had it handled." I waved away the bad like it wasn't major. It was. I just wanted to focus on the good. "But people line up to get in. You worked hard and made it a cool place to be. That made me smile, not the other part."

"Fuckin' hell." He wrapped me in his arms and smashed my face against his chest. "Only you can do this shit."

"What shit?"

"Make me happy."

God.

God.

My heart squeezed, and I knew I was in trouble. So much trouble.

I gnawed my lip before a thought popped into my head. Luckily, when I opened my mouth, my question popped out and not any of my other thoughts. "How did you know I was at Voodoo if your phone's broken?"

"Killer told Frankie, Frankie told me. Edge keeps Ray in her VIP area and doesn't let anyone close, so knew you'd be good. But if I'd known you were wearing *this*," he teased a finger along the back of my dress, just above my ass, "the bachelor parties could've gone to hell."

That someone cared enough to keep tabs on me was not an unpleasant sensation. Far from it.

"Love that you're here," he continued. "Needed you here. Otherwise, might've lost my damn shit and ended up in cuffs."

"It almost makes me happy Peter was at my place."

I hadn't meant to say anything. Not because I was protecting Peter or hiding it. Lars' day had been shitty enough without me piling on the drama.

Plus… I'd kinda forgotten. In Ray's words, the dicking down really was that good.

But at my blurted admission, all the tension I'd helped alleviate permeated Lars' body worse than before. "Peter?"

"My, uh, ex."

His voice was low and even and a little scary "And *why* was he at your place?"

I shrugged. "I didn't give him the chance to tell me. I got out of the Uber, saw him, and got right back in to come here."

"You came here."

It wasn't a question, but still I answered as I held out my arms. "As you can see."

"Not to one of your girls or your sisters."

Huh. One of those probably would've *made sense.*

Piper lived in the opposite direction of Wicked, but her house was a little closer. I'd rather run into traffic than face Nora while I was drunk, but it would've been a quick ride to Ruth's.

"I didn't even think about them." Even if I had, I'd have gone to Lars anyway.

"You didn't. You came here."

"Yes..."

"To me."

"Yes," I repeated, still lost. And growing nervous. His blank expression was freaking me out. As was the way he kept repeating himself, as if I'd done something wrong but was too tipsy to piece it together.

He clearly wasn't mad I'd shown up. Not unless he fucked every uninvited guest—an image I did *not* want to picture.

And it wouldn't make sense for him to be pissed at me about Peter. I hadn't invited him to my house. I didn't want him there.

I'd be happy to never see his arrogant face for the rest of my life.

As far as I could tell, I hadn't done anything wrong. If Lars was about to be a dick, I'd just go home.

Because sometimes badasses Uber away from their problems.

Right as I was about to snap at him, his eyes went melty hot. Lust and affection swirled like dark and white chocolate.

"Fuck." Lars grabbed my hand and pulled me toward the door.

"Where are we going?" I squeaked.

Oh shit.

Lars

Motherfucker.

Up until that moment, I hadn't completely hated Joss' ex. 'Cause if it weren't for him being stupid enough to cheat, I wouldn't have her. And if it weren't for him being such a douche, my sorry ass wouldn't look so good by comparison.

I owed him one.

Or I had before he'd been stupid enough to show up at my woman's house.

Not a goddamn reason he should be visiting her to begin with, but uninvited in the middle of the night?

Fuck.

That.

Reaching the hall, I told Frankie I was leaving. My crew could handle closing Wicked.

I had a man to threaten.

Gouge.

Maim.

Everything else Joss liked to teasingly accuse me of, all the while knowing it was still the straight up truth.

"Wait, wait, wait," Joss yelped as we headed to the back lot. When I didn't wait, she tugged me to a stop. I could have easily kept going, but I didn't want to risk her tripping on her pretty heels. "What're you doing?"

"Going to your place."

"Why?"

"See what that asshole wants."

She gave a flick of the wrist wave. "I'm sure Peter's long gone by now."

"Then we'll climb into bed, and you can ride my dick."

At her happy little gasp, said dick jerked in response.

Truth be told, I was hoping that bastard was still there. I didn't want him to show up again when Joss was home alone.

Once I dealt with him, then we could get to her riding my dick.

And maybe my face, if I asked nicely.

She watched me for a moment as I helped her into my leather jacket. Realizing it'd be pointless to argue, she gave a sigh. "Can I at least have my panties back?"

"Fuck no." I pulled her close. "If he's forcing a confrontation, it'll be while you're wearing my leather with my come dripping out of your sweet pussy."

A tremor went through her that had fuck all to do with the cold. Probably had fuck all to do with my dirty words, either.

My woman just liked that someone had her back since I'd bet my life her sorry excuse for an ex never did.

Without another word, I helped her onto the bike and climbed on. She tightly wrapped her arms around me before I even started the engine. Knowing she was bare. That my come was leaking outta her. That her body was pressed to mine.

I nearly said fuck it and took her to my place around the corner.

But I didn't.

Because I wanted to make sure she was safe and comfortable in the house she loved so much. And because I needed time to get my shit locked down. Otherwise, I'd open my stupid mouth and tell her I loved her. That it started the first time she'd smiled at me.

It'd been on the tip of my tongue when she'd called me baby, looking so damn pretty. I'd damn near choked on the words during sex, when she'd broken her rule by letting me fuck her in my office. Begging me to.

But when I'd found out that she'd come to me instead of any of the closer options. That she hadn't even thought about going to anyone *but* me. That control unraveled into a thin thread.

The only reason I held back was because I didn't want to tell her while her ex was taking up her headspace. That bastard didn't get to encroach on us. I didn't want him tied to *our* memory.

Once I dealt with him, I'd tell her.

I was done being a little bitch about it. If she didn't feel the same way, I'd make her.

There was no other option.

I'd start by threatening—maiming, gouging, whatever—her ex and then continue by making her come while she rode my face and dick.

It was a solid start to forever with Joss.

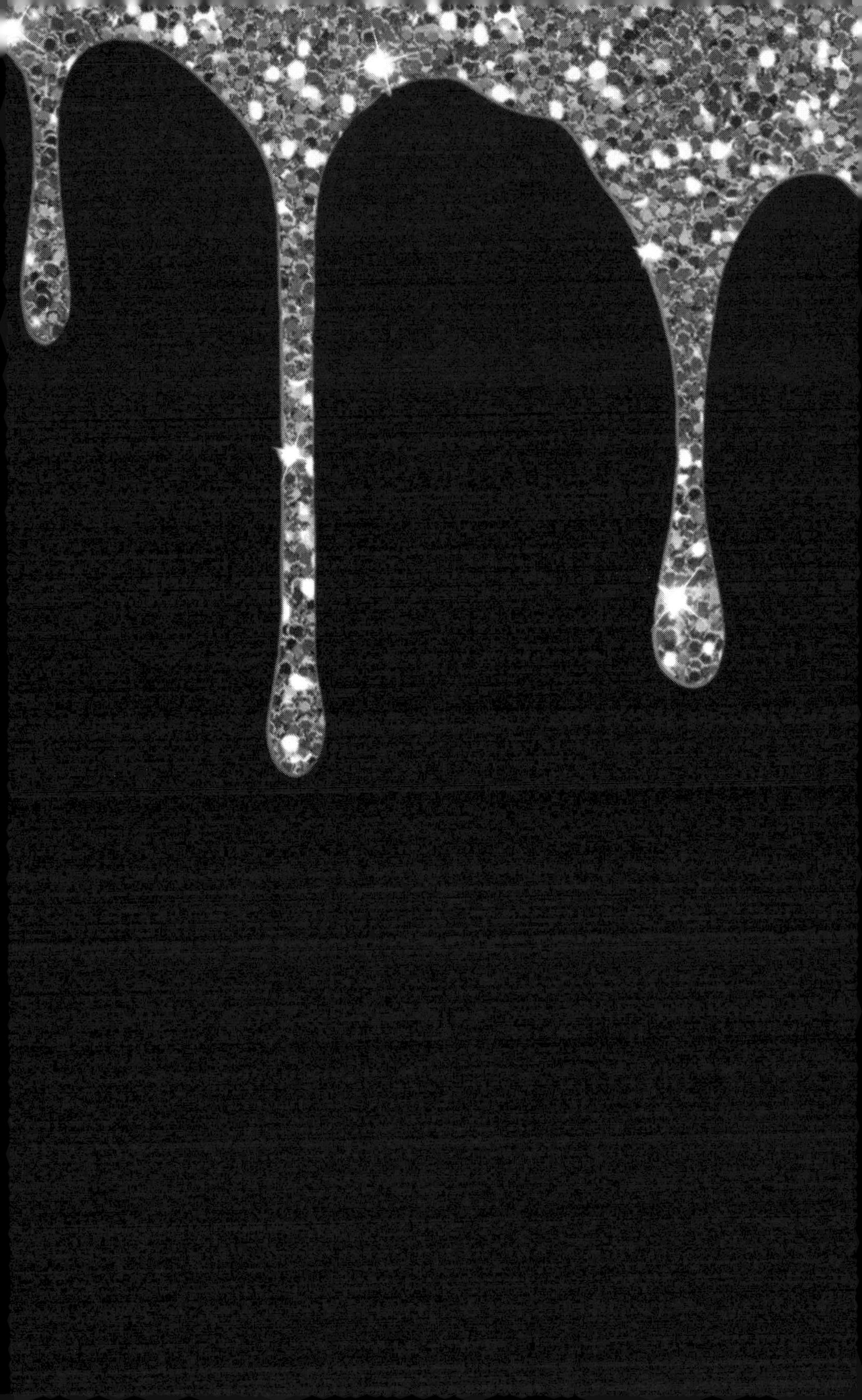

TWENTY-FOUR
Pigeon Homeschooling Services
JOSS

Joss

PETER, IN TYPICAL PETER FASHION, HAD BROUGHT nothing but bad luck.

First, by the time Lars and I had gotten to my house, Peter had been gone. That was also good news, but it would've been nice to tell him off with Lars at my back.

Then, Lars had wanted to thoroughly check the house for any signs of bullshit. By the time he'd finished, I'd been asleep. Dead-to-the-world, no-waking-me, *asleep*.

That meant there'd been no dick riding to end my night. And since Lars had left before I was awake, there'd been no dick riding to start my day, either.

As I sat on the front steps at my parents' house, playing with my nephews and waiting for Sunday dinner, I realized my bad luck was far from over.

Because much to my shock and rage, he'd brought the worst thing of all...

Himself.

My jaw was on the ground as I watched him gently ease his overpriced cellphone of an electric car to the curb before climbing out.

He looked ridiculous.

It was a Sunday. The day of rest. And there he stood, wearing clothes that were too starched with hair that was too styled, like he was meeting a celeb client and not crashing a family dinner.

No sexy buzzed head. No tattoos. No motorcycle made for long, peaceful rides.

His stupid car was stupid flashy for the sole purpose of letting everyone know he had money.

I knew why I'd fallen in love with him as a teenager. I just had no clue why I'd kept loving him after he'd changed so drastically. No clue how I'd ever let him hurt me so bad. Embarrass me.

Most of all, I didn't understand how I'd ever let him *dull* me. Diminish me.

Belittle and control me until I was boring. Drab.

He'd made me fuckin' beige when I deserved to be technicolor.

I *was* technicolor, dammit.

"Go inside," I muttered to my nephews.

"Gladly," Jasper muttered back. None of them had liked Peter much.

Or maybe at all.

He was stuffy and way too fake. Kids had good instincts when it came to that. Better than most adults—myself included.

As Peter approached, I stood. I wanted to follow my nephews and haul ass inside. Not because it hurt to see him or because I needed to go lick my wounds.

My wounds were pretty much healed thanks to time, Lars, and my own damn self.

I wanted to get away because I honestly didn't care. Not about the past, him, or his excuses. Why should I be forced to listen to him twist shit around until he made himself feel better?

I didn't give him the finger and flee, though. Because Peter had already shown up at my house. He'd wined and dined—or coffeed and manipulated—my mother. Worst of all, he'd somehow found out about Sweets You Rock, and I didn't need him showing up there.

So even though Lars wasn't at my back—and his come wasn't dripping out of me—I was beyond ready to tell Peter off. It was long overdue.

Under the false impression I wanted to chat, Peter's expression softened. Rather than his signature smile that was meant to charm and connive, he gave me his real one.

The boyish one.

Way back when, that smile had gotten me to agree to our first date. To agree to let him see my boobs. Then touch them.

It'd gotten me to agree to marry him even though we were sheltered babies who didn't understand the real world.

It forced me to dim myself.

Then I'd realized it wasn't the same effortless and easy look of love. He'd weaponized it. It was just another tool in his belt of bullshit.

So I was ready when he said, "Jossy Bean—"

I held my hand and my head up, silencing him. From my position on the porch steps, I was looking down at him.

A power play because I'd learned from the worst—him.

"You need to leave me alone, Peter." He opened his mouth to speak, but I continued. "I'm not kidding. I'm not running so you'll chase me. I'm not playing games. You need to leave. Now. Forever."

"Joss, I just want to talk."

"I don't."

His eye twitched. Good. He wasn't used to badass Joss who stood up for herself without worrying about being called a bitch or shrill or difficult.

"Is this because of *Lars*?" he bit out.

"How do you know about Lars?"

He waved his hand in the air, dismissing a very freakin' valid question. "It doesn't matter."

"Yes, it does. How?"

He must've realized I wasn't going to drop it, and he looked annoyed. "I went to your house to talk a few weeks ago and saw you leave together on a *motorcycle*." He spat the word with disgust, even though the Harley likely cost more than Peter's car—especially with the upgrades Lars had admitted to purchasing just to see me.

"Okay, but how do you know his name?"

He flushed a little as he tugged at his collar. "Some of the guys from the firm have been to his strip club."

Right. He had all the guys from his firm with him when he came to talk, loaded in like a clown car, and one of them recognized Lars.

Makes complete sense.

Not that he, oh, I dunno, recognized Lars because he himself has visited Wicked.

Sure. I'm totally stupid enough to believe that.

I let his lie go because it didn't matter. I had other burning—and creepy—questions. "How did you even know I was working at the bakery when you ratted me out to my mother?"

He held his hands in the surrender position. "That was a coincidence, I swear. Maggie picked up muffins from there and saw pictures of you and the owner. She fished around and found out you work there."

Maggie was a kiss ass and a big mouth from his office. I bet she'd savored that tidbit like some of Piper's cream cheese frosting.

"So?" he prodded. "Is it because of *him*?"

"No, it has nothing to do with him and everything to do with not wanting to talk to you. Not whenever you came over. Not when you were waiting on my porch like a freakin' stalker. And not now."

But he acted like I hadn't even spoken. "You were on the back of that bike. Then you were at that club last night, partying and drinking and dancing in that damn dress for anyone to see. I thought you wanted to see me but the security wouldn't let me talk to you." Anger made his handsome face contort into something ugly and red. "You're my fucking fiancée and they wouldn't let me talk to you."

Shuddering, goosebumps spreading across my crawling skin.

I didn't bother to ask why he'd want to see me or why he was there. His buddies loved places like Voodoo. They brought Sweater-Set-Miffy to the country club and family dinner before having their secret fun on the wild side.

Instead, I focused on the more important part of his unhinged rant. "I'm not your fiancée."

Nostrils flaring, he inhaled and gave me dopey puppy eyes. "I fucked up, Joss. I know it. You've let me suffer long enough. It's time to talk about us. You owe me this much."

It was incredible. Astounding, really, that someone could be that dumb.

I hadn't let him suffer.

He'd brought *that* on himself. And the idea that I *owed* him because he was sad?

I slow blinked, at a loss for words. But then I found them. "Were you homeschooled by a pigeon?"

His head jerked like he'd been smacked. I'd never spoken to him like that. I may have thought it, but I'd never said it.

It felt good.

He must've realized his charm was getting him nowhere because he switched tactics. His smile turned mean. A shark hiding his killer teeth as he sniffed for a weakness. For blood.

Ah, the gaslighting portion of the evening is about to begin.

"It doesn't make sense, Joss." His faux concern was laced with cruelty. "He's around all those women, day after day. Night after night. You're hot, Joss. I've always thought so. But those dancers are paid to be *sexy*. That's a completely different thing. You're not naïve enough to think he's not sampling the product before serving it to his customers..." He let his words trail off, letting them hang in the air like a scripted pause before finishing, "Are you?"

He'd put the wounds on my heart. In my soul. They were his fault, and he wanted to tear them open and pour salt in them. To fill my brain with doubt and my relationship with toxicity.

At his words, memories rushed through my head.

Of him and his accelerated heart rate.

The stripper in his car, riding him.

Lars and all the gorgeous dancers he was surrounded by. Day after day. Night after night.

As I stood there, mulling over Peter's words, I couldn't help it.

I tried, but I couldn't stop myself.

I started laughing.

Loudly.

Aimed right at Peter's shocked face.

Lars didn't dip his pen in company ink. It didn't matter how gorgeous the dancers were. To him, they were professionals there to do a job, and his job was to protect them. That was it.

Hell, he'd made a special point to emphasize that I wasn't an employee. I was an independent contractor. Totally different in his eyes.

More than that, though, Lars' word was everything to him. Same with loyalty. If he wanted someone else, he'd end the relationship he was in. Simple as that.

He was too much of a man to play little boy games.

And if he'd never cheat on anyone, he'd sure as hell never, *ever* cheat on me. He had a self-proclaimed obsession. In his words, I was the most gorgeous, sexy, and pretty person he'd ever seen.

He wanted me, and he liked me.

He'd break his own fingers and gouge out his own eyes before he betrayed me. I believed that to my soul.

"Your deviant boyfriend fucking his way through sluts is funny to you?" Peter asked.

"No, you're funny to me. That you think these ugly attacks would accomplish anything is hilarious. There's literally not a single thing you could say that would change anything." I wiped at my eyes, and I did it using my middle finger.

I was vaguely aware of the door opening behind me. As badly as I hated airing my dirty laundry, I needed to get it all out and then send him out of my life forever.

It was beyond time for him to become someone else's problem.

"We're done, Peter. We've been done for over eight months. And if you're honest with yourself, you'll know we've been done for a lot longer than that. We were both just too stupid and stubborn to see it."

There. That sounded nice. Like I was sharing the blame, even though it was totally that douchebucket's fault.

He didn't leave on the high road I'd just paved specifically for him. Nope, he had to play stupid games like he had his heart set on the biggest of the stupid prizes.

His gaze darted behind me before he curled into himself. Just a little, so as not to overplay it. A shark acting hurt to lure well-meaning yet tasty humans closer. "I just wanted to talk to you. To apologize. But you're being cruel. This isn't you, Jossy Bean. This is because of that man you've been seeing."

Someone gasped behind me, and I could've throttled Peter.

Oh, you absolute dickass.

Again, that wasn't enough for him. With my mom, and likely my dad, as our watchful audience, he decided to continue ratting me out. "He isn't a good man. You've seen his s—" He was smart enough to catch himself because if he mentioned Wicked, he was also admitting there. "His club. It's full of dangerous people. He's dangerous. And he's manipulating you."

Indignation filled me as I steeled in my spine and held my head high for myself *and* Lars. He'd worked hard to make Wicked something amazing. Did I want to tell my parents? No, not right then. I wanted them to meet Lars first. Get to know him and see that he wasn't the stereotypically skeevy strip club owner in a velour tracksuit.

I wanted them to see how smart and genuinely charming he was. How sweet he was with me. How caring. How much he respected and adored me.

But Peter was trying to sabotage that.

"You're right," I agreed, my voice low and even. "He's not a good man."

His eyebrows shot up, but that didn't stop the smug smile from curving across his smarmy face.

It died there when I finished, "He's the *best* man. Because he would never cheat on me. Ever. He'd cut his own hand off first. He doesn't raise his voice at me. He doesn't look at me with disapproval when I change my hair or do my makeup or wear what I want. He likes me exactly as I am." I leaned forward, my voice no longer even. It shook with rage. "And if you ever say anything bad about him again, I'll..." I hesitated as my mind blanked.

I'm gaining traction as a badass, but I haven't had to dole out any real threats yet.

The scariest one I make is to contact a parent, but that's not...

Bingo.

"This is going to be the last conversation we have, Peter. You're going to leave my family alone. You're going to leave my boyfriend alone. And you're going to leave me alone." He opened his mouth, but it was too late. He'd earned his stupid prize. "If you don't, I will send the video of you and your special friend to your mother."

Suck on that. You're not the only one who can rat people out to their moms.

He blinked a few times before it sank in, and his face drained of color.

The short video I'd taken of the stripper riding him.

When we'd canceled the wedding, he'd lied to his parents and the rest of his family. The nasty emails and DMs I'd received had made it clear he'd shifted all the blame onto me. I hadn't cared enough to set the record straight then. It'd been easier to let it go.

But that wasn't me anymore. I made waves when things were worth fighting for.

Like Lars.

And my inner peace.

"There's no video," he whispered, terrified his mom would find out he wasn't her innocent, perfect boy.

Barf.

He was right... kind of.

Once we'd gone our separate ways, and I'd thought he was out of my life, I'd deleted the video. But nothing stayed gone forever. I still had the same cell, and I was betting someone I knew was tech savvy enough to retrieve it.

I didn't share any of that. "Is that a risk you're willing to take?"

A throat cleared loudly behind me. "Think it's time you left, son."

It might've sounded like a suggestion, but nothing in Noah Lennon's tone brooked any argument.

Peter was a handsome man. He was a personable man. He was a charming man.

But he wasn't a smart man.

Despite my very real threats and Dad's very real... Dad-ness, he hesitated. "I don't understand why you won't just listen."

"Because I just don't care," I shot back, staring him down.

"She's made her feelings clear," Dad cut in again. It wasn't the same as having Lars at my back, but it was far from bad. "It's time to move on. It's for your own good. If my daughter says she'll do something, she will. Easier to go your separate ways and stay there."

Peter didn't give me a last look. No goodbye. No wistful sentiment. He knew my threat was real. He knew I'd had the footage. And, since I was the new, improved, kinda badass Joss, he knew I'd share it.

So with his tail tucked between his legs, he hurried to his car and sped off.

Leaving me to deal with... my own personal hell of a clusterfuck.

Since the best defense was a good offense—or something like that—I turned around and skewered Mom with a glare. I cut off the outrage brewing on her tongue with my own. "Did you invite Peter here knowing what he did to me? How he *hurt* me?"

I was spreading it on thicker than peanut butter, but I needed any leverage I could get.

"What?" My mom put her hand to her chest like I'd stabbed her with my peanut butter knife. "No. I'd never do that."

Damn.

It was good my mother hadn't facilitated the sneak attack. That would've actually hurt. But it also meant I had nothing to push back with when they came at me about the secret boyfriend.

And they would. All of them. My whole nosy family.

Damn and *shit.*

Surprisingly, Mom didn't launch in straight away. Taking pity on me, she gave me a warm smile and a tender squeeze. "Let's go eat before the cube steak turns into ice cube steak."

I started to follow her when my dad grabbed my shoulder. He wrapped an arm around me and pulled my side tight to his. "I don't think he's dumb enough to come around again after you laid him out, but you tell me if he is."

My throat clogged at his protectiveness. "Thanks, Dad."

"One thing I've learned in all my years as a husband and father..." He pressed a kiss to the top of my head. "Never underestimate a Lennon woman."

It was true.

A good lesson.

One I'd have been smart to remember.

Because after everyone was at the table, the cube steak was served, and it was quiet, Mom looked at me. Looked me dead in the eyes.

And then she announced, "Joss has a boyfriend."

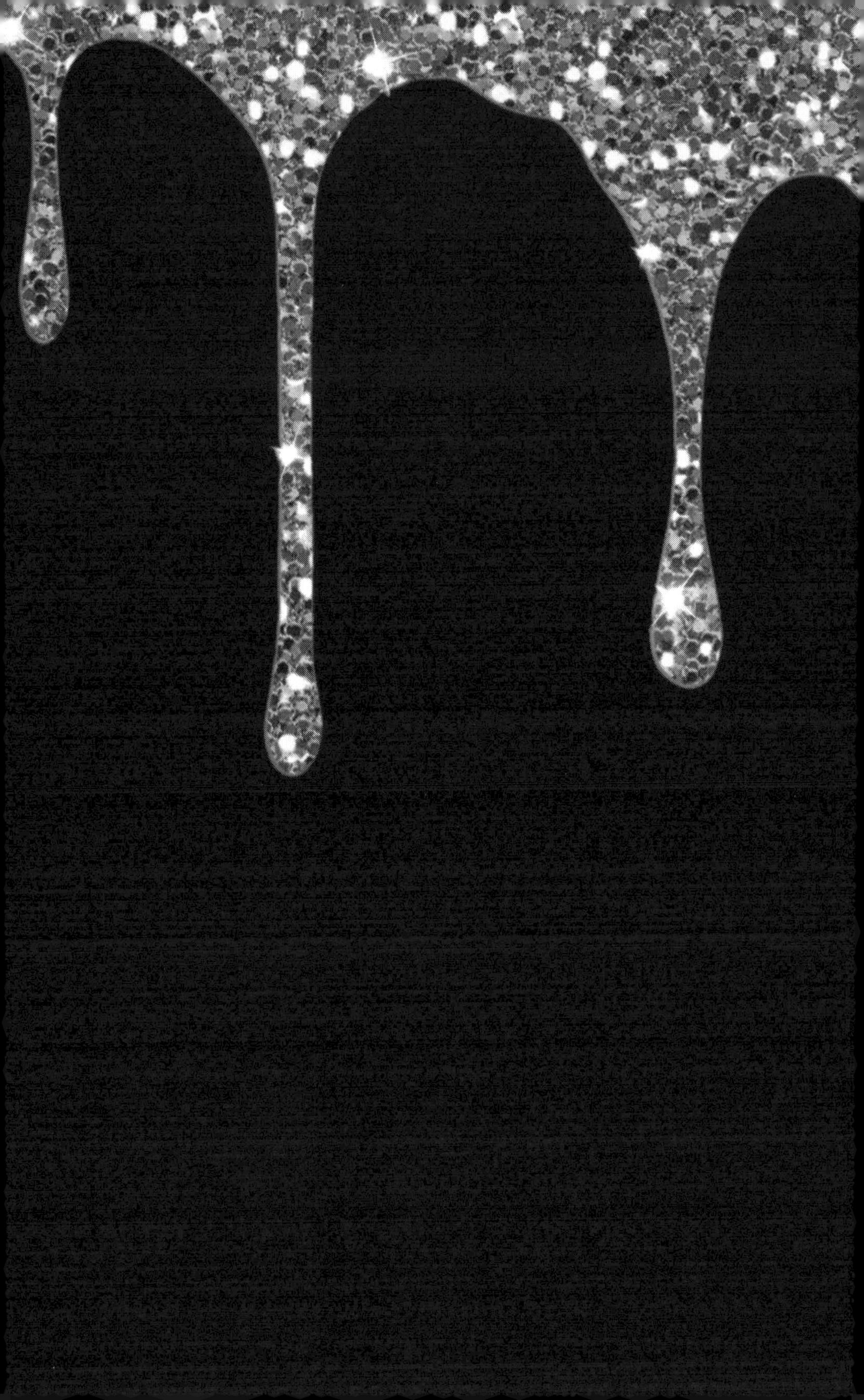

TWENTY-FIVE
Grab Your Glow Sticks, It's a Butterfly Rave

JOSS

IN MY LONG—LIFE LONG, IN FACT—HISTORY OF FAMILY dinners, I'd never experienced one quite like *that*.

Mom had dropped her juicy gossip bomb and then sat back to enjoy as everyone attacked me with questions.

We really were more alike than I'd realized.

I hadn't answered anything, which had backfired and only stoked their curiosity. It was clear I'd need to bring Lars over sooner rather than later.

But I was still gonna drag my feet for as long as possible because they were a *lot*.

I was related to them, and even I thought so.

Mentally exhausted—but physically full of a delicious dinner—I pulled into my driveway and grinned to see a familiar Harley parked on the street.

I'd barely climbed out of my car when I was suddenly pushed against it.

"You were gone too fuckin' long, hotcakes." When Lars' mouth hit mine, the day washed away. Everything except being in my man's arms.

"I didn't know you'd be here," I panted when he tore his mouth away. "You need a replacement phone."

"Already picked it up."

"Why didn't you text?"

"Wanted to surprise you."

It's the second surprise visit from a man today, but the only one I actually want.

He snagged my wrist and started for the porch, more impatient than usual. That was fine by me, and I almost went before remembering my mother had sent me home with leftovers. Leftovers I did *not* want to leave in my car overnight.

"Hold on." I grabbed my stuff before returning my wrist to his strong hold.

We made it all the way to the porch before I came to another abrupt halt with my hand on the rail.

The sturdy rail because someone had fixed it properly.

I briefly noticed new lights bracketing the door, but it was the lovely porch swing hanging from the ceiling that stole my focus.

My gaze shot to the side to find Lars regarding me. "That's not the one I bought."

"Sorry, baby." He wrapped an arm around my shoulders. "The wood on that sucker was warped beyond repair."

That was unsurprising since it'd been sitting in the box, exposed to the elements, for over a year.

The first time I'd toured the house, my heart had squeezed as I'd imagined sitting on a porch swing or rocking chair, looking out at the world. Cars driving by. People walking their dogs. Neighbor kids playing.

My own kids playing.

After signing a million papers to make the house officially mine, I'd gone straight to the store to buy the cheapest porch swing they had. At the time, I'd still been trying to make things work with Peter and had thought we'd hang it together. Laughing, drinking lemonade, the whole cliché romance montage.

Unsurprisingly, he'd never had time. He'd never *made* time. My dad and brothers-in-law had offered, but it became a stubborn point of contention and resentment for me. I was happy to let it sit there, neglected until it was useless.

Poetic.

There was nothing cheap about the one Lars installed. Natural wood with a seat so wide, it was large enough to stretch out on. He'd even bought pretty pillows.

Pillows.

If sitting on a plain porch swing had been a goal, lounging on that cushy one with a good drink and an even better book was an absolute dream.

I wanted to do that. I couldn't wait to do that.

But I *needed* to do something else first.

It was my turn to snag Lars' hand and tug him inside.

"Do you want to see the rest?"

There's more?

It didn't matter, my answer was still the same.

"No."

"Got it." In the blink of an eye, I was in his arms with my legs wrapped around his waist.

I tossed the leftover container and my bag to the side as we moved, not really caring if gravy spilled on my floor. That was a problem for the future me.

When he reached my room, I was already trying frantically to strip him. Needing to touch him. Feel him. Lars' desperation was just as strong, his mouth and hands working to taste and touch as much of me as he could without dropping me.

My back hit the mattress, our clothes were strewn about, and then he was on me.

In me.

With one powerful surge, he was buried to the hilt. He drew back until just the tip remained before slamming in. Making my breasts bounce. Making my body shift up the bed. Filling me so completely, I wasn't sure I could take it.

But I did.

Over and over.

I couldn't get enough.

I'd *never* get enough.

I shoved at his shoulders, unable to form the words to verbalize the request. He knew, though. He always knew. It was something I liked to do often just because I could. Because he liked it.

More importantly, because *I* liked it.

Keeping our connection, he carefully rolled us so I was on top and his head was elevated by pillows so he could watch.

Watch me ride him. Watch me stretch around him. Watch me greedily take what I needed.

And he gave it. He gave me everything. *Always.*

Without me nagging. Without him complaining. Without resentment or monotony or stipulations. Effortless and easy, Lars took care of me in more ways than I could count.

It was overwhelming.

My chest was tight. Butterflies raved in my belly, a mosh pit of twisted flutters. Putting my hand to Lars' muscular chest, his heart was racing, too.

And *that* was my undoing.

My voice was little more than a hoarse whisper. "Say it."

His gaze shot from our connection to my eyes. His hold on my hips tightened as he planted himself deep. In typical Lars fashion, he read my face. My body. My soul.

Without a moment of unsurety, confusion, or hesitation, he did as I ordered.

He said it.

"Love you, Joss."

I usually disliked when he used my actual name. It was irrational, but I preferred *baby* or *hotcakes*. Right then, though, it was perfect.

His heart pounded under my palm as I closed my eyes. I let the moment settle into me. Not just my brain or my heart. No, hearing Lars Luthor rumble that he loved me seared itself into my very being.

Into my DNA.

I wasn't confused. I wasn't unsure. And without another moment of hesitation, I opened my mouth to hand him my vulnerable, scarred heart. And I'd do it knowing he'd take care of it. Just like he took care of the rest of me.

Before I could, Lars put a finger to my mouth. "Be sure you get what you're saying."

My brows furrowed. I'd been dying to tell him how I felt. Working up the nerve while dying, but still. I'd never been more sure of anything in my life.

"You give me you, all of you," he continued, "and I'm never giving you back."

My heart squeezed with a pain so damn beautiful, it rocked me to my core.

Before his finger had even fully moved, I said, "I love you, too."

Bending his knees so his legs were against my back, Lars sat so our torsos met. I was surrounded by him. Filled with him. Obsessed with him. His hand wrapped around my neck to tip my chin up. "Say it again."

"I love you." I moved, the angle hitting a new and wondrous place.

I only controlled it for a moment before Lars took over. Using his hold on my hip and throat, he rocked me. My clit ground against him and the tip of his dick rubbed that spot deep inside me until I was shaking. Tightening his fingers against the side of my throat, he cut off my air before taking my mouth to steal the rest.

When he released his hold, my lungs filled, my head rushed with everything and nothing, and the orgasm he'd been fueling erupted. His filthy words of lust, tender words of love, and grunts of pleasure filled my ears as we came.

Stripped raw.

Flayed open.

Exposed.

Vulnerable.

But safe.

And *loved*.

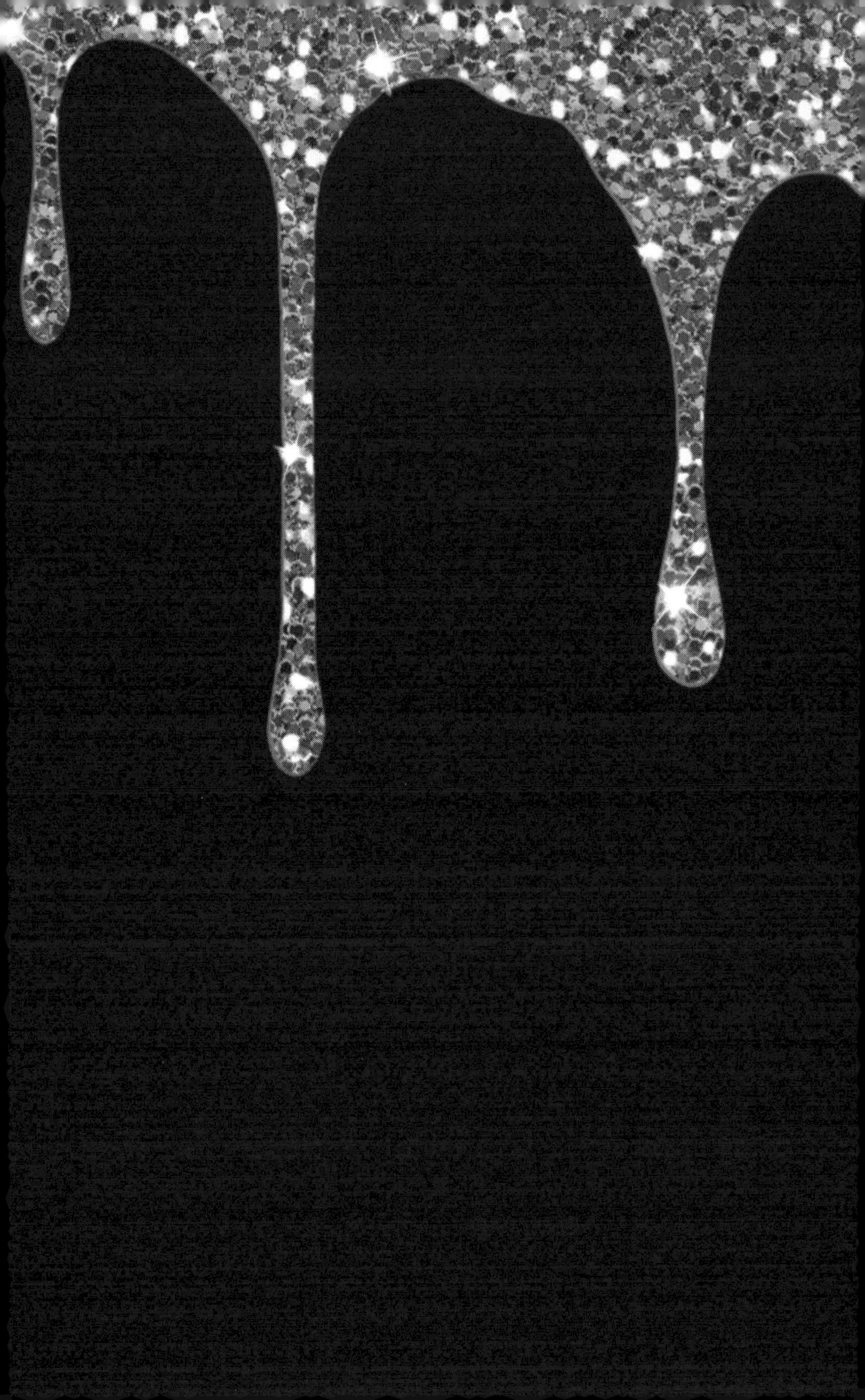

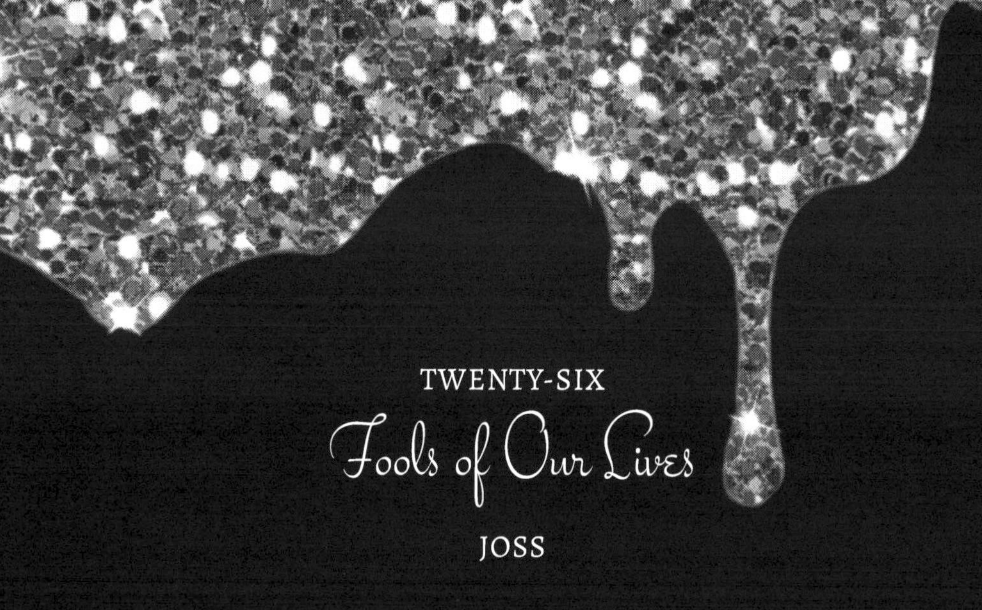

TWENTY-SIX
Fools of Our Lives
JOSS

EVEN THOUGH I'D HAD A BOYFRIEND IN HIGH SCHOOL, we'd never been one of the couples who made out in the hallway. Definitely never in a classroom. My teachers would've ratted me out to my parents, earning me detention *and* extra shifts at the hardware store. Even if I'd been willing to risk that, Peter had not. It would've gone against his *golden-boy* image.

But I was no longer a student. I was the teacher.

Which meant making out in my classroom on a Tuesday afternoon was totally fine.

Holding an iced coffee in one hand and Lars' neck in the other, I enjoyed the thrill of kissing him for all the baby dolls, dinos, and building blocks to see. While standing on the quiet time rug, no less.

"Wanna break in one of the nap mats?" Lars murmured between kisses.

Yes.

"You've got work, and I need to pick up my friends from PE."

His voice and smoldering expression dripped sex. "I wanna be your friend."

I fought the urge to melt into him. If I did, we'd end up rolling around the rug, and there was no way I could be quiet on it.

"You are." I lifted my cup. "You brought me coffee."

"Good to know it's that easy."

I shrugged since he wasn't wrong. For him, it really was that easy.

With one last kiss, he headed for the door, speaking as he moved. "Love you, hotcakes. Counting down the minutes."

It took a moment to get my brain working again. It took an even longer one before I had enough control to go to the gym rather than chasing after Lars.

We were on the way back, walking in a not-so-silent line by the office when Ms. Clara opened the door. The PE high they were riding peaked as they fervently spoke over each other to share their every thought with their favorite staff member.

For probably the first time ever, she didn't give the kids an indulgent smile. Her attention was on me, and it was etched with concern.

Uh-oh.

"Mr. Henry wants to see you."

Extra uh-oh.

Time with Mr. Henry took weeks to schedule. An immediate meeting was almost as bad of a sign as the foreboding expression on Ms. Clara's kind face.

"I'll take your kids back to the room and get them settled." She reached out to give my arm a reassuring squeeze.

I gulped, trying to swallow over the lump that'd formed in my throat.

Will they still be my kids after this meeting?

Not wanting to prolong my anxiety, I lightly knocked on his office door and opened it without waiting for a response.

Mr. Henry didn't offer a smile or bland greeting. He simply gestured to the chair in front of him. "Have a seat, Miss Lennon."

I wish he'd go back to not knowing my name.

Clutching my hands, I hoped my nerves weren't obvious. Because internally? I was a piece of tissue paper in a tornado.

Without delay, he cut to the awful chase. "We've had a complaint."

My stomach bottomed out. Not to the floor. Or the basement. Or the layers of dirt beneath the building. No, my stomach had taken a journey to the center of the Earth.

I'd never had a complaint made against me. Not even as a student teacher. Logically, I'd known it would happen. It was inevitable. Every teacher eventually had a parent or colleague they didn't mesh with.

But nothing bad had happened. My little friends were thriving. After arranging the evening at axes, the teachers thought I was a rock star. No one had given any indication there was a problem.

I was blindsided.

Stunned, my voice was flat and numb. *I* was flat and numb. "What was it?"

"It's been brought to our attention that you're involved with a man who has questionable..."

When his words trailed off, I pushed, "Questionable *what*?"

Mr. Henry broke eye contact and fidgeted with the pens on his desk. "Questionable employment choices."

That was a load of shit. "And?"

"And it's been pointed out that parents may feel uncomfortable with their children being exposed to that lifestyle."

"Then it's a good thing I've never taken them on a field trip to his club."

"But he has been in the building. Just as recently as today."

Plenty of spouses visited. Spouses who, if teacher's lounge gossip was to be believed, made much more questionable choices than Lars ever had.

But no one said a word about them.

"Yes, while my kids were gone. *Not* because I think he's some sort of nefarious influence," I emphasized, "but because I don't like to introduce distractions or disruptions to their schedules. Like, for instance, pulling their teacher away from them right after the most hectic part of their day."

His nostrils flared, but he kept going. "What you do in your personal life is your business. We obviously can't police that. But there are certain expectations we hold our teachers to."

"When have I not met expectations?" I asked, riled all the way up at the insinuation. The *insult*. "I go above and beyond for my kids. Every eval has shown that. And I go above and beyond for this school. Lars has, too, all while eating the cost. Thanks to him, you avoided a school full of disgruntled teachers on the verge of a mass exodus."

His stern expression wavered. "And I appreciate that. But my back is against the wall here. They said if it didn't end, they'd go above my head."

"*It*? My relationship?" I reared back like I'd been punched right in my damn face. "You're giving me an ultimatum?"

I was fairly certain that was illegal, but even if it wasn't, I didn't care. I was done. Why would I want to keep pouring my blood, sweat, and tears into a school where I was treated like garbage?

Mr. Henry vehemently shook his head, as if an HR nightmare danced in his brain. "As I said, what you do in your personal life is your business. I'm just asking that your visitor not return."

"Fuck that," I bit out, not caring if it was unprofessional. They'd come for my livelihood *while* insulting my boyfriend.

Since neither the students nor the parents had met Lars, it wasn't coming from them. The staff, though? Most of them had seen him, albeit briefly. I needed to know who'd been smiling to my face as they talked shit behind back.

"Who complained?" I pushed. "Was it another teacher?"

"You know I can't disclose that," he said even as he gave a small shake of his head.

"A staff member?"

Another subtle shake.

"So, it was a parent," I surmised, deflating faster than a pool floatie that'd been stabbed in the back. It still hurt, but nowhere near as bad.

"I can't disclose," he repeated, all while shaking his head.

What the hell?

"Do you even know who did it?"

And, surprise, surprise, yet another shake.

I wanted to smack him for being a spineless bobblehead.

"Let me get this straight," I seethed, forcing my tone to stay low. I'd already sworn at my principal, I couldn't yell at him—even if he did deserve it. "You've dragged me away from my students. Dragged my personal business into my work. Badmouthed the man who saved your ass with a *free* event. And threatened me because of an anonymous complaint?"

At my summary, Mr. Henry had the good grace to look sheepish.

With a resolute nod, I stood. "Fine. Then I quit—"

I didn't even get the chance to mention my union rep and attorney before he jolted from his seat. "Miss Lennon, that's not what I want. If this goes above me, it'll be completely out of my hands. I won't be able to help you."

His earnestness rang true. His delivery sucked, but his heart seemed to be in the right place.

"I don't like this any more than you do," he continued. "When I received the email—"

"Wait, it was an email? Can I see it?"

He clicked a few buttons on his computer before turning it so I could read.

It was a weird sensation, being filled with relief and rage at the same time. It warred within me until my brain swam and my chest wanted to implode.

"I'll handle it." With that, I stormed back to my classroom, seeing red-hot-rage.

Or blood.

I'd planned to tell Lars about Peter's surprise visit.

Honestly. It'd been at the top of my to-do list.

Then Lars had surprised me with all the house stuff, and *he'd* shot to the top of my to-do list.

After sex and love declarations and a trip to his condo for a repeat of both, the showdown with Peter had been the furthest thing from my mind. Lars and I had our own bubble of happiness. No way was I bursting that to let Peter's bullshit seep in like noxious sludge.

That was before he'd sent an email to my principal. He may not have signed it, but it was him.

If parents, the school district, or even the media were to find out about Miss Lennon's involvement with a deviant, they might be uncomfortable with who teaches their kindergartener.

And who runs the school…

. . .

A DEVIANT.

Only one moron had called Lars that, and he'd done it two days before on my parent's porch.

I wanted to drive to his PR firm and confront him myself, but he'd like that too much. A crazy, obsessed ex would be like a crystal trophy for his shelf. The cred boost he'd get would guarantee free drinks and rounds of golf courtesy of his idiot buddies.

Not to mention, I'd have to see Peter again. I'd already made it clear that wouldn't happen.

I had a better plan.

I'd texted Lars that I needed to see him, but when I arrived for my exciting evening of bookkeeping, it was Frankie waiting for me outside. We weren't as close as I was with Killer, but Frankie liked me. Mostly because I shared my dinner leftovers, but that was fine. I wasn't above bribery.

We might not have been BFFs, but he took one look at me and frowned. "What happened, Teach?"

"Just a long day. How's your shift?"

He wasn't deterred. "Need me to kick someone's ass?"

I laughed, though it wasn't actually a joke. "Maybe next time."

He just nodded and stepped aside so I could enter.

As soon as I moved down the long hallway, the swinging door on the other side slammed open. Lars' sharp gaze did a quick sweep of me, like he was searching for injury. Seeing my appendages were still where they should be, his long legs closed the distance before he pulled me into his office and slammed the door.

"Thanks for walking me in, Frankie," I called, glaring at Lars for his rudeness.

Lars wasn't fazed by my intimidating stare. "Just saw your text. What do you need?"

"How did you track down Controversy LLC's owner?"

His brows shot up even as the rest of him became guarded. "Nox has a couple guys who are good with technology. Why?"

"Could they restore something I deleted from my phone?"

"Probably." He crossed his arms. "I'll repeat... *Why*?"

I quickly filled him in on Peter's visit, my video threat, and the email to my principal. I left out that Lars himself had been the focus of the email.

If he found out Peter was trying to use him to hurt me, there'd be no chance at civility.

Once I was done with the minimal details, I held up my cell. "Can you see if one of his techy guys knows how to recover the video? I'm not going to send it to Peter's mother." I paused and amended, "Not yet, at least. I think sending him the proof that it does exist will be enough of a threat."

Without a word, Lars pulled his phone from his pocket, his thumbs moving across the screen. It beeped before he'd even put it away. "Dair will be calling you on the office phone in ten to walk you through how to do it."

"Thank you," I said slowly, my eyes narrowed.

That'd been easy.

Too easy.

My suspicions were confirmed when he ordered, "You can thank me by telling me where this motherfucker works."

"Baby—" I started, going for the sweetness before he cut me off.

"No. That bastard was waiting at your house in the middle of the damn night. He showed up at your parents' house. And then he had the balls to email your boss? No, Joss. You can handle it your way. Send the video to him. His parents. The rest of his family, his friends, his first-grade teacher. But I'm still gonna have a word with him myself."

I'd expected that. I would've been shocked if he hadn't insisted. And maybe it made me a shitty person, but I wouldn't stop him—as long as he promised not to maim or gouge. Threaten, though? I was surprisingly okay with that.

Peter deserved the consequences of his own actions for one.

I crossed my arms over my chest to mirror Lars' stance. "No violence."

"Can't promise that."

"Then I'm not telling you where to find him."

Already angry, his body tightened until he looked two second away from tearing the door off its hinges. Despite his fury, he didn't yell. "Why're you trying to protect him?"

I didn't poke the bear. I rolled my eyes right in his face. "I'm protecting you, you dumbass. There are too many cameras near his office, and he is too litigious. He'll press charges and sue and drag it out. We'll never get him out of our lives."

Lars was still pissed as hell, but he softened at that. "*Our* lives?"

"Yes. Now promise."

"No violence." He uncrossed his arms and pulled me closer. "Unless he starts it."

That was fine because it'd never happen. Peter didn't start fights. He also didn't finish them. They could ruin his image—literally and figuratively.

Holding my glare a second longer, I told Lars where Peter worked. Before I could regret my decision, he kissed me until I forgot what regret even meant and then left.

I was officially making waves.

And it was about time.

When the office phone rang, I didn't pause. "Hello?"

"Aye, lass, it's Dair." The loud background noise of clinking and conversation cut off. "What can I do fer ya?"

"Are you out to dinner?" I hadn't even considered the time difference if Dair wasn't in the states.

"Nah, just following whispers."

I had no clue what any of that meant because Nox's profession—and, by association, Dair's profession—was rarely discussed. It wasn't illegal, per se, but it was in the gray.

It was also none of my business, so I explained my issue. Or overexplained it. Because rather than just saying I'd deleted a video, I filled the poor man in on what the video was of, Peter being an asshole along with a cheater, and my threatening plan.

When I reached that portion, thick laughter filled my ear before the accented man weirdly said, "Aye, the talent in the states is well good."

Again, I had no clue what that meant, but it sounded like a compliment.

"Let's help ya get the thick cunt outta yer hair, aye?" With the patience of a saint, Dair dumbed down the technical terms until I could follow his instructions. Within minutes, the video was rescued from the dark, creepy crevices of the cloud.

I thanked Dair and let him get back to following whispers.

Now what?

Lars

Walking into the yuppy building, I expected to have to bribe or bullshit my way past security, but I wasn't stopped. I moved straight to the elevator with confidence, like I belonged there, and no one batted an eye.

I followed Joss' directions, got off at the tenth floor, and continued past offices until I found the one I was looking for.

Without knocking, I pushed the door open and savored the way the douchebag's expression morphed from startled annoyance to panic.

Fuck yeah, he knew who I was. And, shocking as shit, I knew who he was, too. Not by name, but I'd seen him at Wicked over the years.

Which meant he was even stupider than I'd thought. Why would he pay to have women flirt with him when he had Joss at home, in his bed?

The man was a fuckin' fool.

"I'm calling security," he snapped.

"Go ahead. It'll take them at least a minute to get up here, and I can do a lot in that time."

His scowl deepened as his gaze darted from his phone back to the door. "She made her point. She didn't need to send her guard dog."

Fuckin' hell, he was giving me warm feelings. First, he wouldn't say her name. Then he called me her guard dog. How the hell was I supposed to dislike *that*? But then he had to fuck it up by lying that she'd made her point.

Closing the distance so only his desk sat between us, I leaned over. "Yeah? Then why'd you run to her principal like a cowardly rat?"

He leaned back. I waited for a lie, but it didn't come. "I sent that email weeks ago."

Not denying he'd sent it, just denying the timeline.

And, fuck me, I believed him. It was still jacked, but it could've been worse.

"Ya know, I like you," I said.

His eyes narrowed in suspicion, and his shoulders were at his ears from how tense he was.

"I can die happy," he bit out sarcastically.

I continued like he hadn't spoken. "You fucked Joss over so bad, it makes me seem like a good choice when I sure as shit don't deserve her."

"We can agree on that."

"You don't deserve her, either, dipshit. But thanks to you, she's insane enough to want me. To love me. And I'm gonna bust my ass to make sure she doesn't regret that decision for a single moment in *our* lives. Starting with making sure you never breathe her air again."

Peter gripped the arms of his chair until his knuckles went white. "What? Are you going to kick my ass?" He was trying to save face, but fear drained the color from his face until it matched his knuckles.

"Nah. Promised Joss no violence." I shot him a vicious smile. "Unless you start it."

If he leaned back any farther, he'd topple the chair and knock himself on his ass.

"I don't have to do jack shit other than be at her back while Joss deals with you." When the moron's brows lowered, I shook my head. "You underestimate her. My girl's got her own kinda badass streak."

Better than we could've planned it, Peter's phone dinged, and I glanced down to see Joss' name on a text.

No, not Joss.

Jossy Bean.

Bet she hated that shit.

Peter sat up fast, a small smile playing at his lips. He forced it to grow into a smirk. The smug expression made me want to punch it off his face, but it was the small, tender smile that had made me murderous. No one should be smiling like that about *my* woman.

He swiped at his phone, and the sound of wind and birds filled the room. Then the sound of muffled—yet fake-as-hell—moans took over.

Joss had been able to restore the video. *And* she'd sent it.

Christ, I love her.

His arrogant smile dropped like he'd been punched in the gut.

Or the crotch.

"Like I said," I started when it looped back to nature sounds, "she'll handle it. And if you think she won't blast that out to your family, friends, and anyone else, you don't know her."

"I did know her." His glare cut to me, the sound still looping in the background. "But then you ruined her. *My* Joss was sweet and loving and quiet and—"

"And then you cheated on her."

"I made a mistake!" he roared before his eyes widened. Closing them, he gathered his composure. "It doesn't matter anyway. She's always acted like she's so perfect on her high horse. But now she's just another rude bitch who plays like she's better than me. Enjoy the uptight prude."

There he was, giving me warm feelings again and making me grin. "If she was an uptight prude with you, that says something about you, not her. 'Cause my Joss is still sweet and loving, but she's snarky and fiery and fuckin' *wild*."

I could've let it be. I'd made my point, and Joss sure as shit made hers with that perfectly timed video message. Peter was a dumbass, but I doubted even he was stupid enough to keep going. He was all bluster and bullshit. I could've let him have that shred of dignity he was clinging to.

But he didn't deserve that.

I reached out, and he flinched before glowering. The memory of that alone would haunt him. I bit back a smile and picked up the picture frame from his desk.

Joss' smiling face hit me in the chest, gut, and dick.

I'd wanna look at it all day, too. But just 'cause I understood it didn't mean I'd allow it.

I started undoing the back of the frame as I spoke. "You can sit up here, in your mid-level office, and try to convince yourself you're better off. You can stick your little prick in toxic snatch until it rots off. You can bad mouth Joss, twist the narrative, and tell whatever lies you need to feel superior. But we both know the truth. She's not acting like she's better than you. She *is* better than you."

Peter continued glaring like his stare could make my head explode, but he said nothing.

"Think I made it clear, but lemme make it crystal. Stay away from Joss. Move the fuck on, or I'll help her ruin your life. Got it?"

After a long, silent moment, he lifted his chin.

I tossed the empty frame to the desk, pocketed the picture, and started for the door before pausing. "And stay the hell outta my club."

With the same confidence as when I came, I left the building and headed back to my woman in my club.

And hoped like hell she'd break her rule again by riding my dick in the back office.

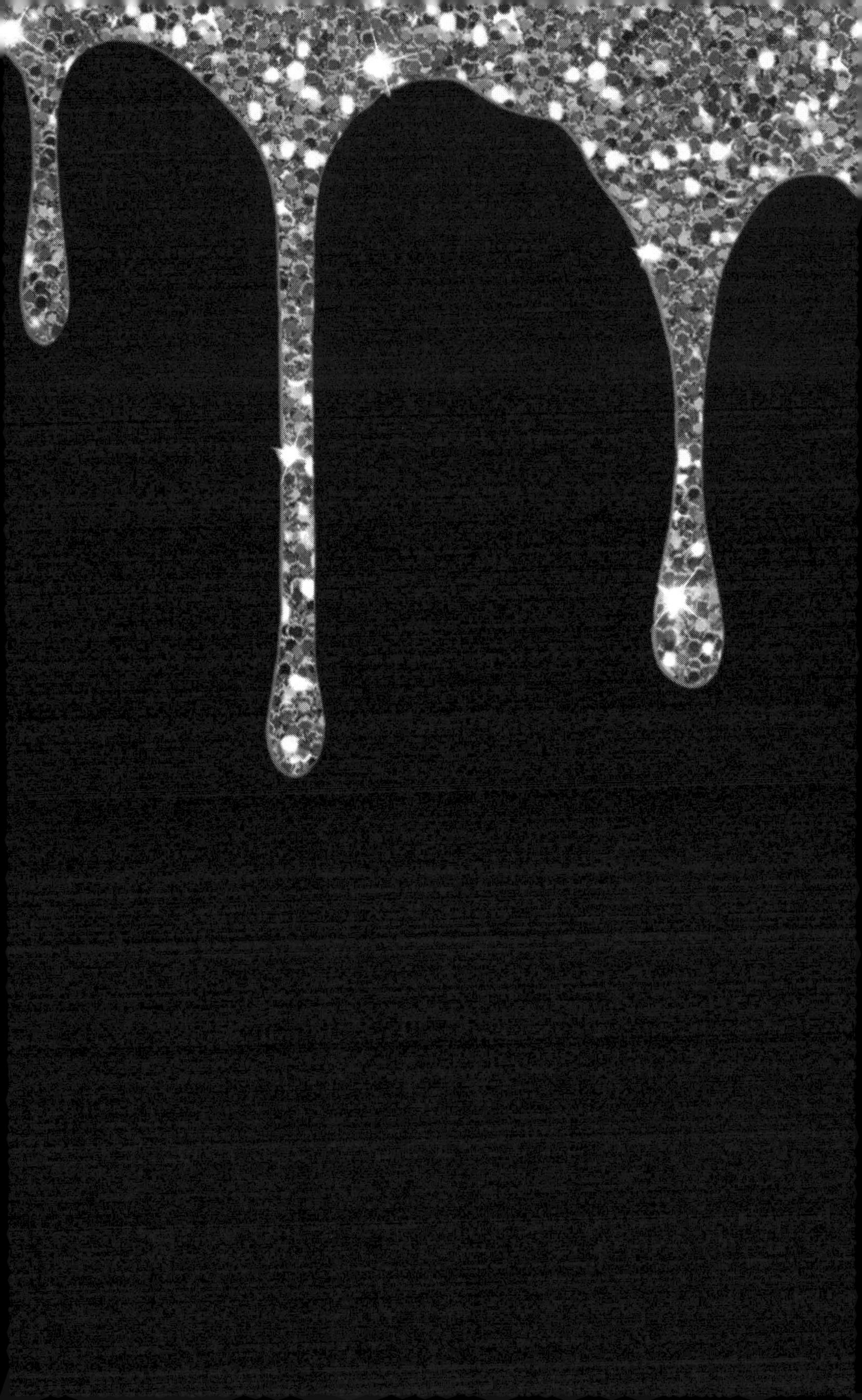

TWENTY-SEVEN

One Small Step for Man, Three Chocolate Cookies for Orgasms

LARS

"HARDER."

My good girl loved my cock no matter how she got it but riding me was her favorite.

Slouched on her couch, with her still in her sexy-as-fuck dress and me still in my clothes, she didn't try to hide how much she loved it. The proof was on her face. In her stuttered breathing. In the wetness that coated her thighs and my dick.

My control had been razor-thin all night while we'd belatedly celebrated Nox and Gus' engagement. I was glad they'd waited for the dust to settle after they'd moved her grandma from Tennessee to an assisted living facility in the city. That meant instead of going stag, I'd had Joss with me. Pressed tight to me. Touching me. Tormenting me.

All night, I'd pictured getting her pussy around my dick. And every time my eyes had landed on the rock on Gus' finger, I'd imagine my ring on Joss'.

Following her order, I gripped her hips and slammed her down my length harder. Taking her rougher. Knowing how she liked it. I added my thumb to her clit and watched my girl ignite around me.

Watched her let go of all that pent-up wild.

I followed soon after, but not before wringing another from her so I came with her pussy choking my dick.

Dropping her head to my shoulder, Joss' breath evened till I thought she was asleep. Fine by me. Didn't matter that I was supposed to leave for Wicked. I could've happily fallen asleep with her on my lap and my dick inside her.

But she sat up a moment later to give me a sleepy smile. "I think I better get to bed."

"Yeah."

"Are you still going to work?"

It killed me, but I nodded. I'd taken more time off in the previous month than I had since I'd opened the place. Not that Sasha was complaining about the extra hours. She was making a shit-ton. Not to mention, she loved being in charge. She was good at it, too.

But Fridays got crazy, so I told her I'd be back after dinner.

That'd turned into after dinner *and* sex, but that was better. At least I'd be calmer.

Kissing Joss till I was ready for round two, I grudgingly peeled myself away—but not before using my finger to press my come back inside her. I cleaned up in the bathroom and returned to find her waiting by the door, practically swaying on her feet.

I need to stop waking her all the time just so I can feel and taste her.

Maybe one of these days, I won't be so desperate.

And maybe one of these days, I'll walk on the moon.

The two have the same odds of happening.

"Lock this after me," I ordered.

"Always do."

Once I heard the lock click and the alarm beep, I left. I was halfway to Wicked when my phone rang. Checking the display, I connected the call. "Miss me already?"

Rather than biting out an insult, Nox was serious. "Where are you?"

"My car, why?"

"Dair is here."

"Eh, how's ye bonnie hen? Video work then?"

Nox and Dair were both Scottish and Irish, but Dair still lived overseas. It meant his accent was thicker, and it always took me a second to get what he was saying.

"Yeah, it worked. What's going on?"

Nox and I were tight, but he wouldn't call me to shoot the shit. Especially not when we'd just seen each other.

And especially not with the way he'd spent his night eyeing Gus like he wanted to take her against the wall in the middle of the restaurant.

Would've given him shit about it had I not been counting down till I could get Joss on her couch.

"Followed some whispers," Dair said. "Involving the Irish. They've teamed up with Nash."

Why am I not surprised?

The Irish mob was loud, crazy, and ran in the open. They wouldn't know subtlety if it kicked them in the balls.

Made sense they'd hook up with Nash. They were a perfect match.

"What's that gotta do with me?"

"There are rumblings that they wanna grow. And they wanna use Wicked to do it."

I hadn't busted my ass to make Wicked someplace good just for some crooked bastards to roll in and fuck it up. Eddie had tried that, and he was deep in the ground. I didn't bother to ask how my club factored into their expansion. Didn't matter 'cause the answer was the same.

"Fuck no."

"This the first yer hearing about it?" Dair pushed.

I didn't like the insinuation in his tone even if I understood it. A lot of greedy bastards wouldn't be able to resist the money and power that came from teaming up with the Irish mob. Even more cowards didn't have the balls to go against them.

Neither applied to me, and I said as much. "I'd cut off my left ball before I handed over everything I've worked for. So, yeah, this is the first I'm hearing about this."

"Aye, that's what I told him," Nox said, not happy about the insinuation, either.

"Had to be sure before I put my ass on the line. I'll put the right whispers into the right ears that Nox and I have yer back. I'll also remind them that Wicked falls in Italian territory. Doesn't matter if yer paying for protection or not, the Italians don't stand for poaching."

"That'll work?" I was skeptical that a few threats would be enough to scare away the goddamn Irish mob.

"The Irish are ballsy, but they're not suicidal. It'll work."

"Nox?" I prodded, wanting his input.

"Aye, it'll work. Be aware, if you have any mob patrons or employees, they'll drop off. Could be you show up to work tomorrow and only a tumbleweed blows through."

Fine by me. I'd rather that than a building full of crazy mobsters who want to use my club to funnel their shit.

We talked for a couple minutes more until I pulled up to Wicked. I'd expected flashing lights, a fire, or the building to be razed.

But it looked the same as it did every Friday night.

Packed.

Thank fuck for Joss and that calm she gave me.

I'm gonna need it.

Joss

"Long overdue girls' day."

My focus moved from the register to where Piper stood close by. Alarm shot through me.

Last time we'd had a girls' night, it'd been because of her diagnosis. For a brief moment, I worried she'd gotten more bad news she wanted to share—or be distracted from. But there was no sadness on her face.

She looked happy. Maybe even excited.

"How can it be long overdue?" I asked. "We just went out last night for Gus and Nox's engagement dinner."

"Yeah, that was with other people. This is just us."

"Voodoo again?" I needed to mentally prepare myself. It wasn't that I didn't want to go out. It was just...

I didn't want to go out.

The preparations. The actually leaving the house. The late night.

It was exhausting.

We hadn't even stayed out too late the night before, but after the fun on my couch with Lars, I'd crashed. Hard. I would've slept through my alarm had Lars not woken me.

I could've tackle-hugged Piper when she shook her head. "Harlow's place after work. Unless you're busy."

Even if I had plans, I'd have rearranged them because a Saturday afternoon at a beach house with my friends sounded too perfect to miss.

"I'm in," I said.

"Good. Chinese delivery. Margaritas. It'll be chill." She turned away then stopped short.

When I looked over my shoulder, I saw Sophie standing behind us with a tray of sticky buns. Thankfully, nothing fell, or we'd have a customer riot on our hands.

It was fast. So fast, I may have been way off base. But for the briefest second, Piper seemed to hesitate. Just as quick, though, the pensive look was gone. "We're getting together at Harlow's," she told Soph. "Just a chill girls' day after we close. Are you free?"

Sophie frowned, her disappointment clear. "I have a hair appointment."

"Perfect, that fits with the self-care theme of the day." She gestured to the chaos around us. "Just come when you're done. Once I do all my stuff, you'll probably beat me there."

While Piper sent Soph the address, I looked across the store as Lars entered. As soon as he saw me, a smile spread across his handsome face.

All at once, my heart squeezed, my stomach fluttered, and my thighs clenched.

Such was the power of Lars' smile.

Grabbing a bag from the side, I rounded the counter and met him halfway, not stopping until I was in his arms.

We both knew he hadn't driven out of his way for a cookie, but after he kissed me hard and hot, I still handed him the bag.

Peeking inside, he rumbled, "Three cookies, hotcakes?"

"One for each…" I started, my cheeks and body flushing at the memory of the three orgasms he'd given me the night before and that morning in bed.

His mouth was much better than an alarm and impossible to sleep through.

He opened said mouth, likely to say something obscenely sweet, but I quickly covered it. We were in public, and the customers weren't even trying to be subtle about listening.

Nor were Soph and Piper.

I felt his smile before he nipped my palm between his teeth.

"Ow. You fight dirty." I pulled my hand away to dramatically shake it out despite the fact it hadn't hurt.

"And you like it," he shot back.

It was true. I did.

"I'm going to girls' day at Harlow's later," I told him.

"Sounds good, baby." He hooked his index fingers in my belt loops and tugged me closer until I could feel his cock hardening against my stomach. "This mean you're gonna come to Wicked, drunk and horny?"

"Maybe," I admitted.

"Call me when you're done, I'll come get you."

"I'll Uber."

"Call me." He dipped his head to my ear. "Or I'll plant your ass on my desk, eat you until you're about to come, and then stop. Over and over."

A shudder went through me—and not an unpleasant one. Still, I immediately changed my answer. "I'll call you."

"That's my good girl."

With another kiss, he swaggered out of the bakery.

Leaving me a pile of happy goo.

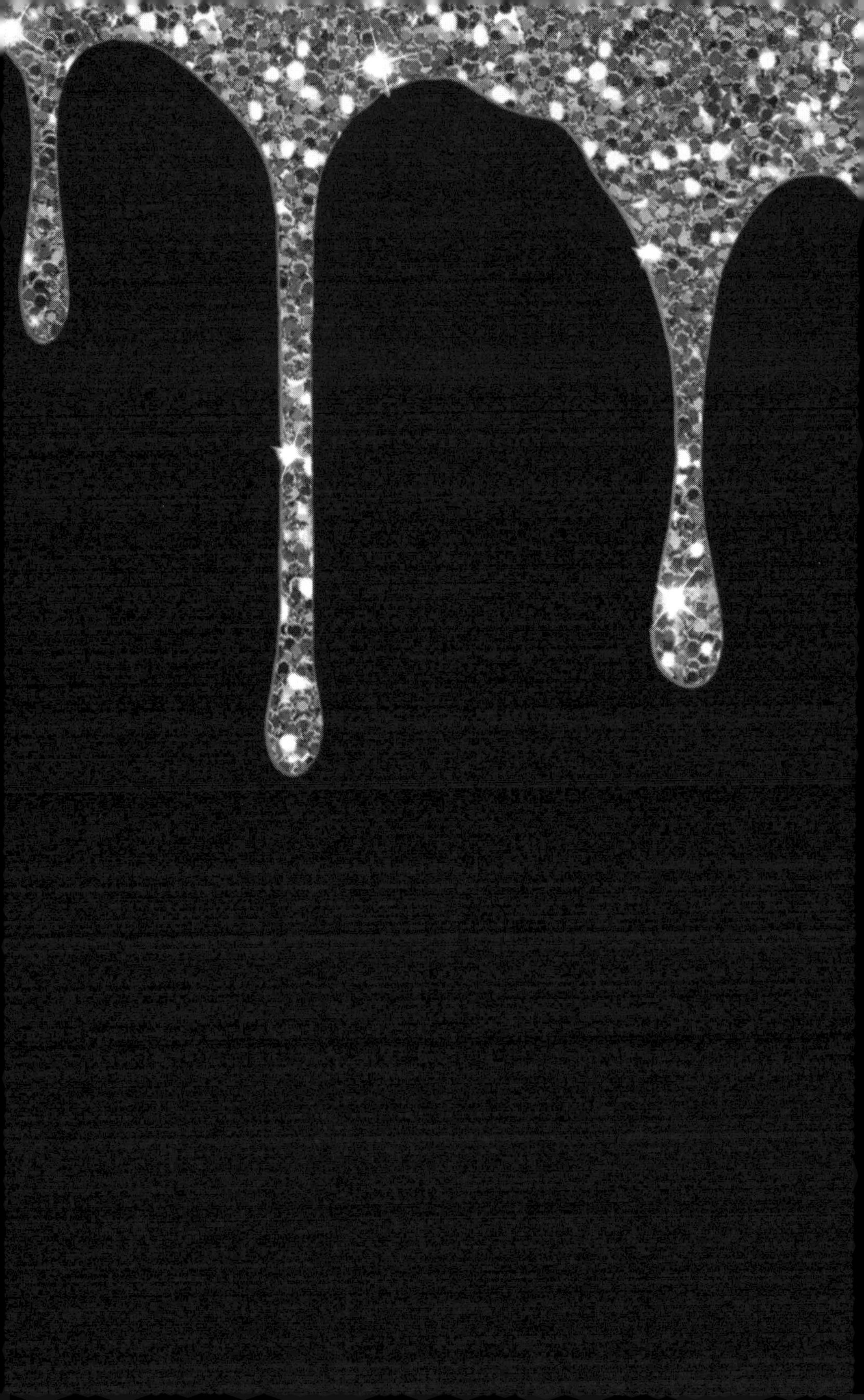

TWENTY-EIGHT
Hot Noods and Cold Truths

JOSS

NOTE TO SELF:

Get a dog.

Follow up note to self:

Get a house on the water with lots of room for said dog.

I wasn't sure if it was because I'd been the first to arrive or because I'd come armed with salty snacks, but for whatever reason, Harlow's two dogs had decided I was their new best friend. They'd followed me everywhere. When I'd tried to help Harlow and Kase in the kitchen, it'd quickly become obvious the dogs and I were in the way, so I'd lured them outside.

Standing on the back deck of the insane waterfront house, I pet Chewy—a massive dog. The small one, Boba, was running through the sand like it was the first time he'd ever seen the outside world.

Not that I blamed him for being in awe. I'd been to the house before, but I was still struck by the beauty of it.

Kase, the romantic, had it built with the dream of a family. He already had his found family, but once he married his red-haired beauty, his dream would be a reality.

I'd be envious if I didn't already have my own romantic badass.

One who'd been texting me filthy things all afternoon. Even though I'd agreed to call him, he'd decided to tease me anyway.

Since my sexting skills were improving almost as much as my badass ones, I was happy to fight fire with fire.

I was also happy to count down the hours until I could break my no-sex-at-Wicked rule, which was pretty much no longer a rule.

The wind picked up, and Boba trotted over to the door, signaling he was ready to go inside. Chewy stayed pressed against me, not moving until I did.

When Lars picks me up, I wonder if he'll assist with a little light dognapping.

I herded the boys inside just as Harlow was slipping on her shoes.

"I was just coming to get you." She handed me a margarita.

And not the premixed kind served in a red plastic cup.

On her kitchen island sat a literal margarita machine, proper glasses, salt and sugar for the rim, assorted flavored syrups, muddled fruit, and a bottle of tequila. Not to mention, bowls and platters of chips, veggies, dips, and other snacks.

And I thought Mary Lennon went all out for get-togethers.

"Jake and Piper just pulled up." Kase pulled Harlow in tight. "You good, ipo?"

"Perfect. Thanks, baby."

"You can pay me back tonight with drunken lani pussy."

Harlow's face went as red as her hair, and I turned away, pretending I hadn't heard a single thing.

"You're the worst," Harlow hissed.

"You love it."

She made a disgruntled harrumph. "You and your ego better leave... Provided your big head can even fit in Jake's car."

"My big—" His words were cut off, but not with her hand over his mouth. I glanced over to see she'd silenced him with her own mouth.

Why didn't I think of that?

They broke apart when Piper entered without knocking. Her gruff husband followed, carrying bags while her hands remained empty, except for her purse.

God, I loved that.

Just because she was capable of carrying all that and more didn't mean she had to.

She lifted a shoulder in a little shrug. "I went a little overboard."

"Sweets, this is a little overboard like I'm a little overbearing," Jake said, not looking one bit upset about either fact.

She rolled her eyes. "Whatever."

He dropped the bags on the couch before tugging Piper into his arms. I didn't just avert my eyes.

I left for the kitchen while they said their goodbyes.

Once the men were gone and the PDA coast was clear, I returned. "Is Ray coming?"

"No, she's stuck in her shop all evening with appointments."

Damn. I'd saved some inspiration pictures of tattoos, and I was antsy to talk to her about them.

"Buncha workaholics," I scoffed, like I didn't work three jobs. I handed Piper the glass Harlow had given me since I hadn't taken a drink yet.

She passed it right back. "Not yet."

"Okay..." I drawled.

Before she could explain, there was a knock on the door. Harlow opened it and gasped. "I love it."

Sophie entered, her hair bouncy in that irreplicable fresh-from-the-salon way.

Her *dark* hair. The lighter color had been replaced by a beautifully rich brown that complemented her skin and features.

"Oh, thank God." Soph carried in bottled water and a couple bags. "I was worried it was too dramatic."

We spoke over each other to assure her it looked amazing.

Harlow grabbed some of Sophie's load and guided her into the kitchen to add her goodies to the already impressive spread.

Once the coast was clear, I leaned over and kept my voice quiet. "Which guy prefers brunettes?"

Piper's eyebrows shot halfway up her forehead. "I didn't even think about that. Key is open. Rhys is particular about a woman's... uh, *disposition*, but not their appearance." She tilted her head, practically bouncing on her toes with excitement. "He's not a dick about it or anything, but I've only ever seen Xavier with brunettes."

I could see Xavier with Sophie.

I could *so* see it.

The way she'd smiled at him had been so cute.

Xavier was hot, hardworking, and, it bore repeating, hot. Once, when he'd helped at the bakery, he'd called me *mama*. If I hadn't already been crushing on Lars, I may have imploded.

He wasn't as outgoing as Kase, but he also wasn't as silent as Key. They would be a good match.

"I just need her to ask for my matchmaking help," Piper whispered, more to herself than me.

Girls' day has a new mission.

Soph came back in, shaking her head. I was worried she'd overheard us until she hooked a thumb over her shoulder. "I thought you said it was going to be a chill day. That is *not* chill."

"It will be." Piper grabbed one of the bags Jake had dropped onto the couch and shook it. "I got face masks."

As she unloaded the bags onto the coffee table, there were indeed face masks. There were also face scrubs, blackhead strips, serums, and half the beauty aisle.

"Okay, I kinda agree with Jake about you going overboard," I half-joked.

"Self-care Saturday, babe," she shot back with a smile that wobbled as she grabbed her purse. "Plus, I brought, uh... these."

Turning it over, she dumped a dozen or so pregnancy tests on the couch.

Suddenly, two things made sense.

Why she hadn't been drinking at the engagement dinner and had declined the margarita I'd handed her.

And why she may have hesitated to invite Sophie.

As awesome as Soph was, her comments to Piper at Voodoo may have stung. She'd meant well and had thought she was being encouraging. Like she'd said, she didn't have many friends. She'd grown up too sheltered. We just needed to show her how it worked. Not get her out of her shell, per se, because there was nothing wrong with being an introvert.

But maybe she'd get comfortable enough to peek her head out a little more.

If that led to her finding an alpha badass who liked her quiet, I knew from experience how well that worked.

Or maybe I was reading too much into everything. That was also possible.

All our eyes shot to Piper, and she lifted a shoulder. "I'm late. I figured if it's good news, great. If it's bad, then I've got margaritas and my girls."

"You didn't see the fertility doc yet, right?" I asked, worried I'd missed something.

"No, I'm supposed to call when my period starts so I can go in for testing."

Harlow picked up one of the tests and flipped it over. "Unless you're pregnant."

"Unless I'm pregnant," Piper confirmed, wishful longing moving unbridled across her face as she stared at the pile.

"Go test," Soph prompted, handing her one.

"Later. I'm not ready yet."

We grazed on the snacks as we talked, the boxes sitting on the couch like an elephant in the room. It was driving me nuts, my stomach churning with anticipation and nerves. And I wasn't the only one losing her mind.

Harlow sat forward suddenly and grabbed four boxes. She tossed one to each of us, keeping the last for herself. "We'll all do it."

Relief loosened Piper's muscles until I was worried she'd melt to the floor like whipped cream frosting left in the sun. She masked the emotion and stubbornly lifted her chin, her tone grudging. "Okay, but you owe me."

"Kung pao chicken for dinner. Got it."

"And don't put all the lo mein in the fridge this time," Piper added, a fierce negotiator.

"Who puts noodles in the fridge?" Soph whispered with a sneer, and I shrugged.

"Fine," Harlow agreed.

Piper nodded before deflating. "But you have to go first."

"Fine." Harlow headed to the bathroom that was off the kitchen.

"You still owe me chicken and hot noods," Piper called before looking from Soph to me. "Since I'm technically your boss, and I'm pretty sure there are some blatant HR violations here, you don't actually have to do it."

"I don't want to miss out on the fun." Before she could get the wrong idea, I tacked on, "I've been on the pill for eight years and have never had so much as a scare, so it won't actually be exciting."

Soph looked at the box in her hand. "I'm still putting the *I* in *single*, so it'll be negative." Glancing up, she gave a tight smile. "But if you're okay with wasting the test, I'm okay with taking it."

Piper flinched, guilt mixing with the nerves that were already palpable. "It's really okay. I didn't want to be the only one doing it, but Harlow's—"

"I'm what?" Harlow asked as she returned.

No one had the chance to say anything before Soph bolted up and hustled into the bathroom.

"Shit, shit, shit," Piper whispered. "If she doesn't quit, it'll be a miracle. I know I can be a lot. Like, I'm pervy and swear too much and I'm overly friendly and completely unprofessional."

"All the reasons I love working for you," I reassured her honestly.

"But I don't think Soph feels the same. Here she is, crushing on Xavier, and I'm rubbing her singledom in her face. Did you see how *sad* she looked?"

"Wait." Harlow was a hundred pages behind since she'd missed our conversation about who preferred brunettes and then Soph's reaction to the pregnancy test. "She has a crush on Xavier?"

"We think," I clarified.

Tilting her head, she made a thoughtful expression before nodding. "They'd be a good match."

"I agree," Piper said. "Which is why I need her to admit her feelings and ask for help. Otherwise, my matchmaking hands are tied." She frowned again. "But before any of that, I need her to *not* quit."

We sat back, aiming for casual as Sophie returned.

"I'm up." I carried the package into the bathroom and paused.

Originally, I'd planned to simply run the test under water, but as I closed myself in the room, the sense of excited comradery got to me. I knew it would be negative, I wasn't expecting any different.

But it was fun to play pretend.

Or maybe even imagine my potential future.

After reading the directions, I used the test, put the cap on, and carefully placed it next to the others before covering it with a piece of tissue like they'd done. I was so tempted to peek at Harlow's test, but I fought the urge.

Barely.

Washing my hands, I returned to the living room and dramatically threw my arm out to Piper. "Last but not least."

With a nervous smile, she practically ran into the bathroom.

We sat in silence for a moment. And, in that moment, Harlow shifted, leaned forward, slouched back, crossed and uncrossed her legs, and a million other fidgets that betrayed her concern for her friend.

Giving up, she stood. "I'll get her margarita prepped, just in case."

"Good idea." I grabbed my still untouched cup and followed to freshen it up.

When Piper was done, she set a timer on her phone. We tried to pretend we weren't watching the seconds slowly tick, but our conversation was stilted.

When the alarm beeped a century later, Piper just silenced it. She didn't move. I wasn't even sure she breathed.

After a minute, Harlow offered, "Want me to look?"

"No, I will." She inhaled deeply and went in for a moment. When she returned, the sad smile curving her mouth said everything even before she grabbed the margarita and took a few huge gulps.

I wrapped an arm around Piper. "You've got a plan and a fertility doc referral. That's major headway because you recognized something was up and took it seriously. Whatever happens, you've got this."

She leaned her head onto my shoulder. "Thank you. That's just what I needed to hear."

Meeting my gaze over Piper's head, Harlow tilted her head and snuck away to the bathroom, likely to clean up the reminder.

Steel in her spine and restored happiness in her eyes, Piper stood fully. "It wasn't the news I wanted. But, like I said, at least I have margs and my girls." She raised her drink. "To plans."

I clinked mine with hers. "To plans."

"Wait!" Harlow nearly slipped in her rush, sliding across the floor. "Who put their test in spot three?"

"Me," I started before taking in her frenzied excitement. My breath froze in my lungs. My heart started slamming away like my ribs were a xylophone. My stomach may as well have been out sailing the ocean with the way it twisted and turned.

But there was no way I was reading her expression correctly.

Nope.

No way.

I couldn't be...

Harlow flipped a test around to show two pink lines.

Two of them.

Not one.

Two.

So dark, I could see them from space.

Everything else, all the chatter and questions and my surroundings, faded away. It was just me and the two lines and the haze of a dream.

A nightmare?

The world snapped back into place as Harlow put a firm hand on my shoulder and pushed me onto a stool. "Joss, doll, sit."

I reached for my drink, but someone snatched it from my hand.

Oh. Right. I couldn't have alcohol. Because I was pregnant.

Pregnant.

A million thoughts filled my head, rushing in a whirl until I couldn't isolate one. It was white noise. Static.

Chaos.

Until finally popped out to overpower the rest.

"This is impossible." My crazy eyes shot to Harlow and the test she held. "I've never missed a pill. I even take my placebo week."

"You're a much better adult than me," Harlow said. "I kept skipping the placebo week and then forgetting to start a new pack. That's why I got an IUD. It's easier since I never have to think about it."

It was good advice had I not already *fucked the hell up*.

"Have you ever been late taking it?" she asked.

Shame coursed through me as I thought about the handful of times I'd been too wrapped up in Lars. My alarm would go off, but then he'd use his hands, mouth, filthy words, or some combination of the three to distract me. I'd still taken the pills, but not until later.

Much later.

I'd planned to adjust my dose time from dinner to morning, but it was a whole process. I hadn't gotten around to it.

"It's still impossible," I said. "I don't feel sick. No cravings. Nothing."

"Uh, you've been yawning a lot lately," Piper shared, which was news to freakin' me. I knew I was wiped out, but not that there'd been a noticeable increase in my yawning. "I just chalked it up to late nights with Lars."

God.

Lars.

"He's going to hate me," I whispered. My heart broke at the thought. Shattered.

My despair was interrupted by Piper's laughter.

God.

Piper.

Like she said earlier when she thought she was being a bad friend...

Shit, shit, shit.

There she was, wanting a baby. And there I was, totally freaking out because I *didn't* want a baby.

Okay, that wasn't true. I was freaking out, yes. But there was much more than that. I just couldn't allow myself to think about it.

Looking at my friend, I braced for anger. Resentment. Heartache. Any of the very valid emotions she had every right to experience.

But her laughter wasn't bitter or harsh. It was genuine.

And it was aimed at me.

She was laughing *at* me.

"Girl, if you think that, you have not been paying attention. Have you seen the way that man looks at you? I wouldn't be surprised if he switched out your birth control for sugar pills. Or PEZ, since I doubt he'd be subtle about it."

"I was the one to tell him not to use condoms," I shared.

"Okay, and? Did he argue?"

I remembered his very sexy reaction. "Uh, no."

"Exactly.

"But he could still think I trapped him."

Piper wouldn't hear it. "Bullshit. That man wants to trap you. If he could get you to tattoo his name on your ass to label yourself as his, he would. You two having a baby together? He's gonna freakin' die of happiness."

Maybe.

Or maybe not.

I knew he wanted me. That he loved me. His self-declared obsession made that clear. But we'd never talked about marriage or kids. For all I knew, he didn't want either.

Shit. This is probably the kind of thing people talk about at the beginning of relationships.

Harlow gestured to the dogs at my feet. "This explains why the boys have elected you their queen. Don't animals have an instinct for this kind of thing?"

"I thought that was cats and death," Piper said.

Harlow waved a hand. "Cats are assholes, so of course they'd sense death. Dogs are angels."

"Wait, wait, wait. Are we even sure the test is right?" Sophie pulled the instructions from one of the boxes and flipped to the FAQ section. "Aren't false positives a thing?"

Where Harlow and Piper didn't attempt to hide their joy at the surprising turn of events, Sophie seemed to match my panic. It was almost funny that we were older than the other two, yet we were the ones freaking out.

"I had one early on in my relationship with Jake," Piper shared, something I wasn't aware of. "But the line showed up after the time limit and it was faint. This was within the timeframe and *dark*."

"Yeah, but it could still be wrong. A bad batch. Before she gets too ahead of herself, she should double-check." Soph worried gaze darted between us. "Right?"

"She has a point," Harlow admitted, visibly working to tamp down her glee. She grabbed one of the water bottles Sophie brought and handed it to me. "Get chugging so you can get to peeing."

"At least hydration fits with self-care Saturday," Piper added. "Now you just need a face mask."

When we went into the living room, Sophie sat close. I braced for well-meaning comments that might drop a fireball on my already raw nerves, but there were none.

Concern lined her face as she watched me.

Nervous for me.

Making sure I was okay.

Offering reassuring smiles and a first round pick of the face masks.

She asked about school, my family, and other random topics to give me the distraction I needed. Harlow and Piper quickly joined in. Between the three of them, I almost felt calm.

Almost.

A while later, when my face felt like the softest peach and smelled even better, I moved next to Piper to whisper, "I'm sorry."

Pulling back, she eyed me like I'd grown five heads. "Why?"

"Because you… and then I…"

She rolled her eyes, but she did it with a warm smile. "I'm not sorry. Do I wish I was pregnant, too? Of course. But *too*. *Also*. Along with you, not instead of you. There's a big difference, yeah?"

I nodded and returned her smile. "You sounded like Jake at the end there. I think you spend too much time with your husband."

"That's not a thing."

The ball of lead in my stomach—one that may or may not have been sharing space with a zygote—lessened at her reassurance. It still wouldn't allow me to eat, and it churned with every sip of water I forced myself to take. But at least I wasn't about to throw up all over Harlow's dog.

When I couldn't take the waiting any longer, I grabbed another box from the couch and went to the bathroom. That time, I didn't absentmindedly set the plastic stick down with distant daydreams coloring my thoughts.

I stared at it.

It reminded me of flipping a quarter to make a decision. In that millisecond while the coin hovered in the air, neither heads nor tails, there was always a moment of clarity. A sinking in my gut or swelling in my chest that told me what I truly wanted.

As the moisture made its way across the display window, I knew to my bones which way I wanted the metaphorical coin to land.

Because it wasn't dread that filled me. It wasn't fear. It wasn't apprehension.

It was hope.

I hoped to see a second line.

And within seconds, I did.

I'm pregnant.
Now what?

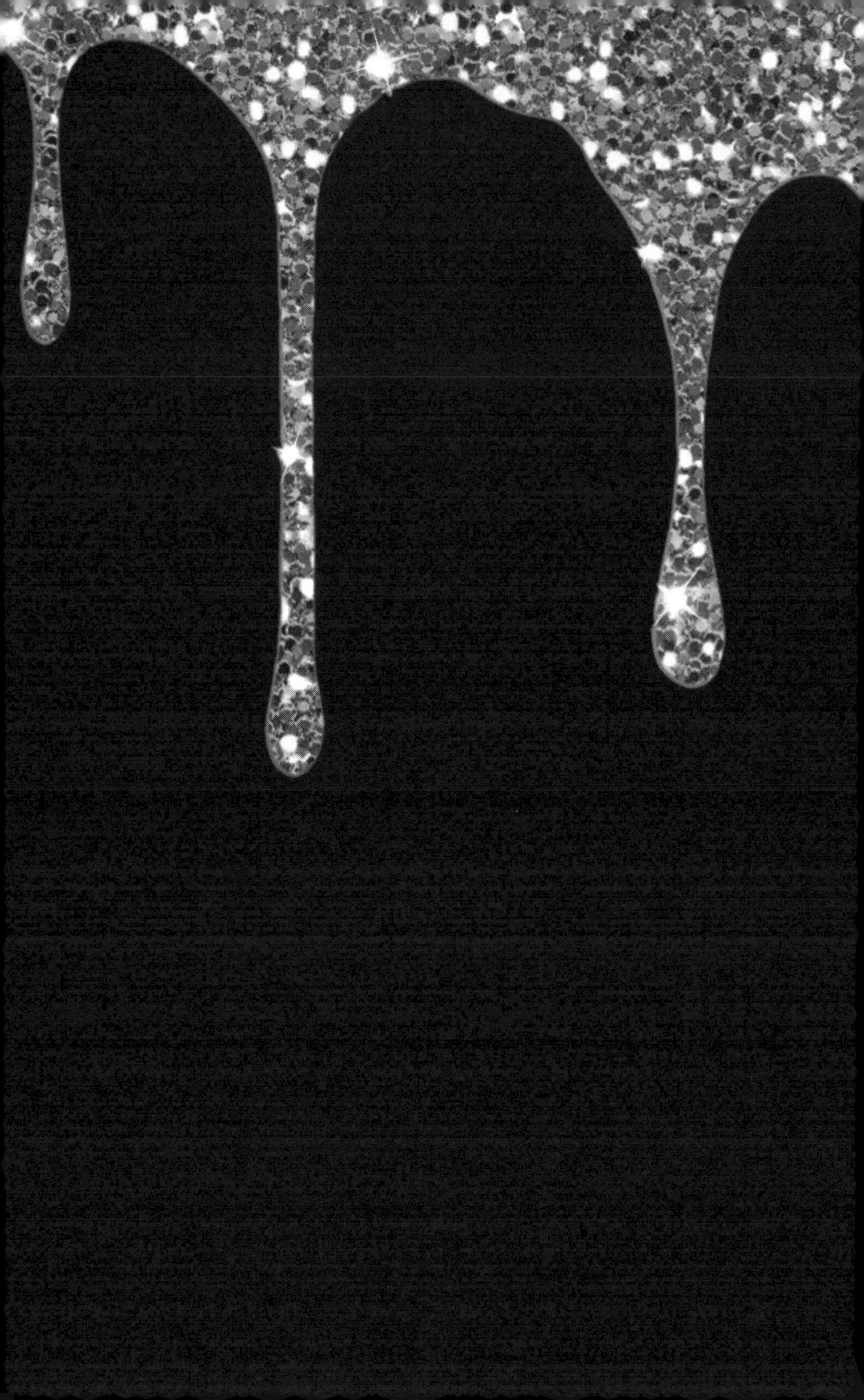

TWENTY-NINE
Ground Control to Major Ick

JOSS

OH NO.

No, wait, worse than that.

Oh fuckin' shit balls.

Standing on my porch, I looked down the driveway to see a bike blocking my car. A familiar bike that was accompanied by a familiar man.

A pissed off man.

Lars' arms were crossed as he leaned against the Harley, his outstretched legs crossed at the ankles. I hadn't heard him pull in, which meant I'd been in the shower.

Knowing I couldn't face him the night before, I'd texted Lars that I wasn't feeling well and would be driving home sober. When he'd climbed into my bed, tenderly pulling me to him, I'd pretended to be asleep.

My guilt at lying had grown exponentially when I'd gone downstairs in the morning to find soup, bagels, stomach meds, my exact brand of tampons, and chocolate.

He hadn't known if it was a stomach bug or a period, but my thoughtful man wanted to cover his bases.

Thankfully, tampons didn't have a short expiration date because they'd be sitting under my sink for a while. Forty-plus weeks or so.

Along with the stash, he'd left a note with strict orders to call before I left the house. Orders he'd repeated via text.

Orders I'd been in the process of ignoring.

To be fair, I hadn't planned to go to Sunday dinner. I'd wanted to sit home, watch TV, and relax.

As perfect as it sounded, there'd been a flaw in that.

Me.

I was the flaw.

Being alone with my thoughts was enough to drive myself crazy. I'd gone from refusing to even think about the pregnancy to looking up everything about the pregnancy. Birth control side effects, test accuracy, symptoms, due dates. After I'd somehow ended up on a parenting message board that would scar for life, I'd decided the distraction of my family was a welcome one.

I just hadn't shared that decision with Lars. Not because I was avoiding him.

I was just... Okay, I was avoiding him.

For good reason, though. I needed time and space to get control of my emotions.

I'd assumed Lars would be so busy at Wicked, he wouldn't notice.

I'd assumed wrong.

He pushed his aviators down, his intense gaze freezing me in place even as he crooked a finger at me.

For a wild moment, I thought about bolting inside.

He must've known, too, because he rumbled, "Don't even think about it, hotcakes."

"Or what?" I challenged.

"Or I'll chase you. Inside. Across town. Around the whole fuckin' world." He pushed his shades onto his head so I could get the full, scary effect of his glower. "Now get your fine ass down here."

I was tempted to run just for the thrill of him chasing me.

But not when I was dangerously close to throwing up, passing out, or both. Because Lars was mad, and it wasn't about me not texting. That didn't warrant a stakeout and a glare.

Something else did. Something one of the gossipy men might have shared. It circled through my head like an annoying song on repeat.

He knows.

He knows.

He knows.

Bracing, I jogged down the steps to him. "If my IPA neighbor was mad about the knocking, he's going to write me an even sterner letter for yelling about my ass."

"I wish the motherfucker would," he shouted, aiming his glare over my head.

I didn't try to shush him because I had my own ass to worry about. Plus, my neighbor kind of deserved it. Instead, I smiled sweetly up at him. "What's up?"

His gaze dropped to my mouth. "Not gonna work this time."

Damn.

But what I said aloud was, "What's not gonna work?"

His rough voice was even gravellier than usual. "I've waited for you to talk to me."

Oh shit.

"To explain."

Oh no, no, no, noooooo.

"I've given you time," he continued.

It hasn't even been a day.

"Outta patience."

Not even a day!

"Tell me why you don't want me to meet your family," he demanded.

I could've passed out. I actually had to grab his shirt to stop myself from slumping.

"That's why you're mad?" I blurted.

Of course, Lars being Lars, caught what I'd said *and* the relief that dripped from my words like honey. His eyes narrowed. "What else would it be?"

"Nothing." I waved my hands like they could hypnotize him or explode with smoke and glitter as a diversion. "I just wasn't sure what had your panties in a twist."

"You know I don't wear anything," he rumbled, making me grasp his shirt for a totally different reason. "Tell me why."

"You work Sundays, and—"

"Try again. You know all you gotta do is ask. No. You don't even have to do that. I've already been cutting back my Sunday hours. Can't always give you the whole day, but I give you a big chunk of it."

I opened my mouth to argue, but he was right.

He made time for me, always.

"It's not that I don't want you to," I started, but even I didn't believe my bullshit.

"Fuck," Lars whispered. Unconcealed hurt tightened his expression and clenched his jaw. "You're embarrassed."

"Baby, no." I prepared myself for him to pull away. To refuse to listen to me. But he was Lars, not Peter. He didn't play games. We communicated.

We weren't toxic.

Slightly dysfunctional, sure. Codependent? Maybe. But the good kind.

I owed him the same bluntness he always gave me. "I'd never be embarrassed of you. I'm embarrassed of *them*. My family is crazy."

"Whose isn't?"

"No, you don't get it. They're the stereotypical, uptight suburban family. Nosy. Passive-aggressive. My mom's antics are exhausting. My dad is old fashioned and more exhausting. My sisters can be borderline bitchy. Well, one can. The other is just bitch-line bitchy." I clutched his shirt and leaned back to meet his eyes, hoping he saw the honesty in mine. Because I'd rather he knew all my vulnerabilities and flaws than to ever think I was embarrassed of him. "You are the best thing I have in my life. The best thing I've ever had. I wanted to selfishly protect our bubble of happiness before they stab their way in with probing questions, shitty attitude, and pandemonium." I inhaled for basically the first time in my run-on spiel before adding, "But they know you exist. They know I have a boyfriend."

I left out the fact they knew courtesy of Peter since that didn't matter.

"'Our bubble of happiness'?" Lars parroted, his hands moving to cup the sides of my neck.

"Yes."

Using his thumbs to tip my chin, he studied me for a long moment before nodding. "Okay, hotcakes. We'll wait until you're ready." Not giving me the chance to speak, he lowered his face until it was in mine.

Until it was all I could see. "But so you know, no one can pop our bubble of happiness. Not with questions. Not with pandemonium. Not even if they chased me out the door with literal knives. 'Cause that shit is ours, baby. And I'll protect it till I take my last breath."

I closed my eyes, needing a moment to let that love wash over me. Needing several to choke down the words on the tip of my tongue. As much as I wanted to keep communicating, standing in my driveway wasn't how I wanted to do it. So I kept my mouth shut on that and said, "I don't want to wait."

It was the truth. I'd only been worried about his reaction to my family, not their reaction to him. I didn't give a shit if they disapproved of his tattoos, his semi menacing vibe, or that he owned a strip club.

They'd throw a fit and get over it.

That's what family did.

And maybe I'd get another loaf of apology bread out of it.

But now that I knew he wasn't going to be scared away, I was ready. He was going to be in my life no matter what. I'd felt that way even before getting the positive pregnancy test.

Lars' thumbs stroked along my jaw. "You sure?"

"You promise to still love me after?"

"Try to fuckin' stop me."

"Can we take your bike?"

"You wanna rip the Band-Aid off like that, then fuck yeah."

"Then I'm sure.

Kissing my forehead, nose, and finally my mouth, Lars let me go and helped me gear up before we took off.

As we rode, I didn't feel nervous. No trepidation. No doubt. There was something about being on the back of the bike that cleared my head. There was something about being pressed close to Lars that made me think about how lucky I was to have him.

A wildness that brought serenity to my life. Peace to my soul.

By the time we pulled in front of my parents' house, almost all my nephews were waiting on the porch. I wanted to take credit, being their favorite aunt and all, but they likely wanted to see what was causing all the noise.

"Whoa. Bad-A, Auntie Josie," Parker called when I pulled my helmet off.

"Parker!" Nora shouted from the doorway.

"I didn't swear. I said *A*. It's a letter. I can't get grounded for saying letters."

"Kid's gonna be a lawyer," Lars muttered with a chuckle as he wrapped an arm around my waist.

"Let's hope. I'm never sure if he'll use his powers for good or evil." I looked down to see his other arm loaded with an abundant bouquet and a few bottles of wine.

"Where'd that come from?" I asked.

"Saddlebag."

"You brought flowers and wine?" I arched a brow. "Kinda cocky. What would you have done if I hadn't invited you?"

"Told ya, hotcakes." He pressed his lips to the side of my head to whisper, "I'll chase you anywhere."

I was, like, ninety percent sure he was joking, and he wouldn't have actually done that.

Okay, it was fifty-fifty.

He pulled away and started for the porch.

Here goes nothing.

I was surprised. It took until we reached the steps before Nora was joined by Dan, Ruth, and Benny. They were off their game.

Without a hint of snark or defensiveness, I greeted the gawking crowd before saying, "This is my boyfriend, Lars."

"This is your boyfriend," Ruth repeated after a long, awkward moment.

It wasn't a question, but still I answered, "Yup."

I understood their shock. First, Lars really was ridiculously hot, and it left me speechless sometimes, too. Second, the only guy I'd ever been with was Peter. They were used to seeing me next to someone who wore khakis and polos. It was a sharp contrast to Lars in his black jeans, black shirt, leather jacket, and shitkickers.

Thankfully, they found their manners to introduce themselves. Even Nora didn't say anything snide or judgy. Out loud, at least.

The screen door rattled a second before my mom came out. "So, we're just heating the..."

Her sentence trailed off when she saw Lars. Then her already wide eyes went saucer huge when she saw his arm wrapped around me.

"Hey, Mom," I said like it was no big deal. Just a normal Sunday dinner. "This is my boyfriend, Lars."

"Mrs. Lennon." Lars handed over the wine and flowers, not coming on too strong. Playing it cool. Or just being cool since he was and didn't have to play at it.

"Thank you," she said automatically, blinking a few times before turning a disappointed-mother scowl my way.

Oh shit.

I gotta be honest, I thought we'd make it a little further into the evening.

But she wasn't upset about Lars. She was upset at my impoliteness.

Her voice was chastising. "You didn't tell me you were bringing someone. I don't have a place set. One of the boys will have to grab an extra chair from the basement."

"Sorry, Mrs. Lennon, that's on me. Didn't tell her I was stopping. She was on her way out and was sweet enough to invite me."

I made a mental note to give Lars a kiss for taking the fall. I made another mental note to give him an enthusiastic blow job for saying he was stopping by and not returning after spending the night.

And also because I wanted to give him a blow job.

I focused on the conversation just in time to hear my mom order everyone inside.

Lars held my hip, slowing his steps and mine. When there was some space between us and the others, he leaned closer. "Where was your head just at, baby?"

"In your pants," I whispered.

He shot me a look of mock horror. "In front of your family?"

There was no humor in my voice when I answered honestly, "Always."

"That's my good girl."

I was his good girl.

But I may not have been his smart girl. If I was, I wouldn't have let my guard down even a millimeter.

"What the hell is this?" my father bellowed suddenly, making me jump out of my skin. Standing at the end of the entry hall, he crossed his arms over his chest and glowered our way. "Get your hands off my daughter."

We weren't big on PDA in my family. Ruth and Benny were married, and Dad still scowled any time she simply kissed his cheek. That said, Lars' touch wasn't inappropriate. No throat hold. No ass grab. His hand wasn't even low on my hip.

But Dad's face was splotchy red and thunderous, like he'd caught me having public sex on the Michelson's lawn.

Putting on my dutiful daughter voice, I started, "Dad, this is—"

"I know who this damn man is. Do you?"

"Who is he?" Mom raised a hand to her chest, nearly whacking herself in the face with the flowers. "Was Peter right?" She stepped back. "Is he dangerous?"

Lars' body tightened, but when my gaze shot to his face, it was blank. Soft, even. Only I felt his reaction to Peter's name and the insinuation he'd made—one I'd specifically omitted from my recap.

"Worse," Dad said. "This man owns an *adult* establishment."

"My mom loves adult things," my nephew Jasper proclaimed. "She keeps them in a locked drawer and says they're just for adults."

Even in the midst of the tense showdown, everyone's attention shot to Nora.

Her face was nearly as red as Dad's when she exclaimed, "Chocolate! It's where I keep my chocolate. Otherwise, they eat it all and leave the wrappers for me to clean up."

"I knew it," Parker hissed, betrayal contorting his face.

"Dad," I said, getting us back on topic—although I'd be giving Nora shit about *that* for years and years. "How is that worse than being a criminal?"

"Well, it's... It's... It's not good!"

"It's sure as hell not bad." Defensiveness and indignation filling me on Lars' behalf.

Not that he was bothered. He was as cool as the rum and Diet Coke I desperately wished I could have. If anything, the firm squeeze he gave my hip and his stroking thumb seemed to be meant to calm me down.

It wasn't working.

I opened my mouth to keep at it, refusing to let Dad insult Lars, when a thought popped into my head. I didn't want to know.

I *really* didn't want to know.

But I couldn't stop myself from asking, "How do you know what kind of business he owns?"

When Peter had tried to throw Lars under the bus, he'd been careful not to implicate himself. Dad had been too reactionary. He hadn't taken the same precaution.

At my question, the angry redness blanched from his face.

It was quickly followed by a suspicious accusation tightening Mom's as she prodded, "Well, Noah? How?"

The heavy silence wasn't long, but it felt like it lasted eons.

When it finally broke, it wasn't my dad who spoke.

It was Lars.

"We've seen each other at Small Business Owners of Boston meetings," he explained as he stepped forward—dragging me along for the potentially disastrous ride. "Never met officially, though." He extended his free hand.

My dad's jaw was clenched so tight, it was a wonder his teeth didn't crumble from his mouth like sand. Even the veins on his forehead throbbed ominously. Still, he grudgingly shook it before a flash of something crossed his face.

He judged everyone by their handshake. According to him, it said a lot about a person.

I'd never shaken Lars' hands, but I'd felt them on me.

Masculine.

Calloused.

Confident.

The kind that said he worked hard, used them often, and wasn't afraid to get them dirty.

Or, in Lars' case, bloody.

I was unsurprised by the flash of approval, but there was something else in my dad's reaction.

Before I could piece it together, it was gone, and he was back to being surly. It was worse than his normal temperament, but better than it'd been when he'd seen Lars.

Progress.

"No use letting the food get any colder," he eventually grumbled. "We'll finish discussing this in private."

"Nothing to discuss." I moved into the kitchen, pulling Lars over to the far corner because I did, in fact, have something to discuss. "Are you really a member of SBOOB?"

"They gotta change that damn name."

"If they changed it to Business Owners of Boston-hyphen-Small, it'd be boobs," I pointed out.

"That I could get behind."

My mind went into the gutter as I grinned up at him, but I didn't let him off the hook. "You didn't answer my question."

"Nah, hotcakes, I'm not."

"Then how did you..." My stomach churned, and I shook my head to clear a wave of major ick. "You know what? Never mind. I don't wanna know."

"Probably a good idea," he muttered, making my stomach lurch again.

That was the expression I couldn't place.

Gratitude to Lars for covering his post-SBOOB boobs visit.

Ew.

How has no one invented brain bleach yet?

It was more awkward, more formal, but no less loud and chaotic as we set the table. Every time I picked something up, Lars plucked it from my hands and carried it for me.

It was already thoughtful, but it was even better when I saw the brownie points he earned with my mom, Nora, and Ruth. Especially because it was obviously not an act. Lars was being himself. Real. Natural. And bossy-as-hell with all the rumbled orders for me to hand stuff over and relax.

Once everyone sat and food had been dished out, Lars grabbed my chair and hauled it right against his. His arm went behind me while he used the other to eat.

And again, it earned him brownie points with the women while the men obliviously ate.

Everyone dug in, but they did it quietly. The adults, at least. The kids didn't have the capability to be quiet. I was fairly certain they'd explode if they tried.

There was a clatter at the head of the table, and I looked over in time to see Mom nudge Dad's arm. Based on her constant glare in his direction, I wasn't sure she believed Lars' explanation. Dad was smart enough to realize the same thing, and he followed his angry wife's nonverbal order to make conversation.

Clearing his throat, he met my gaze. "We drove by your place on the way to dinner last night, Josie."

My black sheep instincts kicked in, and I braced to get in trouble.

What am I doing? I'm an adult. He can't ground me.

Although going to my room sounds pretty amazing right now.

"You put up the porch swing," Dad said finally. "Did you get around to fixing that railing while you were at it?"

I tilted my head. "Lars did. He put in new lighting, too."

Dad's gaze barely cut to him before returning to me. "Still need to replace the windows before it gets too cold. I'll get you some phone numbers."

"Already happening," Lars said, taking my dad *and* me by surprise. "Correct ones were backordered, but installation should be starting next week at the latest."

I hoped like hell the right ones were also the cheap ones because I was going to pay him back every penny. Paying for dinner was one thing. Paying for a nice porch swing was pushing it.

But paying for new windows?

That was on a different planet.

I kept my thoughts to myself since the dinner did not need any more dramatics. Lars knew I was silently seething—of-freaking-course he did. Not that he apologized or offered an explanation. He just gave a nearly imperceptible chuckle before twisting a lock of my hair around his finger.

And pulling.

His tender touch, possessive closeness, and caveman insistence on doing everything for me had endeared him to the women in my family.

I'd have thought that smoothly covering for his secret visits to Wicked would've done the trick with Dad, and maybe it had. But not as much as him fixing up my place.

For a moment, at least. The look of growing approval on Dad's face was wiped out suddenly, replaced by the mottled cheeks and angry vein.

"Oh, what now?" I muttered, exhausted and frustrated and hoping like hell Lars wasn't going to run for the hills.

"Why're you spending so much time and money to fix up a house that's not yours, son?" my dad asked.

Lars' answer was immediate. "'Cause Joss loves that house, and I wanna make sure she's safe and happy in it."

God, I would've climbed in his lap and kissed him if it wouldn't undo the progress he'd made.

Like he hadn't just said the most perfect thing in the world, he took a bite and swallowed before saying yet another perfect thing. "Best manicotti I've ever had."

Mom was practically giddy at the compliment. "It's a process, but I think it comes out well." Her glow dimmed for a brief moment as she skewered me with another look. "I'm just glad I had enough for an unexpected guest."

The buildup and tension of the evening paired with Mom's statement was too much. An unladylike snort burst from me.

"Joss Lennon," she chided.

"Mom, you literally have enough to feed everyone on the block. Twice." She opened her mouth, but before she could speak, I took my lumps. "But you're right, that was rude of me. I'll let you know when he's coming from now on."

It was a loaded statement, and, surprisingly, Parker was the first one with something to say about it. "So you're coming over again?"

Lars raised his chin.

"On your motorcycle?"

"Probably not anytime soon." Lars didn't ignore Parker, nor was he condescending to him. He took the time to explain his reasoning. "It's getting too cold. Not good for the bike, and the roads get dangerous. I wouldn't take your Aunt Josie out when it's not safe."

Parker gave him wide eyes as he bounced in his seat. I recognized that look. It was the one so filled with childish delight, I'd agreed to get him his own extra-large tub of popcorn at the movies.

A decision I'd regretted when I'd had to clean his buttery vomit from my carpet.

I knew what was coming even before he gave a firm nod. "Then you'll give me a ride today."

"Parker, no." Nora sighed and rubbed her temples, following the day's theme of disappointed mothers.

He didn't acknowledge his mom or any of the adults at the table who spoke. He didn't tear his focus away from Lars.

"No," Lars said, and I watched in real time as Parker deflated, totally crestfallen. Until he continued. "When the weather warms up, maybe. That'll give us time to get you some gear. Let your parents get to know me. Then we'll see."

Parker's skeptical gaze studied him, likely trying to figure out if it was a real maybe or an adult maybe that always meant no. "You'll be around that long?"

Without a moment of unsurety, confusion, or hesitation, Lars lifted his chin. "Yeah."

"Cool."

Yeah.

Cool.

Everything settled into a tense kind of truce as we finished eating. Mom popped open one of the wines Lars brought before discovering it wasn't just a nice bottle.

It was a *nice* bottle.

After learning that, Mom discreetly tucked the other two aside, likely to whip out at one of their dinners to impress their friends.

I was good with it. For one, I didn't drink wine even when I could've, so I wasn't missing out. For another, I was sure Mrs. Michelson was going to be filled with opinions about Lars and me riding up on a loud bike. I'd love to see the look on her face when she found out the expensive bottles were from my badass.

When the older kids began to clear the table, Ruth stood. "Joss and I are going to dish out dessert."

I tilted my head back so it rested on Lars' arm as I met his gaze. "It seems I'm dishing out dessert."

He pressed a light kiss to my mouth. "Can't wait."

Knowing he was not talking about the chocolate layer cake in the kitchen, I rolled my eyes. But I did it while clenching my thighs.

I walked into the kitchen to find Ruth standing at the far corner. She waved me over before quietly asking, "So did you find a genie and make a wish for the exact opposite of Peter?"

"Accurate, but no. I thought you were getting dessert."

"And I thought we were sisters," she seethed. "Yet, you didn't tell me about Lars."

"You're literally sitting directly across from him at dinner."

"Yeah, a dinner where you two are looking awfully close. Like you've been seeing each other for a while. Like it's serious."

"We are, we have, it is," I agreed.

"And yet this is the first I'm hearing of it." She shook her head, looking more enraged. "No, wait, Mom told us last week. *Mom* knew before me."

I grabbed small plates from the cupboard and let her rant it all out. "Hmm, I wonder why I didn't bring him around sooner. Might have something to do with my insane sister yelling at me while I'm trying to get some cake."

She slapped my arm. "Oh, shut up." Her voice lowered as she stepped closer. "He owns a sex club?"

"What? No. A strip club."

"Oh." She almost looked disappointed, and that was not an avenue of thought I wanted to stroll down.

I'd had enough mental scarring for the day.

"It's not one of those seedy ones," I shared as I cut into the cake.

"I figured. Motorcycles like his and those bottles of wine don't come cheap." She tilted her head, still not helping me do the chore she'd volunteered us for. "Did you know he knew Dad from SBOOB?"

I shot her a look. "Don't ask."

It took her a moment before her eyes widened and her face went a little green. "Gross."

She peppered me with more questions as she finally began helping. I was about to call for the boys to help serve the plates when she grabbed my arm. "I dated a guy like Lars before I met Benny. He was hot. Wild. So intense, it was impossible to resist him. He had these tattoos..." Her gaze went over my shoulder, wistful and daydreamy before she gave herself a little shake. "The point is, I got so wrapped up in him, I didn't know which way was up. It was a lot of fun, right until he left to be someone else's fun. Then it was misery."

"If that's the case," I said, firm but gentle, "then he wasn't a guy like Lars."

After a tick, her concern morphed into a grin. "No, I guess not. Especially because he never called me *hotcakes*."

For what felt like the millionth time since arriving, I let out an exasperated sigh. But I did it smiling.

The boys helped us pass out dessert, though I didn't take any for myself. All the anxiety, tension, and drama—not to mention, far too much manicotti—had left me nauseous.

It could've also been something else, but I wasn't thinking about that.

Lars used his hold on my hair to tug my head back. "You good?"

Well...

My dad frequented my boyfriend's strip club.

My dad didn't like my boyfriend thanks to said strip club.

My mom looked ready to rip my dad's head off, again thanks to said strip club.

I had no idea what Nora thought—and likely wouldn't until one of my nephews blabbed about her talking shit behind my back.

My nephews who were, at that moment, making graphic poop jokes using the chocolate frosting as visual aids.

My family was overbearing, nosy, and totally nuts.

And I was likely pregnant.

None of that stopped me from smiling. "That depends... Did they scare you away?"

"Told ya, hotcakes, you'll have to pry me off with a crowbar."

"Then I'm good."

Or I will be. Just as soon as I confirm this pregnancy and get this heavy secret off my chest.

Then it'll be nothing but smooth sailing ahead.

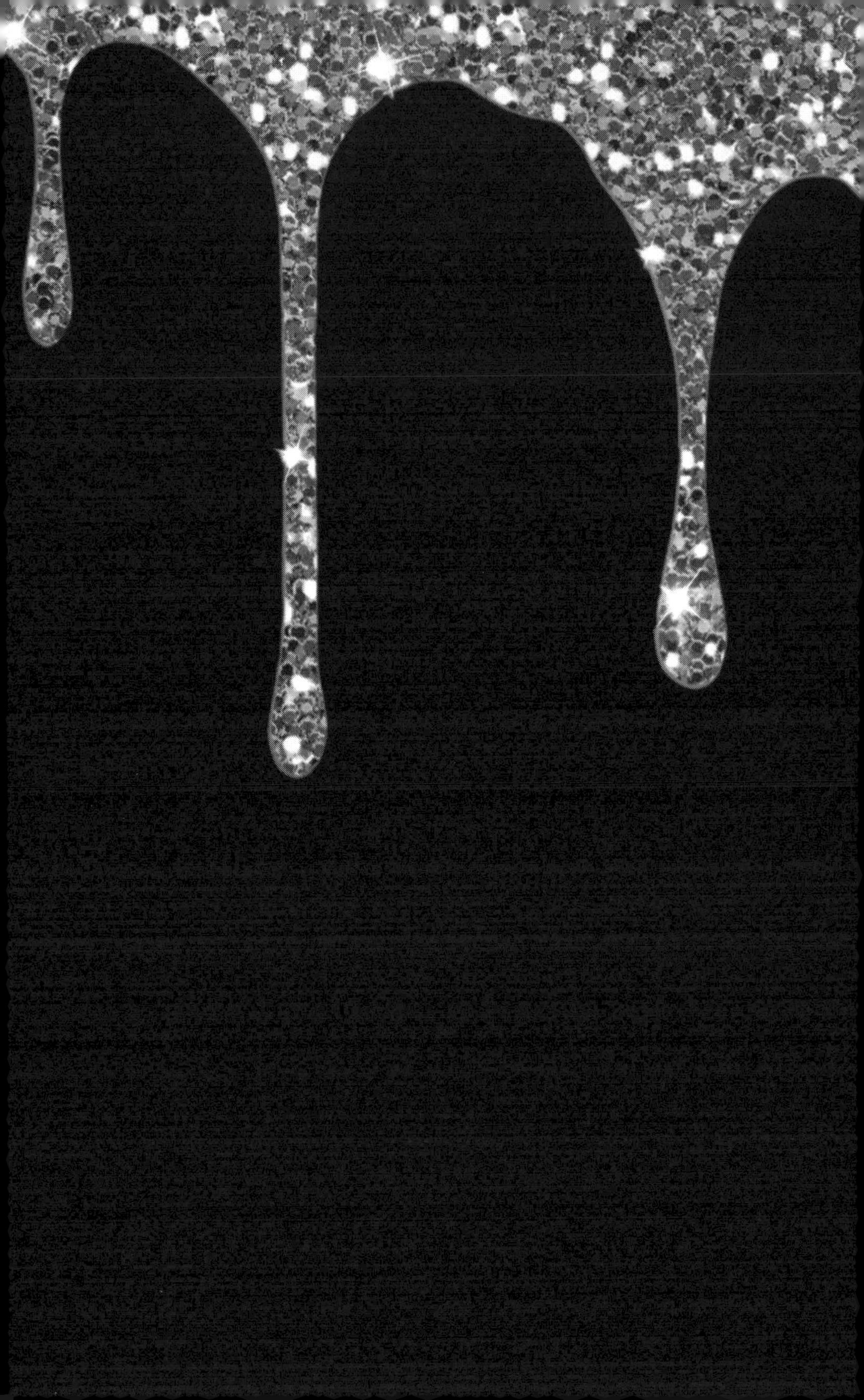

THIRTY

A Lovely Fookin' Nightmare

JOSS

IT'S...

I...

Wow.

When I'd called my doctor first thing Monday morning, I'd naively assumed I'd get a quick appointment. I'd been wrong. According to them, they didn't see expectant women until closer to nine weeks. According to me, that was insanity.

Because I'd been taking the birth control pill—and the fact I'd sounded like a crazy lady on the verge of tears—they'd agreed to squeeze me in at the end of the week.

Keeping a secret was *hard*. Keeping one from Lars, the man who read my brain and body like he'd been studying them for centuries? Nearly impossible. It'd been on the tip of my tongue all week. In the quiet moments. In the haze of twilight sleep. Each time he'd pulled me onto his lap and kissed me stupid. When he'd flirted or made me laugh or made me feel so much love, I'd ached with it.

I'd choked the words back, though. Not because I was worried about his reaction. Well, not *too* worried—irrational and illogical hormones were having a field day with my head.

I'd wanted to be sure before I got ahead of myself. Before I let myself feel the excitement that bubbled under the surface, like my blood was made with champagne.

Sitting in my car outside the doctor's office, I stared at the ultrasound for a few moments longer before carefully sliding it into my hoodie pocket. It was official.

I, Joss Lennon, was pregnant.

We were having a baby. Well, a sac and a tiny... frog leg? Alien? A dot of something. Something that would hopefully grow into a healthy baby.

Which meant I could finally tell Lars.

But not on a Friday. I could have texted him and he would make time for me—he always did. But the news was too major to drop in the midst of chaos.

I wanted us to have time to celebrate.

One more day won't kill me.

ARMED WITH MORE bags than I'd planned, I climbed my porch steps a couple hours later.

I'd thought keeping the secret would be the hardest part. I'd been wrong. Deciding how to tell my badass boyfriend without it being cliché or corny or underwhelming was literally impossible.

Pinterest was loaded with ideas that took more time and effort than I had. Not to mention, my art skills weren't as lacking as Harlow's, but they weren't great, either. I'd decided to make it easy by framing our alien's first picture. Still special, but not fussy or complex.

I was also going to make a big bow out of a motorcycle print ribbon I'd found because Mary Lennon would chew me out if she found out I didn't even make a bow.

The horror.

I'd planned to buy a little onesie or sleeper to go with the picture, but when I'd peeked my head into the baby section, it'd been too daunting. I'd slowly backed away.

Other than the frame and ribbon, the rest of my bags were filled with groceries.

There was no way Lars could complain I only had gerbil food with as much as I'd bought.

I wasn't sure if it was a psychosomatic reaction, but I was *starving*. It suddenly made sense why I'd brought so many salty snacks to Harlow's. I wanted to dive mouth first into a giant vat of honey mustard pretzel pieces.

With my mind on whether I wanted to make the bow first or go to town on some pretzels, I wasn't looking at the knob while I unlocked it.

That's the only reason I saw it.

My peephole was dark before going light.

Someone's in there.

I set the bags down before backing away. I was being dramatic. It was likely a shadow or my imagination or a million other things. But I kept thinking about when Lars had picked me up for our first date. He'd known I was there because the peephole darkened.

Grabbing my phone, I almost dialed 911. But my alarm wasn't blaring. My security company hadn't called to say a sensor was triggered. It seemed overzealous, bordering on insane, to call the police and tell them my peephole was dark.

I'd seen it and even I didn't believe me.

Just because I wasn't willing to the call the police didn't mean I was going to be all stupid-chick-in-a-horror-movie by rushing inside to investigate. Instead, I called the man I knew I could count on to protect me even if there was nothing to protect me from.

As soon as it connected, loud music came across the line. Since I rarely called, especially not on a Friday night, Lars' gruff voice was edgier than usual. "What's wrong?"

"I was on my porch," I said quietly, "and my peephole went dark."

"Fuck. You outside?"

"Yes."

"Get into your car and drive here. Right fuckin' now, baby. I'll call the cops and meet them at home."

I'd have smiled at him calling it *home* had I not been so rattled. "That's not—"

"Now." He pulled the phone away to bark orders to someone else. "I'll stay on the line."

I was almost to my car when movement caught my eyes. Glancing over, I gave a relieved laugh that it wasn't a summer camp serial killer in a hockey mask. "Oh my God. Don't scare me like that."

Except my body didn't loosen as an unexpected wariness slithered down my spine.

Lars

"What was that, baby?"

Nothing.

Silence.

"Joss, you there?" I tried again. "Say something."

When I'd pulled my phone away to yell for Killer, I'd thought I'd heard her laugh and say something. The laugh was good. The silence? Not so fuckin' much. 'Cause even though our call was still connected, she didn't speak.

Couldn't speak?

Using Killer's phone, I called 911 and gave them Joss' address before grabbing my keys.

"Tell Sasha I'm leaving." If Killer had something to say, I didn't stick around to hear it.

The whole drive to Joss', my gut twisted as I listened to our connected call. A breeze. The occasional car. But mostly silence.

Dead-fucking-silence.

Broke every speed limit and got flipped off by an old lady, but I made it to Joss' house in record time. Nearly beat the cops since they were leisurely climbing from their squad car when I pulled up. I'd asked for LeVar, but they'd sent Tweedledee and Tweedledumbass.

Gonna be useless.

I recapped Joss' call as one of them took notes. When I finished, they used my key so they could check the house. The door frames. The windows. Finding nothing, they had me walkthrough with them so I could see if anything was different.

It wasn't.

No signs of a struggle.

No signs of a forced entry.

Not so much as a broken glass or a crooked picture frame.

With no evidence of foul play, they weren't concerned.

The alarm hadn't sounded, but people forgot to arm them. Her cell wasn't working, but phones broke. Her car was still there, but that didn't mean anything.

She could be on a walk.

In an Uber.

She could've gotten a ride from someone else. Maybe a *friend*.

Fuck, it'd taken every goddamn ounce of control in my body not to knock the officer's teeth out for the way he'd said that. The insinuation. Like my woman was off cheating on me, giving someone else the body that belonged to me.

But me getting locked in a cage for assaulting a cop wouldn't help a damn thing.

Joss needed me.

They took a report and scanned the area, but there wasn't much more they could do there. They wanted me to come to the station, but fuck that. Sitting in a dingy room with a Styrofoam cup of shitty coffee wouldn't help me find Joss.

But I knew who could.

Waiting until the patrol car rolled away, I took out my phone and was about to end the call with hers when I heard it.

Not my girl.

Not voices.

Footsteps.

My footsteps.

I walked back and forth until they were loudest. Not seeing anything around me, I dropped to the ground and reached under her car.

And pulled out her phone.

My gut soured as I stared down at the shattered screen.

She'd never leave me worrying about her, and she sure as hell didn't routinely store her phone under her car.

Going inside, I called reinforcements.

"Aye?" Nox answered.

"Joss is gone," I forced out past the boulder in my throat.

"What do you mean the lass is gone?"

I told him about her call and everything that'd happened after. "You got LeVar's number to call him directly?"

"Aye. I know you want all the help you can get, but I can find her through my channels a fook of a lot faster than he can through his." He paused. "Might wanna hold off till you see who's involved... Or till you decide how you wanna handle them."

"Good point." 'Cause depending on who it was, I might not want to wave as they get hauled away in the back of a cruiser. I might wanna get my hands dirty first.

"You check with other lads, see if their women know anything?" Nox asked.

"No. If she was with Harlow or Piper, she'd have called me."

"Aye, you're probably right, but check anyway. I'll call my boys. Text me her address."

I clicked off and shot him the address before calling Kase.

"You finally burn Wicked down so you can have a normal life? We're at Rye and—"

"Has Harlow talked to Joss?"

I didn't have to say shit beyond that. He heard it in my voice, and all the joking humor that'd lightened his was gone. "I'll ask."

Christ.

His reaction was exactly why I hadn't wanted to tell Teo. To dredge up bad memories. I'd been with him when Harlow had become payment for missing drugs. It'd fucked with his head to be that helpless. I'd seen it.

It was my turn to experience it.

"She said no," Kase said. "Piper hasn't either. Where are you?"

"Joss' place."

"We're on our way."

"No, it's—"

"We're on our way," he repeated before hanging up.

Sitting on her couch, I closed my eyes, hung my head, and went through everyone who'd want to fuck with her.

I wasn't the only one obsessed with all of Joss' sweetness, so it was a short list.

Peter.

Fuckin' Peter.

When I'd talked to him, he'd seemed done with her. Joss had put him in his place, and I'd made sure the door was locked and bolted. But maybe my instincts were off. Maybe he hadn't been over Joss and her snark and her fire.

Maybe that dumb fucker wanted to come after what was mine.

I grabbed my phone and sent Nox another text.

Me: Peter something. Works at Saul Strategies. Find me his address.

Nox: On it. Five minutes out.

The list of people who'd fuck with Joss was short, but the list of people who'd fuck with me? A mile long.

Every asshole that'd crossed our paths was a suspect. The guy who'd touched her at Wicked. Her boss. Anyone I'd tossed from the club. Hell, maybe her IPA neighbor had accelerated from leaving a bitchy note. I found myself second-guessing the loyalty I had from Killer, Frankie, and the other bouncers who worked the back hall.

Maybe they didn't like Joss.

Maybe they liked her too much.

The possibility that any of this was my fault was like drinking battery acid.

Jake and Piper were the first to arrive. Piper was pale, concern bleeding from her.

"Teo and Harlow behind you?" I asked.

Jake shrugged. "They were comin' from Rye. We were still at Hyde."

"Any word?" Piper asked.

I gave a sharp headshake.

Jake pulled his wife close until her back was to his front and his arm was around her upper chest.

Like Teo, I was betting Jake's head was on the betrayal he'd faced at the hands of a trusted friend.

Like she could read where his head was at, Piper reached up to hold on to her husband as she spoke to me. "Anyone paying extra attention to Joss? Creepy notes? Random flowers?"

"Just her ex sniffing around."

"You think he'd do something like this?" Jake asked

I ran my hand across the top of my head, thinking on it before shrugging. "Wanna say no, but you know better than most how crazy finds a way to hide itself. Nox is getting me an address so I can find out for sure."

"Good."

"Anything happen at the bakery?" I asked. "Customers coming around too often or paying her too much attention.

Piper gave me a brittle smile. "Just you."

We sat in heavy silence, lost in memories or nightmares or what-ifs.

Teo and Harlow arrived, but it was more of the same. No idea where she was. Hadn't seen anyone bother her. No clue where to fuckin' start.

Nox, Beck, and Matt showed up last, and shit got official.

Shit got real.

Nox's job was all about finding things. He grilled me on her schedule. Her life. Work. Everything. Once he was done, he asked, "She do anything different today?"

"No," I answered.

"Yes," Piper immediately corrected.

My gaze cut to her. "What changed?"

And why the fuck didn't I know about it?

"She had a doctor's appointment." She flashed me a reassuring smile, but it didn't reach her eyes. Not anywhere fuckin' close. "Nothing bad, just a routine thing."

I didn't care if it was for a flu shot and a sucker. I wanted to know.

Also wanted to know what the hell Piper wasn't telling us. Knew she was a good person. Also knew she loved my girl like a sister. So it wasn't guilt or involvement. She was near fuckin' tears with worry. But there was something.

Watching her closely, I asked, "You know something else?"

"No," Piper said. Lied? No fuckin' clue.

Pissing her off—thereby sending Jake at my fuckin' throat—wasn't gonna get me anywhere, so I let it go. She wouldn't risk her friend's safety by withholding something important.

"Other than the Peter fooker, no one else has an issue with the lass." Nox stroked his beard, eyeing me. I knew what he was thinking.

No one has issue with her…

But who has issue with *me*?

I answered his unasked question. "Fired a bouncer a while back for leaving his post. I'll get you his name. Had a beer distributor pull out, and I've thrown around threats of breach of contract. I'll send that info, too." I tilted my head. "Usual customer bullshit, but nothing sticks out. Haven't had to break any hands or faces lately. The Irish?"

"That was my first thought, so I had Dair reach out to all his contacts. It's not them. They took his warning seriously and moved on to other options. They weren't risking war with us or the Italians over one club when there are hundreds of others."

"He's sure?"

"Not even a whisper, and those tools have big mouths."

All I was left with was one more name that'd been lurking at the back of my head.

One more motherfucker.

Nox was thinking it. His boys were thinking it. Kase was probably thinking it, too, after all the shit that'd gone down with Harlow.

Elliot Nash.

He'd been quiet since I'd confronted him at his office. He'd backed off. But it wasn't the first time he'd tried to play nice. It wouldn't be above that cowardly bastard to go after a woman 'cause he couldn't take on a man.

Nox turned to Matt and Beck. "Pay Nash a visit."

Harlow made a strangled gasp. She'd heard the graphic details of what Nash did to women. She'd been threatened with it.

And now Joss could be with that same monster.

Fuck.

Fuck.

I was coming outta my skin.

Nox's dinging phone pulled my focus before I shattered one of the picture frames Joss lined her wall with. "Dair got an address for the ex. I'll head over there while they track down Nash. We'll be in touch if we find anything."

I stood. "Fuck no. I got the ex."

"Don't be thick."

"You should stick close in case Joss shows, yeah?" Jake added.

"Fuck no," I repeated slower. Enunciating each word. "Can't just sit here with my thumb up my ass."

"Fine," Nox relented, "but I'm coming so you don't get yourself hauled away for killing that gobshite."

"Jake and I will check the bakery and her school and shit," Kase said.

"And Piper and I can wait here for Joss," Harlow volunteered. "For *when* she comes home."

"No." My voice was firm. "Not when we don't know if this house is safe."

"I'll put men outside." Nox typed as he talked. "Make it the safest place for them."

It didn't sit right with me. Nox and his boys were professionals. They knew the risks and carried the hardware to face them. But Kase, Jake, and Piper weren't trained fighters who wiped out human filth in their spare time.

Harlow had stepped on a man's balls until they'd popped like stress balls. She was a wild card.

I may not have liked it, but none of them were backing down. And I wasn't about to waste more time trying to convince them to.

I had a *gobshite* to see.

IT WAS A LONG DRIVE—BUT still far too fuckin' short for my liking—from Joss' to Peter's overpriced townhouse development. I barely threw my car in park before I was out and pounding on the front door.

It was opened a moment later, no suspicious delay.

Not a promising sign.

Also not a promising sign? The genuine surprise on Peter's face.

It morphed to fear he attempted to hide behind annoyance. "Threatening me at my office wasn't enough? How'd you even—"

I pushed past him, scanning the place. Nothing broken. No physical sign of the fight she'd have given. And no emotional sign of the insults she would have ripped him apart with.

Still, I turned to face him. "You seen Joss?"

"No. Now get the hell out of my house before I call the cops."

"Talk to her?"

"Not since she sent me her little blackmail." His gaze went to the door. "Who the hell are you?"

"A lovely fookin' nightmare. Nice place. Compensating for something, eh?"

"Get the hell out. Both of you."

"You haven't seen her?" I asked again.

"No, why?" A nasty smile curved Peter's mouth. "Wait... She left your ass, didn't she? Knew it was only a matter of time."

I let his smug gloating go. It didn't matter 'cause he didn't have her.

I'd never felt so damn helpless. Not as a kid. Not even during my time inside. Never.

Peter held out his arms. "As you can see, she didn't come here. Even if she did, I wouldn't let that bitch in. Not after you ruined her."

I closed the distance and was about to choke him with his own polo when Nox grabbed my arm.

"This is why I had to come with, you muppet." I didn't know which of us Nox was talking to, but it didn't matter. He pulled me away. "Don't waste time on this tool. Gotta find your lass. Focus on that, aye?"

"Wait, is Joss missing? Like, actually missing?" Peter asked, proving again he had nothing to do with Joss 'cause the fucker had no control of his face. Didn't like him, but I'd invite him to poker night.

"Yes," I gritted out.

Disgust curled his lip. "What'd you drag her into?"

That time, Nox had to use both hands to haul me back, and it'd still been close. "A thick himbo, aren't ya?"

Peter was stupid.

But he may have also been correct.

Turning, I stormed from the house to my car. To go nowhere 'cause we had no other fuckin' leads.

Throwing open the door, I didn't get in. It felt too small. Like a Hot Wheels. Like a cage. Like I couldn't breathe. I slammed my fists against the roof and hung my head, fighting to clear away the bloody, mangled horrors that taunted me.

A hand landed on my shoulder, and I nearly swung before I saw it was Nox.

"Get in," he ordered.

"Gimme a minute."

"Don't have one. Matt is calling." He pointedly looked around, making his point. It wasn't a call he wanted to take where someone could overhear.

With a chin lift, I did as he said.

The phone rang, and Nox put it on speaker. "Anything?"

"No sign of Joss, boss."

My gut clenched. Not that I wanted Nash to have her. I just wanted to know where the fuck she was. "You sure?"

"Positive. Tapped into his security feeds. He's been in his back office at NashVille's all night. Saw some shit to discuss. Saw some shit I'll need a therapist for. But no sign of Joss. No visitors. No messages. Nothing but his usual fuckery."

"What do we have to discuss?" Nox asked as I started my car.

I'd heard all I needed.

"He took Lars' rejection and shifted his attention to Mayhem. They rejected his gift of girls and guns, so he is working to find a new route. Didn't say what."

He'd tried something similar with me and Nox and had gotten exactly nowhere. Court of Mayhem was a local motorcycle gang Nox worked with on occasion. If he trusted them enough to team up, it meant they weren't the kind of people who'd fall for Nash's shit. Whatever his new route was, it would be a wasted effort.

"I'll give Judge a heads-up." Nox went through a couple more details with his boys while I drove. Since I had no clue where to go next, I returned to Joss'. After that...

I wasn't sure what the hell to do.

About a block away from her place, Nox shifted in his seat. A moment later, he pulled his gun. "We got a tail."

That close to Joss', it'd be impossible to shake them before we arrived. I could keep going but I wasn't wasting my time. I had more important things that needed my attention.

"Let's see what they want then." I turned into Joss' driveway and pulled the DoubleTap from my ankle holster.

We climbed out just as the car parked at the curb. Taking aim, I waited.

After a long moment, Peter got out of his car with his hands up.

"Coulda shot you, you himbo," Nox muttered, shaking his head as he reholstered his weapon.

I didn't follow. "What're you doing here?"

"Can you put that away?" Peter asked. "Or at least stop pointing it at me?"

I didn't do either.

But I also didn't shoot.

He lowered his arms slowly. "I'm here to help."

My eyes narrowed. "Why?"

"Joss and I are over," he admitted with overdue finality, "but that doesn't mean I want to see her hurt."

I may have been a possessive prick, but I wasn't a stupid one. Not when it came to Joss' safety. Since we'd gotten together, I'd made it my business to know *her* business. I hung on every damn word she told me about the bakery or school or whatever. But there was a lot I didn't know about her life before me.

But Peter would know.

Which was why I lifted my chin and lowered my gun.

His shoulders deflated. "I'm still friends with her mom and one of her sisters on socials. They both posted about doing stuff tonight, but no mention of Joss." He started for the porch. "You'll see, they're tight."

"Already saw," I said.

If my girl wasn't missing, I may have smiled as he stumbled at my words. Had to give him credit, he didn't get pissy like I expected. "I bet that was interesting."

"You'd bet right."

We got inside to find Jake and Kase had already returned. Piper's expression was blank as she eyed Peter.

Harlow's wasn't. Her gaze was filled with contempt on behalf of her friend. Her word was more bite than greeting. "Peter."

It took him a moment before he connected the pieces. "We went to high school together, right?"

"Right." It was one word, but it dripped with acid.

Peter looked like he had more to say, but when Kase wrapped an arm around Harlow, he smartly kept his mouth shut. "The place looks the same." He tilted his head. "I think we both knew I wouldn't be living here with her. That this was her dream house. She decorated it how she wanted, and I was never present enough to notice."

"Too busy pumpin' in your car," Nox muttered, not giving an ounce of fuck or sympathy.

Not arguing, Peter just nodded.

Kase and Jake recapped all the nothing they'd found. Their women had been busy online stalking anyone and everyone from Joss' friends list. Between Peter and them, what they'd been able to find—or, more accurately, *not* find—was scary-as-shit.

Stalking made easy.

"I'll run through the other names you gave me," Nox said.

"I'll help." I didn't anticipate anything but it would keep me from losing my damn mind.

"Hey." Peter looked over his shoulder at me. "How's Joss know Sophia?"

"You mean Sophie?" Piper asked.

"Oh, yeah, that's right."

"You know her?" I asked.

"From work."

Boston may have been a big city, but in a lot of ways, it was small. There was overlap. Everyone knew someone who knew someone.

There were coincidences, and then there was shit that just didn't sit right with me.

"You talk to Sophie yet tonight?" I asked Piper.

She shook her head. "I tried but she didn't answer."

Nox lowered his cell and gave Piper his full attention. "Tell me everything you know about her."

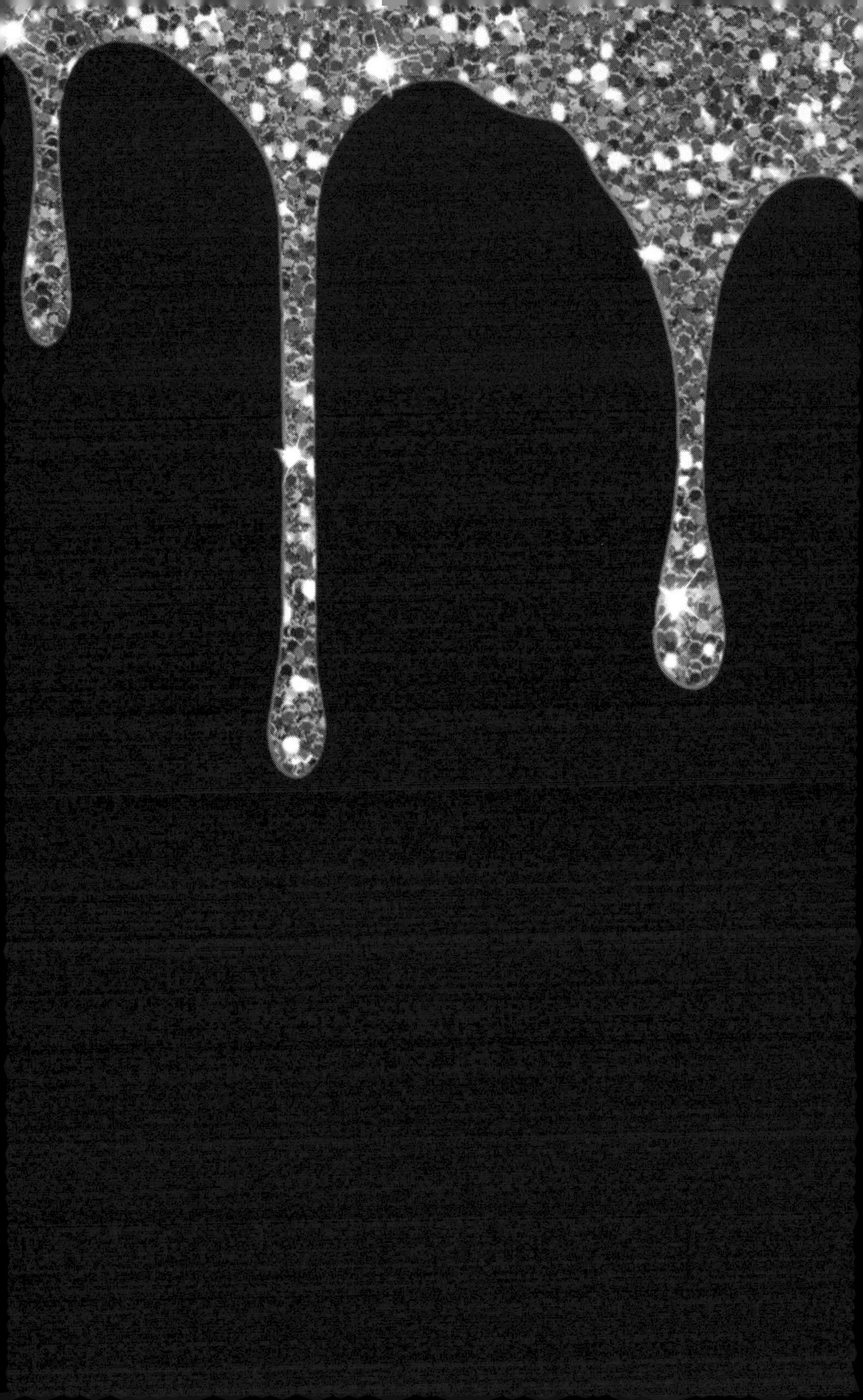

THIRTY-ONE
Just Hanging Out
JOS

Joss

"I WASN'T READY. IT'S NOT TIME. I WASN'T READY." OVER and over and over.

Leaning so hard against the passenger door, it dug into my side, I stared at Sophie.

And the gun in her hand.

When Sophie had jogged down my porch, holding my discarded bags, I'd felt relief at the familiar face.

Only it wasn't so familiar.

She'd looked... off. That morning at the bakery, she'd been wearing the wrap dress I'd given her. Her hair had been pulled into a low bun. Her makeup had been minimal as always.

She'd looked... normal.

But everything was different. Her hair was down. Her makeup was heavier. And she was no longer wearing the wrap dress. She was in my favorite pair of jeans, an oversized sweater I'd swiped from Lars, and even my shoes.

It'd sent a tremor of apprehension through me even before I'd seen the gun in her hand.

After she'd forced me down the street and into her car, she hadn't answered any of my questions. She hadn't responded when I'd tried to engage her in conversation. She kept repeating the same thing.

She wasn't ready.

It wasn't time.

I had no clue what the hell either meant, but I wanted to find out. Later. When I was a safe distance from her and her crazy eyes.

We drove for far too long. Each mile marker was like a taunt as we traveled farther and farther from my house. From the city. From any sign of civilization. I didn't know what direction we were headed because the navigation screen in her car was shattered. Even if I could open the door, dodge a bullet from the gun she kept aimed my way, and survive a tuck-and-roll from a vehicle going sixty, I'd be lost. Lost and left to die in the middle of nowhere.

I was *not* an action hero in the making.

I hadn't been tracking the turns. I hadn't spotted any landmarks to remember. I had no grand plan to rescue myself. All I knew was I had to be smart. Cautious. It wasn't just about me. I had an alien frog leg to think of.

When Sophie pulled in front of a secluded lakefront house, my gaze darted around. There was nothing. No other car. No boat. Not even a bicycle.

And no neighbors that I could see.

"Get out," Sophie ordered. The gun shook in her hand, and my stomach wrenched until bile burned my throat. She wasn't comfortable with it. She didn't know how to properly hold it. Her finger rested on the trigger.

That was how people ended up dead.

I did as she ordered, happy to escape the confined space—though I'd be a whole lot happier once I escaped the psycho, too. When she stuck her head back in, I slowly inched backward.

Boom.

The loud noise echoed around us, mixing with my scream. My instincts kicked in, my brain searching my body for pain as my heartbeat slammed in my ears.

Like my veins were filled with ice, I froze as cold terror ran through me.

But Sophie acted like nothing was amiss as she hefted my bags from the car and closed the door. She came into my space, not even mentioning that she'd fired the gun. It may have been into a tree, but still.

She'd fired the damn gun.

"Inside." Once we were in the living room, she used the gun to point at the empty corner farthest from any windows or doorways. "Sit."

I carefully eased myself to the ground and breathed a small sigh of relief when she lowered the gun. She didn't release it, but at least I wasn't staring into my own mortality.

After she dropped the bags on the couch, she paced and muttered and muttered and paced. Like she didn't know what to do next. Like it wasn't time.

Like she wasn't ready.

Since I was no match for a psycho with a gun, overpowering her and running were both out. I tried to talk to her again.

"Is this cabin yours?" I asked. "It's nice."

Better than dying in a rickety, abandoned cabin like in the movies.

I choked down a sob at that thought, wrapping my arms around my stomach. I felt the ultrasound pictures beneath my arms and drew strength from them before trying again. "Is it yours, Soph?"

It was too clean to be vacant. But if it was hers, or even an Airbnb she'd rented, Nox's guys could find a record of it. Because I had no doubt Lars had called in help. That he was looking for me.

He had to be.

I couldn't allow myself to consider the alternative.

"That's *not* my name!" Sophie said, ending on a screech. "It's not *Soph*. It's not *Sophia*. He always called me *Sophia*. It's been over a year, and it's still *Sophia*, *Sophia*, *Sophia*. No matter how many times I correct him. *Sophia*, *Sophia*, *Sophia*." She turned toward me, her glare filled with so much hate, it stole my breath as renewed panic surged through me. "That was on the rare occasion he even talked to me. When it wasn't *Joss*, *Joss*, *Joss*."

It was impossible to follow her manic rant. I had no clue who she was talking about. The only person who was obsessed with me was Lars, but she hadn't known him for over a year. I wasn't even sure he'd said a single word to her, much less called her the wrong name.

It couldn't be him, so... "Who?"

"*Who*? The man is still in love with you, and you ask *who*." Her face tightened like I'd personally insulted her, and she raised the gun until it was all I could see. All I could focus on. "Peter!"

I jerked, slamming my head into the wall. Blinking away the pain, I tried to piece together what she'd said.

She worked with Peter.

She wanted Peter?

She'd never mentioned him. She'd barely even talked about her day job except to say she was an office manager at a boring accounting office. Nothing about a PR firm.

"Sophie," I said carefully. I'd read somewhere that saying the abductor's name helped bond with them. Or maybe I'd seen it on TV. Either way, it was worth trying. "Peter and I aren't together."

"You might think that, but he doesn't. He loves you. You just can't see it from that pedestal everyone put you on. He talks about you all the time. Did you know he still calls you his fiancée? Of course you don't because the only time you mention him is to talk shit. God, you're such a bitch. This is why I didn't want to meet you. I just wanted to know what he saw in you, but your stupid alarm ruined that."

"My alarm?"

The night the window sensor went off.

Before she even started at the bakery.

It wasn't the wind.

"You made it easy once we were *friends*. You never even asked how I knew your address after we went shopping. You punched in your passcode while I stood right there. You left me alone. So trusting, like no one would ever hurt perfect Joss."

My breathing picked up, panic making my fingertips tingle and my vision tunnel. I worked hard to slow it because if I didn't, I'd pass out.

And if I did that?

I wasn't sure I'd wake up.

Her expression wavered between anger and despair. "I tried being like you. I styled my hair like you. I colored it like yours. I did my makeup like you do. I started dressing like you, talking like you, being you. I sent the message to him to meet at Voodoo. I thought he'd see me in your dress and finally talk to me. But no. He watched *you* all night. He went to *your* house. He wants Joss. *Everyone* wants Joss. No one even notices me."

"That's not true," I said softly, fighting the wave of nausea that roiled through me at her confession. I'd assumed her style changes were for herself or maybe one of the Hyde guys. I'd never put it together that the darker hair and her clothing choices after our shopping trip were because of me.

Were to become me.

She let out a bitter laugh. "Lars walked right by me *twice* when he came to see Peter at Saul Strategies. Not a flicker of recognition on his face either time. Like he hadn't seen me every Saturday for weeks. Piper and Harlow are always talking about you. *Joss is so sweet. Joss is so helpful. Thanks for sending Joss my way.* You think I don't know how much I'm excluded?" She pressed the gun against my forehead, hard enough to hurt. To dig in.

Wincing, I wanted to close my eyes and block out her loathing. Block out the possibility of what was to come. The inevitability? But I couldn't. I watched as hatred and hurt twisted her face into something hideous.

"Even you don't notice me half the time."

Guilt swirled with the terror in my chest because she was right. I worked in silence, my mind either on the night before or my day ahead. I didn't always notice her.

"I'm just tired in the mornings," I explained. "And I've always been quiet. I didn't think you minded."

"Right," she scoffed, lowering the gun again. "Because of course I wouldn't mind being ignored day after day. Being invisible to everyone while they bask in the sunlight of *Joss*."

"You're not invisible."

"And you're not so perfect." Her lip curled in a sneer. "I thought you were being smart for once. Peter doesn't even like tattoos, but I'd have gotten one if you did. I'd have to get one if you did. But you listened. You actually listened to me about them being too permanent."

That wasn't why I hadn't gotten one, but I wasn't about to correct her.

"But then you had to do something worse." Her gun lowered. Not all the way. Just to point at my stomach as hellfire blazed in her deranged eyes. "You had to get pregnant. You had to ruin all my careful planning. I can't copy that. You fucked everything up. You fucked it up! I'm not ready. It's not time."

I could feel her desperation—it was contagious. If I couldn't talk her back from the edge, I'd have no choice but to act. Run or maybe tackle her.

And hope I didn't end up with a bullet in my already occupied belly.

"I can talk to Peter for you," I tried. "I can set you two up."

Another bitter, ugly laugh. "You think I still want him? He had his chance. Peter was a small dream. Insignificant. I'm aiming big. Taking what I deserve. Why would I waste more of my life on him when I could have yours?"

My what?

I had no clue.

"Sophie—"

She put the gun under my chin and used it to tip my head. Slow and sharp, her words carried so much hatred. "That's not my name."

"I said Sophie," I rushed out frantically, unable to hold in my tears. "You said you didn't like to be called Soph, but I said Sophie."

"That's not my name!" She jabbed the gun with every screeched word until it broke the skin, leaving my chin stinging as blood dripped down my throat.

"Okay!" I choked on a sob. "What is your name?"

Like a switch had been flipped, she stepped away.

She smiled.

Moving differently, she went to one of the bags and grabbed the pretzels. She chomped away like we were hanging out. Like it was girls' day. Popping another in her mouth, she pulled her phone out and sighed. "Don't you hate when houseguests overstay their welcome?"

I had whiplash from the change in conversation and the change in her.

When she blinked expectantly at me, I forced myself to whisper, "Yes."

"It's so rude." She turned her phone so I could see the video feed. A live one? I wasn't sure. But I knew where it was.

My house.

My man, my friends, and even my ex stood in my living room. They were talking, though there was no audio to hear what they said.

I tried not to think about how long that camera had been up. What she might've seen. We were beyond that. Her seeing me ride Lars on my couch was the least invasive thing she'd done.

She flipped the phone back so she could see the video. Her nose wrinkled. "What's *he* doing there?"

I braced for more rage at the sight of Peter in my house, but it didn't come.

She just rolled her eyes. "Typical Peter. He doesn't want to accept we're over, and I've moved on."

At her change and her words, a sickening realization hit me.

She doesn't want my ex.

She wants my whole life.

Confirming my suspicion, she kept talking like she was me. "I know my friends love me. And I know how much my man misses me. But this is too much." She tilted her head. "Maybe once my houseguests leave, I'll call Nora and Ruth to have my nephews stay over."

God.

God.

A fresh rush of panic mixed with guilt until my heart raced in my heavy chest.

I was going to die.

I was going to have a heart attack and die, and I'd left the people I loved vulnerable.

Because like an idiot, I'd shared with Sophie. I'd answered all the questions she'd peppered me with at Harlow's. She knew about my family, my nephews, *everything*.

"Never mind, I'm too tired for their shenanigans," she said.

It took everything to hold in my thankful cry.

"I need to just go home and sleep." Another pretzel before she rubbed her stomach. "Sleep is important for pregnancy."

She's not just a little off.

She's an entire tray of cupcakes short of a bakery.

"Why don't we head to your place then." Cautious and watchful, I hoped I didn't push her off the ledge by going along with her delusion. "We'll have a sleepover and ride to the bakery together in the morning."

Her curled lip twitched, and she shook her head with exaggerated pity. "Sorry, but you do *not* want to be there for what my boyfriend is going to do to me later. It'll just remind you how sad and alone you are. How you have no one in the entire world." She took the frame from the bag. It didn't matter that there was nothing in it since the ultrasound printout was safely tucked in my pocket. She lovingly stroked the glass. "He's going to be so happy to hear he trapped me. It's gonna be wild."

"Tomorrow then?" I forced out, my lungs too tight to expand.

"My girls and I have plans. Lots to talk about. Lots of secrets. I'd say maybe if you were around, we'd throw an invite your way. But you won't be." Gently kissing the empty frame, she set it aside and checked her phone. "Oh, good, they're leaving." She turned it again so I could see everyone trailing from my house.

To look for me?

Or giving up?

She gestured with the gun. "Stand."

"Sop—" I started before her unhinged eyes widened. "Joss. Let me hang out here while you go home."

"That's the plan."

That should've been reassuring, but there was something about the way she'd said it that sent alarm bells ringing.

I couldn't wait any longer. There was no opening. I needed to make one.

Without hesitation, I bolted to the side and hoped I caught her off guard.

For a second, I did.

But then my hood pulled taut and yanked me back until I slammed to the floor.

My shoulder hit, and an electric jolt of pain shot down my arm. My head thudded against the floor with a sickening crack. Another wave of nausea whipped through my stomach as my vision blurred.

I lost my breath.

And I couldn't drag in a new one because Sophie was lifting me by the hood she still clutched. The fabric dug into my airway, and my legs flailed, searching for purchase at the odd angle. Once I had my feet under me, the slack loosened, and I gulped a panicked breath.

"Careful," she chided in that saccharine sweet voice. "These old floors are uneven, and it's easy to trip. You could've gotten hurt."

Yeah, because you grabbed me, you scary bitch.

Keeping hold of my sweater, she poked the gun into my back and walked me through the rest of the cabin. Blood dripped heavily from the side of my head, leaving a sick trail until we reached the back door. "Open it."

Oh shit.

The water.

She wants to drown me.

I wasn't an Olympic swimmer, but I wasn't a weak one, either. I could make it to a neighbor or dock.

I could still get away from her, and that was all that mattered.

Hope soared in my chest.

And then it left a crater as it crashed and burned.

Because when I opened it, it didn't lead to the water.

It led to a cold, sterile room with chains, sharp knives, and hooks hanging from the ceiling.

The kind of room my uncle used to break down the animals he hunted.

Pushing me until we were under a hanging chain, Sophie held the barrel flush to my temple with one hand while she grabbed a manacle with the other. When she reached for my hand, I pulled away.

Boom.

It may not have hit me, but I heard and felt the bullet whiz by my head. It'd been close. Too close.

Taking advantage of the distraction and my ringing ears, Sophie latched both of my wrists before I even knew what happened. She checked that they were secure, tugging on the restraints and the chains above me.

"You know what's funny?" she asked conversationally as she worked.

Nothing.

Absolutely nothing about any of this is funny.

"It's nearly impossible to get poison. It's not like in the movies. You can't just order some online or whip it together with common household ingredients so they can peacefully drift away." She shook the gun in her hand, and I let out a stifled scream. "I got this today. *Today.* Fake name. Bad fake ID. No problem." She aimed it my way again, and there was nothing stifled about my scream that time. "A peaceful death is illegal, but a painful one is easier to get than spray paint. Funny, right?"

Tears rolled down my cheeks, and I couldn't pretend to go along with her crazy. "Please, don't do this. Please, don't shoot me."

"Shoot you?" She snorted a laugh and tossed the gun behind her. It was out of my reach, but at least it wasn't aimed at my head. "I could never do that. I'd never kill anyone. I always tell my kindergarten friends to treat others how they want to be treated. That's what I'm doing. I'm treating you *exactly* the way you treat others."

She backed toward the door and pressed a button on the wall. I jolted as the chains I was latched to clattered and rose, taking my arms with them. An unbearable pain shot from my injured left shoulder, but that wasn't enough. Sophie held down the button until my feet could barely touch the ground. Until I couldn't take the strain off my shoulders. Until I couldn't rest a single muscle in my body.

"Once you're gone, you won't be able to make everything about you." Her smile and tone held more elation than a kid on Christmas morning. "They won't go on and on about how perfect you are because they'll finally realize I'm better. They'll finally see *me*."

"You can't do this," I sobbed.

"I'm not doing anything. It's not my fault you're invisible. I'm just leaving to live my perfect life. Moving on without thinking about you. About how it affects you." She shrugged. "What happens to you isn't my problem."

"Sop—" I started before catching myself again. "Hey! *Pleeeeease*!"

But she ignored me as she walked from the room.

"Joss!" I tried.

Nothing.

I screamed. I wailed. I cried. I thrashed around until my wrists bled.

But she never returned.

And my restraints didn't loosen. Not even a millimeter.

Closing my eyes, I thought about my alien frog leg. I focused on keeping my breaths even because I needed to do it for both of us. I reminded myself that Lars would come for us.

"We're okay," I whispered. It didn't have ears, but I talked to it anyway. "He's going to save us."

I know he is.

Right?

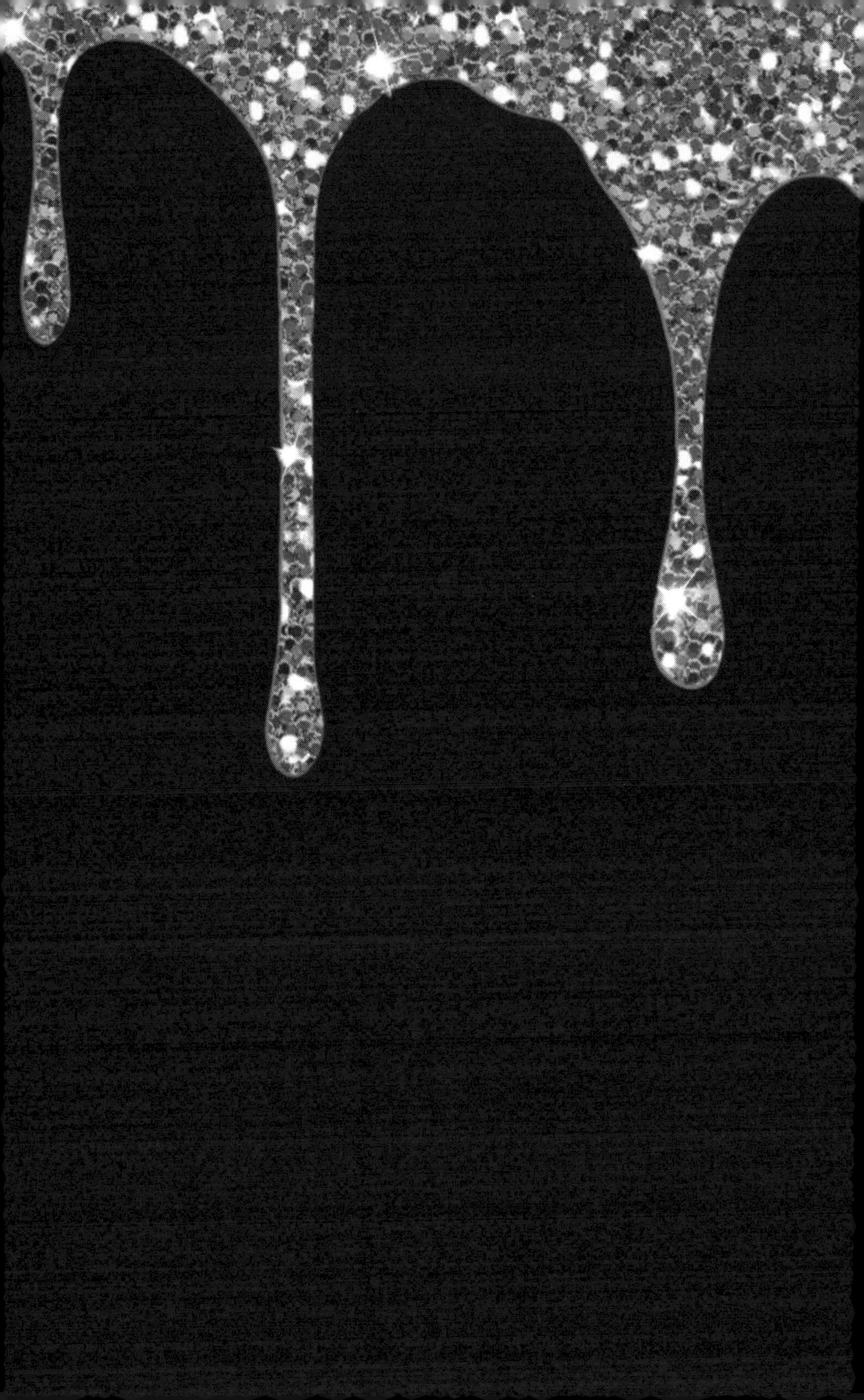

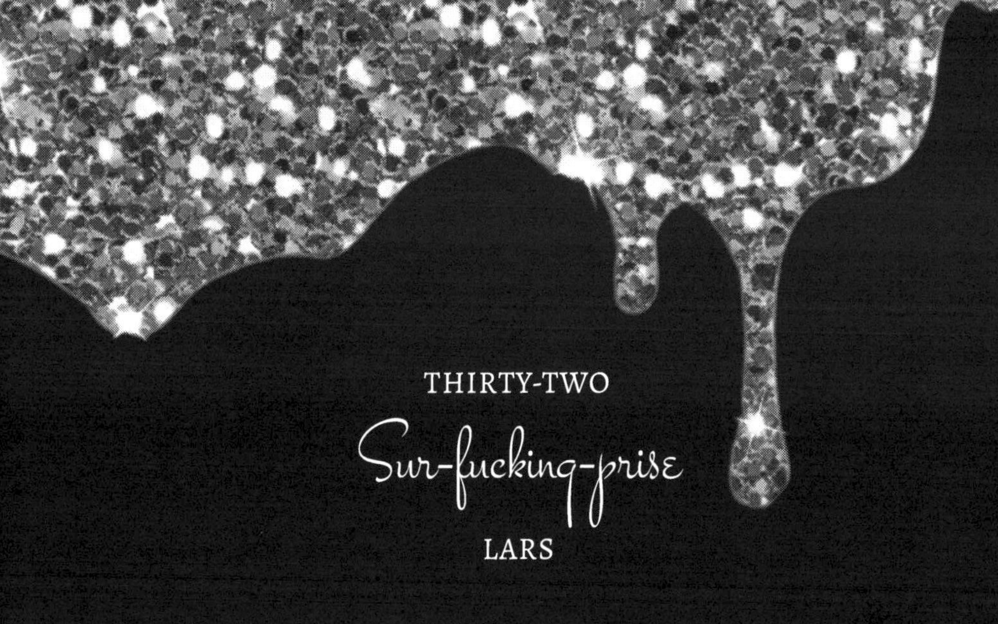

THIRTY-TWO
Sur-fucking-prise
LARS

THE WOMEN AND PETER TOLD NOX EVERYTHING THEY knew about Sophie.

It took less than two minutes.

And it was a lot of contradictory bullshit.

Because unlike what she'd told Piper about an accounting office, she worked at the PR firm with Peter for over a year. That should've been enough time for him to know a single thing about her, but he didn't. Hell, he hadn't even gotten her name right.

Piper knew a little more. Sophie worked the same bakery shift as Joss. She was single. Quiet. Didn't share much about herself except she liked to hike and maybe kayak.

But that was it.

"She's not rude." Piper's lips tipped down. "But she can say things without realizing it comes off as rude. Like when Joss—" Her words cut off suddenly.

"When Joss *what*?"

"I meant me."

"You got yourself confused with Joss?" I snapped.

"Dude," Jake bit out, glaring at me. But he did it while squeezing his wife's shoulder. Like he knew she was being shady, too.

Piper hesitated for beat. "We found out we might not be able to have kids."

Christ, I'm a dick for forcing her to share this.

"When *I* told my girls," she continued, "Sophie wasn't reassuring. She made it worse. I thought it was unintentional, but she has a habit of being a little... judgy. She's more traditional than us. She said she grew up sheltered without much family."

"You think she could've done this?" Nox asked.

She gave a wobbly nod. "I didn't before, but like Lars said, I know how crazy can hide itself. I just don't know *why* she'd do it."

That didn't matter. We'd get to the why after. Once I had Joss in my arms.

"You have her address?" Nox looked between Piper and Harlow.

Harlow shook her head, but Piper nodded. "In my personnel files at the bakery.

Nox sent off a text. "I'll get my guys on it, they'll be faster."

Piper's face was guilt-stricken. It was the same guilt I'd felt when I thought I was to blame.

That I'd brought someone into Joss' life who would hurt her.

"We'll find her," I reassured Piper.

And myself.

It didn't help.

It made it worse.

At my soft words, she burst into tears. Jake gathered her in his arms, whispering to his wife, but she kept sobbing. "It's my fault."

"No. It's mine." At Peter's quiet confession, everyone turned to him, and he held up his hands in the surrender position for the second time that night. "I didn't take Joss," he reiterated. "But Sophie has a crush on me. A big one. People were giving me shit about it, and I complained to HR. She was let go."

"You got her fired for having a crush on you?" Piper snapped, her guilt forgotten as wrath took its place. "Because you're more concerned with your rep than her livelihood?"

Peter shook his head. "It wasn't an innocent crush. She kept lying to people about dates we were going to do, like throwing axes and rides along the coast."

Piper winced. "My bad. I thought you meant it was innocent. Like, she blushed when you talked to her or something. Not that she was being hostile. You had every right to complain."

"I didn't report it until she got inappropriate."

"Inappropriate how?" I asked.

"She sent me a picture of her bent over a little table."

Piper winced again. "A hot pink table?"

"Yeah, how'd you know?"

Jake looked down at his wife. "You include her in your little photoshoot with Joss?"

I'd assumed Joss had used the self-timer to take the picture I loved so much, but her and Piper had clearly made a whole thing of it. At any other time, I'd have found that funny-as-shit.

Not right then, though.

Piper shook her head. "We did it quickly while Sophie was in the kitchen. We didn't want to make her uncomfortable."

"When was she let go?" I asked Peter.

"Today."

Fuck.

That was no coincidence.

Peter checked the time before pausing. "Does Joss still wear a watch?"

"No," I said. "Why?"

"Joss and I had our smart watches synced. That was how she tracked me when I cheated. I thought if she still wore it, we could track it."

"She doesn't." Harlow still didn't look happy to see him, but she'd stopped shooting daggers from her glare. Her words were a different matter. "Pretty sure you ruined them forever, you prick."

If Peter was smart, he'd guard his balls.

Nox's phone beeped. "Don't need it. I've got Sophie's apartment number and a cabin she acquired recently."

"How recently?" I asked.

"Month or so ago." He looked up. "She inherited it when her last living relative died—her mom."

"Send me the address of that cabin."

"We'll stay here again," Piper said.

"No." I'd let them stay before, but not again. "Sophie has been here. She was inside earlier without the alarm going off, which means she has the code. Doesn't matter how many men are outside, it's not safe."

"He's right." Nox's words were so quiet, I could barely hear, and he was right next to me. He looked between Piper and Jake. "She could've planted a bug. I'm sending guys to sweep your bakery. She been to your house?"

"Just Harlow's," Piper muttered, barely moving her mouth.

"Got it. Sending some there, too. Go let them in. She been to your place, himbo?"

"No," Peter answered.

"Good. Go home."

He hesitated, opening his mouth before closing it like a fuckin' fish.

I put him out of his misery. "I'll update you later."

He lifted his chin and followed the others out the door.

We didn't speak again until we were in my car. After punching the address into my navigation, Nox called Matt and ran through the orders while I drove.

While I floored it.

Once he was off the phone, I called Killer at Wicked. "Clear the place out. Fast. Tell the dancers I'll square up with them later."

"Got it, sir."

"I mean it," I said. "I want the place empty in five. Walk every woman to their car and get the hell out."

He didn't waste time asking questions before clicking off to do as I'd order.

I wasn't sure if Sophie would go to Wicked, but I wasn't fuckin' around with their safety.

When we'd gone to Peter's, I'd been hopeful. Joss hadn't been missing for long, and my instincts said Peter wouldn't hurt her. Maybe he'd grab her and try to force her to listen, but she could've handled him.

Speeding out of the city, that hope wasn't there. Not when Joss had been gone for so long. Not when it seemed likely Sophie was a crazy cunt.

Terror poured through me. I didn't know what we were walking into, and the possibilities made it feel like I'd swallowed glass with a salty lemon juice chaser.

By the time we found the secluded house, I was coming outta my damn skin. Bypassing my DoubleTap, I grabbed my Nighthawk from my glovebox and climbed out. I was ready to kick the front door down before Nox held up a finger and pointed toward the house.

He checked the windows from different angles before shattering the glass in the door. Shining a light, he nodded. "No tripwire or explosives."

Guns drawn, Nox and I cautiously entered the house. Other than pretzels spilled on the couch, there was nothing off in the living room.

The pretzels were enough.

In a cabin in the middle of the woods, bugs should've been crawling all over them. But there weren't.

Which meant they hadn't been there long.

"Lars," Nox whispered.

When I saw what he was aiming his light at, the air was knocked from my lungs.

Blood.

Not much.

Not a deadly amount. But if it was my woman's blood, it was still too damn much of it. Enough to form a trail. We followed it through the house until we reached a windowless door that I threw open.

What I saw didn't knock the air from my lungs.

It slammed into me, rocking me to my fuckin' core.

Joss. My Joss. My woman.

Her arms were pulled taut over her head in a way meant to bring optimal pain.

Torture.

Her left arm was out of whack. I didn't know if it was broken or just dislocated. Her face was red and wet with tears. Blood dripped down her chin, forehead, and wrists.

Lifting her head, her wide eyes went wild and the chain clattered until she realized it was me. She settled.

And then she smiled. Didn't matter if it was small and scared and wobbling.

She.

Fuckin'.

Smiled.

"I knew you'd find me," she rasped.

And then she started sobbing, each shudder pulling at her arms and making the pain worse.

"Baby, fuck." I ran to her and lifted her off the ground to support her weight. To ease the strain while Nox found a way to lower the restraints she hung from.

Like she was a buck to be hoisted and skinned.

A mechanism roared above us, and the chains began to loosen. I held her carefully, waiting until there was enough slack to sink to the ground with her in my lap. Going slow and easy, I checked her injuries. Checked her restraints. Brushed her hair from her face.

"Call an ambulance," I barked to Nox, but he was already doing it.

As he spoke on the phone, he tossed the cupboards and drawers. Clicking off, he asked me, "You got bolt cutters in the car?"

"No."

"There's nothing here."

Joss sniffled in my lap, her body tight. Panicked.

"We'll figure it out, baby. I promise. You're good. I got you. I got you." I pressed my lips to her hair and kept repeating that. I wasn't sure if it was for her benefit or mine, but it didn't matter.

All that mattered was it was true.

"She left me here to die like this." Joss stared at the chains, her voice and body shaking.

She.

"Sophie?" I confirmed.

Lifting her chin, Joss looked at me with haunted eyes. "She thinks she's me."

"She's a crazy cunt if she thinks she'll ever be you."

"Literally, Lars. She literally thinks she's me. She kept talking about how you guys were at her house, and how she wanted to go home." She gasped, and her panicked eyes swung between Nox and me. "She talked about my sisters and nephews."

"I'll discreetly put my guys on them," Nox assured her, already typing out a message. "How'd she know we were at your house? She have cameras planted, little one?"

Joss nodded. "Just one, I think."

Nox lifted his chin before holding out his hand to me. "Cops are on their way."

I handed over both my guns. He'd stash his with mine in my car since neither of us were legal to carry, given our records.

I kept Joss in my lap, stroking her hair and listening as she filled me in on the batshit ramblings of a batshit cunt. When sirens sounded from outside, her shaking started again.

Cops barreled in and separated me from Joss. It gutted me, but I moved away from her without a fight. Anything to hurry along the process. When she cried and shook while they cut through her restraints, it didn't gut me.

It killed.

Once they realized I wasn't a threat—and that Joss was close to a meltdown—they let me return to her. As soon as I was standing close, her violent tremors eased to shocked shivers.

"This yours, sir?" One of the cops pointed to a gun and eyed me like I'd tried to pull some bullshit.

Which I had, but not that stupidly.

"It's hers." Joss' tears started again. "That's how she got me here."

"You got your answer," I gritted out. "Mind putting that somewhere so it stops traumatizing my woman?"

He didn't touch it. "Why'd she leave it behind? She seemed too thorough to be so shortsighted"

Joss didn't say anything as she stared at the gun on the floor. I was about to bag the damn evidence myself when she finally spoke. "She thinks she's me. She wouldn't need a gun because I'd never have one."

I was two seconds from losing my temper when the medics entered. Those two did *not* fuck around. In seconds, they wheeled in a stretcher, secured her, and brought her out to the ambulance, moving in sync while one checked her vitals and the other pushed.

Tossing Nox my keys so he could follow, I climbed in and stayed the hell out of the way as they hooked Joss up to the machines.

"My baby," Joss rushed out.

For a second, I thought she was talking about me. And I couldn't say I minded the possessive statement. But when I looked at her, her eyes weren't on me.

They were on the medic.

And her hand was pressed to her stomach.

"Your what?" I rumbled.

The medics shared a look that said they were expecting drama. That it wasn't their first time with something like that. Otherwise, they kept working as one asked, "You're pregnant, ma'am?"

Moving gingerly, Joss reached into her hoodie pocket and pulled out a picture that looked like TV static. "Barely, but yes."

Yes.

"You're pregnant?" I asked, like I hadn't just heard her answer the question. Like she wasn't holding the proof.

"I wanted to do something special to tell you." Her eyes were brimmed with fresh tears as she held out the picture. "Surprise."

Sur-fucking-prise.

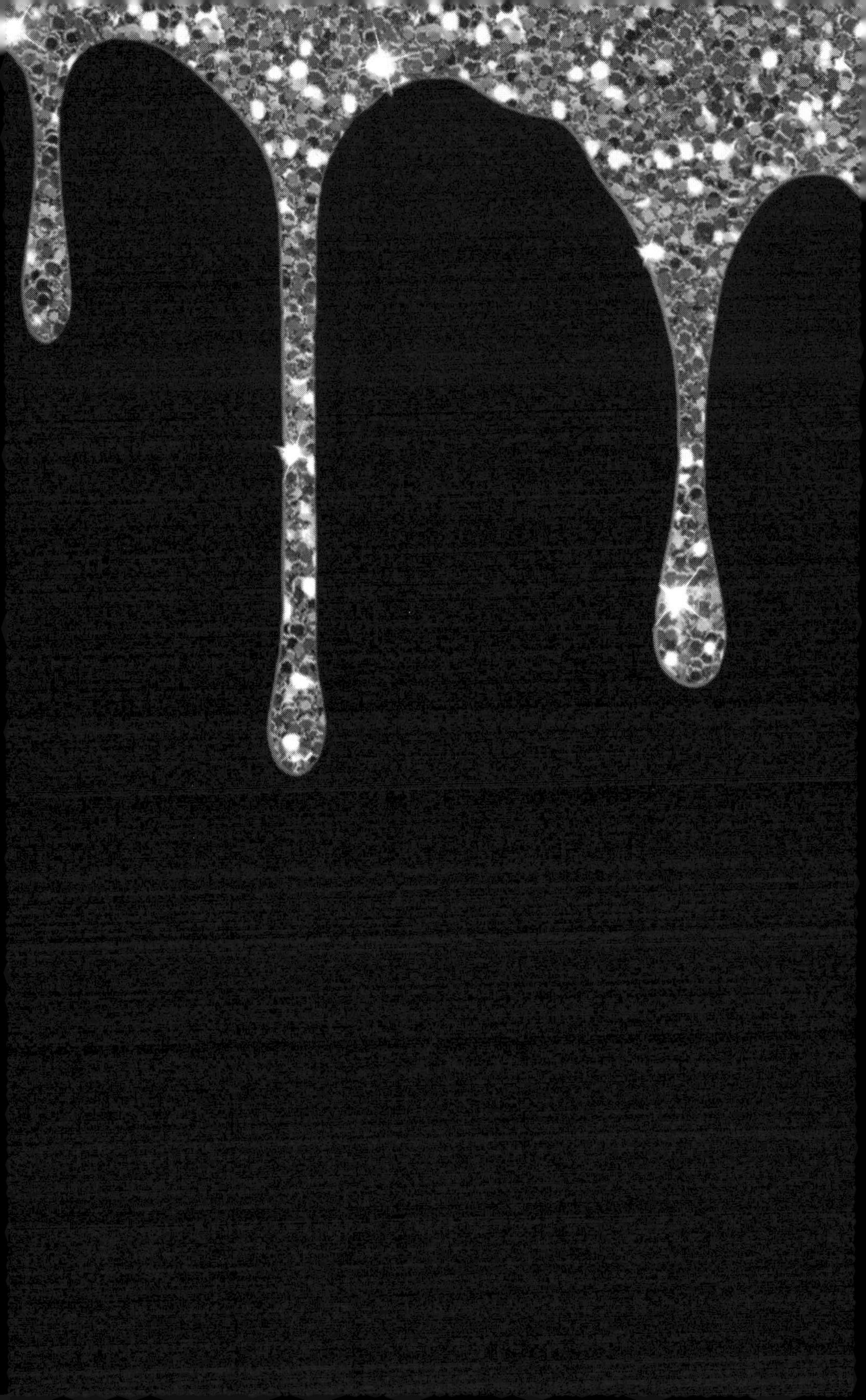

THIRTY-THREE
Alien Frog Leg
LARS

STANDING IN THE HALLWAY A WHILE LATER, I HIT accept on the call. "Yeah?"

The doctors were still with Joss. I'd had to lock down my anger every time they made her hiss in pain—which was too damn often—and be the calm she needed so she didn't try to kick my ass out of the room.

Not that I'd leave her side.

Except to take that call.

"We got her."

It wasn't the voice I wanted to hear.

On the drive to the cabin, Nox and I had talked about our options once we found Joss—and Sophie. It'd been his attempt to keep me sane. Give me something to plan. Reassure me we'd find her.

I wanted to string that bitch up. I wanted to torture her. Fuck with her head. I wanted her to hurt, emotionally and physically, like she'd made Joss hurt.

Nox could've had Matt or Beck grab her so I could do all that and more. I wished it was one of their voices telling me they had her.

But Joss wouldn't want that.

She'd want Sophie to pay, yeah. In the legal way. An official way. A way that would involve a restraining order and Sophie seeing the inside of a cell.

Once we heard that Sophie believed she was Joss, Nox had texted our cop friend, LeVar.

LeVar, who frequented Wicked.

LeVar, who occasionally passed info along to Nox.

LeVar, who'd immediately gone to wait at Joss' house.

LeVar, who was calling to say Sophie had gone to what she believed was her house. And he had her.

That meant I wouldn't get to hang her from chains and terrify her with a gun. But it also meant my girl was safe. That she could breathe easy.

So I'd take the frustration.

"I've touched base with the cops at the cabin," LeVar continued. "We're getting a warrant for her apartment to see what else we find. We'll have to talk to Joss, but I'll push to wait until tomorrow."

"Owe you one," I said.

I didn't.

I owed him a lifetime.

"Lars," he interrupted before I could end the call and get back to my woman. "She believes she's Joss."

"Nox told you that."

"No. She *believes* it. Honest to God, she showed me Joss' ID and swore it was her. They look a little alike, but not enough to pass for her. But she's convinced. Hasn't wavered."

"I know," I repeated.

"Giving you a heads-up, prepare for that defense."

Knew that, too.

I clicked off and went to the waiting room to find more than Nox waiting.

Kase, Harlow, Jake, and Piper were there, too.

"How is she?" Harlow asked.

"Banged up and shaken, but okay."

"And the..." Piper started, gauging my reaction.

The secret she'd been keeping made sense.

I'd have to have a talk with my girl about her friends knowing shit before I did, but at least she had trustworthy people in her corner.

That was hard to find.

"We don't know about the baby yet," I told her.

Harlow squeezed my arm. "I'm sure it's fine."

Telling them to go home—not that they'd listened—I returned to the room to find Joss and a doctor in a stare down.

"Ms. Lennon," he said, "you need to get that shoulder x-rayed."

"I will. *After* I see if my baby is okay."

The doctor stupidly looked at me like I could change Joss' mind. Just 'cause he underestimated her didn't mean I would.

After a long, heavy silence, he sighed. "I'll send someone in."

Once it was just the two of us, Joss asked, "Everything okay?"

"Police have Sophie."

Joss didn't sigh.

She deflated, sinking into the bed. "I wondered if you'd call the cops or let Nox... handle it."

"Wondered that, too," I admitted.

"I'm glad you did it this way so she can get the help she very obviously needs." She flashed me a smile that turned into a wince from pain. "Less fun, I bet."

"You'd bet right."

"Less eye gouging, too."

"Night's still young, baby."

She laughed, but it turned into a pained noise. "How does laughing hurt my shoulder?"

Cupping her cheek carefully, I dropped my forehead to hers. There was a lot I wanted to say. To ask. But I didn't. I closed my eyes and listened to her breathe. I felt her.

'Cause she was alive.

The door pushed open, and I grudgingly lifted my head.

A man pushed a big machine that looked like a retro TV into the room. After asking Joss some questions to confirm her identity, he started it up and prepped before putting a wand...

Not on her fuckin' stomach.

I let her claw my arm as she braced against the intrusion. Running my free hand across her head, I tried to soothe the lines that tightened her face. They were gone a moment later, but it wasn't because of me.

It was because of the screen.

A dot. A fuckin' speck. And in the middle of it, a fluttering blip.

"Everything looks perfect." The man clicked on the keys. "There's the heartbeat."

It was a dot.

It was a fuckin' speck.

And I'd never been so instantaneously in love.

Seeing Joss hanging from those chains had rocked me to my core.

But seeing our little speck rocked me to my damn soul.

"It's our alien frog leg," she whispered, her voice full of the same love.

"Remind me to name our baby," I whispered back, making her laugh.

Our baby.

Joss

I WAS SORE as hell.

Hanging from a hook for all eternity did that to a gal.

It may not have actually been an eternity, but it'd felt like it. And for all that eternity, I'd never doubted that Lars would rescue me. He was always there when I needed him.

My shoulder had been dislocated and badly bruised, but it wasn't broken. In between short visits from my friends, I'd been cleaned up, patched up, and sent home.

But not my home.

No.

After Sophie's creepy invasion, I wasn't sure I'd ever feel comfortable going back to the house I loved so much.

Surprisingly, it wasn't the exposed brick, quiet neighborhood, or lovely porch I'd miss. It was no longer the house itself that I loved so much.

It was the memories I'd made there.

Having sex with Lars for the first time. Or saying I love you for the first time. Or every night he'd hauled his ass across the city just to climb into bed with me for an hour.

I hadn't had to tell Lars I was too freaked to go home. He was Lars, after all. He'd known and had driven us to his condo.

After helping me into bed, he'd forced me to drink an entire cup of water because the doctor had mentioned I was slightly dehydrated.

He must've missed the key word—*slightly*—because as soon as the glass was empty, he went to refill it. When he returned, he set it on the nightstand and sat on the edge of the bed next to me. "We gotta talk, hotcakes."

I nodded solemnly. "I know. I'm sorry for not telling you sooner. I wanted to be sure before I said anything. But I had a doctor's appointment today that confirmed it, so I was going to tell you. I promise."

"Not about that." He regarded me for a moment, his displeasure clear. "Though, gotta be honest, not a big fan of Piper knowing about your pregnancy and appointments before me."

"What do we need to talk about then?"

Because he wasn't mad about the pregnancy. That fear was officially dead. Squashed. RIP, six-feet-under, DOA, *dead.* Murdered by his reaction to the ultrasound.

Wonder.

Amazement.

Love.

It may not have been planned, but it was not unwanted by either of us.

"We're getting married next week, so if there's anyone you want there, invite them."

His statement was said so simply. Like when he'd told me about our first date, there was no question. No confirmation.

But unlike our first date, I had objections.

"We're not getting married," I said even as a rush of adrenaline spiked my veins like espresso brewed with an energy drink instead of water.

"We are."

"You can move in. Or, even better, I'll move in here. We'll go from there."

"I already moved in."

"No..." I started before thinking about my closet and dressers.

Standing, he moved to his closet and opened it.

It was basically empty.

Little by little, Lars' clothes had begun showing up at my place. It'd made sense since we spent most nights there, so I hadn't even questioned the convenience of it.

I gave him the stink eye. "You moved yourself in."

He returned it with his own unapologetic shrug. "Got tired of waiting."

"That's fine. We'll live together."

"We will. But we'll also get married next week."

"Baby," I said softly. "Today was a crazy day. I can't imagine how scary it was for you to not know where I was. And then the baby stuff? It was a lot. A whole fuckin' lot. This is not the time to make a rash decision."

Lars tilted his head. And then he smiled.

God, I loved his smile. I loved it most when I was making him do it.

Except when he smiled at a weird time, and I wasn't sure why.

I didn't trust *those* smiles.

"What?" I prodded.

He pointed to the nightstand. "You never snooped."

"No," I drawled, not sure what that had to do with anything. "Some of us respect people's personal space."

Not that I minded when he enlisted the help of his electronic coworkers from my bedside table, but I wasn't telling him that.

He gestured again. "Look."

With shaking hands, I opened the drawer and peered inside.

A velvet black box.

The kind of velvet black box that held jewelry

The kind of velvet black box that held engagement rings.

He grabbed it, along with a scrap of paper. The paper was what he handed me. "Check the date."

Weeks.

He bought this weeks ago.

"Warned you that if you gave me you, I was never giving you back. Meant it then. Mean it even more now that you're giving me you *and* a baby. Won't even be able to pry me away with a crowbar."

"You're okay about the baby?" I already knew but I needed the reassurance of hearing it in his bluntly honest way.

He shook his head, and my stomach dropped until he continued. "Not okay. Fuckin' thrilled. Making a family with you? Perfect, Joss.

And the thought of you carrying my baby? Fuck. You don't know what it does to me." His voice went rough, his hooded gaze doing nothing to hide the volcano of lust that was dangerously close to erupting. "Why do you think I always pushed my come back inside you so not even a drop leaked out?"

"I didn't know that's what you were doing," I breathed, suddenly too overheated.

Too needy.

"Tried to keep you distracted when your alarm went off so you'd miss your pill. Didn't know if it would work. But I wanted it to. So goddamn bad. And it did. My baby is growing in you. Fuck."

I waited for him to kiss me, but he didn't move.

"Kiss me?" I wanted it to be a firm order, but it came out an airy question.

He gave me a sharp shake of his head. "You need rest."

It'd been the most emotionally and physically exhausting day of my life. Despite the pain meds from the hospital, my shoulders ached. My heart cracked. My memories hurt.

But I didn't need rest.

I needed the reminder that I was alive. That I hadn't been shot in the head. That I was breathing, safe, and in his arms.

He needed that, too.

"Kiss me," I repeated, my voice thick with the desperation we both felt.

The volcano may have exploded, but Lars was careful as he kissed me. Moved me. Stripped me and then himself.

With my shoulder, I had no choice but to be on top, but that was good with me.

It was my favorite place to be.

Lars' fist wrapped around his length, holding it steady while I carefully eased down. Up and down. Up. Down. Taking him more and more each time I sank down until I had all of him. Until he was planted deep. I tried to rock, but he kept a firm hold on my hips, guiding me. Usually, I loved that, but he was being too gentle. Too cautious. I was hurt, not broken.

"Harder," I tried.

He did the opposite.

"I can take it," I swore.

He slowed.

"Baby," I breathed, swirling my hips. Smiling at him. Doing anything to goad him into losing control.

"Say yes."

"That's sexual manipulation," I huffed through my frustration as I tried and failed to move.

"You know I fight dirty."

"And I love it."

"Then say yes. Not 'cause of our alien frog leg. 'Cause I love you. Been in love with you since you smiled at me from behind the counter. 'Cause I can't live without you. 'Cause I want all your wildness and snark and sweet smiles for the rest of my life till I take my last breath."

How could I argue that?

I didn't try. It was the easiest question I'd ever answered.

"Yes."

"That's my good girl." Lars took out the ring before tossing the box to the side. Sliding it on my finger, he pressed my palm to his chest. "Never let you regret this, baby." He gently tugged my hair, bringing my head down as he leaned up to meet me halfway. When his mouth took mine, I opened wider, giving him the access he demanded.

The ownership.

Of the kiss. My body. *Me.*

And I did it knowing I had the same ownership of him.

His wild. His wicked.

It was all mine.

He was all mine.

My obsession.

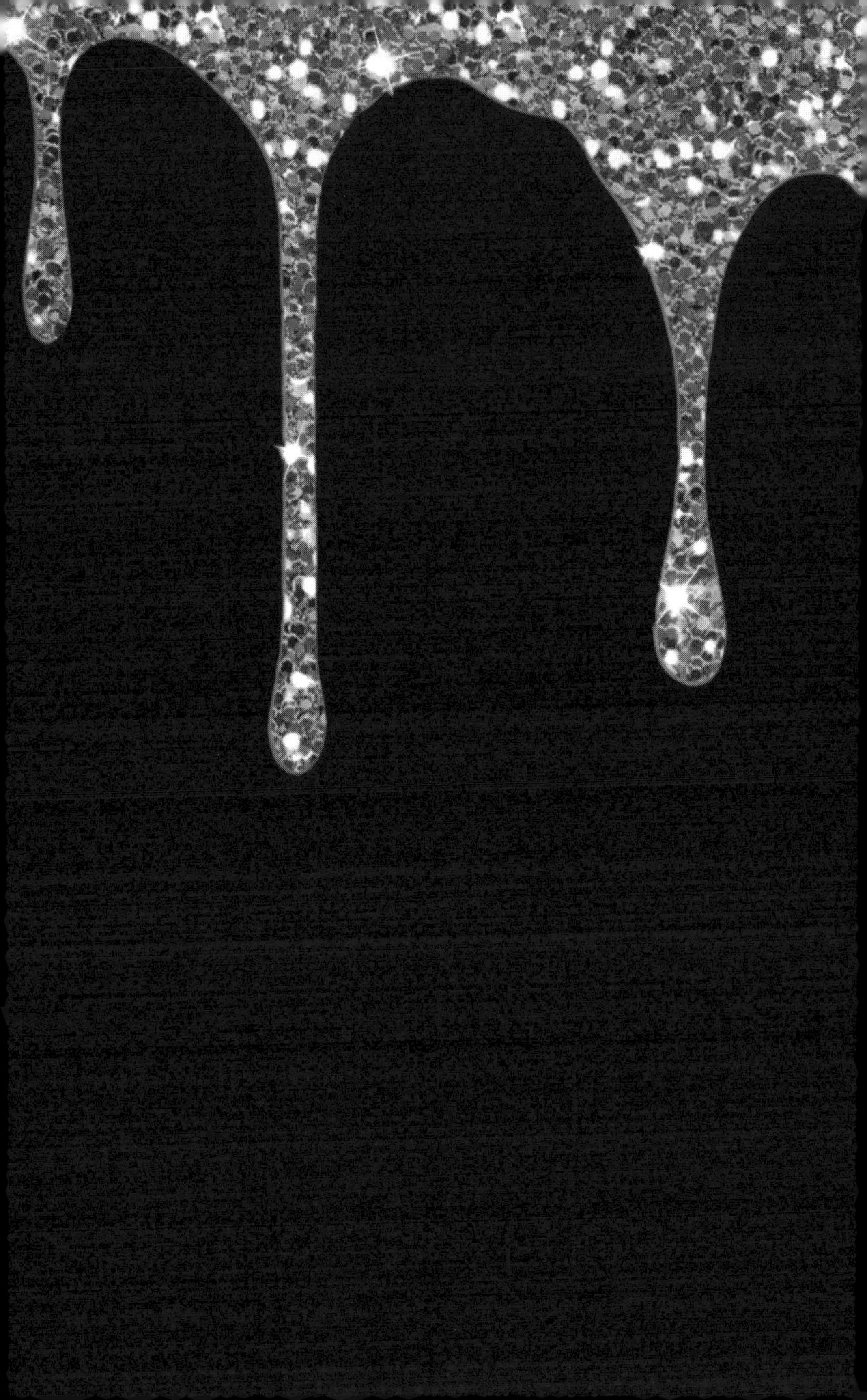

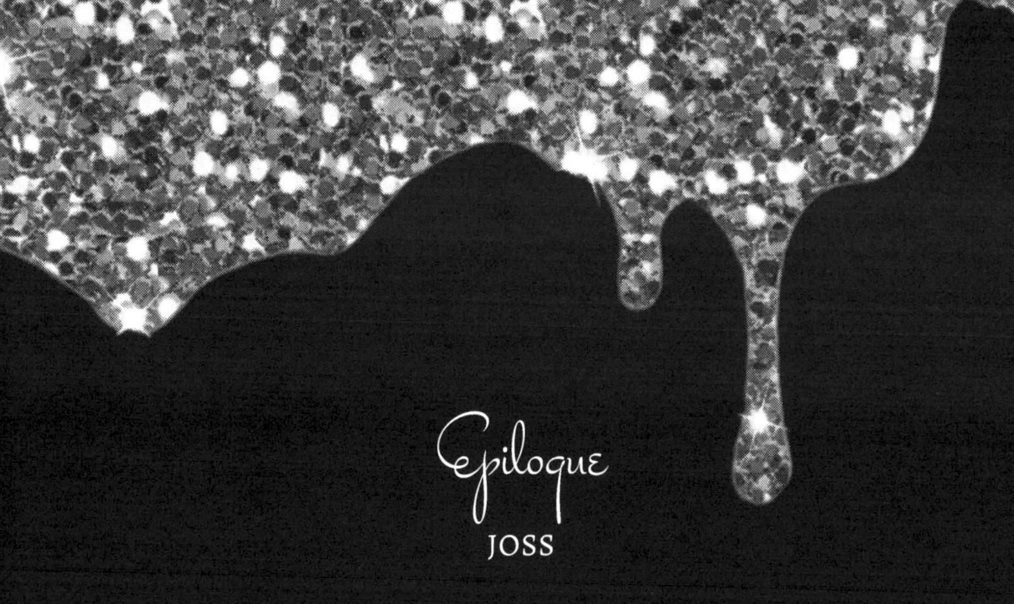

Epilogue

JOSS

FIVE WEEKS LATER

IT WAS OFFICIAL.

I, Joss Luthor, was a married woman.

Much to my husband's chagrin, we'd had to wait two weeks instead of one. Not by choice. Lars could control a lot, but not the weather. Rain had postponed our outdoor wedding for one week, but it could've been worse.

My mom had wanted us to wait *months* while she planned something big. A few months wouldn't put us in the running for *Longest Engagement Ever*, but it would still be too long.

Lars hated the idea, but he would've gone along with it if it was what I wanted.

It wasn't. I hadn't wanted anything big. Nothing fancy. I hadn't wanted a room full of guests and pomp and fussiness.

I wanted Lars.

And as I looked down at the paper that'd come in the mail, it was all legal and real.

I had him.

According to him, I'd always had him. Ever since the first time he'd come in for a chocolate chip cookie, and I'd smiled at him.

That was fair. He'd had me since then, too.

Walking through his condo, I went to wait for him in the bedroom so I could watch him strut out of the bathroom with a towel wrapped low around his hips—a favorite sight in a long list of many favorite sights. It would also save time because once he saw the marriage license, he'd want me in bed.

Or in the hall.

On the couch.

The kitchen counters.

The shower turned off a minute later. It was another couple minutes before he walked out, smelling like soap and mint and *him*. All his muscles and ink were on display, like my own personal art exhibit. His newly tattooed hand clutched the front of his towel. Below that inked hand was something big and beautiful and growing harder by the millisecond.

According to him, the clock tattoo wasn't a reminder to give me his time. He didn't need that. It was a symbol of how much he loved to take his time with me. He'd told me all about it while he'd buried deep inside me, that tattooed hand wrapped around my neck like my favorite necklace.

There was already heat in his eyes when he saw the way I watched him. But it stoked into a wildfire when he saw what was in my hand. "That what I think it is, hotcakes?"

I unfolded the paper and held it up. "Yup."

We were already together. Already married. A paper shouldn't be that big of a deal.

But my husband loved every reminder that I was his wife.

Taking me to the bed, Lars' towel ended up on the floor and the marriage license was... somewhere. I had no idea where it'd landed because I was focused on touching him while his mouth took mine.

Just when things were getting good—which was saying something because they were always good—he pulled away. His face and voice were loaded with so much tenderness, it made my chest ache. "Gotta go, baby."

I knew that.

I just didn't want to.

Lars' blue eyes studied me, going soft and melty. "We can wait."

I knew that, too. We'd already postponed a couple times because I hadn't been ready. Lars would wait eons if I said I needed them.

But I was sick of waiting. Sick of being a coward. I needed to put on my big girl panties and at least pretend I was brave. "I'm good."

Lars kissed me again, but that time it was slow and sweet and leisurely, yet no less hot. When he stood to get dressed, I'd planned to do the same, but then his naked body distracted me.

Hypnotized me.

I was only human.

"Keep looking at me like that, hotcakes," he rumbled, tugging a pair of faded jeans over his deliciously taut ass, "we won't be going."

I was fine with that, but I moved anyway.

Going to the closet, I grabbed a pair of jeans and tugged them on. And then I sucked my stomach in, did a little jig, and wrestled the button to get it to latch. I was only, like, five minutes pregnant, but the bloat was real.

Dressed and as ready as I'd ever be, we got into the car and made the drive to my house.

My home.

The place I'd loved since the first time I'd seen it.

The place I no longer felt comfortable in.

I'd wanted to sell it. Lars had shot me down. Not for good, but for a little while. He'd asked for time, and I'd given it.

Inhaling deeply, I climbed out of the car as Nox stepped out of my house. When I reached him, he squeezed my arm. "Good to see you, lass."

"What about me?" Lars asked, playing wounded.

Nox glowered at him. Even though I knew they were tighter than brothers, and there was no real venom in the look, it was still scary as hell. I felt bad for anyone who was actually the target of his ire. "Never good to see your ugly mug, you thick bastard."

When Nox stepped aside, it took me a moment to work up the nerve to enter. My pulse pounded in my throat, like I'd swallowed my heart and was choking on it. My palms were clammy and sweaty. My legs shook like al dente noodles as they gave me a tour.

But the more Nox and Lars showed, the more the panic subsided. They pointed out the new system panel. The new windows and doors. The locks. The alarms, outdoor cameras, and sensors.

Utilizing Nox's expertise, Lars had redone every inch of security. He'd made sure no one could get in.

He'd made sure I could feel safe in the house I loved.

Nox handed over a paper that listed all the instructions and temporary codes before leaving us alone

Moving *way* into my space, Lars curled his hands around my neck and used his thumbs to tilt my head back. "What do you think?"

"I'm not sure—"

"Know it's been hard, baby," he interrupted.

"I just—"

"You didn't let Peter ruin this house for you." Lowering his head, he brushed his lips across mine before shifting away just enough to meet my eyes. "Don't let that cunt take anymore away from you."

That cunt—as he so lovingly referred to Sophie—*had* taken a lot.

For a while, there'd been a dark cloud over the bakery. It was still there, but it was fading.

Slowly.

She'd taken my restful sleep, leaving me with nightmares. I'd started seeing a therapist so I could deal with them before the baby arrived.

We couldn't both wake up screaming in the middle of the night.

And Sophie had almost taken away my wedding day.

Despite the chilly weather, getting married on the beach outside of Harlow and Kase's house had seemed like a dream. The gorgeous ocean view. The changing leaves. The relaxed atmosphere.

But when I'd looked out the window after getting ready, I hadn't seen our small group of family and found family. I hadn't seen Kase waiting to officiate. I hadn't seen the beautiful scenery. I hadn't been at Harlow's.

My dream had turned into a nightmare, and I'd been back at Sophie's cabin.

It'd taken a while for Harlow and Piper to talk me down. Once I'd been thinking rationally again, my stubbornness set in.

My life had come precariously close to ending next to water. It was the ultimate *fuck you* to keep living that life next to water, too.

For five weeks, she had successfully taken my home from me. I hadn't stepped foot inside since that night. Not until my man had busted his ass to make it safe for me again.

If only he'd let me tell him as much.

"I was trying—" I started.

Again.

Right before Lars interrupted.

Also, again.

"I know, baby."

I rolled my eyes. "You interrupt a lot."

"Wanna give me detention?" He lowered his hold to grip my ass and pull me tight against him. "'Cause I know you don't wanna take away play time."

He was right. I didn't.

"What I was *trying* to say," I snapped, "is that I don't know how I got so lucky to have you as my husband. The house is perfect. I think it may be more secure than a bank vault, but that's okay." I inhaled deeply, and I did it easily. "I feel safe."

He grinned down at me, and, God, it was beautiful. "Safe enough to try staying the night?"

"That depends."

"On?"

I paused for dramatic effect. Sue me. "I still haven't had outdoor sex. If we stay, can we fuck on the porch swing after it gets dark?"

"Can do that even if we don't stay. Gimme a couple hours, I'll put a porch swing up at the condo."

"That's appreciated but not necessary. I'll try staying here."

His fingertips dug into my ass as he squeezed hard enough to take me onto my toes. "That's my good girl."

Lars

FIVE MONTHS LATER

"You do know I'm already pregnant?" my wife bit out. Her cheeks were pink from exertion and self-consciousness.

I'd have thought she'd be used to it. But every time I spread her legs to see her perfect pussy full of my come, she would blush and try to shift away.

And every time, I held her in place.

Memorizing what was mine.

"Actually," she amended, rubbing her rounded belly, "I don't think I could get any more pregnant."

That wasn't true. Her beautiful stomach would grow before our daughter joined us. Then, once it was safe, I'd start trying to knock Joss up again.

Hadn't shared that plan yet since I liked my dick where it was. And if she knew I was already thinking about getting her pregnant before she'd given birth, she'd rip it off with her bare hands.

My cell rang from the pocket of my jeans I'd discarded.... somewhere. Out in the hall maybe.

Joss took advantage of the distraction and closed her legs. "Go answer your phone, you perv."

"You love it," I shot back.

Her smile was full of so much love, it hit me in the gut. It always did. "I really do."

I had to go partway down the stairs to grab pants. The ringing stopped only to start again. "Hey."

"You got a minute?"

At the edge in Nox's tone, I jogged down the rest of the steps before answering. "What's up?"

"Just caught some whispers. Nash is in the wind."

That was not news.

He'd been laying low. So low, no one had been able to find him. And they'd been searching.

Nox.

His boys.

After Nash orchestrated a break-in at a nurse's apartment—a nurse that Judge had claimed as his—the Court of Mayhem brothers had joined the search in a big way.

"We knew this," I pointed out.

"So in the wind, even his crew doesn't know where he is."

That was surprising. Orders were still being carried out. We'd assumed he was calling the shots from wherever 'cause fuckery was still afoot.

"You sure they're not bullshitting to cover?" I asked, not trusting it.

"Positive. He ghosted everyone. Lots of tension growing in his clubs because no one trusts each other. Rumor has it, some of the higher-ups in his hierarchy of fuckery are trying to find their balls to go for the throne of filth. He wouldn't sit back and let that happen."

Well, shit. That is *interesting.*

But not the good news it seemed. I didn't believe that Nash was gone. There was no power or money in that. If he went to ground, it wasn't to retire on some island in the sun.

It was to plan his next act of bullshit.

"Beck's crushed," Nox bizarrely added.

"What the fuck? *Why*?"

He chuckled. "Nash's fortress of dickheadery was stocked with an arsenal that made a military armory look like a tea party. I'd finally given the order to light the match that would send the whole thing to hell, taking Nash along with it, but now the bastard is gone. Beck says he's got arson blue balls."

Working at Wicked, I saw and heard everything. I didn't judge.

But Beck was a straight up freaky bastard.

"What's your plan?" I asked.

"Keep looking. Keep following whispers. Someone's gotta know where the fooker is."

That was true. 'Cause if he really was drinking margaritas on an island somewhere...

Who was giving the orders?

With that question rolling around in my head, I clicked off with Nox and checked my watch. Needed to leave for Wicked, but I had enough time.

Even if I didn't, I'd make it.

I always did.

I climbed the steps two at a time. Didn't matter that I'd just had her.

When it came to Joss Luthor, I'd never get enough.

Entering our bedroom, I slowed my steps, moving quietly.

I'd always been willing to go knuckles with any fucker, no matter how big and badass they thought they were. I'd broken fingers. Wrists. Noses. If it came to Joss, I wouldn't hesitate to gouge some eyes out.

But even I wasn't brave enough to wake my pregnant wife.

No fuckin' way.

Joss

FIVE YEARS LATER

STANDING IN THE storefront of Sweets You Rock, I listened.

And I waited.

Years ago, I'd done the same thing, listening for the rumble of Lars' Harley. The noisy bike and its rider always sent a thrill through my body.

While that was still *very* true, it wasn't the roar of a motorcycle I was listening for. It was something far sweeter.

I didn't have to wait long before I heard it.

"Mama!"

I turned just in time to see a flash of long brown hair before a tiny human collided with my legs.

"Easy, pancake," my husband rumbled, his free arm stretched out to steady me.

Even though it wasn't a weekly thing, he knew the routine.

Like Harlow had always done, I only worked the bakery on the occasional Saturday when Piper needed me.

Or, more often, when I needed a morning with my friends.

Weekday shifts before school were long over, too. Not that I'd left my best friend high and dry. I'd waited until she'd vetted and hired replacements.

A lot of them.

The love people had for Piper's baked goods hadn't waned. Not even a little. Since her hands were more than full, she'd needed full-time staff, not just part-timers.

And she'd needed space.

When Jake and Piper had designed the building, they'd included extra units to rent out. Instead, they'd each expanded until it was just their shops—minus Posey's recording studio. Eli's wife had offered to give up the space, but he'd threatened to quit if she did.

He was just as over the top as the rest.

No matter how much things had changed, if I was working a Saturday, Lars stopped in for a kiss and a cookie. He just didn't come alone anymore.

I scooped Remy up and opened the display case. She grabbed her dad's cookie and handed it off before putting her chubby hand to her chin. "I dunno what I want."

I'm shocked.

When she started to lean up, down, and all around in a way that pressed on my bladder, Lars plucked her from me while smoothly shifting our sleeping toddler son into my arms. It was the kind of flawless maneuver that made me think, in that one tiny area, we were totally nailing the parenting thing.

Just in time to shake things up.

Once Remy was armed with a marshmallow treat in one hand and a sprinkle cookie in the other, she happily skipped away to cause adorable chaos.

I pressed my lips to Mylo's sleeping head when Lars wrapped my ponytail around his hand and gently tugged. "You excited to tell everyone?"

"Tell everyone what?"

We both looked over to see Piper standing behind us, her face completely blank.

"She already knows," Lars surmised, shaking his head. I had no pity for him. He'd known what he was getting into when he married me.

And he loved it.

"Knows what?" she tried, but it was too late.

"If it helps," I told him, "at least you knew first."

I'd found out about Remy during girls' day at Harlow's. Piper had been the one to tell me I was pregnant with Mylo after I'd only wanted raisin cookies.

Who in their right mind wanted raisin cookies unless they were pregnant?

Since I'd recognized the symptoms on my own that time, I'd waited until Lars was home to test. I'd thought we were doing well keeping the secret, but it'd been coconut cookies to betray me that time.

"And she's sworn to secrecy," I continued, "so you still get to tell everyone else."

"And I still have no clue what you're talking about," Piper kept on because she was a real friend.

There was a clatter from the kitchen followed by a familiar high-pitched giggle.

"My cue," Lars said.

But he did it smiling.

No, he did it grinning.

It didn't matter that Remy was five going on sixteen. He loved every second of her shenanigans. Her fire. Her snark.

He always said it reminded him of someone else he knew.

Don't know who that could be...

A mini badass came strolling from the kitchen, followed closely by an even smaller badass. "Ma."

Gathering all his three-year-old gruffness, Linc mimicked his big brother. Kinda. "Mama."

Rhett crossed his arms—a move that was again copied by his brother. "Dad said to tell you we're going to the park with Uncle Lars."

Ma.

Dad.

Uncle freakin' Lars.

My heart.

Linc must've forgotten about his plan to mimic Rhett because he threw his arms in the air. "Park, park, park!"

I caught a flash of tears brimming Piper's eyes before she hid the emotion.

It'd taken nearly two years and a lot of medication, but Piper was eventually able to get pregnant. When Linc was two, they'd decided to add to their family again.

That time by adopting Rhett.

At seven years old, he'd had a rough life that had *not* improved in foster care.

It'd improved with Piper and Jake's love, patience, and time.

Not to mention, the rest of our found family's unconditional love —even when Rhett had claimed he didn't want any part of it.

Since he'd slowly started referring to Piper and Jake as *Ma* and *Dad*, it was clear he'd accepted the inevitable.

He was stuck with us.

"Where is your dad?" Piper asked Rhett, and I could almost see the hearts and rainbows that dripped from the question.

"Outside."

Piper scanned the storefront. It was a lull before the afternoon rush hit. There was still a line, but her staff could handle it.

Even still, she checked with everyone before leaving her post to walk her boys out.

Lars came from the kitchen, dangling Remy over his shoulder. "You seen my little pancake? Wanted to take her to the park, but I can't find her."

"Dad, Dad, Dad," she squealed in delight. "I'm right here."

He flipped her right-side up and set her on her feet. "There you are."

Remy danced around, patiently waiting while Lars pulled me in close. She was used to our goodbyes.

After kissing me stupid, he took Mylo and reached his hand out to Remy. Her grin was just as big as her dad's when she happily took it.

In his worn jeans, white t-shirt, and leather jacket, my badass husband was already hot.

But right then, being effortlessly affectionate with his kids?

He'd never been hotter.

And that was *really* saying something.

If I wasn't already pregnant, I'd have a serious case of baby fever right now.

"I'll be done soon," I said.

"Don't rush," he shot back with a devastating smile. "We've got time.

And we did.

A lifetime of it.

The end

Flip through for a sample of Little Dove

OUR WHITE CASTLE

Juliet

"GET IN."

"What?" I asked, taking rapid shuffling steps to keep up as my father gripped my shoulders and propelled me backward. I stumbled, nearly falling, but he didn't stop.

Throwing open the small pantry door, he shoved me inside. "Don't come out no matter what you hear. Got it?"

I had no idea what was happening, but I knew better than to question Shamus McMillon, especially when he was in a *state*.

His graying red hair was in disarray and his wild eyes kept darting to the side. Each breath he huffed my way smelled like cheap whiskey and a keg of Guinness.

So instead of the fifty-billion questions that danced on my tongue, I said, "Okay."

"I mean it, Jule-bug. Don't open the door until I say so." He scanned my face, his expression tense and anxious. With a sigh, he closed the door, leaving me in darkness with stale crackers, canned Spam, and likely a mouse or two.

I'd just gotten home from errands and grocery shopping when Dad had dragged his butt off the couch to raid the food. His eyes had gone toward the front window before he'd dropped the peanut butter jar to the ground in order to push me into the pantry.

I had no clue what he'd seen that'd freaked him out. We lived at the end of the long dirt road behind Dad's gym and the only visitors we got were his buddies.

If anyone should be freaked by that, it was me. His friends were assholes who gave me the creeps.

Whatever this is, I hope it's fast. I splurged on ice cream, and Vegas doesn't seem to understand February is winter. My precious cookies and cream goodness is probably melting right now.

Maybe it's dinner delivery and I don't have to cook for once. Or maybe it's the few people I like from the gym bringing cake to go with my ice cream. Maybe, just maybe, my father didn't actually forget my seventeenth birthday and is trying to surprise me.

And maybe I'll find a rainbow in the box of stale, store brand Lucky Charms and ride it to a pot of gold.

I knew better than fanciful dreams. It wasn't the first time my dad had forgotten my birthday. The fact it was on Valentine's Day should've taken the guesswork out of it, but he'd still have to care enough to remember.

He never did.

There was a pounding on the front door before it opened so hard, it banged into the wall.

"Boys!" Dad greeted, his voice traveling easily through the paper-thin walls. "What brings you to my castle?"

I barely held in a snort.

If this is a castle, it's owned by the Burger King.

And his Dairy Queen.

It's their humble White Castle.

I'm so hungry.

"If ya wanna book me," Dad said, "ya gotta call my girl. She schedules my fights."

I rolled my eyes. He always gave that line, like he had some big-time agent or manager handling his fight bookings.

I was his girl. Just me and a tattered desk calendar in the backroom of the training gym he owned.

"We had a meeting today," a deep voice rumbled—calm, cool, and collected.

Whereas my dad sounded nervous, jittery, and forced. "Oh! Was that today? Must've slipped my mind. What'd you need?"

"Rough loss on Saturday," whoever said.

Wait. I thought he won.

He hadn't said as much, but he also hadn't gotten blackout drunk —or worse—like he always did after a loss.

"Yeah, that sp—kid," he said, catching himself before he used the slur, "has a helluva right hook."

There was a lot to despise about Shamus McMillon, and his casual racism was high on the list.

"That's funny," the mystery man said in a tone that made it clear there was nothing humorous about it. "'Cause I talked to Jose's trainer. He said his right hook is weak. Not only that, but he sets his left foot. Everyone knows about it. He's trying to break him of the habit."

"Must've missed it. I'm gettin' old, not as sharp as I used to be."

"That so?"

"Yeah, I've actually been tossing around the idea of hangin' up my gloves and focusing on training the young guns at the gym."

That was news to me.

Dad gave a chuckle. "But if you're interested in booking my grand finale fight, Max, I'll—"

"Maximo," the voice rumbled.

"Huh?"

"My name is Maximo. *Not* Max."

The name didn't sound familiar. Knowing who my dad associated with, I could just picture the wannabe hotshot with a pot belly and greasy face who thought he was one of the Rat Pack.

I just hoped, whoever Maximo was, he hurried up and said what he needed to say. I had to eat, and after being on the go all day, my feet were killing me.

"Right, right, Maximo," Dad said. "I'll get you my girl's number, and she can help you out."

As if my dad hadn't spoken, Maximo continued. "After I talked to Jose's trainer, I went to see someone else."

"Who?"

"Carmichael. He had a lot to say about you, Shamus."

"Yeah?" A pitch of nerves hit Dad's voice. "We're old friends. Haven't seen him in a while. Probably about a year or so."

That was a lie. Mugsy Carmichael was one of the wannabe gangsters Dad liked to run with. He came by the gym all the time and totally creeped me out. He'd just been there earlier that week.

"You know what I hate, Ash?" the man—Maximo—asked.

"What, boss?" a new voice answered.

"Liars. Fucking hate them."

Something slammed against the wall, making me jump.

"You took the fall," Maximo bit out, his volume low, though he might as well have been shouting. There was a bass rumble to it that I could almost feel.

"I'd never—" Dad started, but based on the sound of flesh hitting flesh—the soundtrack to my life—someone punched him before he could finish.

"Don't lie to me again," Maximo said. "You took the fall after you bet on Jose."

My dad was a lot of things. A drunk. A gambler. A racist. A crap father.

And greedy.

I hadn't thought he was a cheat, though. His name, title, and reputation in the boxing world were the most important things he had. He valued them above all else—including his only daughter.

"Your loss cost people a shit-ton of money, Shamus. People who are not happy. People who are accusing me of running crooked fights. I don't like liars or cheats, and I sure as fuck don't like being accused of either."

"I didn't fall," Dad claimed.

But it was a lie.

And the sound of punches meant they knew it.

I reached out and gripped the doorknob before hesitating.

It wasn't the first time someone had come to rough Dad up. He had his share of enemies. In the fight world. In the casinos. All across the US.

I wouldn't be surprised if the sisters at Mother Mary's in New York spit when they heard his name.

At least whoever was out there had gone straight to Dad instead of roughing me up in his place. It wouldn't have been the first time that'd happened, either.

Dad was a professional boxer. He could take care of himself. There was nothing I could do except put myself in danger for nothing.

I let my hand drop from the knob.

"I can make it right!" Dad shouted, and the commotion died down.

"I think you're underestimating how pissed people are. They want their money back."

"I just need a little time, but I'll pay." Dad's panic was growing, and he didn't try to hide it. "I'll find a way. Sell the gym. Do something."

Oh, Dad. What'd you get yourself into this time?

"Pit me against one of your new guys," Dad pleaded, "and I'll do whatever. Win or throw the match, whatever you want. I'll make it believable so no one knows."

"Are you fucking kidding me?" Maximo roared, the sound rattling in my ears. "What part of 'I hate liars' does he not get?"

"No clue, boss," whoever said.

"Let's get this over with."

"Whoa, fellas. Max...imo. Maximo, man, sir. Come on." Dad lowered his voice until I had to press my ear against the shared wall to hear him. "The gym, the car, *everything*. You can have it. Take it."

"I don't want your shit, Shamus. It's as worthless as you are."

"C'mon, man, seriously, I get it. I fucked up. I'll find a way to pay and then I'll retire. I'll steer clear of the tables. But if you kill me, you'll be out the money. Dead men can't pay."

Kill?

Did he just say kill?

I threw open the door and launched myself into our small kitchen. I turned toward the entryway to the living room just as a boom filled the tiny house. Filled my head. It bounced around, leaving a ringing in my ears.

But I barely noticed the echo it left behind.

Because my focus—the entirety of it—was on my father.

My dead father with the hole in his head and his brains splattered on our crappy couch.

I'm never going to get that stain out.

I'd thought my words were in my head, but I must've spoken them out loud because every set of eyes shot to me.

Well, every set except Dad's.

Vomit lodged in my throat.

"Shit," a black-haired man bit out.

The man to his left lifted his gun and pointed it at me.

Right.

At.

Me.

I had nowhere to go. There was no way I was getting through three goons and a monster of a man. The old backdoor behind me didn't open anymore. If I jetted down the hall, I might be able to break one of the painted-shut windows, but it was more likely I'd be shot in the back.

If I'm dying, running will not *be the last thing I do on this earth.*

Trapped like a defenseless mouse surrounded by vicious predators, I stayed where I was. I steeled my spine and raised my chin.

I waited for death.

"Wait," the black-haired man said, pushing the other man's arm down. He studied me with dark eyes, running a tattooed hand through his hair and then across his stubbled jaw. Seeming to reach a conclusion, he gave a single nod. "She comes with us."

Oh no.

At that, I did turn and run.

There were fates worse than death.

And if that was what I was facing, I'd take a bullet in the back instead.

I took them by surprise and gained some distance, but my short legs were no match for the goon's much longer ones.

Thick arms wrapped around my waist, and I thrashed. I screamed. I bit. I kicked and punched and clawed.

I'd fight.

I'd die.

But I'd never go with them.

"Fucking hell," the man cursed, squeezing me like I was the rabbit Lennie pet too hard.

I caught him with a lucky kick to the junk. His hold loosened enough for me to wiggle free and punch him in the throat.

I started to turn to take on whatever was behind me, but before I could, everything shifted. The world went sideways.

And then it went black.

Also by Layla Frost

THE HYDE SERIES

Hyde and Seek

Best Kase Scenario

Fate Nox

Wild Wicked Obsession

Ring Around the Posey

COURT OF MAYHEM

Until Mayhem

Finding Mayhem

THE DILLON SISTERS

Damaged by Layla Frost

Deathly by Brynne Asher

THE FOUR

Styx

Stoned

Broken

Bones

BLACK RESORTS

Little Dove

Little Sunshine

Little Goddess

STANDALONES

About the Author

Growing up, Layla Frost used to hide under her blanket with a flashlight to read the Sweet Valley High books she pilfered from her older sister. It wasn't long before she was reading hidden Harlequins during class at school. This snowballed into pulling all-nighters after the promise of "just one more chapter".

Her love of reading, especially the romance genre, took root early and has grown immeasurably until it was time to write her own stories.

When she's not writing, Layla Frost is an insomniac with a deep love of iced coffee, tchotchkes, plants, and her hens. She's also the world's okayest mom, but her kids think she's cool... ish.

JOIN MY READER GROUP:
www.facebook.com/groups/LaylaFrostCupcakes

facebook.com/LaylaFrostWrites
instagram.com/laylafrostauthor
amazon.com/stores/-/author/B00VJMSYKQ
bookbub.com/authors/layla-frost
tiktok.com/@laylafrostauthor

Made in the USA
Columbia, SC
01 July 2025

60192860R10250